P9-ARN-337

Praise for

DARK LIGHT OF DAY

"A spectacular debut novel."
—Faith Hunter, *USA Today* bestselling author

"A great debut from the urban fantasy world. Ms. Archer is now down on my 'never miss' author list."
—*Night Owl Reviews*

"A fascinating story line . . . Archer has created a dark world that will grab your attention from the very start."
—*The Reading Cafe*

"[A] well-written and fast-paced urban fantasy with unique characters and a multilayered plot."
—*A Dream Within a Dream*

"There is a fresh new voice in urban fantasy, and she has a unique take on Armageddon . . . With her unusual heroine, Noon Onyx, Archer has created a brilliant character who struggles against fate to find her place in the world. Set against the backdrop of university life, there is an abundance of adventure, mystery, and passion!"
—*RT Book Reviews* (4 stars)

Ace Books by Jill Archer

DARK LIGHT OF DAY
FIERY EDGE OF STEEL

FIERY EDGE
OF STEEL

JILL ARCHER

PEABODY INSTITUTE
LIBRARY
DANVERS, MASS.

ACE BOOKS, NEW YORK

MAY 2 9 2013

THE BERKLEY PUBLISHING GROUP
Published by the Penguin Group
Penguin Group (USA) Inc.
375 Hudson Street, New York, New York 10014, USA

USA I Canada I UK I Ireland I Australia I New Zealand I India I South Africa I China

Penguin Books Ltd., Registered Offices: 80 Strand, London WC2R 0RL, England
For more information about the Penguin Group, visit penguin.com.

FIERY EDGE OF STEEL

An Ace Book / published by arrangement with Black Willow, LLC

Copyright © 2013 by Black Willow, LLC.
All rights reserved. No part of this book may be reproduced, scanned, or distributed in any
printed or electronic form without permission. Please do not participate in or encourage piracy
of copyrighted materials in violation of the author's rights. Purchase only authorized editions.

Ace Books are published by The Berkley Publishing Group.
ACE and the "A" design are trademarks of Penguin Group (USA) Inc.

For information, address: The Berkley Publishing Group,
a division of Penguin Group (USA) Inc.,
375 Hudson Street, New York, New York 10014.

ISBN: 978-0-425-25716-6

PUBLISHING HISTORY
Ace mass-market edition / June 2013

PRINTED IN THE UNITED STATES OF AMERICA

10 9 8 7 6 5 4 3 2 1

Cover art by Jason Chan.
Cover design by Lesley Worrell.
Interior text design by Laura K. Corless.

This is a work of fiction. Names, characters, places, and incidents either are the product
of the author's imagination or are used fictitiously, and any resemblance to actual persons,
living or dead, business establishments, events, or locales is entirely coincidental.
The publisher does not have any control over and does not assume any responsibility for
author or third-party websites or their content.

If you purchased this book without a cover, you should be aware that this book is
stolen property. It was reported as "unsold and destroyed" to the publisher, and neither
the author nor the publisher has received any payment for this "stripped book."

ALWAYS LEARNING   PEARSON

Acknowledgments

In writing this book, I was inspired by a number of things, among them an old French imposter case, two children's songs, and a fairy tale. Chapter 8 includes portions of the international student hymn "Gaudeamus Igitur," chapter 17 includes a traditional Irish toast, and chapter 18 includes portions of John Milton's "On the Death of a Fair Infant Dying of a Cough."

Continued thanks to my agent, Lois Winston, for her timely advice and never-ending encouragement. To my editor, Jessica Wade, for her insightful comments and astute suggestions. It's great to work with someone who knows your characters almost as well as you do and who always has their best interests at heart.

To the rest of the team at Ace: Brad Brownson, my publicist; Michelle Kasper, production editor; Mary Pell, copy editor; Jesse Feldman, assistant editor; Lesley Worrell, art director; and cover artist Jason Chan—thank you! There are myriad things that need to be done behind the scenes to produce a quality novel, and I am grateful to have had help with all of it.

Thank you to Joan Havens for assisting me with the Latin phrases again. This time, I modified one of the loose translations to fit the story. Any and all errors of interpretation are mine.

A big, huge thanks to my family and friends, who support me in ways too numerous to list. Without you, this book would not have been possible.

And, finally, to my readers, thank you for choosing to read *Fiery Edge of Steel*. I hope you enjoy it!

I

A woman knows the face of the man she loves like a sailor knows the open sea.

—HONORÉ DE BALZAC

Chapter 1

ॄ

In pre-Apocalyptic times humans stoned their criminals to death by throwing rocks, sharp pieces of metal, and other debris at the wrongdoer until they were so bloody and beaten, death was inevitable. It was said that, until jaws were broken or skulls were smashed, all wrongdoers cried for it to end.

Everyone got their wish.

Stoning demons is impossible, of course. Trying to kill a demon by throwing rocks at it would be like trying to take down an alligator by blowing soap bubbles at it. So, in modern times, public executions call for a *Carne Vale*—a "farewell to the flesh" ceremony where waning magic is thrown instead of stones. The practice is even more brutal than its ancient counterpart, but just as cowardly.

Ari Carmine and I stood elbow to elbow in Timothy's Square, waiting for the awful thing to begin. Beside me, Ari squeezed my hand. He likely meant the gesture to be reassuring, but it made me feel trapped and I pulled my hand free. I glanced up at him, quirking my mouth in a half smile meant as an apology. He looked down at me, expressionless, but I could feel his signature, that wispy magical aurora that allowed uncloaked waning magic users to sense one another's presence. Ari's signature was warm, as always, but today it was laced with blistery bits, as if the glowing embers of a dying fire had been kicked at me. It made standing next to him uncomfortable.

Around us, the crowd of Hyrkes—humans with no magic—continued to build as students from both St. Lucifer's and the Joshua School gathered. The heat from the unrelenting overhead sun was oppressive. Since there were no trees in Timothy's Square, there was no shade. There was no cover. Nowhere to hide from what was to come.

Peering over my shoulder to check for possible unobserved routes of escape, I made the mistake of catching Sasha de Rocca's gaze. Sasha was a distant cousin of mine, but that didn't mean we were close.

He sneered openly at me.

"Dressed for a funeral, Noon? Do you really think mourning is appropriate for a *Carne Vale*?"

Automatically, I glanced down at my indigo sheath. In Halja, midnight blue—the color of the sky when Lucifer was struck with the lance that killed him over two millennia ago—was the color of mourning.

"The thing deserves to die," Sasha said, his low voice burbling up out of his thick barrel chest. Suddenly his cold, crinkly eyes and dirty blond beard seemed far too close. I stepped back.

It wasn't that I was afraid of Sasha. My power was far greater than his. But, unlike Sasha, I hated using mine, and he knew it. I hadn't thrown magic since last semester when my demon client had almost killed me. The St. Lucifer's faculty had given me leave to table my magic use over the semester break, but now that classes were back on, my "recovery" was officially over. I was expected to come out of my self-imposed dormancy today, and I was expected to come out of it so that I could participate in the one thing I abhorred.

Killing.

Sasha, Ari, and I were Maegesters-in-Training here at St. Lucifer's, which meant we were being taught to become demon peacekeepers. When we graduated we would be expected to serve the demons that ruled Halja—as counselors, judges, even executioners. Since I was a pacifist at heart, it was a line of work I'd come to reluctantly. In fact, it was fair to say I was still having a great deal of difficulty accepting some parts of my future job description.

My resentment at being forced to participate in today's *Carne Vale* ignited and I leaned toward Sasha. "If you feel so strongly that the demon deserves to die, why don't you go up there and do it yourself?"

Sasha had been needling me, with bitter barbs of both words and magic, for a week. I'd ignored him. Until now.

"I can't," he said finally, shrugging.

"Can't or won't?" I snapped.

Sasha stared back at me, his ice blue eyes unaffected by the withering heat. But beneath his long, scraggly beard and his limp, lackluster hair, Sasha was sweating. If he said *can't* again, he'd be admitting how weak he was. That he didn't have enough power to bring down a demon on his own. Of course, I didn't think that was anything to be ashamed of. And it certainly wasn't uncommon. Most Maegesters-in-Training couldn't bring down a demon alone. But someone like Sasha would be loath to admit it.

If he said *won't*, though, he'd be admitting he was a coward. *Won't* meant that, even if he could, he wouldn't take on the moral obligation of killing a demon in cold blood. That he wouldn't walk right up there, look the demon in the eye, and execute it. I suspected that's why *Carne Vales* were designed the way they were. Not because it took a village to put down a demon, but because it took a village to hide the guilt when we did so.

Our argument drew the attention of an Angel from the Joshua School. Once, Angels had been our enemy. During the Apocalypse, the Savior and his Angels had fought against Lucifer and his Host. But that war was now ancient history. In modern-day Halja, descendants of both armies worked together all the time. Angels often assisted Maegesters with their cases, acting as scribes, interpreters, and field assistants.

This Angel was dressed as if he were going to a bovine roast, which I found particularly distasteful under the circumstances. His tanned legs poked out of a baggy linen kilt and his dark gray, short-sleeved tunic was barely even laced. Luckily he had another shirt underneath. Still, his whole look was so casual and inappropriate for a *Carne Vale*, that I took an instant dislike to him.

"I take it you'd rather get this over with," he said to me. "Do it right. Put the guy—and his woman—out of their misery without all this pomp and . . . circumvention."

Ari tensed. The Angel's comment, and his directness, momentarily stunned me. I stared at him, the Angel's taupe-eyed gaze meeting mine.

"That's what you're telling him, right?" the Angel said, gesturing toward Sasha, "that he ought to put his magic where his mouth is. So, what about you?" he said, looking back at me. "Would you do it? *Could* you do it?"

No! Never! I wanted to shout, but suddenly all eyes were on me. What had been a discussion between a few Maegesters-in-Training and an Angel now became a preexecution spectacle for anyone who happened to be standing nearby. I was Noon Onyx, the only female Maegester-in-Training in all of Halja. My father, Karanos Onyx, was head of the Demon Council. I was *Primoris*—the top-ranked waning magic user in my class. *Everyone* wanted to know what I was capable of.

Except me.

"What woman?" I said, diverting attention to another question. "There aren't going to be two executions, are there?" I glanced at Ari.

"No, the accused has a . . ." He paused, considering.

"Wife? Paramour? Accomplice?" The Angel mused. He slid his hands into his pockets and rocked back on his heels, as if he were trying to decide between vinegar or mustard in a condiment line. "What do you think, Ari? Was Ynocencia actually a victim?"

Ari stared at the Angel, his eyes dark. The Angel stopped rocking, but kept his hands in his pockets and his stance relaxed. He wore an expectant expression as he met Ari's stare.

"I think Ynocencia has lived her whole life between the demon and the deep," Ari said slowly.

"Yes, but who's the real demon, hmm?" The Angel waggled his brows and Ari scowled.

Forget about that, I thought. "Who's Ynocencia?" I asked, completely lost. Sasha rolled his eyes.

"Weren't you paying attention in class today? Ynocencia is Jezebeth's lover. Jezebeth?" he repeated after seeing the blank look on my face. It galled me that Sasha knew more about the *Carne Vale* case than I did, but I guess that's what I got for keeping my head out of the books since I'd been back. "The Demon of Falsehoods and Lies?" Sasha prodded.

I shook my head. I had a vague suspicion Jezebeth was the demon we were supposed to execute today. I shifted nervously on my feet and risked another glance through the crowd, calculating my chances of ducking out unnoticed. By then, Sasha had turned his attention to the Hyrkes around us and was doing a hack's job of explaining the case to them.

By all accounts, Ynocencia had been a dutiful wife to an abusive husband. Then, seven years ago, Ynocencia's husband sailed down the Lethe to seek greater fortune. Ynocencia would have been happy had that been the last of him, but he returned last fall a changed man—stronger, smarter, kinder. Unfortunately for Ynocencia, she'd forgotten (or willingly chose to ignore) that, in Halja, perception and truth are not always the same.

Six months later, Ynocencia's real husband returned— as weak, stupid, and mean as he had been before he left. He challenged Jezebeth's identity and declared him a fraud. He claimed Jezebeth was a drakon who had used his human form to sleep with his wife and steal his farm. At first, Ynocencia's neighbors rallied around her, swearing that Jezebeth was Ynocencia's loving husband. The town began formal proceedings to oust the "newcomer" but things got ugly, provoking the drakon to shift into his true form. When Jezebeth realized he might lose his human lover, he went mad and terrorized the town. One woman and three children were killed. The neighbors withdrew their support and Jezebeth was put on trial for adultery, fornication, duplicitous conduct, theft—

Wait! Jezebeth was a drakon? I didn't think they existed . . .

To the east of the square, I heard scraping and clanking. The crowd rippled and swelled back as if a giant had stepped into its edge. "But drakons are a myth," I said quickly, turning toward the sounds. They were mythological creatures, winged demons supposedly born to human mothers.

"As much of a myth as a female member of the Host with waning magic," Sasha snorted. I blocked him out. I was trying to block it all out.

I don't want to be here, I thought. *I can't do this. I won't do this.*

I was the girl who went out of her way not to step on ants. I put house spiders in cups and took them out to the curb rather than squashing them under my boot heel. And I was expected to help kill someone I'd never met just because someone else said they deserved to die? Even if I had paid more attention in class, someone else's case notes wouldn't have been enough to convince me to end another's life. Frankly, I didn't know if I was capable of executing a demon in cold blood. But what I did know was that if I was going to be asked to take on the moral responsibility of ending another's life, I was damn well going to be deciding for myself whether they deserved it or not and I wasn't going to be participating in an execution purposefully designed to be cruel.

At the edge of the crowd, my father was ascending the wooden steps of a hastily erected platform. Waldron Seknecus, St. Lucifer's dean of demon affairs, and Quintus Rochester, one of our professors, stood near the platform with several upper-year Maegesters-in-Training. My father walked to the center of the platform and held his hands up. The crowd immediately fell silent. He gestured to his left and a young man was led up the stairs.

Rail thin and filthy, the man stared defiantly out at the crowd. But when a woman's cry pierced the silence, his defiant look turned to one of terror. *He hadn't known she would be here,* I thought. I could feel it in his signature. The anguish, the anger, the remorse. Suddenly I heard a thump and the crowd shifted again in response to something happening. Jezebeth strained against his captors, twisting his body from side to side, trying to break free. But more than mere muscles held him in place.

Had his human lover thrown herself against the base of the platform?

Was that the thump I'd heard? The thought of her desperation suddenly made me sick. Why was she being forced to watch?

The crowd swelled. I felt the waning magic around me intensify. Beside me, Ari's waning magic flared and I suddenly felt like I'd emerged from a dark house into blinding sun. Instinctively, I shielded myself from him. He glanced down at me with a small, stiff smile. In the midmorning sunlight, his eyes were the color of caramel.

"Ari . . ."

I didn't have to finish my thought. Waning magic users couldn't read minds, but some of us—the more powerful ones—could feel one another's feelings. My redlining signature told Ari everything he needed to know. I was ready to bolt.

"Don't. Everyone will see you leave," he said in a low voice, leaning close to my ear. "You're standing right next to me so no one will know if you don't participate. My magic is strong enough for both of us." He stared at me, waiting for me to respond. I shook my head and clenched my fists, keeping my head down. I didn't want Ari throwing my stones for me. Or seeing me cry when I did so. Up front, the drakon's lover continued her pitiful sobbing as she begged my father to set him free.

"Unveil him," my father commanded, motioning toward Jezebeth. The Archangels on the platform cast a spell and suddenly Jezebeth—the real Jezebeth—was before us.

Fyrhto, I thought. My mouth went dry and my throat seized up so that swallowing was impossible. If that wasn't this creature's name, it should be. Waves of fear and fury pulsed from it. Whatever human shape the thing had possessed fled, leaving a massively horned, thickly tailed and scaled greenish black demon facing the crowd. But this thing's horns weren't only on its head. A good half dozen long, ridged spirals splayed out from the top of its shoulder blades, each one ending in a tip as sharp as a lance. The thing crouched and suddenly the horn tips that had been harmlessly pointing skyward leveled at the crowd. They *were* lances, I thought breathlessly, wondering what it would be like to have bones that were built for battle. Behind it, the creature's wings unfurled like leathery sails rigged with bones and sinew.

Enraged, Jezebeth clawed deep gashes into the wooden floor of the platform, snapping his jaws and snuffling, the wet sounds in his throat at war with the dry clacking of his teeth. He tossed his head back and roared, some awful combination of hyena laugh and wild boar grunt that caused the crowd to step back even farther from the platform. A few Hyrkes turned and ran. I wanted to do the same.

"Jezebeth"—my father's voice boomed through the square—"you have been found guilty of murdering four human Hyrkes. Those sins are punishable by death. The Council has determined, due to the heinous nature of your sins, that your death must not only serve as punishment, but also deterrence. Your death will be needfully painful and prolonged and you will be subjected to all of the moribund degradations and dying humiliations that the traditional *Carne Vale* method of execution entails."

And then, with no more emotion than if he were signaling someone to dim the lights before a theatrical performance, Karanos gave the signal for the stoning to begin—*"Exsignare." Extinguish his signature.* He looked right at me when he did it, his face unreadable. Did he regret that I had to participate? Or was he worried I'd make a poor showing and embarrass him?

The thumping renewed with the stoning. Jezebeth's woman was trying to reach him again. Her screams and shrieks made it clear she'd stop at nothing—even her own death, which was what approaching him while he was being stoned with waning magic would mean for a human Hyrke—to be by his side. It made me wonder what her real husband was like. It said volumes about the man who'd left her that she'd rather die by the side of this hideous creature than go back to a life with him.

Jezebeth's awful porcine roar turned into hoarse braying. To me, it sounded more desperate than determined. Had he even been able to control whether he changed or not?

Maybe he was just trying to tell the woman good-bye . . .

Jezebeth fell to his knees and I knew I couldn't do it. Wouldn't do it.

I ran.

Grateful for its unoccupied silence, I took refuge in the stacks of Corpus Justica, our law library. I strode past the lone desk clerk, avoiding his eyes and hoping my face didn't appear red and splotchy. I took the stairs to the second-floor study carrels two at a time and made my way back to the one I usually used—a tiny desk set in a far corner of the unpopular tithing and tax section. Unfortunately, I'd forgotten there was a small window in this part of the library, one that overlooked Timothy's Square. I'd never given the window much thought before, but now I wished fervently that it wasn't there. Why hadn't I kept running? Why had I taken refuge in the academic heart of the very place I despised?

I walked over to the window, wrestled with the catch, and then pressed it wide open. Jezebeth's bloody, steaming corpse lay sprawled on the wooden platform as the crowd dispersed. People's expressions varied. Some were disgusted; others were shocked; a few just looked confused. Something must have happened to have brought such a quick end to the *Carne Vale*. But instead of feeling relieved that Jezebeth's suffering was over, I felt miserable.

I couldn't see Ari and wondered if he was on his way to find me. Part of me wished he wouldn't (what was I supposed to say to him about what had just happened?) but the other half acknowledged that I'd run here because it was the first place he'd look. Just as I was about to close the window, I saw the taupe-eyed Angel—the one who'd asked me if I could, or would, execute Jezebeth alone and in cold blood. He stood at the edge of the square, staring up at me, his hands still in his pockets, his expression contemplative.

I guess he had his answer.

Suddenly, I remembered the cry that had first started the Apocalypse: *Beware! Angels at the gate!*

I slammed the window shut.

Chapter 2

ح

I waited for Ari at Corpus Justica for another half hour. He didn't show so I packed up and left. I went to Alba's, a.k.a. "the Black Onion," a tiny café where my study mates and I ate when we wanted to get off campus.

Alba's has been serving lunch on the corner of River Road and Widow's Walk for three generations. Alba's husband had been a fisherman. When Estes, mighty Patron Demon of the Lethe, chose to take her husband's life, Alba made do by selling vegetables from a cart on this very spot. Her daughter (conveniently named Alba too, as was *her* daughter, the current owner), had traded in the cart for a café. Alba's was mostly a Hyrke hangout, but I loved it because the menu was perfect for a waning magic user—there was no fresh produce. Apparently Alba the Second had had enough of farm fresh with her mother's cart. Here, everything came fried, baked, battered, or stewed.

I chose a seat at a table near the big bay window overlooking the Lethe, wondering (as I did nearly every time I came here) why Alba the First would choose to live the rest of her life in sight of the very thing that took her husband from her. But then, maybe the answer was in the question. Maybe she hadn't wanted to forget.

Alba the Third shuffled over to me as soon as I sat down. We knew each other well enough. After all, except for Rickard Building (where my classes were), Megiddo (my dormitory), Marduk's (our campus' underground pub), and Corpus Justica, I spent most of my time here. Which was to say *not much*, but enough so that she knew I was a student at St. Lucifer's Law School.

She asked me what I wanted and I told her "bread" and "soup" without specifying what kind (there was only one kind of each here, the daily special). She nodded, but kept her substantial hip resting on the edge of the table. She looked down at me, her gray eyes still clear despite her age. Finally, she reached into her apron pocket and withdrew a dollar bill. She smoothed it flat on her leg and then put it on the table and pushed it toward me. I stared at it, puzzled. *Shouldn't the money go the other way?* Alba slid into the chair opposite me.

Behind her, I could hear the sizzling sounds of fish on the grill as her cook prepared the day's catch. All around us, the pungent smell of garlic and onion filled the air.

"I want to hire you," Alba said. I gave her a blank look.

"I need to tell you a secret," she continued in a raspy whisper. "You know, attorney-client privilege."

I glanced between her and the dollar bill, not bothering to tell her all the problems associated with the arrangement she was suggesting. (I was being trained to represent demons, not Hyrkes; it was really my word that kept my mouth shut, not money; and worst of all—*a dollar?*—I wasn't sure what she valued least: my services, my silence, or her secret.)

I sighed and pretended to accept the dollar. I'd give it back to her as part of the tip anyway. I'd have kept her secret without it. I could already tell she wasn't hiding anything truly horrifying.

"What's up, Alba? Has one of your suppliers been sub-
stituting catfish for grouper?"

She frowned at me and shook her head, waving a hand
in the air to dismiss an obviously ludicrous idea. "As if,"
she mumbled. "No . . . I . . . Noon, when's the last time you
had one of my black onions?"

I chewed the inside of my cheek, wondering how to tell
Alba the truth. The fact was, Alba's onions were infamous.
Every kid in Halja had probably eaten at least one. That's
why Alba's café was also known as "the Black Onion."
Legend had it that a real black onion would tell a sailor's
fortune (and *only* a sailor's fortune). Those who sailed the
Lethe could ask it a question (*any* question) and then peel
the onion for the answer. The sailor's answer would be
buried within the onion, written on paper as thin as, well,
onionskin.

But Alba's onions were fake. First off, anyone could use
one (convenient for the Albas, since that meant any cus-
tomer could buy one). Second, the question asked had to be
a "yes" or "no" type question (*Does he love me?* and *Will I
be rich?* were popular choices). Over the years it had been
determined that Alba's black onions revealed only twenty
or so standard answers (*Not so much* and *Never!* were unpopular answers). No one complained, though, because at
least half of Alba's onions revealed answers the asker
wanted to hear. The last time I had one?

Never!

But, savvy as she was, Alba was already one step ahead
of me, guessing my answer before I voiced it. She pursed
her lips and looked unhappy.

"Uh-huh," she said, nodding. "I thought so. Truth is,
Noon, I *do* have a supplier problem. The Angel I've been
getting my black onions from is moving on. He graduated
from divinity school and found a ward. He says he no longer has time to keep me in onions." She looked completely
put out that her co-conspirator was going legit. I tried to
hide my smile.

Angels were spellcasters. Unlike Maegesters, whose waning magic was innate, an Angel's magic came from faith and constant practice. Apparently Alba had found an Angel willing to create bogus black onions as part of his daily workout routine.

"You want me to help you find another Angel to work with," I guessed.

"Bah! No. I'm sick of Angels, sick of spells. I want the real deal—black onions made by Luck's hand."

"Alba," I said slowly, "I'm training to be a Maegester. My magic is waning, not waxing. I can't grow anything. Every plant I touch turns to dust. You need a Mederi."

"I know you're not a Mederi," Alba said, rolling her eyes. "But your mother is. And word on the street is that she's got a blackened garden. I'll pay good money for some black onions. Real ones. I'll even offer to make her a partner, with respect to the sale of the onions only, though." Alba waggled her finger at me, as if I'd already agreed to handle the contract negotiations. "Tell her we'll raise the price. Won't get as many people buying 'em," she grumbled, as much to herself as me. "Although . . . maybe we'll get more—"

"I don't know, Alba," I said, cutting her off. I didn't want her to get too excited about an idea that wouldn't work. "My mother doesn't grow anything anymore . . ."

But this time it was Alba's turn to cut me off. She barked out a laugh and said: "She wouldn't have to grow 'em. She'd just have to dig 'em up! *Luck* makes a sailor's fortune."

I raised my eyebrows at her. *Didn't Luck make everyone's fortune . . . or lack thereof?*

"Look," Alba continued, "I hired you so I could tell you what I'd done without you reporting me. I wasn't trying to trick anyone; I was trying to make a living. And the fact is, Hyrkes like to have a little fun with magic too."

Magic, fun? Hardly.

Alba must have seen my mood change because her expression suddenly became serious. She slipped her hand back into her apron pocket and withdrew it a second time.

This time she moved her hand toward me with a closed fist. When her hand was close enough to almost touch me, she uncurled her fingers and deposited something on the table in front of me. It was a small, black onion, about the size of a clove of garlic.

I stared at it.

"Go on," Alba urged. "It's the last real one I've got. Even a waning magic user can touch it without spoiling it."

"Trying to trick *me* wouldn't be wise, Alba," I growled, but she scoffed at my words, clearly unafraid of me.

"I may be ignorant, but I'm not stupid. The black onion is yours." She grabbed my hand and plopped the small bulb into it. "Take it. Your mother doesn't even have to say yes. Just *ask*."

Finally, I groaned and nodded and slipped the onion into my pocket. Alba smiled and left to place my order.

Since no one else was there that I knew, I took out my copy of *Manipulation: Modern-Day Control of the Demon Legions* to keep me company. I would have preferred the company of anyone else to that book, save the next person to enter—my father, whose entry set Alba's tiny doorbell tinkling in a happy fashion that was completely at odds with the person who had caused it.

The appearance of Karanos Onyx at the Black Onion had a stilling effect. All conversation stopped, as did the scraping of metal spatulas on the grill in back and the clinking of utensils on dishes out front. A fork fell off of a table and clattered to the wooden floor. My father glanced pointedly around the room and people fell back into their previous rhythms immediately, even if those "natural" rhythms now seemed deliberate. My father was the highest-ranking Maegester in all of Halja. He was executive to the Demon Council. No one wanted his gaze directly on them. Solo patrons buried their noses in books, and groups of twos and threes restarted stalled conversations with gusto, laughing a little too loudly and speaking a little too quickly. For my part, I simply frowned and watched my father's slow progress toward my table. I knew why he'd come.

"Don't see you in here much, Father," I said. "Seems like Empyr or the Dominion would be more comfortable lunch haunts for you."

"I take lunch wherever I am most needed, Nouiomo."

Instinctively, I searched for signs of emotion in his signature. *Just how angry was he that I'd run out on Jezebeth's execution?* But, as usual, his signature eluded detection.

"How come I've never felt your signature?" I asked. "Are you *always* cloaked?"

"Yes," he said peremptorily. And then something mildly shocking happened. He expanded his answer. "It wouldn't do for the executive not to be heavily warded at all times." His being so forthcoming prompted me to ask another question before I could think better of it.

"Who's your Guardian Angel? I've never met them."

To say Karanos glared at me would be giving his unblinking stare far too much emotion. "Noon, you only just declared your status as a waning magic user four months ago. There are a lot of people you don't know yet."

Alba sidled up to the table, looking pleased. However unpleasant this conversation might be for me, I couldn't help feeling the least little bit happy for Alba. Serving the executive lunch (as well as retelling the story of it) would definitely put more money in her till. I'll bet she wished she had saved that last black onion for him. Although Alba couldn't know that Karanos had even less of a chance convincing my mother to return to her garden than I did.

"What'll it be, Mr. Onyx?" she said. "Bread, soup, or fish?"

"Fish," my father said and Alba left. It wouldn't do to keep the executive waiting.

"You ran out on the execution today," Karanos said. "Ari covered for you."

I ground my teeth, but otherwise kept my expression neutral. It never paid to let my father see how upset he made me. Ari covering for me was the last thing I'd wanted, but my father continued his narrative of the morning's events, unconcerned with my concern.

"After you left, Ari threw a blast that instantly killed Jezebeth. His actions weren't merciful; they were . . . misguided." Karanos paused, allowing the full impact of what he was—and wasn't—saying sink in.

All Maegesters-in-Training were held to the highest standard of behavior. When you had the power to start fires with a thought or a touch and you theoretically had the power to control a demon legion, well, obviously the ruling elite took a close interest in your personal and professional development. Pursuant to both law and scripture, anyone born with waning magic had to declare it before the spring of their twenty-first year and then start training to become a Maegester—a demon peacekeeper or modern-day magical knight—because waning magic was the only kind of magic in Halja that could keep the demons in check. My Maegester career wasn't a choice. It was prescribed by my birth, required because of my blood and my magic.

Waning magic users whose actions were considered rogue were killed. No one, *no one*, defied the Demon Council and lived. Which was why hearing my father speak of Ari's actions as "misguided" sent a small fissure of alarm down my spine. He'd meant them to. I nervously twitched under his stare until our food arrived.

My soup turned out to be a creamy tomato flavored with the garlic I'd smelled earlier, as well as olive oil, vinegar, and sea salt. As Luck would have it, Alba's was serving their fish dish whole today. Apparently the cook had been given free rein and had come up with a dish that might have tasted good, but looked grotesque. Karanos' entire plate, save one tiny ramekin of sauce, was taken up with the body of a charred red snapper. I knew it was mesquite and not magic that gave the fish its blackened appearance and bulging eye, but still I blanched. My father, however, had no such reservations. He slit its back with a knife and then unflinchingly stabbed his fork downward, neatly detaching the skin.

"Where is Ari?" I asked, fighting to keep my voice steady. Gone was my false bravado when I had confronted Karanos earlier about his lack of signature and missing

Guardian. Here I'd been nursing a grudge because Ari
hadn't come after me when I'd fled to Corpus Justica.

Was Ari in trouble?

Across from me, my father continued to peel the skin
from his fish. He looked up at me, his black-eyed gaze
meeting mine. Only Karanos could fillet something and not
get a single speck of flesh on his impeccable suit.

"He took Ynocencia home," he said matter-of-factly,
peeling and slicing. "I ordered him to because I wanted to
talk to you."

I took a sip of my soup. It was ice-cold, which I wasn't
expecting—clearly it was meant to be served chilled. I
made a moue of distaste, which Karanos saw. The corner
of his mouth twitched in what may have been amusement
or, more likely, derision.

"When I was young, I wanted to be a mechanic," he said.
I dropped my spoon in my soup and a few drops of orange
splashed out onto my white paper place mat. I looked up
at my father in surprise. The comment was so personal,
so revealing. So unlike anything he'd ever shared with me
before.

"Hmm? Oh, yes," he said in a bland voice with a bland
expression that was only a smidge away from facetious. "I
spent all of my free time with Mark Grayson. The Hyrke
mechanic who lives on the Petrificai estate?"

I nodded. I knew Mark, although we'd never had much
to say to each other. Maegester magic didn't mix well with
machines.

"Grayson, and the Petrificus family, were gracious
enough to let me onto their repair docks. Luck knows how
much longer Grayson's repairs took with me hanging about,
but he never said a word. Everyone was always friendly,
very accommodating."

I swallowed, not wanting to say anything that might
interrupt one of the only stories I'd ever been told of my
father's life before becoming the executive. Across the
table, Karanos delicately deboned the fish. He placed the
spine and rib bones on top of the pile of discarded skin.

He stared at me then, and for just a moment the deadness of his stare reminded me of the snapper's bulging eye.

"What happened?" I said in a soft croak.

"I grew up," he said sharply. "I turned twenty-one. I declared."

With a single neat motion, Karanos sliced off the snapper's head and pushed the plate toward me.

"Jezebeth was guilty and deserved to die," he said stonily.

We stared at each other for a few moments. The deliberate conversational hum in the room became more forced. Hyrkes couldn't sense my magic heating up, but they could see the flush in my face and my clenched hands on the table. But then Karanos got up, dropped his napkin in his chair, and walked out.

Just before he left, he called over his shoulder, "The snapper is for you. I remembered how much you hate filleting them."

I wanted to remind him that I hated eating them too, but I knew he remembered. That's why he'd ordered it.

Chapter 3

ॐ

After the snapper incident, I had no appetite, but I didn't want to offend Alba so I ate half my bread and managed to choke down the rest of my soup. *Damn* my father, I thought viciously. We were all damned anyway, or so some believed, but saying it helped keep my anger in check so I didn't burn down the Black Onion. I left an enormous tip that included Alba's dollar and enough to recompense for the untouched fish, grabbed my books, and headed back to Corpus Justica. I stayed at the library until close, reviewing doctrines, defenses, and demons because, in one very important way, survival at St. Luck's was no different from in Halja as a whole.

Ignorantia legis neminem non excusat. Ignorance of the law excuses no one.

When I returned to my dorm room it was after midnight and Ivy, my roommate, was already asleep. I dropped my backpack as quietly as I could, stripped off my clothes, and slipped into bed without even brushing my teeth or washing my face. Why bother when I'd be up again before the sun anyway? But five hours later, when I awoke feeling completely unrefreshed, I thought better of my mini rebellion and scrubbed and brushed extra hard. Heading out into the warm, humid air of a midsummer morning, my skin glowed, my teeth shone, but my eyes were still bleary and bloodshot. Nothing short of a spell could disguise the tired, haggard look of a St. Luck's law student.

Manipulation class, the class that taught us how to manipulate our magic and control our demon clients, was starting at the Luck-forsaken hour of 8:00 a.m. All future Maegesters were required to take it. Manipulation was held in Rickard Building, where all of our other classes were held, but the classroom was on the fourth floor, an unoccupied, almost forgotten section of the building, furnished with decades-old desks, lithographs, and inkwells. Not that anyone actually used the inkwells these days. The rationale for such an old-fashioned venue was that visiting demon clients (who were sometimes centuries old) would feel more comfortable there, but I thought the real reason might have been to keep the Hyrke students happy. Most Hyrkes worshipped a demon or two but not many would actually want to meet one.

I entered the classroom as I always did, tense. Even if my own client had not tried to kill me in this very room last semester, the room, its occupants, and what we discussed here still would have made me tense. I concentrated on keeping my signature in check. I'd learned a lot about how to control my magic, but unfortunate accidents still happened from time to time.

Quintus Rochester, our professor, was leaning against the front of his desk, his bulk nearly hiding it, glancing at his watch. I had sixty seconds to get to my seat or I'd be sure to be his first victim.

Why didn't I get here earlier?

Because I couldn't stand to be in this room for longer than what was absolutely necessary. I nodded to Mercator, the only other student in the class besides Ari who would nod back at me, and scooted into my seat. The seat next to me, Ari's seat, was empty. I guess he hadn't made it back yet from escorting Ynocencia home. I couldn't imagine how horrible that assignment must have been, making sure the lover of the demon he had just killed made it back safely into the arms of her abusive husband. But Karanos wouldn't have seen it that way. After Ari's protocol breach yesterday, Karanos would have viewed the escort assignment as the perfect test of fealty. *Huh.* Now that I thought about it, I was surprised my father hadn't demanded that I *eat* the snapper he'd ordered for me. But as it turned out, my father had a far greater test planned for me.

If revenge is a dish best served cold, then knowledge is a dish best left untouched.

"Ms. Onyx," Rochester's gravelly voice erupted from his mountainous being like a lava spill, slow moving but unmistakably deadly. "Define duty."

Ugh. My mental musings about fealty and my father had inadvertently brought about the very thing I'd sought to avoid: Rochester's attention. It was tempting to blurt out something about *ad valorem* taxes or import duties in an effort to misdirect the discussion, but such an attempt would be academically disadvantageous, as well as completely ineffective. Rochester always got right to the point and he expected his students to do the same.

"A duty is an obligation that one person has toward another."

"So a duty is the same thing as an obligation?"

"Not necessarily. 'Obligation' implies that something was received in return for the duty owed."

"So all obligations are duties, but not all duties are obligations?"

"No . . ." Jeez, I was losing ground already and Rochester was only two questions in. To my left, Brunus Olivine, a nasty, lecherous, repugnant Maegester-in-Training whose signature always made me think of rotten cabbage, snickered.

"A duty is something that's owed," I said, correcting my earlier answer.

"Why would someone owe something for nothing? Isn't one of the basic tenets of contract law consideration?"

"Yes," I said slowly, thinking, "but duties can be imposed by all kinds of things, not just a contract."

"So all contracts are duties, but not all duties are contracts?"

I nodded. Rochester stared. I swallowed. I knew he would have preferred an unequivocal "yes" to a nod but my analysis felt shaky. To my detriment, I'd glossed over the duty readings last night in favor of the demons and defenses. Little wonder why, but now I'd pay for my poor choice. As if on cue, Rochester started windmilling his massive arm in an attempt to get me to answer faster.

"And how does that work?"

"Duties can arise from all sorts of things. Contracts, promises, moral and ethical obligations, emotional attachments—"

"To whom are duties owed in those situations?"

I opened my mouth and closed it. The examples were almost limitless. Duties were owed to the Council, to clients, to Luck, to those we lived with, worked with, loved. The demons owed duties to those who followed them; the Angels to the wards they were sworn to protect. Now that I'd been forced to think about it, Halja had infinitely more duties than demons. Anyone who had ever had any kind of a relationship with anyone had owed some kind of duty at some point. I said as much to Rochester, who finally nodded at something I was saying.

"Right. *Relationships* create duties. Your first answer was correct, Ms. Onyx. Duties and obligations are nearly synonymous, because every relationship confers benefits on its participants. Just by virtue of being in a relationship, a party receives something so a debt is then owed to the other."

"Yeah, *benefits*," Brunus sniggered, glancing over at Mercator. "Do you think your benefits with your fiancée are the same as Noon's with Ari?"

Mercator's signature pulsed and Brunus grunted. He looked ready to throw something fiery in return but Rochester cleared his throat. There was no official policy on when it was appropriate to throw waning magic in Manipulation. Class rank was established based on magic use so, of course, there was some showing off. But Rochester always reined us in when small eruptions threatened to become major interruptions.

"Ms. Onyx, what is the duty of an outpost lord?"

"To provide for his people."

"That's not a literal obligation, is it? Outpost lords are just figureheads, right?"

"No," I said, my tone almost ominous. "It *is* literal. Like everything else in Halja," I muttered. And that was the crux of it, I thought. My problem with Halja. My problem with St. Lucifer's, this class, and yesterday's execution.

Under demon law, when a person owed a duty of care to a stranger, it didn't mean be careful. It meant *care*. A person had to care about the person you owed the duty to, which was ridiculous. Only the demons would try to legislate caring and concern. *As if.* But I knew why they'd done it. Because it was the only way they could do it. The only way they *could* care about perfect strangers was on paper. Demons didn't understand the difference between words and actions. "Do as I say, not as I do" was a Hyrke phrase. Humans understood the nuanced agonies and emotional intricacies involved with ethical dilemmas, but not demons. To the demons, everything was black and white. Morality was a math equation. They never had to worry about guilty consciences because (even if they had consciences) their own law gave them an out. If the law said a person had to die for their sins, they were executed. And no one would feel bad about it. Because there was no duty of care owed to criminals. And if demon law didn't require a duty of care . . . Well, the demons just didn't care. So where did that leave waning magic users like me?

Grinding my teeth.

Rochester paced the front of the room. The way he intentionally bumped his signature into ours when he was questioning us made me think of a mortar and pestle. Rochester was the pestle and we students were the mortars—

empty ones, of course, because if we'd had anything to buffer the grinding crush of his signature against ours, then Rochester wouldn't get as much perverse pleasure out of our discomfort as he did. He turned around to face his desk and rummaged around in the stacks of papers and books, finally pulling out a thick leathery envelope with trailing ends of loose string and a broken wax seal. He threw it to me just as Ari walked into the classroom.

"The case file for your first field assignment, Ms. Onyx," he said when I caught it. "And you too, Mr. Carmine," Rochester said, addressing Ari. "As *Primoris*, Ms. Onyx has been selected as the lead investigator. As *Secundus*, you will be her partner." Ari nodded at Rochester and then turned toward me.

Suddenly, all the conflicted emotions I'd felt yesterday flared up again: my anger over the fact that there was very little mercy (if any) in Halja, my shame at running out on Jezebeth's execution, which had left Ari covering for me—the last thing I'd wanted. And my horror over Ari's swift execution of Jezebeth. I knew Ari, who had freelanced for my father as a demon executioner before enrolling at St. Luck's, was no stranger to executing demon wrongdoers, but *still* . . .

I met Ari's stare. Neither one of us smiled. If Rochester was aware of the tension between us, he ignored it.

"In your case file, you'll find an accusation—a demon complaint—filed by an outpost resident with the Demon Council. Locate the complaint and read it."

I did, wordlessly passing it to Ari when I was finished.

COUNTRY OF HALJA

DEMON COMPLAINT

- ☐ CITY OF NEW BABYLON
- ☐ TOWN OF ETINCELLE
- ☒ OUTPOST: <u>THE SHALLOWS</u>

ACCUSER: <u>ATHALIE RUST</u>
ACCUSED: <u>VODNIK, PATRON DEMON AND OUTPOST LORD</u>
DATE FILED: <u>SPRING</u>

CASE NO.: <u>2013 OSH 00000001</u>

NATURE OF COMPLAINT:

TO THE HONORABLE KARANOS ONYX, DEMON COUNCIL EX-
ECUTIVE, C/O THE BOAT MAN,

FIFTEEN. THAT'S HOW MANY MEN DISAPPEARED LAST WEEK.
ALL FISHERMEN, WHO KNEW THE MARSHES AND SHALLOW
LANDS. THEY WOULDN'T HAVE GOTTEN LOST. THEY WOULDN'T
HAVE LEFT. THEY LOVED US. AND BESIDES . . . THERE'S NO-
WHERE TO GO.

WE'VE BEEN HUNGRY. (VERY HUNGRY.) SO OUR DEMON
PATRON LED THE MEN INTO THE DARK WATERS TO FIND MORE
FISH. HE TOLD US THEY'D BE SAFE, BUT HE LIED. LORD VODNIK
AND OUR GEREFA, STILLWATER, WERE THE ONLY ONES TO RE-
TURN FROM THE DARK WATERS. WHEN WE ASKED THEM WHAT
HAPPENED, ALL THEY SAID WAS—GRIMASCA GOT THEM.

BUT GRIMASCA ISN'T REAL. VODNIK IS.

AND VODNIK IS THE ONE WHO KILLED THOSE MEN.

MAY LUCK FAVOR YOU (AND FIND US),

ATHALIE RUST

After Ari was finished reading, Rochester summarized
the contents of the complaint for the rest of the class.
"Who's Vodnik?" he then barked out. "Has anyone read his
Demon Register entry?" This was another of Rochester's

favorite assault tactics, accusing us of not spending enough time with Halja's demonicopedia.

Sasha's hand shot up and Rochester nodded at him.

"Vodnik is a water demon and the current outpost lord for the Shallows, a poor fishing community in the far eastern region of Halja. The Register says he was spawned in a polluted storm drain somewhere along River Road . . . sometime in the last half century . . . I think."

Sasha paused. Rochester frowned.

"Well over four centuries ago," Mercator corrected. Sasha gave him a cool look, which Mercator ignored. In Manipulation, we learned almost as much from Mercator's extracurricular readings as we did from the big man himself. Mercator continued.

"Sometime around 1593, Vodnik and a group of followers set sail down the Lethe. They'd intended to sail as far as the sea, but six months into their journey they hit the trifecta of travel woes: sickness, spoiled food rations, and shallow waters. Vodnik convinced the party their bad luck was really Luck's hand, guiding them to settle there."

"And Grimasca?" Ari said, looking at Rochester first and then Mercator. "There's no Grimasca listed in the Demon Register. Which demon is Ms. Rust referring to?"

Rochester gave the class a hard look. "Some of your mothers must surely have warned you about Grimasca?"

To my surprise, Mercator, Sasha, and Tosca all nodded.

"Well, what did your mothers say? Speak up," Rochester commanded.

Tosca answered first, saying that his mother had called Grimasca the Demon of Hunger. "She said he was spawned before Armageddon, which makes him even older than Luck. She said he was the biggest and baddest hellcnight that ever lived."

I'd never heard of Grimasca, but I'd heard of hellcnights. They were a particularly vicious and venomous type of demon. All demons can shape shift, usually into horrifying beasts, creatures, or natural phenomena like wind, rain, plague, or fire. But hellcnights could shift into a mirror image of any living thing. But what really made them dangerous, and something to be extraordinarily cautious of, was the fact that, in addition to their ability to manipulate their physical shapes, they could also mask, manipulate, and mirror signatures. So even I wouldn't be able to distinguish a real person from its hellcnight imposter.

Sasha told us his mother had referred to Grimasca as Lucifer's Spy. According to her, Lucifer used Grimasca's uncanny ability to impersonate in order to gather information and infiltrate enemy groups. His favorite alias? A Hyrke butcher. According to Sasha's mother, Grimasca had three parallel scars on his cheek that he'd put there himself.

"But Grimasca wasn't just a spy," Mercator said quietly. "He was also supposed to have been an assassin. Luck used his butcher alias not just to gather information and infiltrate enemy groups, but also to execute his adversaries. Grimasca's bite, as well as the bite of all hellcnights, is poisonous. Anyone bitten by them succumbs to a deep and unbroken sleep. It's interesting that your mother called him the Demon of Hunger, Tosca. There's a rumor that after Armageddon, when Halja was starving, Grimasca and his hellcnights went for so long without food that they no longer needed it. That they found other sources of sustenance."

"Yeah, well, what did *your* mother call him?" Tosca asked Mercator, as if Mercator had called his mother's honor into question instead of just suggesting there might be more than one interpretation of Grimasca's legend.

"The Grim Mask of Death."

Everyone got quiet after that. Mercator's mother's moniker for Lucifer's spy slayer seemed to sum up all of the horrid things all the mothers had said about him.

I considered the stories I'd just been told. Most demons lived for centuries, not millennia. And the fact that Rochester knew Grimasca's story had likely been told to students by their mothers had me thinking Grimasca sounded like more of a myth than a drakon did. In fact, Grimasca actually sounded more like a children's boogeyman than anything else. But we lived in Halja, a country where anything was possible and all demons, no matter how mythological they might sound, were potentially real. When it became clear Rochester wasn't going to comment on the stories' veracity—or lack thereof—I asked him outright: "Are any of those stories true?"

Rochester carefully folded his hands across his belly, contemplating me.

"You and Mr. Carmine will have to tell us," he said finally. "That's part of your assignment—determining the truth of the accusation. What really happened to the fishermen? Is a demon responsible? If so, which one? Needless to say, any demon that is found guilty will have to be dealt with on-site."

"Dealt with?" I said, my voice steely. "Don't you mean executed?" This assignment wasn't about testing my academic skills or my magic. This assignment was about testing *me*.

Could I? Would I?

Bizarrely, an image of the taupe-eyed Angel's contemplative gaze from yesterday popped into my head. Underneath my desk, I dug my fingernails into my thigh.

"That's exactly what I mean, Ms. Onyx," Rochester said. I didn't nod. I couldn't. I just sat there, staring at Rochester, who stared back at me.

The classroom was eerily silent. Sure, half my classmates resented me (I'd joined this class late in the first semester and, due to circumstances I'd rather have avoided, had been involuntarily catapulted into the *Primoris* position), but even the most resentful of them must have realized the gravity of the situation. First, the trip to the Shallows would be dangerous all on its own. Traveling conditions had improved only slightly in the last four hundred years. Sickness and hunger might not be a problem, but rough waters, *rogare* demons, and other unseen river dangers were still very much a threat to any party sailing the Lethe. Second, no demon would welcome Council involvement in outpost affairs. Sure, Vodnik would be obliged to put us up and allow us to investigate, but he was a demon. He would be planning all sorts of cunning ways to make our deaths in the Shallows look accidental. And, life being what it was out there in the eastern hinterlands of Halja, staging an accidental death would be all too easy. Third, and worst by far, was the fact that the assignment wasn't random. If my investigation proved that either Vodnik or Grimasca (if such a demon even existed in the first place) was guilty, I would have to execute it.

"You won't be without help," Rochester said. "In addition to Mr. Carmine, who's had some prior field experience, your captain, Ferenc Delgato, will also act as a guide and mentor. Delgato is an old friend of mine. He's going to continue your Manipulation training en route." I swallowed and nodded slowly. I was glad to hear there would be a more experienced Maegester accompanying us.

Rochester rummaged around in his desk, finally pulling out a silver vial on a silver chain. He walked over to my desk, the tiny vial swinging gently from his finger.

"Is there a demon in there?" I said, eyeing the vessel suspiciously. Last semester, Rochester had delivered a demon familiar to me in a silver filigreed ball that looked disturbingly similar to this piece.

"Even if there were, Ms. Onyx, you'd be bound to accept what help I offered you." When I still didn't reach for it, he grunted and said, "It's an alembic full of waerwater."

"Waerwater?" I said, reaching for the vial. "Never heard of it."

"Let's hope not," Rochester said. But instead of handing me the alembic, Rochester unclasped the chain and motioned for me to turn around. I did and a moment later Rochester had fastened the chain around my neck. I held up the silver vial, examining it more closely. There were no filigrees or scrolls. Nothing etched on its surface. The whole thing was as smooth as a mirror. I dropped the alembic and it thudded heavily against my chest.

"Waerwater is a type of truth serum," Rochester explained. "Any demon accused of a sin punishable by death has the right to request trial by waerwater. Have you used waerwater before, Mr. Carmine, when you were working for the executive?"

Ari nodded grimly.

"Good. Then you can instruct Ms. Onyx in its use should the need arise." But instead of nodding again, Ari just looked at me warily. I had the feeling I wouldn't like hearing what Ari had to say about using waerwater. The alembic suddenly felt even heavier around my neck. But Rochester was moving on. Class was almost over.

"The last bit of assistance," Rochester said, returning to stand at the front of the room, "will be provided by the Joshua School." He addressed everyone now. "This semester, each of you will have a chance to select a Guardian Angel to work with during your field assignments. Your Guardian Angel will travel with you and train with you. Select carefully. Some of these pairings last for a lifetime.

"Okay, that's it for today. Later tonight, read your case files. Everyone leaves in three days, immediately after Angel selection."

There was no time after class to speak to Ari privately. Instead, we walked to our lockers among a sea of students. I didn't want to talk about the *Carne Vale* or our assignment. Or what Ari had been doing before class or my lunch with Karanos yesterday. For now, I just wanted Ari to know I was glad he was back. When I shut my locker door, he was behind it, waiting for me. My gaze met his. On impulse, I reached my hand behind his head and pulled him toward me. I stood on my toes and pressed my lips to his for a long moment and then released him, glancing around self-consciously. Possessive displays weren't my usual habit, but the look on Ari's face assured me it was the right move. His expression softened and he gave me a slightly wondrous smile.

I always thought that Ari softened my edges, but sometimes it was the other way around.

Chapter 4

After Manipulation, we had Sin and Sanction and then Oathbreaking. That meant sitting through another four hours or so with almost a hundred other people—mostly Hyrkes, because Ari was the only other Maegester-in-Training in my section—who had no idea we'd just been given the Assignment of Death. In between Professor Telford's dry lectures on anticipatory repudiation and the ensuing duty of mitigation, I decided to satisfy a different duty that evening—my duty to my own curiosity.

They say Curiositas killed Cattus.

But no one really knows.

Curiositas was a fairly youngish demon living in the twelfth century, only a few decades old, when he met the gorgeously supple and fiercely feline demoness Cattus. When he asked her what she most wanted to do on their dates, Cattus kept telling Curiositas, "You don't want to know." But Curiositas, being Curiositas, kept at Cattus day and night, although mostly by night, because Cattus was nocturnal. Curiositas, on the other hand, was a day creature, all flecked with gold and shining brilliance. His preferred haunt was the Lethe and the two met at the docks every day at dusk.

Cattus would stare into the great murky depths of the Lethe, searching for any sign of Curiositas. Sometimes her ears would twitch. Sometimes her tail. Sometimes her eyes would grow big as saucers and her haunches would wriggle in anticipation. Curiositas never fully breached the surface of the water. He liked to tease Cattus, as she teased him. He gave her glimpses only of himself: a tiny bit of fin, a stream of bubbles, a patch of orange gold twisting just beneath the surface, sparkling, shimmering, just out of reach.

There's a romantic version of the story the Hyrkes like to tell. Some nonsense about the two demons being doomed lovers. But that's not the version I was told, nor is it the version I believe. Unlike the Hyrkes, I don't have any romantic notions about demons. They're much worse than Maegesters. *Much.* And that's why I know—although I wish I didn't—what Cattus most wanted to do with Curiositas. And that's why I believe the version that puts an end to Cattus' hunger.

Ivy, my Hyrke roommate, never gets my version of the story.

"Ends Cattus' hunger?" she always asks, frowning and exasperated. "What does that mean? Did Cattus finally catch Curiositas? Or did Curiositas really kill her?"

And, every time, I always wink and tell her:

"You don't want to know."

Yep, I thought, strolling with Ari to the very docks where Cattus—or Curisoitas—had been killed, *there are lots of things I don't want to know, about myself, about others . . . But surely, knowing what sort of person our new teacher, Captain Delgato, would be wasn't one of them.*

After all, forewarned was forearmed, right?

* * *

We skipped a cab ride in favor of a brisk walk to the docks but the humidity and my high-collared shirt meant that ten minutes in I felt sticky and gross. New Babylon was a major urban city, with tightly packed, tall buildings and loads of people—most of them Hyrkes. I followed in Ari's wake, elbowing my way through the congested streets, grateful that I'd stashed my books in my locker before I'd left. As we got closer to the docks, the crowd thinned. The commuter ferries docked farther west than the outpost boats, so before long it was only us and the gulls. They flew high above us, their raucous cries competing with flapping sails, lapping water, and squeaking ropes. When we finally reached the edge of the Lethe, I stood by Ari's side, my hand shielding my eyes from the brilliance of the setting sun flickering across the water. Tonight's Lethe wasn't dark and murky; instead, it shined like fire, although little difference it made to anything hiding beneath its surface.

Who would have thought that darkness and fire could be equally obscuring?

I dropped my hand and lowered my eyes, fishing in my pocket for the envelope Rochester had tossed me. Somewhere inside of it would be the name of Delgato's boat and its dock number. But instead of the envelope, my hand found Alba's onion and I withdrew it. In the warm honey glow of the setting sun, it looked grayish purple instead of black. Funny that I couldn't use it now even if I wanted to—I'd never sailed the Lethe. Sure, I'd traveled the width of it countless times, but never its length—and never on a boat with a sail.

"What's that?" Ari asked.

"A black onion," I said. "A real one. Alba gave it to me."

Ari's eyebrows shot up in surprise. "Are you sure it's real?"

In answer, I held it out to him in my palm. He didn't reach for it, though, just watched. When it was clear it wasn't going to rot, he nodded and smiled.

"I guess you won't have any problem with this semester's assignment," he said, laughing. "Just ask the black onion what happened to the fishermen."

I frowned. "Execute a demon based on a few words revealed to me by one tiny vegetable? Would you?"

He shrugged. "Magic doesn't lie."

"Maybe not. But it distorts the truth all the time." I slipped the black onion back in my pocket and reached for the other divination tool I'd been given recently, the alembic full of waerwater.

"Tell me about this," I said, sliding the vial gently back and forth on its chain. "Rochester said waerwater is like a truth serum. Do demons just drink it and then the magic forces them to answer questions truthfully?"

Ari grimaced. "A waerwater trial is as brutal as a *Carne Vale*. But it's the demon's choice. And anyone who survives it is set free."

I shook my head. "I don't understand."

"Waerwater trees are old, rare, and very strong. They grow out of ancient tar pits and their bark is like iron. They're so strong, in fact, that waning magic has to be used to drive the spile into the tree's base in order to tap it. Waerwater is the tree sap. You have to be careful when collecting it, though, because it will burn right through the skin of any waning magic user."

I dropped the alembic and reached up to unhook the clasp, but Ari stopped me.

"It won't hurt you in the alembic. And if it's around your neck, there's little chance that you'll lose it."

"What do you mean that anyone who survives it is set free? If it burns right through a demon's skin, what do you do with it?"

"The accused drinks it. Voluntarily. It's not a punishment. It's a right. Legend says some demons have survived. And anyone who does must be set free."

"What? Why?" I said, outraged. "Just because they were brave enough—or stupid enough—to play with magic and not get burned?"

Ari's look was piercing. "No, they're set free because

their survival is considered evidence of Luck's divine intervention."

"Do you believe that? Do you believe that a demon who survives drinking waerwater is automatically innocent of the sin he was accused of?"

Ari took a long time to answer.

"It doesn't matter what I believe."

"You told Rochester you'd used waerwater before. Have you seen a demon die after drinking it?"

He nodded.

"How many?"

At first I thought he'd refuse to answer. In the past, Ari had been reluctant to tell me much about his days as a demon executioner. But then he said, "More than a few."

"Have you seen any live?"

He shook his head.

"So it's really just an offer to let the accused fall on a sword?"

Ari just stared at me, his signature dimming. Around us, the wind kicked up. My black hair streamed out behind me like a flag as the myriad boats, tugs, dinghies, and dahabiyas that were tied at the water's edge bobbed up and down.

"Was Jezebeth offered a trial by waerwater?"

"Yes, but Ynocencia talked him out of it. Trial by waerwater is a painful way to die."

"More painful than a *Carne Vale*? How do you know all this anyway? Did you and Ynocencia have a heart-to-heart just before you dropped her back off with her abusive husband?"

The words just slipped out. Until then, I'd ignored all of my conflicted feelings over yesterday. But now that I'd voiced them, they sounded more vicious than conflicted. It wasn't fair, really, grilling Ari like this. He'd only done what he'd had to do. What the law required him to do. What the executive—*my father*—had ordered him to do. Hadn't it been mere hours ago that I'd actually been worried about him? Worried that his covering for me at the *Carne Vale* would get him in trouble?

Ari blew his breath out. He looked out across the Lethe and then finally back at me. In the deepening twilight, his eyes glistened like two pools of black ink.

"I didn't take her back to her husband."

Maybe it was how he said the words, or maybe it was the fact that his signature was now as tightly wrapped as I'd ever felt it, or maybe it was his defensive, closed stance, that had me look at him anew. And really see him for the first time that night.

Ari was exhausted—physically, magically, and emotionally. Dark circles ringed his eyes and a day's worth of stubble covered his chin and cheeks. His eyes had a slightly haunted look. Like he'd only just realized how much he had to lose. That missteps had consequences that went way beyond himself.

"Where did you take her, then?"

"Somewhere he'll never find her."

"But . . . ?"

"You think I should have done what your father asked?" he said quietly.

Yes. No! Luck, I didn't know. For an instant, I was just glad I hadn't had to make the decision. And then I was struck with the most horrifying shame I'd ever felt. Because—*again*—Ari had thrown my stones for me. The only reason he'd been asked to take Ynocencia back was because of something *I'd* done (or failed to do). I covered my face with my hands and just stood there, feeling angry, embarrassed, and weak.

Minutes passed and Ari did nothing but stand beside me. But it was enough. More than enough. Because, Luck knew, I wasn't perfect. Far, *far* from it. And he'd always stood by me. I finally lowered my hands, happy that my eyes had stayed dry.

"I'm sorry," I said, stepping close. Ari's heart beat wild and fast, despite his darkly serious expression. He moved his hands to the base of my neck. Lacing his fingers together, he then used his thumbs to gently tip my head back. His face was no more than an inch from mine or I might have missed his next word.

"Nouiomo."

When Ari's lips met mine, his signature released, as if he'd been holding a deep breath and had just exhaled. Unbidden and slightly out of control as always, my magic responded to his. Suddenly, I felt as if I'd just swam from Etincelle to New Babylon—underwater. I gulped and Ari slid his hand down so that it rested gently against my heart. Beneath his palm and the linen of my shirt, my heart beat madly and my demon mark stung like I'd just been shot with Eros' arrow.

After a few moments, I reached my arms behind Ari's back and clasped them together. I pressed my cheek into the coarse cotton of his shirt, smelling sweat instead of the clean, vanilla-laced scent I was used to. I didn't care.

"You know when I first fell in love with you, Noon?"

His words were low and muffled. I pressed my ear tighter against his chest and shook my head.

"Last semester when you killed Serafina."

I stiffened immediately but he put his arms around me. Serafina had been the small demon familiar that my father had sent me to "practice" with. Within a day, I had roasted her into oblivion.

"She deserved to die," said Ari. "She'd burned one of your friends, a defenseless Hyrke, right in front of you."

I remained mute. What he was saying was true, but it was only half the story. The real reason Serafina died was because I couldn't control my magic well enough to control her. Killing her hadn't been necessary; it had been a mistake.

"I'd never met anyone whose magic was so strong . . ." Ari said almost wistfully, "but whose heart was so soft."

I didn't think it was possible to stiffen any further. Ari had to know his words were making me feel worse. *This* was the story of how he fell in love with me? He'd just scored the hat trick of insults: Reminding me I'd killed something; reminding me I'd done it out of ineptitude; and then telling me I was really soft on the inside . . . That my heart had the strength of a soft-boiled egg.

"Ari," I said carefully, "I don't want to be weak."

He laughed. "You're the farthest thing from it."

"No. I mean on the inside."

He tried to tighten his hold on me, but I pushed back so that I could see his face. In the rising moonlight, there were lots of shadowed spots, portions I couldn't see. But I could tell he wasn't smiling.

"You can't fight my battles for me," I said.

He stared at me for a moment, his face dark and unreadable. Finally, he sighed.

"I know. *I know.*"

He seemed to be trying to convince himself as much as me.

Later, we looked for Captain Delgato and the boat we'd be sailing to the Shallows, but it wasn't in its slip. So much for satisfying my curiosity. Considering Cattus' fate, however, maybe it was for the best. Meeting my new teacher could probably wait.

Chapter 5

❦

Some say Evander Joshua was motivated by self-interest; others say he was a perfect Angel. What is known is this:

Joshua was an Angel who lived sometime in the early centuries after the Apocalypse, circa 100-200 AA. His mother had been a Mederi healer (a female descendant of Lucifer's Host born with waxing, or healing, magic) and his father had been an Angel (a descendant of the once-great but now-defeated Savior's army). At the time, relations between Host and Angel families were still strained. In spite of, or perhaps due to, his parents' ostracism and the frosty welcome he himself received from both sides, Joshua reimagined a Halja where Angel and Host lived, loved, learned, and worked side by side. He created the Guardian/Ward relationship and became the first Guardian Angel, serving Magnus Antimony, one of the earliest Council executives.

Was Joshua a romantic idealist or a keen political strategist?

Who knows? What I did know was that I was due to

report to the House of Metatron, a grand name for a small, dark ceremonial courtroom over at the Joshua School, at seven Wednesday morning to begin the tedious process of Angel selection—otherwise known as *Voir Dire*, or "to speak the truth."

Well, we'd see about the truth part. There was bound to be some embellishment, aggrandizement, and general blowing of horns. The Joshua School was just as competitive as St. Luck's. Angel students had until they graduated to find a ward or they'd face a lifetime of endless research in the never-ending stacks. Of course, some preferred academia to the field (and, having just been assigned my first field assignment, I wasn't sure I blamed them), and some became artists or winemakers, but most wanted a ward. Wards meant more money—and more prestige, which Angels loved as much as Mederies loved gardens and Maegesters loved fire (at least most Maegesters did . . . personally, I had a love/hate thing going with fire, but that's off topic . . .).

Angels. The point is that they are our protectors. Our paid protectors. But they also take an oath to guard their wards and, like everyone else in Halja, the Angels take their oaths very seriously. A good Angel would know how to hide their ward, how to heal them, at least until a Mederi could be found, and how to make them more deadly with all kinds of "booster" spells (lately, many second-semester Maegesters-in-Training—*ahem, Brunus!*—had been pouring over Angel *curricula vitae* in the hopes of securing the deadliest partner imaginable). Great Angels also knew all three of the primary demon languages and a handful of other, more obscure ones because an Angel's other purpose, in addition to being a Guardian, was to serve as interpreter and scribe for the Maegester they worked with.

But, unlike Brunus and the rest, I didn't want someone who would make me more deadly. I didn't care about spell-casting ability or linguistic scores. I didn't care about offensive, or even defensive, ratings. I just wanted to find someone who wouldn't make me want to jump overboard during our trip to the Shallows. Someone who would blend into the teak woodwork of whatever sailboat we were going to be sailing. Someone who wouldn't be obnoxious or offer unwanted opinions or ask unwarranted questions. Maybe even someone who would be fine not talking to me at all . . . Because I'd learned the hard way last semester that an Angel could turn on you just when you needed them the most.

Wednesday morning I woke cranky and irritated. It wasn't that it was still dark out when I woke (although who in their right mind would make plans before daylight in a country ruled by demons?); it was that it *wasn't* dark, at least not in my room. After one hundred eighty-one days of successfully ignoring the nearly all-consuming urge to set my morning alarm bell on fire, I'd finally gone and done it. And in spectacular fashion too. In those few seconds between sleeping and waking, I'd torched the whole thing into a mini mountain of melted copper and bronze that glowed like a night lamp and smoked like a volcano belching toxic fumes. I was so ticked off; I left it there to harden, uncaring of whether I would later be able to remove it from my desktop.

Ivy had left a note:

Noon—

Went to get coffee and biscuits. Meet Fitz and me in Timothy's Square at dawn to discuss Angel candidates.

Ivy

p.s. Wear something sexy. I heard Holden Pierce is a hottie!

I groaned. I'm surprised they didn't make an exception to the "Future Maegesters Only" rule for Manipulation for

Ivy. She was a master manipulator, even if she didn't have waning magic. This was her MO, always dropping very unsubtle hints about my need to bare my demon mark. As if the whole world didn't already know I was the Host's version of a Hyrke strong girl in a carnie sideshow. Despite Ivy's postscript, I made sure I wore something that covered my mark, but I amped up the vamp more than I would have otherwise. It wasn't to attract whoever this Holden Pierce was (I had my own hottie and was more than happy with him); it was to bolster my own confidence with superficial gloss.

Two minutes before sunrise, I left Megiddo and headed for Timothy's Square, garbed in a shockingly short, gray linen skirt, high platform satin sandals with black ribbon laces, and a hibiscus pink top that was sleeveless but came nearly to my collarbone. In fact, the shirt had a little extra detailing at the top in the form of a thin, slightly ridiculous, summer scarf. I strode over to the bench where Ivy and Fitz—Ivy's cousin and my other closest friend—sat waiting for me, my attitude a combination of haughty (another coping mechanism I was practicing for later), irritated (*still* at my melted alarm bell, not at Ivy or Fitz), and (the reason I kept focusing on the first two) *worried*—Big Time.

"Hey, Noon," Fitz said, giving me a salacious full-body stare that would have been offensive if it had been given by anyone other than Fitz. He winked and nodded slowly. "Looking good." Then he grinned and handed me a steaming paper cup and a small white paper bag. I smiled back and sat down.

I opened the bag and inhaled, hoping to replace the lingering toxic smell of metal burned by waning magic with the warm, doughy, sweet scent of breakfast biscuits lightly dusted with powdered sugar. I stuck my nose deep in the bag and breathed as if I were ridding myself of hiccups, but a second later Fitz smacked my arm, clearly impatient for news. Startled, I sucked in a lung full of powdered sugar and came up choking. My scarf came loose and one end of it got tangled up in the top of the bag. Ivy narrowed her eyes, sighed, flipped the end of the scarf over my shoulder, and pounded me on the back.

"What's up, Noon?" Fitz said, ignoring the hacking attack that he'd caused. "We've barely seen you this semester. Ivy and I want the skinny on All Things Dark and Scary."

Hmm . . . How to answer?

I cleared my throat.

Well, after ditching Jezebeth's execution, my dad tracked me down at the Black Onion and told me if I ever ditched again, I'd sleep with the fishes. Then I went to Manipulation class and got the Assignment from Hell, er, Halja, and walked with Ari to the docks, where he confessed to hiding a wife from her lawful husband despite having been ordered to do otherwise. Now I'm heading in to pick out a spellcasting partner. And I have no intention of actually working with them.

Of course, I didn't say all that. But, in between bites of biscuit, I did mumble something similar to that last line.

"We figured you'd say that," said Ivy. "That's why we took the liberty of thumbing through the Angel CVs and selecting the candidates *we* thought best suited to you." She took a big swig of her coffee, which was laced with steamed milk, licked the foam off her lip, and gave me a winsome smile.

I grimaced.

"Really, Noon, it's not that bad. I know you feel like—after what Peter did last semester—no Angel can be trusted, but some of these candidates look pretty good. Great, in fact."

"Then you work with them," I said petulantly. I knew I was being childish, but Fitz and Ivy were my best friends. If anyone understood how I felt about Angels (besides Ari), it would be them.

Ivy ignored me. "Let's start with Holden Pierce," she said. I looked to Fitz for his reaction, thinking maybe Ivy just wanted to vicariously man shop, but he was all business. He had my bound copy of the Angel CVs open to Pierce's page and was looking expectantly at me.

"I agree," he said to Ivy. "Pierce is ranked first. We should discuss him first."

Ugh. I wiped my hands on a napkin, stuffed it in my bag, crumpled the whole thing up, and neatly tossed it in a nearby trash can. Fine. If Fitz was getting down to business, I would too. And, frankly, I had less than an hour before I was supposed to report to the House of Metatron. In a fit of pique (*ahem*, sometimes I could be stupidly stubborn), I'd refused to review these CVs earlier. I supposed I should know something about the candidates I was expected to interview.

"What's his defensive rating?" I said.

"Ninety-eight point four," Fitz said, handing me the book. I skimmed Pierce's CV. It was as impressive as any top-ranking Angel candidate's would have been. Pierce was twenty-five years old; his parents were Bertrand and Samantha; he was in his third year at the Joshua School; he knew Hunnic and Dacian, in addition to Vandalic, Venetic, and Vestinian, the three primary demon languages. His *potentia* (an Angel's ability to stay focused and continue casting spells) was listed as "meritorious." His grades in Post-Apocalyptic History, Linguistics, and Spellcasting were as admirable as mine were in Sin and Sanction, Evil Deeds, and Manipulation. In short, he was an amazing candidate, except . . .

I grunted.

"Yeah," Fitz laughed. "You see his offensive rating? Is that unbelievable or what?" He grabbed the book back and stared at Pierce's CV like Pierce was some sort of Hyrke super toy that Fitz couldn't wait to unwrap at Yule. "And did you see his specialty?" he asked dreamily. "Enforcement."

"I saw it," I said dryly, looking at Ivy. "*This* is the guy you wanted me to dress up for? His 'noteworthy' spells are Painfall, Damage Cascade, and Hemorrhage. *Really?*"

Ivy had the good grace to look chagrined. "Well, he *is* ranked first . . . And so are you! Why not?" she asked, eyes blazing indignantly.

"Um, maybe because him and Brunus already have *'Amici Optimi In Aeternum'* tattooed on each of their arms."

She sighed, frowning, resigned to the inevitable. Fitz sighed, smiling, eyes closed, still unwrapping imaginary toy army Angels. I snatched the book back from him.

"Hey!" he cried, opening his eyes. He refocused on me. "Lambert Jeffries."

"Ranked second," Ivy said, flipping to his page. "His academic scores and field ratings are almost as good as Pierce's. His *potentia* is listed as 'commendable.' And he speaks Aquaian. That might come in handy. Didn't you say your field assignment was in one of the outposts? Which one?"

"The Shallows."

"Whoa. That's . . . Well, it's . . ." Ivy didn't often sputter. She didn't have magic, but she was usually very self-assured.

"So you've been there?" I asked, thinking that I remembered Ivy saying once that she'd been to every out-post. "What's it like?"

"A thin and watery place," she said softly. "A hungry place."

She glanced guiltily at her empty biscuit bag. "I was only there once, when I was small, maybe seven or eight years old. I don't remember much."

We were all quiet for a moment and I sensed the only other memories Ivy had of the Shallows were bad ones, and not very helpful.

"Who's your captain?" Ivy said finally, with forced cheer.

"Ferenc Delgato."

"Odd," said Ivy, her freckled face screwed up with concentration. "I've never heard of him. Maybe he's new . . . ?"

"He's an old friend of Rochester's. He'll be our captain,

as well as our new Manipulation teacher." I looked at my watch. Twenty minutes to go.

Fitz suddenly sat up straighter. "I could go with you," he blurted out. "Get a job as the mechanic or cook."

I frowned, thinking the last thing I needed was a defenseless Hyrke that I cared about coming along. At least the river Hyrkes were well versed in the dangers they faced. Ivy just laughed.

"What in all of Luck's great land do you know about machines . . . or even cooking?" Then she hooted and guffawed and slapped her knee while Fitz glared at her, and then we all got down to business again. But I was touched that Fitz had offered.

"Okay," I said. "Lambert Jeffries. Number two. Lay it on me."

"Well," Ivy said, "like I was saying, he speaks Aquaian, which could come in handy since you'll be sailing the Lethe." She paused and glanced at Fitz. "Aquaian is what a lot of water demons speak."

"I know that!" Fitz awkwardly ran a hand through his hair and turned away. His carrot-topped mane was always in shambles and he'd just made it worse. I sensed this was the wrong time to tell him.

"Fitz, who would you pick for me?"

"Me?" he said, turning back around to face me.

"Yes, you. You and Ivy have obviously spent some time with these CVs. What do you think?"

I was genuinely curious. I knew Ivy would make her preference known regardless of who anyone else thought would be a good choice. But Fitz was likely to go along with her suggestion once it was made and I wanted to know what his choice would be.

"Fara Vanderlin," he said, after a brief hesitation.

"Fara! You can't be serious!" Ivy practically jumped up from the bench. She suddenly became very animated, gesturing wildly, almost knocking my coffee cup out of my hands. Luckily, it was empty.

"She's ranked fourth, Ivy. Luck, it's not as if she's not any good."

"But her voice. It's like a shrew's. How can any Angel talk like that? It's got to affect her performance."

"Obviously it doesn't," he said huffily, as if Ivy had just called his own competency into question.

"Vanderlin, huh?" I said. "What's her specialty?"

We were sitting on a bench facing south. Behind the Joshua School, the sun was just poking up. Fitz glanced left for a moment at it and I did too. The city's low skyline looked like a series of black bricks set against pink foil. For a moment, what we saw was simple and beautiful, dark shapes against a cotton candy sky. But I knew as the sun rose higher it would shed its light on all the hollow, unseen spots. The ugly spots that were better off left in the dark. The spots full of dirt and filth, age and disease, and sometimes, even a demon or two.

"She's a gap filler," Fitz said quietly, not looking at me.

"What's a gap filler?" Ivy asked, amazed that Fitz seemed to know something she didn't.

"An Angel who finds spells that will fill in the gaps of their ward's experience level," I said, sensing why Fitz had been reluctant to tell me his choice. "My father calls them 'Gum and Pin' men. Get it? *G-A-P*?"

Ivy frowned, clearly confused. "What are you talking about? Chewing gum? Hat pins?"

"The term isn't complimentary. He thinks of them as jacks-of-all-trades, masters-of-none. Why do you think she'd be good for me, Fitz?"

"Because she can cast Clean Conscience."

Ivy just pursed her lips together. I did too. I'd never heard of the spell Clean Conscience, but its name said it all. I guessed if I were teamed with Fara, executing Jezebeth would have been a slam dunk. Kill first, ask for magical moral whitewash later.

I stood up and reached my hand out toward Fitz, motioning impatiently. I needed my book of CVs back and I needed to get on over to the House of Metatron *now*. Fitz stared at me for a moment and I had the oddest thought: when he was serious, Fitz actually looked handsome—in a rough, uneven sort of way. He placed the book in my hand and stood up too. I said my good-byes and started walking toward the Joshua School, feeling as if I were carrying a backpack full of five hornbooks, instead of just a slim bound copy of a dozen CVs or so.

Fitz caught up to me just as I was getting ready to cross Angel Street. He tapped me on the shoulder and I turned toward him.

"We care about you, that's all," he said. "You're a good person, Noon, and we don't want anything to happen to you."

I thought how funny we must look together. Me, in high satin sandals and a full face of makeup, and him in ripped cargo pants and a shirt upon which he'd hand painted the words, *"Roccaturi te salutant!" We who are about to rock salute you!* It was a phrase our Council Procedure professor, Darius Dorio, was overly fond of.

"If I'm such a good person," I said, "then I don't need an Angel who carries guilt erasers in her pencil pack."

The light changed and I tapped my finger against the letters on Fitz's chest. I gave him a mock salute and raced across Angel Street and toward the Joshua School.

Chapter 6

❧

Leaning against the beige brick wall of the Joshua School, just outside its entrance, was the taupe-eyed Angel who'd cornered me at Jezebeth's execution. His back was to the bricks and one leg was bent, sole resting against the wall. His sandy blond hair fell in disorderly waves to his shoulders, partially obscuring his face. As I neared the door, he raised his hand to his mouth and puffed on a cigarette. A shiny silver bracelet on his right arm caught the sun, flashing brilliantly a second before the tip of his cigarette turned first fiery red, then grayish black, and then disintegrated completely.

I put my hand on the door handle, happy that his ragged mop of hair prevented him from seeing me as much as me him. I had no desire to be peppered with another round of obnoxious, intrusive questions.

That's what you're telling him, right? That he ought to put his magic where his mouth is. What about you? Would you? Could you?

I sneered to myself and yanked open the Joshua School's heavy glass door.

"Who's your friend?"

I paused and released the door handle, glancing over at the Angel. I guess he'd noticed me after all.

The Angel gestured across the street to where Fitz still waited. Fitz gave me a small wave and turned back toward St. Luck's.

"Love the shirt," said the Angel, smiling. He shook his head like he couldn't believe anyone would wear anything so stupid.

"My friends are none of your business, spellcaster," I snapped.

"Probably not," he said, looking down at my bound copy of CVs. "Have you picked out which one of us you want to work with yet?"

Ugh. Us?

"*You're* in the pool?"

He nodded and exhaled while looking straight at me. It wasn't quite blowing smoke in my face.

"No worries, firestarter. It won't be me. I'm ranked dead last."

I yanked open the door again and disappeared inside. *Whatever.*

I hadn't been in the Joshua School since last semester, before my ex–best friend, Peter Aster, had betrayed my trust. Peter wouldn't be here this morning (he was completing his studies off campus, in a place even more prestigious than the Joshua School), but the place still made me feel queasy. Like no one could be trusted, like everyone was wearing a glamour, like what you saw *wasn't* what you'd get.

The Joshua School was amazingly contemporary looking for folks who made their living off of ancient knowledge. The whole place gleamed with bubbled glass, oiled iron, and bleached wood. Odd, funky furniture covered with slim cushions in block patterns were tastefully arranged throughout the room. One entire wall (the one behind the Angel's gatekeeper, the building's security guard) was lined with square cubbies full of mail, letters, scrolls, feathers, ink pens, and leather pouches, all likely full of charms, both ensorcelled and not, and myriad other things people had left for the Angels and that the Angels had left there for themselves. It was their equivalent of a post office and locker all in one. But locks weren't required for the "lockers" because no one in their right mind would steal from an Angel. You'd likely be poisoned, cursed, or worse.

Joshua School's lobby was crowded with groups of twos and threes. There was a hum to the place and a general mood of excitement. I gathered *Voir Dire* was as much of a big deal to the Angels as it was to the Maegesters-in-Training.

I knew immediately that Ari was somewhere in the lobby because I felt his signature. It felt reassuringly warm and vibrant, like sunshine. *This* must have been what the person who first used the term "sun kissed" had been feeling.

I smiled to myself and moved through the crowd, following Ari's strengthening signature, until I found him at the far end of the room, talking to an ethereally beautiful woman. I knew instantly that she was an Angel. Angels loved three things: ancient languages, history, and telling a good story. They were natural poets, bards, and actors. Grand spellcasters cast their spells as if all the world was their stage. This confidence, combined with the strength of their beliefs, was what separated the mediocre from the erudite, the middling from the transcendent.

This woman held herself as if she were ringmaster for every beast in Halja, and since Halja's beasts were mostly demons, just the act of portraying such confidence was in and of itself quite a feat. She had long, flaxen hair and moss green eyes. She didn't smile, nor did she frown. Her gaze was focused intently on Ari in a predatory, almost raptor-like way. Only when I was within a few feet of them did she break eye contact with him and glance over to me. Her gaze was arresting. Even I, who viewed this whole Angel selection business with a gimlet eye, couldn't help wondering for a moment what sorts of spells this girl could cast. She simply radiated faith magic. I was almost afraid to touch her.

"Nice glamour," I said.

"'Truth has no face but that which we give her.' The Book of Joshua, seventeen, twenty-one."

Her voice was scratchy, like she'd just gotten over a bout with pneumonia or was suffering from laryngitis. I gaped at her for a moment, realizing who she was.

Fara Vanderlin—the Angel Fitz thought I should work with.

She murmured one word and changed her glamour (it was as easy for her as trading one hat for another, which was impressive) and stood before us as a mousy-looking, bucktoothed, pimple-laden, glasses-wearing girl of about fifteen or so. The effect was almost too perfect, too stereotypically bookish.

"Do you prefer this?" she asked. Her voice didn't match this new glamour any better than the last.

"Actually, I prefer no glamour," I said. *I prefer "no Angel" too,* I thought, but kept that thought to myself.

"I know," she said, frowning, glancing at Ari. "He said you wouldn't like working with someone who's constantly veiled. But you'll need to be veiled from time to time in your work and I wanted you to see that I am capable of putting on a good glamour. After all, 'An investigation requires many tools, but a glamour is the handle which fits them all.' The Book of Joshua, twelve, eighteen."

I snorted. "Maybe," I said, "but I always liked, 'We must look demons in the face.' Joshua, one, twenty."

I expected her to look annoyed. Angels usually didn't like it when you quoted the Book back at them, but instead she positively beamed.

"You've read Joshua!" she squeaked excitedly. "I just *knew* we'd be a good match!" She hopped up and down and squeezed Ari's arm. I stared at Ari. He stared back. Finally, Fara's smile disappeared.

"Well, I'll see you both inside, then," she said nervously

and let go of Ari's arm. With one raspy word, she switched her glamour back to "Halja's Reining Ringmaster" and sauntered away. Now I knew why Ivy had reacted the way she had when Fitz had mentioned Fara's name. I could never work with her. Nothing about her was real. Her face changed with the snap of a finger and her thoughts were regurgitated from a book. Who knew who Fara Vanderlin really was? Did she? I doubted it.

"You too, Ari? Fara Vanderlin? I'd sooner work with a demon. At least then I'd know what I was getting."

"Fara can be anything you need her to be. That's why she's a great choice for you."

"Yeah, well, I need her to be paired with someone else."

"You know you'll need to pick someone, right?"

"What about you?" I countered. "Who would be a great choice for you?"

He shrugged. "That depends on who you choose."

"You know you'll need to pick someone for *you*, right?" I said, my tone mimicking his earlier one.

Before he could respond, a gong sounded. Its initial metallic zing tweaked my nerves and the lingering hum of it made my hair stand on end. I wasn't the only one. I felt the collective signature of the other waning magic users in the room expand. For a moment, it felt like the whole room was the inside of a balloon that was about to pop. But then I heard the bang of heavy doors and that expansive feeling seemed to be sucked into whatever portal had just been opened. A sonorous voice boomed from the other end of the lobby:

"Welcome, Maegesters. The House of Metatron is now open for this year's *Voir Dire*."

Immediately the twenty or so people in the room queued up in front of the two giant wooden doors that had just been opened. The doors were carved mahogany, the only dark thing in the room. Near the front I saw Rochester standing with a man I didn't recognize. He must be the Angel emcee. He looked downright jovial next to Rochester. He was average height, slightly paunchy, with curling gray hair. From my place at the back of the line, I couldn't see his eye color or distinguish any other features. In front of me, two Angels I didn't know—a man with an egg-shaped face and hair shaved so short he was practically bald, and a woman with angular features and long light-bright flyaway hair—were whispering to each other. They glanced back at me and I debated introducing myself, but then I noticed that the Angel in front was passing something out at the door.

Shades of last semester! I thought. *What was up with the Angels and their damned door prizes?* Last semester, at the entrance to a ball held upstairs on the thirty-third floor, seraphim had handed out lilies. Real ones. The kind that wither and die instantly when waning magic users touch them. One of the seraphim had been very insistent that I accept his "gift." I'd had to threaten to burn the whole place down before he backed off. I wondered what they were passing out now and whether I'd want it and, if I didn't, whether I'd be able to refuse it.

No one was talking much in line (hard to openly discuss possible pairings with everyone standing twenty feet or so from one another) so I flipped open my CV book to review some of the candidates we'd missed this morning. Lambert Jeffries, the number two Angel, was probably worth taking a closer look at.

Yep, I had squawked up a storm about this whole Angel-selection business—and it was true that, given my druthers, I really would prefer *no Angel* to working with one of these strangers—but the plain simple truth was . . . I doubted I'd survive my upcoming trip to the Shallows without a Guardian. So it was time to shed the histrionics I sometimes allowed myself and get serious.

As Ivy had said, Jeffries' scores and rankings were impressive and he spoke Aquaian. But some of the best things about Jeffries were things I hadn't noticed earlier: his specialty was *lex talionis*, or "adjudication," and one of his noteworthy spells was Discernment, which could really help us during our investigation. The other was Reciprocity. I hadn't heard of that one and wasn't sure of its value. Was it some sort of magic Golden Rule? If so, I could probably work with him. After all, "do unto others" wasn't such a bad motto, right?

I glanced over at Ari, who was staring at Jeffries' page with narrowed eyes. He looked up at me and gently shook his head. I frowned. I hated it when Ari tried to push me to do something (or, in this case, not to choose someone), even if it was supposedly for my own good. Did he still think Fara was a good pick just because she was a gap filler? I switched to her page. It was mostly stuff we'd already discussed but I noticed her other noteworthy spells were an AIR boost and Ascendancy. I bristled.

AIR boosts gave Maegesters greater accuracy and increased range. Ascendancy was known as a spell for weak Maegesters. Ones who had control issues. I clenched my jaw and flipped the page, willing myself not to think about my melted alarm bell.

On the next page was a name I didn't recognize: Raphael Sinclair. I skimmed his bio. Parents were Roderick and Valda, his grandfather had been Guardian to the seventy-fifth executive (mildly impressive), and his younger brother was deceased (that gave me pause; I had a twin brother and didn't want to contemplate what experiencing a loss like that must have been like). But then I saw the rest of his CV. It was absolutely preposterous. His *curriculum vitae*, or "course of life" was practically blank. His *potentia* and noteworthy spells were "TBD," he had no declared specialty, and both his defensive and offensive ratings were "Unknown." He'd gotten Cs in Spellcasting and Post-Apocalyptic History and—I almost laughed out loud—an F in Transcription. His only redeeming mark? An A in Linguistics, which, for an Angel, was like saying he knew how to read. He was ranked eleventh out of eleven. Suddenly, I knew exactly who this guy was.

No worries, firestarter. It won't be me. I'm ranked dead last.

This was the taupe-eyed Angel's page. The one who smoked and asked all kinds of unwanted questions. He was right. I wouldn't be choosing him. Then I did laugh out loud and looked up at Ari. He shrugged and rolled his eyes.

About half the line had gone in already. I saw now that the Angel emcee was offering everyone a sip of wine. *To steel our nerves?* Doubtful. The last thing an Angel would want to do is to decrease tension about an upcoming "show."

Finally, we moved close enough for me to get a good look at the Angel at the door. He held a silver chalice to the lips of the nearly bald Angel in front of me and murmured some words. The student Angel swallowed and accepted the white linen napkin that Rochester offered. After wiping his lips, he looked down at the napkin, peering closely at it. Was it my imagination or did his pale, egg-shaped face get even paler? After a moment's hesitation, he stepped into the darkened room of the House of Metatron.

The process was repeated with the Angel with the flyaway hair. The only difference was that she frowned when looking at her napkin and then stepped through the doors immediately. Finally, it was my turn. I nodded politely to Rochester and turned to face the Angel. He peered at me through eyes that were so milky white I wondered if he was blind. He cocked his head as if he were trying to get a better look at me, his gaze not quite focusing on me. A small fissure of alarm pierced my belly and I was suddenly glad Angels couldn't sense signatures.

"Welcome, Ms. Onyx," said the Angel. "I'm Friedrich Vanderlin, today's master of ceremonies. We've heard a lot about you since your declaration."

He smiled when he said it, but his smile was as empty as his gaze. I couldn't help wondering if what he'd heard about me had come from Peter, which probably meant he thought the worst of me.

"I'm happy to be here," I said. Even I could hear the false note in my voice. Friedrich's mouth quirked crookedly.

"My daughter's looking forward to working with you," he said. "Like father, like daughter, eh?" He reached out to give me a friendly pat on the shoulder and it took every ounce of willpower I had not to back away before he touched me. My reaction was overblown and didn't make sense. *What was he talking about anyway?*

"Friedrich is your father's Guardian," Ari said, frowning at Rochester. Guess Ari thought Rochester should have told me. I certainly thought someone should have, but since that person should have been my father I couldn't be too upset with the rest of them. This little revelation, however, only reinforced my decision not to work with Fara. If daughter really was like father—*no, thanks.*

Friedrich cocked an eyebrow and stared at me, his head tilted just a bit to the left. His white eyes gleamed a bit too brightly, like he was a cat who had his paw on a mouse's tail. Rochester cleared his throat and Friedrich turned around to wipe out and refill the silver chalice.

"You are familiar with Empyr wine, Ms. Onyx?" Rochester asked.

I nodded warily.

Angels were obsessed with apples. They took their love of this fruit very seriously, worshipping it as a symbol of the lost world they once ruled. A common motif in Angel art was the fallen apple that never rotted. Empyr wines were apple wines that were "enhanced" by some of the best Angel sommeliers in Halja. The enhancements were spells. Each batch had its own name, flavor, coloring, and associated spell. They were served upstairs in the Angels' infamous restaurant on this building's thirty-third floor.

I'd had Empyr wine exactly two times in my life. Each time it had produced life-altering effects, although in an indirect manner and not of the kind I could have guessed.

Friedrich turned back toward me and offered me the cup. Inside, the liquid was pink and fizzy and flecked with gold. I reached for the cup and there was a brief moment when I wasn't sure Friedrich would let go. *Was the spell tied to his touch?* I yanked harder and the wine nearly spilled out of the cup as it broke free from his grasp. Rochester's signature nudged mine, like a parent pinching an errant child. I glanced back at Ari, who gave me a tight smile.

I tipped the cup to my lips and drank. Immediately, a bitter, chalky taste filled my mouth. I hid my grimace, finished, and handed the cup back to Friedrich.

"This batch is called 'Fortuna's Favorites,'" Friedrich said. "Think you're one of them?"

Time will tell, I thought, but said instead, *"Fortes fortuna adiuvat."* Fortune favors the bold. Another of Dorio's sayings. Maybe Fitz had the right idea.

Friedrich grunted. Ari grinned.

Rochester held off magically pinching me again. Instead, he handed me a white linen napkin.

"A gift from this batch's sommelier," he said. "Some words of wisdom regarding this semester's assignment."

I choked back a laugh. *From tea leaves to wine tannins, where Angels fear not to tread . . .* I accepted the napkin and wiped my mouth gently. I'd been generous in this morning's application of Daredevil Red lip paint. Who knew what my fortune might be if I added too much of that to the mix? But the laugh died in my throat as I looked down at my napkin. Slowly, a stain of words appeared:

> **When traveling into the unknown, sometimes the biggest danger is the one you bring with you . . .**

The color of the words was entirely uncheerful. In fact, instead of wine or lip color, the words looked like they'd been written in dried blood. I crumpled up the napkin and shoved it at Rochester.

Then I pulled open the carved mahogany doors of the House of Metatron and entered its unwelcome darkness.

Chapter 7

ટ

If hanging out in the Joshua School lobby, with its slanted angles, crazy shapes, and glamoured Angels, had felt like being in a carnival fun house, then emerging from the hallway into the House of Metatron was like entering a dark house of mirrors, one that was lit with candle-filled silver sconces and shimmering chandeliers. The courtroom's mahogany walls curved into a soaring dome that was so high, the top disappeared into darkness. My guess was the Angels, who love white and bright, made this ceremonial courtroom dark in deference to the demons who ruled Halja.

The room was a circle and if one imagined a cake with the center cut out and the outer edges divided into four equal parts, that's how the floor was divided. Two halves of the circle were for visitors or, in Angel parlance, the audience. One quarter of the outer circle was raised and a high ornate bench rested against the curved wall in back of it. The judges and emcees would sit there and, in front of them, the accused and witnesses would give testimony on small stands.

The final outer area of the room was the jury "box," where all the Angels were gathered. Because of the curved walls, it wasn't exactly a box, but it was encased with a decorative railing. Most of the Angels were standing around, talking amongst themselves. One, however, had already taken his seat. He sat in the front row, off to the side, with his long legs stretched out, feet resting comfortably on the rail. All he needed was a straw hat and a piece of grass between his teeth to complete the picture of idyllic unconcern.

Jutting out from the walls around the perimeter were theater boxes reserved for various greater demons. Designing these boxes (which were probably all for show and had never been used) was the closest the Angels would ever get to actually adoring a demon. Still, gazing into some of the darkened boxes—not really knowing if a demon was lurking inside—was unsettling. The nameplates on the boxes flickered in the candlelight, but were legible enough: Alibi, Disobedience, Tyranny . . . Evil's box just looked like a big black hole. I turned away abruptly, my gaze coming to rest on the object that occupied the room's center position.

It was Metatron's statue of Justica, the Patron Demon of Judgment, Mercy, and Punishment.

Legend says Metatron, a first-century Angel scribe, fell fiercely in love with Justica. He revered her impartiality and dispassion, claiming her to be a paragon of law and order, so unlike the other slavering, bloodthirsty deity demons. He commissioned this statue and had it placed in a sturdy oxcart—the first "House of Metatron." He traveled the whole of Halja with it rattling around behind him. He died without ever finding her. Hyrke romantics are very taken with the story, but I always wondered how much money Metatron made. How much had he charged folks for a chance to see Justica's "real" likeness? How much had he charged to bring news from one outpost to another? How much had he charged to unofficially mediate the small disputes he likely encountered along the way? Hyrkes wouldn't fall for a traveling road show or circuit court like Metatron's these days, but back then, well . . . Metatron, like most Angels, had probably been quite the entrepreneurial herald.

From her central position in this modern-day House of Metatron, Justica's stone face appeared to glare down at us with pursed, disapproving lips. Her gray hair was loosely bound in a bun at the back of her head and a formless shift draped her more than ample bosom and hips. *Timeless* and *venerable* were probably what Metatron had been going for when he'd commissioned this, but I couldn't help thinking of the words *old* and *tired* when I looked at her. Justica carried the traditional sword and scales that marked her trade, although her sword tip rested on the ground, almost as if it were too heavy for her to lift. And, of course, she was blindfolded. Metatron, like modern historians, had likely told supplicants that the blindfold represented her objectivity. That Justica, unlike Fortuna, couldn't pick favorites. But, considering the bloody tip of Justica's sword, I rather thought I knew what the blindfold was for, and I couldn't say I blamed her.

Ari came in looking rather sinister in this light. He always did in low lighting. That was part of his appeal. He wore a long-sleeved, iron gray tunic with a black leather vest. The amber-colored highlights his hair sometimes had in the sun were nonexistent in here. His signature, and those of the rest of the Maegesters-in-Training, were banked and, if not at ease, then at least subdued and in check.

Ari gave my elbow a slight squeeze and stood next to me. An Angel with sharp features, light eyes, and ice blond hair stepped onto one of the stands. His voice rang out in the chamber, startling everyone into silence.

"All rise! *Voir Dire* for the eight hundred and forty-sixth academic year is now in session. The Honorables Quintus Rochester and Friedrich Vanderlin presiding."

Most of us were already standing, but Mercator, Sasha, the Angel with the flyaway hair, and Fara all leapt to their feet. Rafe pulled his feet off the rail, stood up, and thrust his hands in his pockets. Rochester and Vanderlin found their place at the bench and we all sat down. Friedrich spoke first.

"Today is the first day of the august and admirable three-day tradition of *Voir Dire*, whereby second-semester Maegesters-in-Training from St. Lucifer's examine the eligible candidates from the Joshua School in order to determine who might be a good fit for them as Guardian. As all of you know, the Guardian/Ward relationship has been practiced since the early post-Apocalyptic days. This time-honored tradition and repeated bonding between our two sides has restored Halja to a harmonious state, a place where Angels, demons, and their Maegesters can coexist."

Friedrich had each of us, Maegesters-in-Training and Angel candidates alike, stand up and introduce ourselves. Many of us already knew one another, but I did find out that the two Angels who had stood in front of me in line (the man with the pale oval face and the woman with the flyaway hair) were Lambert Jeffries and Melyn Danika, respectively. The Angel with the ice blond hair and chilling looks who had introduced Rochester and Vanderlin was the "hottie" Holden Pierce. Rochester took over speaking.

"Each MIT has been given a field assignment designed to test both your academic skills and your magical might. Going into the field is never easy. Halja's outer territories are full of *rogare* demons and other dangers. The Angel you select today could very well save your life, many times over. Student rankings for the Maegesters-in-Training determine the order of questions and selection. Ms. Onyx, you may proceed."

Suddenly, my mouth was dry. Ivy, Fitz, and I hadn't prepared any questions. I'd barely reviewed all the CVs in my packet. I stood up almost involuntarily and glanced down at Ari. He gave me an impatient look. I don't think he realized how ill prepared I was. I cleared my throat and looked over at the Angels. The longer my brain stayed blank, the harder my heart beat, until I finally blurted out, "Who's been to the Shallows?"

Every single Angel stared back at me blankly. Pierce looked like his preference would be to take an oath to kill me, not protect me. Danika scowled and one of the Maegesters-in-Training in back of me snickered.

No one raised their hand so I sat down. After an uncomfortable moment, Ari stood up. He was *Secundus* so I guessed it was his turn to ask a question.

"Ms. Onyx and I have been asked to investigate an allegation of demon wrongdoing set forth in a demon complaint that was recently filed with the Council. The accused is an outpost lord and the complainant is one of his followers. Have any of you ever been involved with a demon investigation before?"

No one had, although Lambert Jeffries had spent considerable time studying Halja's Wergild Index, so he was intimately familiar with the numerous, assorted, and quite imaginative forms of blood payment that we could demand if we found the accused guilty. Melyn Danika knew a few useful investigative spells and Holden Pierce told us that, although he hadn't *yet* worked on a prosecution case, he *welcomed* a chance to do so. He emphasized his declaration by smashing his right fist into his left palm. I was tempted to ask him if, in addition to Painfall and Hemorrhage, he also knew the spell Melodramatic Gestures, but it wasn't my turn.

And so the questions went. On and on. It was endless and not a little boring. The gavel came down for the first time on Thursday, our second day.

I'd started to zero in on Lambert Jeffries as a possible partner. He wasn't perfect (he always seemed grumpy when he answered my questions, which would make for a long sail to the Shallows) but of the possible candidates, he seemed the least bad of the proffered "goods." I mean, consider my choices! Holden Pierce (maniacal, bloodthirsty sadist); Fara Vanderlin (screechy, pulpit-pounding fraud); Raphael "Rafe"

Sinclair (irritating slacker who asked more questions than he answered); and *et al* ("and others" seemed to sum up the rest admirably; there was nothing remarkable about *any* of them).

Late in the day, questioning worked its way back around to me again.

"If each of you could bring only one thing into the field with you, what would it be?" I asked.

Everyone's answers were predictable. Holden said he'd bring a crossbow loaded with diamond-tipped platinum shafts, Melyn said she'd bring her spellbook, Fara said she'd bring *Virtus* (or courage), and Rafe just shrugged. But then he said:

"It depends on where I'm going. But if I were going to the Shallows, I'd bring food."

The room got quiet. Not for any good reason either. It wasn't as if my question was particularly controversial, nor was Rafe's answer particularly surprising. Everyone knew the outpost settlers were usually starving. But, for once, Rafe seemed serious. His eyes reflected the glow of the candlelit chandeliers as he stared pointedly back at me. Was *he* lecturing *me*? After spending nearly two whole days slouching in his chair pretending to ignore the proceedings, I was surprised Rafe knew where any of us were going. But his answer would have been my answer.

Maybe Mr. TBD deserved a closer look.

"Okay, what else? What spells do you know that might be useful in an investigation, prosecution, or a trip to the Shallows?"

"What if I told you I knew the spell Clean Conscience?"

I tensed and so did Ari beside me. Fara Vanderlin sat up straighter and glared at Rafe. He ignored her and continued to stare at me. Suddenly, the rest of the courtroom vibrated with alertness.

"Do you?"

"Do you think it would help you?"

BANG!

Friedrich pounded the bench with his gavel. "Mr. Sinclair, answer the question."

Rafe paused for a moment. Then he shook his head. "No," he said. "I don't."

Oddly, I was relieved. As if I were ever going to actually work with him and be tempted to let him cast it over me. But with Friedrich and his gavel backing me up, I couldn't resist one final question, just out of curiosity.

"What spells do you know, then?"

"Um. Hmm . . . Let's see . . . I think I still remember Bootstrap . . . Pat on the Back . . . Cup O' Cocoa—"

BANG! BANG!

"Mr. Sinclair," Friedrich's voice boomed, "you have taken an oath of honesty."

Rafe blinked innocently. "I know. Oh, I almost forgot. I also know Ladies Man, Lucky Charms, and"—Rafe winked at me—"Wet 'n Wild." I thought Ari was going to go ballistic right then and there, but Friedrich and his gavel beat him to it.

After a five-minute recess we returned to the courtroom. The day dragged on and I became increasingly irritated. In addition to a smashing headache brought on by Friedrich's pounding gavel, my toes pinched beneath my sandal ribbons and my tailored tunic now felt two sizes too tight. I longed for soft baggy pants, bare feet, and a large cotton pullover. I wished we could make our choices and go home. I already knew who I was going to pick: Lambert Jeffries.

Ari leaned toward me and said in a low voice, "Don't go for Jeffries."

Instantly, I could feel my signature swell. I *hated* it when Ari did that. It wasn't that he could read my mind . . . exactly. It was that he seemed to always know what I was thinking. And sometimes, I didn't want him to know my thoughts. Or tell me what to do. I ignored him and, instead, asked Jeffries another question. This was the tenth question I'd asked him today so everyone probably knew he was my top pick. I asked him what spell he would use to subdue a hellcnight if we encountered them on the trip. As Rafe had earlier, he answered my question with a question. But this time, there was no gavel pounding. At least, not at first.

"You know what my specialty is, right?" Jeffries said to me.

"Yes. *Lex talionis*."

"Do you know what that means?"

"It's adjudication by the Golden Rule. 'Do unto others as you would have them do onto you.'"

"No. You've got it backward. It's 'Do unto others as they've done onto you.'"

What did this have to do with hellcnights?

"There are a lot of people in Halja, Jeffries. That's a lot of behavior to keep track of. Wouldn't it be easier to just worry about one person—ourselves?"

"There are a lot of demons in Halja too. Are you saying keeping track of their behavior is too much for you?"

I suppose he was only exercising the Golden Rule—verbally pinning me against the ropes as I had him many times already today—but I didn't like it. Especially since he turned what I'd said around to imply that I couldn't do my job properly. Where was Friedrich's gavel when I needed it? But Jeffries wasn't finished. And when he continued, what he was saying just got worse.

"I don't understand why you'd want to partner with me. We're *nothing* alike. *Voir Dire* means 'speak the truth.' Well, the truth is I don't want to be your Guardian. An eye for an eye is not just some charming colloquialism for me. I truly believe that if someone rips your eye out, you should get to rip theirs out too. Why did you run into Corpus Justica on Monday? Don't you know that Jezebeth deserved—"

"Deserved to die?" I hissed. Finding out that Jeffries really was a poor choice for me, combined with the fact that Ari had tried to warn me about him earlier, made me exponentially angrier than I might have been otherwise. "I *should* know he deserved to die, right? I've only been told that a half dozen times or so by now. But you know what? I don't go around chopping people's heads off just because

I've got a sword in my hand and someone spins me around and points me in the 'right' direction."

"Onyx, you're selfish and irresponsible. You don't deserve the power you have. You should have taken the chance that Peter offered you last semester and pursued the Mederi path. In case it didn't occur to you, there is no peacenik specialty here at the Joshua School. Holding hands and making nice is for the *women* down south."

Until that moment, Ari had thankfully stayed out of it. But at this latest insult, Ari's signature bloomed like blood in water.

BANG!

Ari and Friedrich both stood up, but before either of them could stop me, I shouted:

"Since we're speaking the truth, the truth is I don't want a Guardian. I don't want to work with an Angel. The only Angel I've ever worked with, Peter Aster, betrayed my trust and stabbed me in the back. Literally? No, but he might as well have. He let two people nearly die so he could pursue his ambitions. And instead of kicking him out, the Joshua School made him *Scholar Excellentia* and sent him to finish his studies in the Archives at Satyr Hill. If that's the Angel version of Retaliatory Justice, I want no part of it."

BANG! BANG!

Instantly, the anger that I'd felt toward Peter last semester became white-hot, as if he were sitting in front of me instead of a box full of other Angels who clearly didn't want to work with me any more than Jeffries did. Last semester, after Peter betrayed me, I'd burned off some of my anger by irreversibly destroying an inanimate object. But by repressing my anger, and my magic, in the time since, it had obviously grown. Retaliatory Justice? Ha! I was way beyond that. I wanted to punish Jeffries for all the unpunished pain Peter had caused me. I wanted to hurt Jeffries for all of the horrid things he'd just said to me. Suddenly, I wanted to brand *lex talionis* on Lambert Jeffries' ass.

BANG! BANG! BANG!

My unshed magic was a palpable thing in the room. All

of the waning magic users could feel it, and even though the Angels couldn't, they'd worked with our side long enough to know what was going down.

Oh, Luck. Suddenly, I remembered my melted alarm clock. *T minus 4 . . .*

Jeffries looked shocked and the tiniest bit scared. "You're unstable, Onyx," he cried, leaping out of his chair. *3 . . .*

"And irrational. You're not suitable Maegester material and everyone knows it." *2 . . .*

BANG! BANG! BANG! BANG! BANG! BANG! BANG! BANG! BANG! BANG!

"With your permission . . . ?" Rafe Sinclair's clear, calm voice cut across the chaos. "Now might be the time to let you know I do know Flame Resistant Blanket. Would you like for me to—"

"Cast a spell on me," I threatened, "and you'll be the first to go up in flames." *1 . . .*

As I'd done in the past, I tried to retract my intractable magic. But waning magic is slipperier than a silver coil coated with grease. I pulled back with all my might, but my efforts became more friction for the fire and my frustration became the spark that set the whole thing alight. For one horrifying second my magic became too hot for even me to hold. I let go and the tail end of its whip-like force lashed me across the cheek. Instinctively, I threw up a shield. It acted like a giant cast-iron pot lid, sealing off and smothering the source, but it did nothing to douse the flames that were already out. Dozens of fireballs swirled around the House of Metatron in ever tighter, increasingly faster, circles. Then, like a mighty cyclone collapsing in on itself, my magic converged in the center of the room and exploded. Metatron's statue of Justica disintegrated in a shower of smoke, stone, and disbelief.

There was no more gavel pounding. Friedrich looked as transfixed by the scene as everyone else. The only person who didn't seem completely blown away was Rafe Sinclair, who nimbly hopped the bar of the jury box where the Angels had been sitting and walked over to the pile of dust and sand that had once been Justica.

"Wouldn't dream of casting a spell over *you*," he said, laughing quietly. He picked up a handful of dust and ran it through his hand, mumbling the entire time. The falling sand reversed, looking disconcertingly like an hourglass run backward. In only twice the time it had taken me to destroy her, Justica was restored. Rafe threw the remaining sand over his shoulder as if it were salt that had been spilled on the table instead of dust from one of the Angels' most valued possessions. He clapped his hands together and wiped them on his pants before heading for the door. He might as well have been whistling. On his way past me, he gave me a thumbs-up.

"Luck loves his own, firestarter. Never forget it."

I turned back to the new statue and peered at her more closely.

Justica hadn't been restored; she'd been recast. Gone was the stout matronly figure and her somber disposition. She was now a young warrior woman with a lithe shape and long limbs. Strong arms wielded a flaming sword, held tip to sky, and scales that looked more like a sling loaded with fireballs than something that might be used to measure. Her hair was unbound, and in the magic of the recently cast spell, it seemed to wreathe with fury. Worst of all, Justica's blindfold was gone and we could now see her defiant, daring face.

It was mine, right down to the new searing-hot burn mark on my left cheek.

Chapter 8

ࢦ

Somehow I made it out of the courtroom and back to Megiddo. I was absolutely, amazingly mortified. Sure, I'd never really wanted a Guardian in the first place, but to have left *Voir Dire* under such ignominious circumstances. *Ugh*. I didn't know how I'd ever show my face in class again. I slipped off my sandals, wincing as my tortured feet stepped onto the bare floor and hobbled over to my new wardrobe (my clinic client from last semester had burned my old one, just before he'd whisked me off to my Manipulation classroom to try and kill me). I pulled out old pants and my longed-for pullover.

I debated ordering food and just staying in, but I'd promised Ivy and Fitz I would meet them at Marduk's, St. Luck's underground pub, for dinner. And I couldn't hide forever. I hadn't even spoken to Ari before I'd left. I'd simply walked out. At least this time, I hadn't run.

I grabbed cash, keys, and clear lip balm (I tossed that damned Daredevil Red lip stain in the trash can), and then locked up and left. I was at Marduk's less than an hour after the whole incident had gone down. With any luck, news of it hadn't yet reached this side of campus. I descended the stairs, swung open the door, and stepped inside.

The entire place erupted: catcalls, cheers, jeers, shouting, stomping. I stepped back in surprise and everyone rushed forward to greet me. Dozens of patrons in various states of inebriation wanted to congratulate me, punch me in the shoulder, slap me on the back, or buy me a beer. *Hyrkes*, I thought, mystified. I couldn't be sure, but it seemed this impromptu celebration was in honor of my stupendous loss of control. The fact that I'd made such a spectacular mistake must have made it seem as if I were more like them, Halja's magic-less masses. Of course, it didn't hurt that my little stunt had stuck a thumb in the Angels' eyes. (Hyrkes tended to view Angels as the snobs they were.) I shook my head, nonplussed, and accepted the beer that someone foisted on me. It turned out to be Fitz. His hair was standing up on end as usual and his eyes were wild with excitement.

"Hey," he screamed in my ear. "Did you see what the special was tonight?" The special at Marduk's was never food. "Fireballs!" Fitz hooted. I glanced over at the bar. Lined up at the edge were at least a dozen flaming shots. I now noticed little "fireballs" all over the room. I groaned, but even I couldn't hear it above the din.

"If this place burns," I yelled to Fitz, "it won't be my fault."

He grinned and grabbed my arm, pulling me through the crowd. He led me to a table near the back where Ivy and Ari were waiting. Ari stood up as soon as I was in view.

I swallowed.

Luck, he was good-looking. I suppose it was an odd time to notice it, but it was something that hit me every now and then, especially when I was feeling vulnerable. Ari had changed too. His gray tunic and black leather vest was gone, replaced by faded, fraying black pants and a white shirt that showed off his deeply sculpted muscles. His dark gaze caught mine and he stepped toward me, his signature as hot and viscous as molten glass. He wrapped one arm behind my back while the other cradled my neck. Always in these moments he seemed much bigger than me. I am not a small person, nor (as today's events revealed yet again) am I timid or frail. That said, my *Primoris* ranking didn't mean I was the stronger magic user. Quite the opposite. When I first came to St. Luck's, Ari had been *Primoris*. He was one of the most powerful Maegesters-in-Training Rochester'd ever taught. He lost his top ranking because of me. He'd almost died last semester trying to protect me from my murderous client.

Trapped by Ari's overpowering embrace and ensnared in his all-consuming signature, I went limp and willingly let him tip me back over his arm. But it wasn't fear that made me go soft. It was love.

"Aristos," I whispered. But who could hear in here?

He kissed me then, a deep, thorough kiss that said he didn't care how many people were watching or what they thought of us. Fists were gleefully pumped into the air around us amid woots and whistles and further shouts of encouragement (none of which Ari needed). I closed my eyes and wrapped my arms around him, succumbing to the bliss of having nothing on my mind but *him*.

Well, him . . . and me . . . and the things we might do together later . . .

I broke off the kiss and turned my head. Ari laughed, a low rumbling sound I felt rather than heard. "I can feel your blush in your signature," he said. "I don't need to see it." He released me and I stood up. Ivy (good Hyrke that she was) seemed charmed by the romantic tableau we must have presented. Fitz just looked wistful. Someone fired up the jukebox and Fitz recovered, yelling for a round of boilermakers. Everyone started singing:

Gaudeamus igitur iuvenes dum sumus.
Let us rejoice while we're young.

Ari grabbed my hand in his and led me over to the table. We sat down and joined in and raised our glasses and our voices with the rest.

> *Vita nostra brevis, est brevi finietur.*
> Our life is brief, soon it will end.
> *Venit mors velociter.*
> Death comes quickly.
> *Rapit nos atrociter.*
> Snatches us cruelly.
> *Nemini parcetur.*
> To nobody shall it be spared . . .

I awoke the next morning, my bare legs entwined with Ari's. Everything throbbed, my body (bacchanalian pleasure had been the order of the night), my demon mark (*still* glowing faintly from Ari's firebrand touch), but, most of all, my head (post-*voluptatem*, boilermakers sounded like a horrible idea!). I flung Ari's possessively wound hand off of me and sat up, clutching my head and moaning. Ari continued sleeping, his tousled hair and untroubled countenance suggesting only one of two choices: (a) crawl back under the covers and curl up beside him; or (b) smother him with my pillow. I chose (c) get up, get dressed, don dark spectacles, speak to no one, find shot of espresso ASAP.

I walked to Marduk's and got the A.M. Grab Bag #5, which was a double shot and dry toast. Cradling my paper bag like it was Luck's lost heir, I pulled two pieces of mail from my mailbox and slowly ascended the stairs to my dorm room. *How was I ever going to make it through* Voir Dire *today?*

I was seriously contemplating how I could realistically work my pullover and spectacles into a professional-looking indoor ensemble when I realized, with mixed relief and horror, that I needn't worry. I stared down at the first piece of mail, which was a typed postcard from the Joshua School:

The Joshua School

FOR IMMEDIATE DELIVERY

NOUIOMO ONYX
NEW BABYLON, HALJA
ST. LUCIFER'S LAW SCHOOL
MEGIDDO, ROOM 112

THE HOUSE OF METATRON IS CURRENTLY UNDERGOING NECESSARY RENOVATIONS. ACCORDINGLY, THE THIRD AND FINAL DAY OF *VOIR DIRE* HAS BEEN CANCELLED. GUARDIAN/WARD PAIRINGS WILL BE MADE BASED ON PRELIMINARY INTEREST AND OTHER FACTORS. THE FINAL LIST FOR THIS ACADEMIC YEAR WILL BE POSTED ON QUINTUS ROCHESTER'S DOOR BY CLOSE OF BUSINESS TODAY.

I stopped for a moment in Megiddo's stairwell and leaned against the stair railing. Was Friedrich making the final pairings? Luck, I hoped not. My own shrill voice mocked me: *I don't want a Guardian. I don't want to work with an Angel.* Jeffries might be out of the question now, but maybe I'd be paired with Melyn Danika. She'd seemed unremarkable yesterday, but today (viewed through my sobering morning-after perspective) she seemed downright perfect.

I tore open my second piece of mail, a sealed letter with no return address. By the second sentence, I was sitting on the stairs and the letter was shaking in my hands. I wasn't sure if my shaking was due to anger or fear. Either way, this second piece of news was even worse than the first. Luck, I'd been so *stupid.* I took my espresso and toast out of the paper bag. In between dry bites and forced swallows, I thought, not for the first time, how amazing it was that, in Halja, it took only seconds to go from contemplating your wardrobe to contemplating your own death. The letter was from Friedrich:

Ms. Onyx,

While my daughter, Fara, had been looking forward to working with you, I think it is in her best interest that she be assigned to someone else. You indicated yesterday that you did not desire a Guardian, therefore none will be provided.

Your father has been contacted regarding your destruction of the invaluable and irreplaceable Angel artifact, "Metatron's Justica." We will discuss appropriate reparations. In the meantime, you are no longer welcome at the Joshua School.

Venti secundi;
daemones pauca,

Friedrich Vanderlin
Archangel, 5th District

I crumpled up the postcard and ripped up the letter and stuffed them both in the paper bag with the rest of my trash. Friedrich had signed his note, "*Venti secundi; daemones pauca*" or "Fair winds; few demons." On the eastern Lethe? Not likely. Guess I was on my own. It could be worse (although not much). I could have ended up with Raphael Sinclair. I shuddered. Luck forbid.

Wouldn't dream of casting a spell over you . . .

Grim determination (and not a small amount of caffeine) kicked in. I stood up. I didn't need Angels to survive. I had Luck, right?

Luck loves his own, firestarter. Never forget it.

I gritted my teeth. If only I could.

After a scalding hot shower, a vigorous tooth scrubbing, and a change of clothes, I walked over to Corpus Justica. It was rare to have a Friday with no scheduled classes or activities, but I was glad to have the day to prepare for our trip to the Shallows. Once I was safely sequestered away in the stacks of the library's tithing and tax section, I pulled out our case file and thumbed through the information. The file included the names of two possible witnesses (Thomas Stillwater, outpost gerefa, and Meghan Brun, outpost cearian), a copy of Athalie Rust's bold complaint against her outpost lord ("Vodnik is the one who killed those men"), our scheduled departure place and time (New Babylon, dock twenty-three *E*; Saturday, the sixth day of the sixth month, at 8:30 a.m.), letters of introduction for us to give to Captain Delgato and to Lord Vodnik (not that any diplomatic protocol could spin Ms. Rust's complaint into anything other than what it was: a murder accusation). Finally, there was a suggested packing list:

- ✓ 100 lbs. salt (for mixing with shot and shrapnel)
- ✓ 10 solid shot cannonballs
- ✓ 25 cannonball shells
- ✓ 250 spherical case shots
- ✓ 7 short swords
- ✓ 5 daggers
- ✓ 4 battle-axes
- ✓ 3 morning stars
- ✓ 2 throwing spears

A suggested reading list:

- ✓ Gabinius Hauerite's *Demon Patrons: Duties and Dereliction*
- ✓ Serverlinus Ludwigite's *Hyrke Deaths and Disappearances (Investigative Series)*
- ✓ Bato Vauxite's *Butchery, Bloodshed, and Murder (Criminal Elements Series)*
- ✓ Tullio Trona's *Demon Executions: Prosecution, Protocol, and Practice*
- ✓ Clodianus Agrinierite's *Halja's Outposts: Chronological History and Cultural Analysis*
- ✓ Furius Cinnabar's *Rogare Demons: Survival Strategies*

✓ Diana Elsmoreite's *Estes and the Lethe:
   Cycle of Birth, Death, and Re-Birth*

As well as a suggested route of passage and a map of the eastern Lethe.

I assumed Delgato would be familiar with the suggested route of passage, but I was glad for the map's visual overview of the area we'd be traveling through. The only portion of the Lethe I'd ever traveled was its width. I'd been ferried back and forth from New Babylon to Etincelle countless times (and once, Ari and I had even rowed it, although *not* as part of some romantic holiday, but that's another story . . .), but I'd never gone more than a few miles east of New Babylon, on land . . . or water. I peered closely at the map.

The Lethe, like its own patron demon, Estes, was large and powerful. Here, near New Babylon, it was more than a mile across, but farther east (miles and miles farther), it branched into countless streams, tributaries, rivulets, and runoffs, each more meandering than its nearest neighbor. Some of the streams then went on to merge with other streams. Some rivulets dead-ended, curling around at their end into natural cesspools that seemed to (according to the map anyway) swirl right into Halja's underground. Some tributaries doubled back on themselves, multiple times, producing odd little elbows, doglegs, and liquid switchbacks. On the map, these places were marked as highly dangerous, with the river's currents racing every which way. (In Halja, water could even flow uphill if the conditions were right.) But most troubling were the spots marked as "Wild Territory." These were the spots where we were most likely to encounter water wraiths, the most common form of *rogare* demon in some of the areas we'd be traveling through.

I spent the morning locating the books on the suggested reading list. I added two others: the simply titled *Field Guide*, which was a collection of essays written throughout the years by various Hyrke, Host, and Angel explorers, and a slim paperback volume I'd found by accident: *Oude Rode*

Ogen, Bicho Papao, and Grimasca: Folktales for Children. I had no idea what it was doing in our law library, but when I saw the reference to Grimasca, the demon Vodnik blamed for the fishermen's deaths, I'd tucked it immediately in with the rest. Around midday, I stumbled back to my study carrel and dumped the books onto my desk. They landed with a great big thud. Would anything in here help us? Or would I be better off taking the books' weight in salt instead? Salt was a known water wraith repellent.

"Such a fierce look on such a fair face," said a smooth, cool voice from the shadows. "What are you brooding about, Nouiomo? The merits of spear versus sword?"

"I'm going to be a Maegester, Mother," I said, turning around slowly, "not a foot soldier. My weapons will be wisdom, knowledge, and experience."

Aurelia snorted. Of course, coming from her, it sounded almost genteel. I was surprised to see her. My mother rarely left our estate, let alone Etincelle. She wore a long, flowing, forest green dress in some sort of shimmery fabric. Even in the low light of Corpus Justica she appeared to set off sparks. But it wasn't her magic. She wasn't a firestarter. Far from it. She was a Mederi healer (or, she was supposed to be). Her magic was the soft, nurturing, and creative kind (well, it was supposed to be), but the last time Aurelia had practiced medicine had been the night before my brother and I were born. Before the disastrous mix-up of our twin births.

In the Host, magic is closely related to gender. Males usually inherit waning magic, or the "drop of demon blood," that allows them to control demons, and females usually inherit waxing magic, the "growing magic" that's used for midwifery, field nursing, and medicinal botany. Needless to say, my brother got the green thumb while I got the demon blood. My mother blamed herself, my father did too, and for most of my childhood (despite our wealth and status), my home had been a very unhappy place.

Recently, however, my mother and I had been trying to mend our relationship. It was a prickly path, what with her being the most ferocious Mederi, and me being the softest

Maegester, to have served Luck in over two thousand years. Her gaze rested momentarily on the recent burn mark on my cheek and she raised her hand as if to touch it, but just as quickly she let her hand drop.

"I heard about Metatron's Justica," she said. I cringed, but she laughed, the tinkling sound of it as out of place in this dusty library as a wind chime made of baby spoons would have been. "I would liked to have seen it. Karanos' daughter destroying Justica."

"I lost control," I hissed, upset at my mother's enjoyment of the story. "Someone could have been hurt . . . or killed."

"But they weren't, were they? Everyone loses control from time to time. What's important is that you found a target for your wayward magic. All things considered, I think you performed admirably."

This coming from the woman who'd torched her garden with a match and a can of gasoline. *Why was I surprised?*

"You think Karanos will see it that way?" I asked.

For a moment, my mother looked young and vulnerable. She'd been amazingly beautiful once. The toast of the Host in Etincelle. I always tried to imagine what my parents' life must have been like when they first married. She claimed they'd been in love. It was hard to imagine, except during fleeting moments like this. But the moment passed and her look hardened.

"Your father has never lost control in his life."

Yet another reminder that I'd never live up to his expectations. I sighed.

"Mother, what are you doing here?"

"I came to see you off. And to give you these." She held out two large white wax-paper packages.

I reached for them, but my mother held one back. "Actually, I should probably give this one to your Guardian to hold. Inside it are seeds for the outpost settlers." She handed over the other package. I continued staring at the package my mother still held.

"Mederi-blessed seeds? That's . . . well . . . It's kind of you."

My mother looked sheepish, a look that didn't sit well on her face. "I didn't do the blessing, Nouiomo," she said with a slight huff. "Your brother did. Night came up for a visit a few nights ago. Your father told us the Shallows was going to be your first field assignment."

There was an uncomfortable silence as we both decided not to say what each of us must have been thinking: it was a first assignment that could prove to be fatal.

"Did he say why?"

Aurelia shook her head. "I just assumed there was a job that needed doing and you were the person best suited for it."

Hardly. But it was refreshing to hear my mother speak of me in such glowingly confident terms. And at least Karanos wasn't running around Etincelle telling everyone how yellow-bellied I'd been.

I peeked into the packet she'd given me. It was full of herbs. Dried ones. Or I wouldn't have been able to hold this bag either. A waning magic user's touch is deadly to all growing things.

"I realize your Guardian will be your first line of defense, but it never hurts to have a few medicines on hand. I put a bunch of them in there, all in their own pouches with further storage instructions and dosing directions in case you need them. There's yarrow, arnica, comfrey—hope you won't need that one!—white willow, valerian . . . I even put some damiana in there for you and Ari." She snickered delicately.

"Thank you, Mother," I said quietly, stopping to clear my throat. I looked away, not wanting her to see how grateful I was, how touched I was that she'd brought me something to be used for healing instead of killing. I turned back to her, happy to see that her eyes were also dry. Tears between us would have been way too awkward. I walked toward her, thinking to clasp her hands in mine, but she stepped back quickly, extending her arm so that the bag of seeds was far away from me. I stepped back too.

"So, Noon, who should I deposit these with for safe-keeping?"

Oh. I guess my parents had been told only part of yesterday's story. "Well," I said, laughing in a self-deprecating sort of way, "I guess you can give them to Ari's Guardian. Once we find out who that is."

"Why not yours?"

"Because I won't be working with an Angel this semester," I said summarily. *And maybe not ever,* I thought. But no need to mention that now.

Aurelia stared at me, her face serene as she processed my news. "Serene" with Aurelia almost never meant peace or acceptance.

"It's okay," I said quickly. "Ari's my field partner and he'll have a Guardian."

"Right," she said, her tone suggesting that solution was anything but. "Well, then I'll just keep these for tonight and see you in the morning." Just as she was leaving, the desk clerk found me and handed me a leathery envelope with trailing ends of loose string and a broken wax seal. The only difference between it and Vodnik's case file was that this envelope was thinner and it had red wax instead of gold.

"A messenger just dropped this off for you," the clerk said. "It's from the dean of demon affairs."

With a sinking feeling, I said good-bye to my mother and opened the envelope. It was a second demon complaint.

COUNTRY OF HALJA

DEMON COMPLAINT

☐ CITY OF NEW BABYLON
☐ TOWN OF ETINCELLE
☒ OUTPOST: <u>THE SHALLOWS</u>

ACCUSER: <u>ZELLA RUST</u>
ACCUSED: <u>   ?   </u>
DATE FILED: <u>RIGN 2013</u>

CASE NO.: <u>2013 OSH 00000002</u>

NATURE OF COMPLAINT:

FIVE DAYS AGO, MY SISTER, ATHALIE RUST, WENT MISSING. SHE
LEFT EARLY ONE MORNING WITH OUR DEMON PATRON AND
OUTPOST LORD TO CHECK THE TRAPS. SHE NEVER CAME BACK.
LORD VODNIK SAYS HE LOST SIGHT OF HER AND THAT GRI-
MASCA MUST HAVE GOTTEN HER. BUT ATHALIE WOULDN'T
HAVE WANDERED OFF. SHE'S ONLY EIGHT AND IS AFRAID OF
THE DARK WATERS. PLEASE SEND SOMEONE TO HELP ME FIND
HER. I KNOW A DEMON MADE HER DISAPPEAR.

I JUST DON'T KNOW WHICH ONE . . .

I was glad I hadn't eaten anything all day because I suddenly felt sick. Athalie Rust, the feisty "woman" I'd thought
was one of the fishermen's wives, was probably one of their
daughters. She was the person who had filed the original
complaint, and now she was missing too. And we were
weeks away from helping her. I didn't know Athalie. And I
too had no idea which demon was responsible for her disappearance. But I did know that our trip to the Shallows now
had a priority other than safety.

Speed.

Chapter 9

ꝫ

The fishermen's deaths were tragic, but it hadn't occurred to me that anyone else would be in danger. On
the contrary, I'd assumed the people of the Shallows, and
its patron, would be extra cautious in the aftermath of the
incident. Apparently not. And while life outside of New
Babylon and Etincelle was precarious, and death was to be
expected, it wasn't supposed to come from sources "inside
your fort," the place full of people who were supposed to
protect you. Either Vodnik was killing his own followers,
or this mysterious Grimasca was. It was my job to figure
out which one. And then stop them. I conscientiously ignored the weak-kneed feeling I got when I acknowledged,
if only to myself, that "stopping them" would likely mean
killing them.

I went downstairs and made immediate arrangements to
have my books packed up and sent to dock twenty-three *E*.
Then I left to go find Ari. It was after 5:00 p.m. He should
know by now who his Guardian would be. That left us the
evening to gather our supplies and pack up. I walked over

to Rochester's office, which, along with the rest of the faculty's, was in a building we students none-too-affectionately called the Rabbit Warren.

The Warenne Tiberius Rhaetia Administrative Building was an aboveground maze. The near-windowless building was really one small building and a dozen or so ill-thought-out expansions. Endless narrow hallways twisted around and through the building like square burrows. Locating an office usually meant navigating no fewer than fifteen turns and as many doors. Some had signs. Some not. It all depended on how engaged the occupant was with the here and now. (Administrative work in a demon-run law school wasn't always the paper-pushing job people thought it was.)

I was on my way to Rochester's office when I felt the stink of Brunus' signature. It crept up on me like the smell of a garbage can full of fish heads and bilge water. Sure enough, seconds later Brunus, Sasha, and Tosca—my class' trio of Maegester-in-Training malcontents—rounded the corner. They started laughing immediately.

"Nice burn mark, Onyx," Brunus said, pointing to the still-blistery spot on my cheek from yesterday.

Tosca stopped directly in front of me, forcing me to stop. He cocked an eyebrow at me, daring me to push past him.

It was a little embarrassing. I was immeasurably stronger than all of them put together, but I had control issues and they didn't. Tosca was taunting me. Crazy as it was, I think he *wanted* me to try something. *Here*, in the hallways of St. Luck's! Which was insane. But if things went disastrously wrong, who would get blamed? Me, of course. The girl who'd destroyed Justica.

"Don't bother looking for your Guardian. You weren't assigned one," Sasha crowed, pointing behind him. "Guess you get to work alone, just like you wanted."

"She's not alone." Ari's quietly menacing voice suddenly sounded from the far end of the hallway. "She's with us."

He stepped out from around the corner and a second later someone else stepped out too.

It was Fara Vanderlin, wearing a floor-length, deep purple, embossed velvet gown. She strode purposefully down the hallway, skirts swishing around her ankles, bell sleeves flapping at her wrists, brandishing, of all things (I nearly laughed out loud), a dowsing rod, which she pointed at Sasha, Tosca, and Brunus as if it were a wand.

"Extremum vitae spiritum edere," she screeched. *Uh-oh.* I looked over at my classmates, expecting them to be turned into water or gold or something Fara might have used that dowsing rod to find. But instead, they merely faded, becoming translucent images of themselves right before my eyes. Their voices became muted too, because they suddenly started shouting at Fara and I couldn't hear a thing.

Fara waved her hand in the air toward the trio of ghosts she'd just made.

"'We are all but pale spirits to be poured over the land until the time shall come to be made whole again,'" she preached. "Joshua, five, thirty-four."

With a final flip of her hand, Fara made Sasha, Tosca, and Brunus swirl away as if they were smoke she'd just chased from a fire.

Oh, crap. "Are they coming back?"

"Eventually." She tapped her rod against her leg. "So, Nouiomo Onyx, *solo* practitioner, you know what else Joshua says?"

If only I could swish Fara away with a wave of my hand.

"'He who borrows cannot choose.' Joshua, ten, nine." She pushed her dowsing rod into my shoulder and gave it a satisfied little shove.

Slowly, I raised my hand to the rod and pushed it away.

"Really?" I said, careful to keep my magic to myself. "I always thought it was, 'She who borrows has the biggest closet.'"

A ri chased me out of the Rabbit Warren and into Timothy's Square. He finally succeeded in grabbing my hand when I was almost ready to step onto Victory Street.

He turned me to face him, grabbing my shoulders to prevent further escape.

"Hey," he said.

"Hey, what?" I snapped.

"I didn't choose her. You know that. She was assigned to me. To us."

"No she wasn't and you know it. *No one* was assigned to me. That's how I wanted it."

Ari's jaw hardened.

"Please," I said, exasperated. "Don't go pretending you're upset. Fara was your top pick all along."

"For you!"

"Well, now she'll be on the boat regardless." I softened. "Look, it doesn't matter, Ari." I told him about the second demon complaint that had just come in from the Shallows. "The only thing that matters right now is getting there, and getting there quickly."

O de to Ivana Jaynes, the best friend a girl could have: At the beginning of the week, Ivy was forced to start off her second semester by watching a hideous demon execution in our public square because my father wanted to teach me a lesson. The next day, she returned from morning classes to find the cooled remains of my melted alarm clock cemented to my desk, a chilling reminder of my hot temper. On the third day, she found similar evidence of such in the form of the ashy remains of what had probably been a nice useful stack of treatises, primers, and horn books the night before. By the fourth day, she was told I'd created a whirling fervor of explosive, destructive, out-of-control fireballs. And on the fifth day, she heard a rumor that three people had "given up the ghost" in my presence. Yet . . . today, she wept for my leaving.

Go figure and Luck bless her.

Saturday at dawn, we stood together at the dock saying good-bye. Ivy was a little weepy. *Did she really think I wouldn't come back?* Fitz was a little more sanguine.

"If you don't come back, can I have the books that Waldron Seknecus gave you last semester?"

I glared at him. He smiled unapologetically. "What? Can you blame me? Think about what an edge I'd have if I had access to our dean of demon affairs' student notes."

"You both don't have to wait, really," I said, glancing over my shoulder—again—at the empty pier behind me. The dock was relatively quiet, with very few whistles or bells. The main traffic was farther west, at the main docks where shoppers and day-trippers would be taking the ferries to and from Etincelle. Piers in the twenties were for anyone catching a boat to the east, like us. It wasn't exactly heartening to see that, so far, we seemed to be the only ones.

A low rumbling of thunder grumbled ominously to the east. I didn't believe in weather portents. Luck had controlled the Legion; the weather was beneath him. But still, choppy waters weren't exactly how I wanted to start this trip. The wind was relatively calm, but every now and then an odd gust would blow, a sign of something coming. Too bad it wasn't our boat. I wanted to get my stuff off the dock and under cover, before the storm hit.

Fitz's expression suddenly turned serious as he followed my gaze off to the east. "I meant it, you know," Fitz said quietly.

"Meant what?"

"That I'd go with you."

"Fitz," Ivy said softly. Her voice held a low warning note. "We talked about that. You'd only be a liability to her."

Fitz's jaw set and he said nothing, just stared out at the water. He glanced over at me then, his expression the strangest combination of humility, anger, and . . . yearning?

"Yeah," he said finally, his voice thick with some unshed emotion I couldn't quite place, "well, being a Hyrke sucks."

"Fitz!" Ivy frowned. "Is that your idea of 'fare well'?"

He glared at her and, if looks could kill, she be skewered twice over. But then he relented and grinned, looking much more Fitz-like.

"Fine," he said. "Then Ivy and I will just have to dream up a little lark of our own while we await your return."

Through the hazy mist, two dark silhouettes made their way toward us. Fitz leaned in toward me and squeezed me in a great big bear hug. Just before he released me, he whispered in my ear:

"If you're not back by Haerfest, I'll torch Seknecus' books and him too and then come after you." His threat sounded chillingly real, especially considering, when he was not at St. Luck's, he resided at the Seknecai Estate (his mother was head housekeeper for Waldron Seknecus). I stepped back and searched his face for signs that he was kidding. Thankfully, his earsplitting grin gave abundant evidence of it and my momentary stomach flutters ceased (I simply could *not* go off into the hinterlands wondering what sort of trouble Fitz might get himself into back home).

Without a second glance, Fitz turned and left. Ivy gave me a swift hug too and then departed after him, swiping tears off her cheek. I wanted to yell to her that she'd likely see more drama in Darius Dorio's Council Procedure class than I would on the river, but my throat felt too raw to pull off the joke. I didn't want anyone, least of all, me, falling to pieces on the docks. What sort of first impression would that give our new teacher and captain? So I remained mute.

From the east, the outline of a boat appeared. A low whistle sounded and I waved. When I turned back, Ari and Fara's silhouettes were recognizable. It looked like they were arguing. And when I saw the small, dark, four-legged silhouette that trailed behind them, I thought I knew why. My jaw dropped. She truly knew no bounds. For her trip to the Shallows, Fara had packed two bags and a . . . tiger cub.

"You can't bring it," I heard Ari say.

"He's a good fighter. He'll be useful if we're attacked by water wraiths."

"I don't care. He belongs in Warja, not Halja. I don't care how you got him—or why. He's not coming."

"You know what your problem is? You don't think outside the box. None of you Maegesters do."

"*Praeceptum primum, praeceptum solum*, Fara. Scrupulous rule following is 'the first rule, the only rule.' You know that as well as us."

Fara snorted and dropped her bags. As if on cue, the tiger cub sat.

"There's no rule against owning a tiger," Fara said dismissively. "Morning, Noon." She snickered at her own joke. As if I hadn't heard that one before. "Ready for a fight?"

With who? Her? Her cat? The rogare *demons we'd likely encounter along the way?*

The tiger appeared to survey the dock disdainfully, ears twitching, tail lashing. I sensed absolutely zero signature from it. It was strange to see a nonmagical beast in New Babylon. I didn't want to give Fara the satisfaction of seeing I was curious about her cat so I merely nodded a greeting and turned back to watch the boat dock. Let Ari deal with her. *She's his Guardian, not mine,* I thought with an odd mix of thanks and regret.

The boat was now within a few hundred yards of the dock. I stared at it, thinking how quickly the trip's problems were mounting (and we were only two minutes in!) The boat was beautiful to be sure—a long, low dahabiya with hardwood trim and bright white triangular sails. And she was big—over a hundred feet long and almost twenty feet wide, which was good because it meant I wouldn't have to bunk up with Fara and sleep next to that tiger. But considering where we were going and the length of time it would take to get there, I still thought "claustrophobic looking" and "coffin-like" were more apt adjectives than "luxurious" or "leisurely." Dahabiyas weren't known for their speed. In this thing, we'd be ducks *in situ* for every *rogare* demon along the way.

Ari walked over to me and planted a kiss on my forehead. He put his arm around my shoulders and turned me toward the incoming boat, pointedly ignoring the absurd scene behind us: Fara amid duffel bags, boxes of books from the library, war chests, and the exotic tiger cub.

"I can train the cat to defend your girlfriend, Carmine," Fara called.

Ari gave me a contemplative look. I was just about to say *don't be ridiculous* when someone else beat me to it. My mother. I hadn't forgotten that she'd said she see me off but, not wanting to be disappointed if she didn't show, I hadn't thought too much more about it since yesterday.

I turned to see her walking down the pier arm in arm with this morning's problem number three.

Rafe Sinclair.

His presence was worse than the tiger and the dahabiya, times a thousand. He had a bad habit of showing up when he was least wanted.

What in all of Luck's bloody battlefield was he *doing here?*

Instantly, a deep, sinking feeling formed in the pit of my stomach, something that felt like those little curling abysses looked on the map under "Wild Territory."

"A cat to defend St. Lucifer's *Primoris*?" my mother said, her clear voice ringing across the docks like a bell. "I don't think so. The Joshua School reconsidered," she said to me. "They've assigned you a Guardian."

Rafe stood before us clad in ripped pants, dock sandals, and a lightweight jacket. Over his shoulder he carried a stick. I glanced behind him and saw that, tied to the end of the stick, was a bulging bandana. I just shook my head. Was he going to use his stick the way Fara had used her dowsing rod yesterday with Brunus, *et al*? What would be next? Riding crops? Parasols? Why couldn't these Angels pack something normal? Tigers and bindles? *Really?* Holden Pierce's crossbow loaded with diamond-tipped shafts and Melyn Danika's spellbook were looking pretty good right about now. I forced myself to focus on my breathing so I wouldn't accidentally burn down the boat before we boarded it.

"Is it true?" I asked Rafe. "Were you assigned to me?"

He met my gaze with an unblinking, almost beguiling

stare. If I didn't know better, I'd have thought he was trying to ensorcell me.

"I warned you. *Don't* try to cast a spell over me. I don't care if they changed their minds and you were assigned to me. You're *not* my Guardian."

"Hey, like I said, I wouldn't dream of casting a spell over you." Rafe's voice was a lazy drawl, thick but slippery, like he was talking out of both sides of his mouth. Angels were good at that. "Where do you want the food? I assume you'll take that."

Just as the boat pulled up to the dock, I saw a long line of floating chests trailing behind Rafe and my mother, much as the tiger had trailed behind Ari and Fara during their arrival. Suddenly something occurred to me.

"What's your tiger's name?" I called to Fara.

"Virtus," she said, like I should already know. *Of course,* I thought, nearly smacking my head with my hand. Fara and Rafe might make for bizarre traveling companions, but they'd told the truth during *Voir Dire.* When I'd asked what each of them would bring into the field, Fara had said *Virtus* and Rafe had said *food.* Despite everyone's sidelong glances, I howled with mirth. I'd thought Fara had meant courage. She'd meant her cat.

Virtute non armis fido; the Book of Joshua 24:17. Loose translation:

Courage over weapons; cats over sanity.

Chapter 10

❧

I calmed down, thankfully, before the docking ropes were thrown on the dock. It wouldn't do to thrust my letter of introduction into Ferenc Delgato's hand while giggling hysterically. Ari gave me a worried frown and went to tie off the eastern end of the boat. He motioned to Fara to do the same on the west end and the rest of us barely had time to move our toes out of the way before a large, heavy gangplank clattered to the dock in front of us. At its end was a youngish-looking boy of about fifteen or sixteen with skin darkened from the sun, hair obviously cut with a dull knife or rusty pair of scissors, and muscles probably built up from loading cargo, swabbing decks, and rowing dinghies.

"Nouiomo Onyx?" he asked.

I nodded and was just about to take a step forward when I felt someone squeeze my shoulder. I glanced to my left and saw Rafe's hand resting there. I looked up and, for a moment, our gazes locked. In the early morning light of the oncoming storm, his taupe-colored eyes looked like liquid charcoal, at once both opaque and reflective, a darker version of the swirling clouds and murky waters all around us.

"I'll make the introduction, if you'd like."

For once, my mother kept her opinion to herself. She stood off to the side, holding the large white paper package full of Mederi-blessed seeds, watching us. If I allowed him to introduce me, it would be as good as allowing him on the boat. I looked from the bag to Rafe and back again. I knew what he was really asking.

Would I accept him as my Guardian?

"No. I'll make my own introduction," I said, shrugging his hand off of my shoulder. I turned to Aurelia.

"Mother, please give the seeds to Fara to hold." Without a second glance at Rafe, I took my letter of introduction out of my pocket. My mother, Ari, and Fara returned to the edge of the boarding plank at the same time. On impulse, I threw my arms around my mother and hugged her. She was startled and stiff at first, but then she held me tight.

"*Ad astra*, Nouiomo," she whispered. *To the stars.* It was a sentimental Haljan farewell. I blinked and nodded and, with a final squeeze of her hand, let go.

Fara was hugging Virtus just as fiercely, if not more so, but her tears were unrestrained. She clutched the cub tightly, sobbing. I looked over at Ari. He appeared unmoved by Fara's unabashed display of affection for her cat. In fact, he appeared annoyed and impatient to get on board. I didn't necessarily disagree (the tiger would be a nuisance and hadn't I just yesterday reminded Ari of our need for haste?) but still I couldn't help softening just the least little bit toward Fara. Anyone who loved a beast so couldn't be all bad.

As I made my way across the gangplank, I made the mistake of looking back. The tiger sat hunched at Rafe's feet, looking miserable. Even Rafe, whom I would have expected to have a bored or indifferent expression on his face, looked . . . uneasy.

Feeling guilty without really understanding why, I stepped on board and made room on the deck for Ari and Fara.

"I'm Nouiomo Onyx," I said, handing over my letter of introduction. The boy opened it and glanced over it, nodding. But then he frowned and looked up.

"It says there's supposed to be four of you."

I sighed and was on the verge of answering when he followed up that declaration with:

"And that there's a . . . tiger cub we're supposed to accommodate . . . ?" He looked up once more, his eyebrows raised in surprise. His face transformed as another emotion I instantly recognized took hold. It wasn't fear; it was excitement. The boy stepped to the edge of the boat, spotted Virtus, and stared rapturously at him. It reminded me a bit of the way Fitz had looked when describing Holden Pierce's offensive rating. *What exactly had this boy heard about tigers?*

My sigh turned into a groan. I'd never bothered to read my own letter of introduction. I gathered my pairing with Fara had been so assured, what with her being a gap filler and me being so sorely in need of one, that both the St. Luck's faculty and the Joshua School's had written the letter naming her as my Guardian. Which made me wonder who they'd predicted for Ari.

"Who's the fourth?" I asked.

The boy tore his gaze away from Virtus and peered at the letter once more. "Nouiomo Onyx," he read. I resisted the urge to raise my hand. "Aristos Carmine." Ari gave the boy a curt nod. "Fara Vanderlin." Fara swiped her eyes and croaked, "Here." I rolled my eyes.

"And Raphael Sinclair."

There was a moment of stunned silence as the boy stared at us.

"That's impossible," I said. No one would have predicted Ari's choosing Rafe. "That letter can't possibly say that Aristos Carmine's Guardian Angel is Raphael Sinclair."

"It doesn't," the boy said, frowning in confusion. "It says he's yours."

Things happened fairly quickly after that. The boy looked up at me suspiciously, clearly questioning my identity. No Maegester could be as ignorant as I was about her own investigative team. Rafe crossed the gangplank, jumped on board, and walked over to me, his uneasy expression replaced by one of triumph. Fara rushed to Virtus and (apparently interpreting the letter's contents as trumping Ari's earlier objections to Virtus) wrapped him in her arms and carried him on board. The boy's attention then became torn between me (a potential imposter) and the tiger cub (a four-legged nonmagical demon-fighting beast). In the span of seconds, the whole introduction splintered into potential catastrophe.

"May I?" Rafe said, addressing only me.

Ari's signature flared with some undefined emotion that was so hot, bright, and fleeting, I only had time to marvel at its intensity before he dampened it down with a display of willpower I'd only ever seen in two Maegesters: Ari and my father. From the few interactions we'd had, I knew Ari thought little of Rafe Sinclair. But he likely felt as conflicted about the question as I did. Because we both knew what question Rafe was really asking, again:

Would I accept him as my Guardian?

I pushed the threat of failed first impressions aside and paused. (Did I really care what this crew thought of me? In the grand scheme of things, first impressions didn't matter. Making good choices over an entire lifetime did.)

Would it be better to accept Mr. Eleventh of Eleven, Mr. Dead Last, Mr. TBD, as my Guardian or would it be better to try to navigate this trip solo? I honestly didn't know. I'd joked with myself when I'd first received the news of my solo status that it could have been worse. That I could have been paired with Rafe Sinclair. But I don't know if I'd meant it.

I glanced to the east, toward a sky dark with fury and waters deep with demons. A jagged fork of lightning lit up the eastern sky and a moment later a spattering of rain started falling. Rafe stood beside me, outwardly patient, hands in his pockets, rocking back on his heels, as if he couldn't care less what I decided. But then he removed one of his hands from his pocket. His silver bracelet caught the gleam of a lightning flash as he nervously swiped his hand through his hair.

He wants to come, I thought. For all his show of nonchalance and disengagement, he wanted to be my Guardian. Who knew why. Did it matter? He might have been ranked dead last. And it was certain, based upon his CV and the completely unorthodox way he'd rebuilt Justica after I'd destroyed her, that he was rebellious. (Not necessarily a trait one wanted in a Guardian Angel.) But maybe Rafe deserved a chance to prove himself, to fill in some of those blanks in his "course of life." It's possible—probable—that I also felt sorry for him. The way I'd felt sorry for Virtus earlier when the cub had realized it was being left behind.

I was suddenly nervous myself.

"Yes," I said, almost too loudly. Luck knew, I didn't want to repeat myself, or this decision. *No second guesses,* I admonished myself. I cleared my throat and spoke to the boy. "You're correct about the four." I motioned to Rafe. "Raphael Sinclair will make our introduction to Captain Delgato."

Rafe grinned then, the brightness and ferocity of his smile almost matching the increasing lightning strikes around us. Suddenly, I knew why I was nervous.

Tiger cubs grow into tigers.

R afe huddled up briefly with the young boy, while the rest of us stood around getting pelted by rain. After a few seconds, during which Virtus started squalling and we all put up our hoods, Rafe yelled, "We'll do formal introductions inside. Let's get all the food and supplies on board first."

Fair enough, because the storm was picking up. We spent the next two hours loading cargo, making sure crates of food were properly sealed and stored, and finding places to stash all the books, weapons, and cannon fodder. The rain continued at a steady pace that seemed designed to erode rain jackets, body temperature, and good moods. At one point, I made the mistake of trying to carry too many things on board at once (two duffel bags and a box of books). The box fell, crashed onto the dock, and broke apart, scattering all of the books I'd spent yesterday searching for onto the pier. One of them even went over the side and into the water. I cried out in frustration and mild alarm.

Like Guardian Angels have been doing for millennia, Rafe appeared at my shoulder, ready to assist, I thought. He stood on the pier, water dripping off the edge of his hood, his face partially shadowed and smiling, peering down at me crouched in the rain, gathering the now soaked books into a pile. But he made no move to help. Instead he just shook his head and clucked his tongue at the unfortunate scene. He then knelt beside me.

"Whistling in the Rain might be a good one right about now, hmm? Want me to cast it? When you asked me earlier this week whether I knew any useful spells, I forgot to mention that one. One of my old housekeepers taught it to me." His voice had a singsongy quality to it that made it impossible to tell if he was kidding or not. Until he said *sotto voce*, "But every now and then it gives the target a near permanent pucker." His eyes locked on my lips. I was too stunned to move. Despite the rain, the air around us nearly crackled with dry, static electricity. But it was just a feeling, nothing visual, atmospheric, or even magical. He held out his hands and I placed the pile of books I'd been holding into them. He shifted them to one arm and held his other hand out to me to help me up.

Heavy footsteps pounded on the pier, coming closer. Before I could accept Rafe's hand, Ari stepped up to us. Rafe withdrew his hand and stepped away.

"Noon," Ari said in a weary voice. "What are you doing?"

I looked up at him and a big fat raindrop hit my cheek and slid down my face. *How long had I been crouched there?* I stood up, my legs aching. All of a sudden, I was so tired. A bone-dead, exhausted type of tired. The kind where you just want to go crawl into bed and never get up again. I think it was all the stress. The pressure of the assignment, the trip, preparing, packing up. I'd been too keyed up to sleep much this past week, and this morning I'd gotten up before the sun to come down here. Now we'd just spent the last hour or so loading up heavy gear in the rain. I was wiped and Ari, bless his heart, knew it.

He reached toward my face and gently cupped it with his hand. It was warm and dry. I laughed to myself. Of course. Ari had so much control over his fire, he wouldn't think twice of putting himself on low burn just to get through this. He rolled his thumb down my cheek, wiping the rain away, at least temporarily.

"Get on board and go inside," he said softly. "I'll finish up out here." His gaze found Rafe farther down the dock pushing one of the war chests. I couldn't help thinking that Rafe looked like . . . Well, he looked like he was whistling. Ari's voice hardened. "I'll bet *I* can get your new Angel to cast some practical spells." I felt the barest crack in Ari's signature. It was like the eruptions Rochester intentionally threw off in class from time to time just to make sure we were all paying attention. But I didn't think Ari's eruption had been intentional. It had felt like a slip. I looked up at him in surprise but he turned me around, pointed me to the boat, and gave me a gentle shove.

"Go!" he said.

I went. Just before disappearing inside the cabin, I glanced back at Ari, Rafe, Fara, and Virtus. A tiny dot of fear, more like apprehension, pricked my stomach. It felt like I'd swallowed a pin. What I was feeling now was just the beginning. That one sharp stab that lets you know something's wrong.

I couldn't help remembering Fortuna's prophecy for me: *When traveling into the unknown, sometimes the biggest danger is the one you bring with you . . .*

* * *

Around 4:00 p.m., everything was finally loaded and stashed away, battened down and ready for our voyage. So far, the only crew member I'd met (and I didn't even know his name yet) was the young boy who'd initially greeted us. The cook had been buried in the kitchen (preparing some elaborate first meal, or so I was told, which was a little disconcerting because, weren't elaborate meals usually reserved for *last* meals?) The captain was nearly nocturnal (or so I was told). He let his mate, the young boy, work the ship during the day while he prowled the decks at night. Not having met Delgato yet, I didn't know if that made me feel better or worse.

The dahabiya pushed off from dock twenty-three *E* with a roar of her engines. I nearly leapt for joy upon hearing them. Thank Luck we wouldn't be under sail the entire time. I'd been afraid the trip would push us into next semester. I watched our departure alone from the rails. The mate was steering, and Ari, Fara, and Rafe were below, probably scalding themselves with hot showers and donning warm clothes, as I had an hour or so ago. It may have been the month of Ghrun but today's weather had made it feel like early Rign.

I'd been pleasantly surprised to find out that, despite the dreariness of our intended destination, the boat we'd be traveling in was comfortable, almost lavishly plush. Everyone had their own cabin. They were tiny, but each one had its own bathroom, wardrobe closet, and bedroll. The bedrolls were on frames, but they were covered with soft linens and plump pillows. Accommodations at the Joshua School were more spacious, but Ari and I would feel right at home with the amount of space allotted to us here. In fact, I was used to sharing the same amount of space with Ivy, so my cabin here already felt opulent by comparison.

There was a formal salon and dining area, much nicer than Marduk's, although rougher looking than our dining room back home. But then, I'd grown up on one of the richest estates in Etincelle; our dining room was three stories high and could comfortably seat thirty people; one could hardly expect that on a boat. Besides being a place to eat, the dining room seemed to serve but one other purpose: underscoring the river's dangers. A handful of original oil paintings were scattered throughout the room, mostly on the walls, but some on small easels or sideboards. These paintings featured an astonishing variety of assorted and horrific water demons, performing unspeakable (but not unpaintable) acts of depredation, defilement, and despoilment. The subject matter of the artwork was no doubt risqué, but there was no denying that the scenes themselves were savagely beautiful.

The lounge doubled as the library. I couldn't help wondering what Delgato's arrangement was with the various Maegester and Angel schools in New Babylon. The boat had clearly been designed with students in mind. The lounge/library was the biggest enclosed area, and the most charming (of course, compared to the atrocities displayed in the dining room, an accidental drowning would appear charming). The windows in the lounge were stained glass depictions of various Haljan myths. Cynicism, unfortunately, comes naturally to me and I couldn't help thinking that, though the windows were exquisite, they'd likely been designed to keep attentions directed at the contents of the room, scholarly books and academic treatises. The library's stained glass windows completely blocked the view of the passing landscape outside.

Lastly (though it had, in truth, been the first thing I'd noticed), were the dahabiya's demon defenses. All the windows were equipped with heavy metal shutters, the kind that shut and lock with one pull. The upper uncovered sundeck was surrounded by cannons—contemporary ones that used explosive demon shot and the ammunition we'd brought aboard.

In short, the dahabiya's posh appearance couldn't conceal what it really was—a battleship.

* * *

A nd so it was, in the twilight of Saturday, the sixth day of the sixth month that year, that we set off for the Shallows in eastern Halja, a destination we would hopefully reach, if all went well, in a little over a month.

That night, after the sun went down, our group met in the dining room for the elaborate first meal and formal introduction to the captain. In some respects, that first meal *was* our last. At least our last meal together for a while. After that, one of us would always be on watch. But that first night out, the four of us got to break bread together without much fear of being attacked. As our dahabiya motored through the strong, wide waters of the Lethe, a full moon rose over Halja, icing the tips of each passing, lapping wave in silver. Farther off, the moon's gentle light soothed quietly rustling fields of phlox, larkspur, and goldenrod, sending the unruly wildflowers' riotous reds, violent violets, and shining saffrons into a slumberous mix of dove, sandalwood, and fawn. In short, the staging for our dinner was magical . . . Magical in the way performances are that start with a barker calling: "Want to watch a woman get sawed in half?"

W e collectively decided to dress for dinner. Each of us had brought one formal outfit. Ari showed up in a black cloak, pants, and a bone-colored collared shirt. Fara wore a skintight, stark white satin gown trimmed with black feathers. I was beginning to get a feel for her look. She loved grandstanding. She'd left her hair unbound and it fell past her shoulders in long, lush, lightly twisted, honeycolored curls. Her eyes were bright emerald specked with gold and her lips were candy-apple red. Her beauty was so over-the-top even I might have been pea green with envy had I not known the whole thing was a highly impressive glamour. This was Fara's idea of making a good first impression.

I snorted. None of us had yet seen what the "real" Fara looked like. I supposed she'd keep us in the dark forever.

For my part, I'd taken a risk with my dress. I rarely ever bare my demon mark. For one thing, I'd spent a lifetime hiding it. For years I pretended to be a regular Hyrke. I'd gone to a Hyrke high school and a Hyrke college. I had Hyrke friends and went to Hyrke hangouts. I'd never wanted anyone to know I had waning magic. Waning magic users were men. They were destructive. They started fires and killed things. Their touch harmed growing things. Without the aid of dramatic and powerful spells, I'd never have a garden, eat fresh fruit, or . . . have a child. Even a powerful spell couldn't fix that last one. So, for most of my life, I'd viewed myself as this sterile, unnatural aberration. That is, until Ari came along.

It's a whole other story, but Ari basically put me on the map of femininity. I still don't always feel good about my magic, but I'm getting better. Which brings me to the second reason I'm cautious about baring my demon mark: when Ari touches it, it burns. And the burning feels . . . good. Which means, should anyone witness an unintentional brushing, well—they'd certainly know how I felt about him. His mark worked the same way, but men's clothing designs being what they were, there weren't a whole lot of reciprocal ways I could accidentally show the world my effect on him.

So my dress tonight was risky because it was an asymmetrical one-shoulder black silk gown. The bare shoulder was my left one, the one with the café-au-lait-colored splotchy demon mark. It almost appeared as if the dress was made to show off the mark, which, while not true exactly, was part of the reason I'd bought it. It established my authority immediately.

In the dahabiya's dining room, I nervously fiddled with my drink, an applejack cocktail, my nod to our new partners, the Angels—although I felt like exchanging it for simple grape wine. My own Guardian was late! And we could hardly start without him since he was the one who was supposed to introduce everyone. Thankfully, the captain wasn't here either so I hadn't been put in the awkward position of postponing an introduction I should have made hours ago. I set my now near-to-boiling cocktail down on a sideboard next to a painting of Estes ravishing a young woman in the reedy waters of the Lethe just as Rafe showed up. His "formal" outfit turned out to be a clean pair of pants and a rough-looking jacket. He held a deck of cards in one hand.

"I came prepared to work for my wine," he announced, walking over to where Ari and I stood. On the way he leaned down to give Virtus a scratch (Virtus hissed at him) and whispered something in Fara's ear. She shrugged and followed him. Virtus trailed after her. When we were all gathered in front of *Slaking His Thirst*, the title of the painting of Estes having his way with the voluptuous woman in the water, Rafe fanned out the deck of cards and said:

"Pick a card."

I frowned. I wasn't in the mood for kids' card tricks.

"Working for your wine means acting like a Guardian, not one of the seraphim," I snapped. "Where's the captain?"

Rafe's attention, which had been lightly bouncing among the three of us, now zeroed in on me with sharpened intensity. His gaze started high, took in the straight sweep of my ribbon-bound hair lying across my right shoulder, traveled down the length of my clingy silk gown, and then came slowly back up to rest, briefly, on my mark.

"Now *that's* a black robe Justica would be proud of," he said, whistling softly and broadening his smile to include everyone. I narrowed my eyes at him. There was one skill in which Rafe would always rank first: provocation.

Ari refused to be baited. He reached for a card with a bland expression on his face, his signature as battened down as the food crates on deck. He looked at his card, took a sip of his drink, and gave it back.

Fara took a card, leaned down to show it to Virtus, scratched the cub behind his ears, and slipped it back into the deck. I took mine. It was the nine of claws. I handed it back to Rafe.

"Y'all know real magic when you see it, right?" Rafe said in an affected drawl. "It's not an extraordinary promise, like the Guardian's oath." He looked directly at me. "'I shall do whatever is necessary to preserve and protect the life of my ward,' Nouiomo Onyx."

"The Book of Joshua, twelve, seven," Fara murmured. I stifled a groan.

"And it's not an ordinary act, like protecting you from harm," he said, still addressing only me. "In our story, that will actually come later." He glanced at Fara and then Ari, clearly including them in his next remark. "Real magic happens when I perform an extraordinary act—like revealing a manticore in our midst. So, without further ado"—Rafe's voice rose then as if he were addressing a crowd of three hundred instead of three—"I'd like to introduce our captain, Ferenc Delgato."

And then Rafe did something I'd never seen another Angel do. He motioned quickly with his hands, making a series of complicated signs in the air. He ended with a dramatic flourish and pointed toward the door. A hideous beast materialized there. It was at least eight feet tall with huge, powerful, bulging muscles, a red lion's mane, a slavering jaw full of deadly sharp teeth, and a long scorpion's tail with a barbed tip that looked like a gigantic hornet stinger. The beast's signature felt sharp and prickly, as if the beast was brushing my bare skin with barbed wire. The sensation of it made me feel slightly woozy and in that instant, I realized that, though we traveled upon the surface of the water, we were in deep, deep trouble.

Delgato was a demon.

Chapter 11

I stumbled forward and grabbed the back of a chair to steady myself. Suddenly, it felt like someone had flayed me, doused me with gasoline, and then set me on fire. It took every ounce of willpower I had not to blast Delgato with a warning shot. *Stay away!* I wanted to scream. My reaction was irrational, I told myself as sweat broke out along my upper lip. This was only a physical and magical reaction. *This* was what happened when Host children were raised as Hyrkes. My instant "fight or flight" reaction wasn't normal. It was simply the result of inexperience and fear. Fear of what the demon might do to me. Fear of what I might do to it.

Rafe gestured toward Delgato again and suddenly he was just a man. Well, a man with a signature, but at least the beast was gone. And his signature felt a little less excruciating. Delgato was obviously a very powerful demon. Odd that I didn't remember reading about him in the Demon Register. But then, no demon I'd studied would willingly have traded the title of lord or patron for mere captain, so maybe he was listed under another name. A few deep breaths later I had my magic under control.

Delgato, meanwhile, studied each of us with his eerie, iridescent cat eyes. He finally settled his gaze on Rafe. "If you're the hornpipe for this group, get on with it, then. Burr's dinner is only getting colder and Russ has been on deck since sunup. He's looking forward to me—and one of you—relieving him."

Most Angels couldn't resist a bit of showmanship and Rafe was no exception. As he introduced us, he infused each of our names with just the slightest ping of magic.

"*Raphael Sinclair*," he said, gesturing to himself and bowing. "Son of Roderick and Valda Sinclair nee Gotzon of Etincelle."

"*Fara Vanderlin*," Rafe said, gesturing to Fara. "Daughter of Friedrich Vanderlin, Archangel of the Fifth District and Guardian of the current executive of the Demon Council, Karanos Onyx, and Mary Gamboge of Etincelle." Fara also bowed, and then couldn't resist adding her own bit, from the Book, of course: "'And thus it was said at the End and in the Beginning, friends are now enemies and enemies are now friends. The demons were, are, and ever will be Legion. Welcome, demon. Welcome, friend.' Joshua, one, one."

Delgato appeared unimpressed by this recitation but he nodded politely and turned toward Ari, who was next.

"*Aristos Carmine*," Rafe said. "Adopted son of Steve and Joy Carmine of Bradbury. Former demon executioner for Executive Onyx."

"Bradbury, Mr. Carmine?" said Delgato. "A strange place for a member of the Host to grow up, eh?"

Ari gave an almost imperceptible shrug. I'd been horrified upon hearing that Joy had found him as an infant, floating in a basket on the Lethe. I'd asked him several times since whether he was at all curious about his birth parents, who had apparently sent a child out on the Lethe to drown. But every time, Ari always said that as far as he was concerned, he was born in that basket.

"*Nouiomo Onyx* of Etincelle, daughter of Karanos Onyx, the current executive, and Aurelia Onyx nee Ferrum of the Hawthorn Tribe."

I nodded to Delgato. I'd learned that Host didn't bow to demons, at least not to lesser ones like Delgato. Historically, *they'd* served *us*. He eyed the alembic around my neck and then his gaze dropped to my demon mark.

"So you're Rochester's *Primoris*," he said, creeping toward me. "A woman with waning magic? I'm not sure I believe it."

I narrowed my eyes at him. "What else would I be?"

Delgato smiled and I could see that, though he'd taken human form, he'd retained some of his beastly attributes. He still had four razor-sharp canines. "A demoness? Halja is full of them."

I snorted. "I've never shifted in my life."

"So you say," Delgato growled, but it was really more of a low grumble.

"And this is Ferenc Delgato," Rafe said, finishing up the formal introductions. "Captain of the dahabiya *Cnawlece* and Patron Demon of Shadows, Stealth, and Hiding."

Delgato gave me a low bow and said, "I adore and abhor secrets."

Ah, so Delgato *was* a patron and not just a captain. I suppose it made sense for the demon of hiding not to be listed in the Demon Register.

Virtus, who had hidden beneath the table when Delgato first appeared in the doorway (some demon fighter he'd make!), chose that moment to come out. Tail up, ears forward, he trotted over to Delgato and sat right in front of him. *How remarkably similar they look,* I thought. *Pointy ears, furry paws, sharp teeth, and those glimmering cat eyes, each pair staring at the other.*

Delgato bent to scratch the tiny tiger behind the ears. "And who is this?"

"Virtus," Fara said proudly.

Delgato laughed then, a deep rumbling sound. The cub looked positively blissful under Delgato's ministrations.

"Who's a pretty kitty?" Delgato crooned. Then he turned around and yelled into the kitchen:

"Burr, bring in the fish!"

As Luck would have it, the fish dish that night was charred red snapper. Unbelievable. What were the odds? Did Burr the Cook know Alba the Third? I stared at the blackened, nasty-looking thing with its bulging eye and reached for my filleting knife. I might hate filleting, but there was *no way* I was going to ask Ari to do it for me. So I spent the better part of the first half of dinner hacking off the fish's head, ripping out its bones, slicing its skin off, and generally being glad my dress was black so no one would see the fish goo I was splattering all over myself. Luckily, the fish meat turned out to be delicious. I was so hungry, I ate every bite. A fact that pleased both Delgato and Burr immensely.

After dinner, Burr—a short, stocky man with a ready smile and big, thick, white scars on his hands that may have been the result of galley burns . . . or something else— brought in coffee and sautéed sweet plantains. They were savory, but my eyelids were beginning to droop. That is, until Delgato suggested an offering to Estes.

Now, in and of itself, the suggestion shouldn't have caused much alarm. First off, it was just plain good manners. We probably should have made an offering to Estes long before now, probably when we'd first pulled away from the dock. But with the storm and the loading up, it had slipped my mind—and obviously everyone else's. Second, Estes was one of the most popular patron demons in all of Halja. Offerings were made to him all the time, even by nonsailors. Sailors, dockworkers, and fishermen all made offerings, as well as commuters, travelers, shoppers, vendors, and even restaurant owners like Alba. But there was something in Delgato's tone of voice that sounded a warning. And there was a slight uptick in his signature that portended trouble.

Virtus had curled up on Fara's lap sometime during the

dessert. She sat absently stroking him, only half paying attention to the conversation. (Her focus was likely off somewhere between Joshua 1:20 and Joshua 27:11.) Rafe looked bored—no surprise there. Ari, however, appeared as attentive as I. What I couldn't tell, however, was whether Ari's attention was due to the change I'd sensed in Delgato or because Ari also felt that we should make an offering to Estes posthaste.

Estes was the hearth demon for every single family in Bradbury. The Hyrkes who hailed from Bradbury were all blue-collar, salt-of-the-earth types who built ships, fished, and worked the docks. With my own eyes, I'd seen them burn their most cherished possessions in offering to Estes— because they had faith that Estes would return those offerings three times over.

Ari, the magical and mysterious boy Joy had pulled from the river, had been raised as a hero among his people. Coming from Etincelle, where magic is almost mundane, I hadn't understood. Until Ari's neighbors had asked me to participate in one of their offerings. Only after seeing their rapture . . . their renewed belief . . . their *need* for faith in magic and the satisfaction thereof, did I understand.

"I'll make the offering," I said, getting up. "I have something that would be perfect." The fish dish and thoughts of Alba had made me think of it. "I'll be right back."

It took mere seconds to exit the dining room and walk to my cabin. Quickly, I found what I was looking for: Alba's black onion. I stared at it in my palm. I had to admit, it didn't look like much, just a small, black, irregular lump, which was starting to flake and peel. But inside it was an answer. An answer to a question anyone on this boat might ask. *Any* question. *Any* answer.

I ran back to the dining room, slightly out of breath. I slowed to a walk and approached Delgato. As Alba had done with me, I slowly scooted my hand across the table toward him, palm down, until I was only a few inches away. Then I opened my hand, dropped the onion, and backed away.

Delgato stared at it.

He looked up at me, perplexed. "A rotted vegetable? That's your offering?"

"No," I said quickly, now suddenly wanting to make sure Delgato understood. The last thing I'd ever want to do is offend Estes. I'd given my blood as an offering to the mighty patron demon. I'd *burned* things in his name. The last thing I would want anyone thinking is that this gift didn't matter.

"It's a black onion. A real one."

Everyone in the room (save Virtus) stared intently at it. Delgato picked it up between his thumb and forefinger, peering at it as if it were a gem. I could almost read his mind: *If only he had a jeweler's loupe, maybe he could see the answers to his questions right through the onion skin. He might never have to peel it. Then he could ask, and receive answers, over and over and over again.*

"And you're willing to just throw this into the river?" Delgato asked me. I paused and then nodded. Delgato stared queerly at me. Almost reluctantly, he put the onion back down on the table and shook his head.

"It's the perfect offering," he said, smiling up at me, canines gleaming, gums black as the onion, "for the wrong demon."

Right, I thought, Delgato *is the Patron of Shadows, Stealth, and Hiding. The one who both adores and abhors secrets. What better gift for him than something that would reveal someone else's deepest, most private secret?*

"The onion's not for you, Delgato. It's for Estes."

Delgato's eyes hardened. That little sliver of fear I'd felt earlier started ripping open. How stupid I'd been. *Never show a demon something he desperately wants but can't have.* If Rochester had said it once, he'd said it a thousand times. I walked over to Delgato.

"It's a true offering," I said, snatching the onion back.

Before I could completely withdraw my hand, however, Delgato's paw closed tightly around it. One of his claws pierced the base of my thumb and a tiny drop of blood welled. I couldn't tell if it was an accident or not. Ari was at my side instantly. Both Rafe and Fara leapt to their feet. Virtus hissed his displeasure at being dumped from Fara's lap and ran under the table.

"Release her," Ari said. I swallowed, desperately hoping Delgato would. How many miles from New Babylon were we already? More importantly, how many miles to go? Despite my increasing concerns regarding our captain, I still hoped we could keep sailing to the Shallows. People there needed our help. A girl was missing. And besides, wasn't Delgato an old friend of Rochester's? Of course, now that I thought about it, that fact gave me absolutely zero comfort.

I gentled my signature, my expression, and my voice.

"You're right," I said to Delgato. "The onion's not an appropriate gift for Estes. It's yours at the end of this trip . . . if we all make it back safely."

I could tell Delgato didn't like that last bit. Apparently, it really was unlikely we'd make it back without at least one death. His expression stayed cold and his paw still gripped my hand. Ari's signature expanded. Rafe and Fara moved in to flank us. I could not allow the trip to become a disaster this early on. And for something so minor. I cleared my throat to steady my voice.

"If we're still making an offering to Estes, what do *you* suggest?"

Delgato continued holding my hand. In fact he squeezed his claw tighter and the drop of blood coming from my hand became a slow trickle. Ari fired a blast at Delgato's paw. Delgato howled and let go. Ari was a moment away from blasting Delgato with something heavy, something that might irreversibly change the direction of our trip.

"Stop!" I shouted. "I'm fine." I turned toward Ari and grabbed his arm. "My hand only stings. Delgato's a *bully*," I said, glaring back at him, "but I've given Estes my blood before. It's no big deal. In fact, I'm happy to do it if it makes this trip faster or safer."

Ari grunted, which was probably the closest thing I'd

ever get from him as an affirmative response when it came time to giving demons blood sacrifices. He'd never done it and didn't agree with me doing it either.

"Blood is fine," Delgato growled, "but after your *partner's* reaction just now, I think it would be more interesting to watch you offer a sign of peace."

"Okay," I agreed just as Ari was saying my name in warning. I shrugged back at him. *How bad could a peace sacrifice be?*

Delgato grinned, but with his canines it looked more like a grimace. He shook his injured paw and turned toward Ari. "I sense a *signare* on both of your marks."

A *signare* was like a magical glaze over a waning magic user's demon mark. Ari had explained them to me last semester. Apparently, demons use them to mark their mates. It was, as Ari had put it, like pressing a thumb into a lover's heart and leaving a thumbprint. The *signare* was branded into our marks by our lover's touch. It took reciprocity, both magical and emotional, in order for the branding to work. I don't know what it was like for others, but the effect of Ari's touch on my mark had never really lessened. The branding was still exquisitely pleasurable, and not a little painful.

"From what Rochester has told me and the way you've acted toward one another tonight, I assume you've each marked the other with a *signare*?"

I glanced at Ari. There was no reason to hide it. It wasn't any of Delgato's business; but then again, what was the purpose of a sign if no one saw it? I suppose *signares* were like Hyrke promise pins. It was just a way of publicly declaring your commitment to each other.

"We have," I said boldly. Ari smiled at me then, but it was strained. I knew he didn't trust Delgato.

"Nouiomo Onyx and Aristos Carmine," Delgato murmured as he got up from his chair. "Rochester's told me all about you two. You, in particular, Nouiomo. You're a source of fascination to many," he said, glancing at Ari, "and not just because you're the executive's daughter." Delgato wandered around the room. It reminded me of the way Rochester wandered during class. He came to a stop in front of one of the paintings near the back wall of the dining room. "Tomorrow night I will continue where my old friend left off. I will teach you how to fight. But tonight I want to see how you love. Come," he said, motioning both Ari and me over to view the painting with him. Ari stood up first and reached for my hand. I took it and rose from my seat. The Angels stood at their chairs, alert and wary. Together, Ari and I stepped up to the painting.

It was a painting of Estes embracing a lover at the water's edge. But unlike Estes' conquests in the other paintings, his lover in this picture wasn't a human Hyrke. She was a demon. In the painting, the two lovers stood naked, ankle deep in the shallow waters of the Lethe's edge at sunrise. The dawning sun rose behind them, coating the lapping waves and the lovers in pink. The left, shadowed side of everything in the painting was as black as the just-ending night. Estes had the demoness in a clinch, his mouth pressed against her mark. Her back arched over Estes' massively muscled arm and her long dark hair echoed the shape of her body and the waves of the Lethe.

In the picture, Estes was depicted as a large human man. Mouth pressed against the demoness' breast, he almost appeared to be devouring her. The demoness, however, was depicted midshift. Instead of feet, she had a dark, twisted plume for a tail. Instead of fingers, she had long, bluish black claws. And instead of a nose and mouth, she had a vicious-looking beak. But her cobalt-colored wings were the most mesmerizing thing about her appearance. I couldn't help wondering if an Angel had painted this picture because her wings seemed to flutter as we watched. They beat the air behind her back as she struggled against Estes' embrace.

The painting's title was *Cliodna's Surrender.*

By now, my cheeks and magic were hot. Ari's signature was at low boil too. Did Delgato expect us to enact the embrace in the picture? I was afraid he did.

Fara stood nearby, poised and ready to cast. Rafe sat back down and put his feet up on the chair next to him. He looked disinterested, but I couldn't be sure.

"So let's see," Delgato said. "Kiss her," he commanded, waving to Ari.

Ari looked at me. I swallowed and reluctantly nodded my assent. After all, hadn't Ari kissed me in front of a crowd just two nights ago at Marduk's? What was one small buss? It wasn't even a blood sacrifice. And I knew Ari would keep the kiss brief and chaste. There would be no swooning, no true surrender. Ari leaned toward me and barely brushed his mouth against my mark. It *stung* and I sucked in a deep breath of air. My chest heaved and I sighed in relief as Ari lifted his head. The room suddenly seemed too bright and I knew my pupils had likely dilated to full black. Delgato, Rafe, and Fara were hardly the cheering crowds of Marduk's, but I thought we acquitted ourselves well. Ari stepped back and Delgato laughed.

"That's not it, is it?" he said to me. "Rochester told me you added emotion to your magic to make it stronger. You told me you were able to mark each other with *signares*. Two *humans*. That's powerful waning magic and I want to see it. Look back at the painting I showed you, Nouiomo. What do you see?"

"The demon's predilection for perversion?" I grumbled. Any lingering buzz from Ari's kiss had fled.

"The *kiss* isn't the sacrifice. The *surrender* is the sacrifice. I want to see if you're capable of surrendering to waning magic."

"Of course I'm capable of surrendering to waning magic," I snapped.

"Your past history indicates otherwise. I was told that you declared your magic only days before Bryde's Day last semester, that you first enrolled at St. Luck's as a Hyrke, and that you're one of Rochester's most reluctant students."

I opened my mouth to protest but what could I really say? Everything Delgato just said was true.

"I was told you have powerful waning magic but that you're still having trouble wielding it as you should."

I stiffened. "What's your point, Delgato?"

"I can help you."

I frowned. *Was this some sort of trick?* "How?"

"Rochester's teaching methods are orthodox. They work best with students who use magic in the traditional way. My methods are unorthodox—as are yours. That's why Rochester asked me to serve as your guide and mentor on this assignment. I understand all too well how much more powerful magic can be when combined with emotion."

Out of the corner of my eye, I took a peek at our Angel audience. They hadn't moved. Fara was still at the ready and Rafe looked like he was napping. What did I care what they thought anyway? It was demons like Delgato and Estes that I had to prove myself to, although I wasn't exactly sure how surrendering myself as Cliodna had was going to accomplish that.

"Is this a sacrifice for Estes, a Manipulation lesson, or just an act that will satisfy your perverted curiosity?"

Delgato narrowed his eyes at me. "All of the above," he finally said. "If you want to learn how to better manipulate your magic with emotion, prove it. Make an offering. Show us that you're willing to surrender to waning magic."

I shook my head. "I don't think so."

Delgato's expression darkened and his signature suddenly made me feel as if I'd been stuffed in a sack full of razors.

"I'm offering to tutor and protect you on this voyage and you refuse to offer even one small sign of peace? Of love? Of commitment?"

"No," I said quickly. It wasn't that I had trouble offering those things. "It's just that . . . well, Ari doesn't have to be involved in my sacrifice."

Delgato laughed. "Is there someone else here you care for more?"

I scoffed. "Of course not." But . . .

"How I use my magic with Ari is my business," I said

shrilly. My temper was starting to fray, which meant my magic control was too.

"Of course it is, Nouiomo," Delgato said, his voice almost a purr. "And if your preference is a more savage sacrifice, I'm sure I can assess you while you use your magic to skin, debone, and disembowel Virtus."

I heard Fara gasp but kept my gaze fastened on Delgato. His signature was full of sharp edges, as if he were made of knives and fangs. It was impossible to tell if he was bluffing.

"Fine," I said testily. I swallowed, mentally preparing myself. *What did it matter if I showed everyone here how I truly felt about Ari? It wasn't as if I was ashamed of my feelings for him.* I reached up and clasped my hands behind Ari's head. I drew him down toward me and kissed him on the lips. It was a sweet kiss. A sign that I wanted to do this, and that I forgave him for whatever might happen next.

Gently then, I lowered Ari's head to my mark. He bent me back over his arm as Estes had Cliodna. My hair broke free of its ribbon and swept the floor as Ari's mouth came down on my mark more forcefully than before. I cried out, going involuntarily stiff. Waning magic pooled in my mark and for one frightening moment, I thought I might lose control. But then I softened, gentling myself and my magic, and attempted to tame the answering waning magic I felt rising up in Ari. But trying to limit both my body's and my magic's response to Ari's touch proved too much. I slumped in Ari's arms. He held me up, my head tipped back, his head still pressed to my chest, the stinging, burning, erotic sensation of his mouth on my mark nearly more than I could bear.

I was almost—but not quite—to the point of no longer caring what happened next when Delgato leaned toward me and whispered, "When you've had enough, surrender. Your magic is destructive, Nouiomo. Surrender to it. Commit to it. *Embrace* it as Aristos is embracing you and shape it into a weapon of war. Even when all you're feeling is love, you must learn how to think violently."

That was it. *That's* what did it. I'd like to think that I am capable of surrendering, for the right reasons, but clearly I'm unable to do so when provoked.

The volatile mix of magic and emotions I'd gathered exploded and sluiced off of me. I was afraid I might repeat what had happened at the House of Metatron when I had destroyed Justica, so instead of fireballs, I willed it into the shape of a giant dove. The flaming bird circled the room in lazy, whooshing swoops. Ari rested his forehead briefly against mine before releasing me from his embrace. I stood up and walked over to a window. I fumbled with the catch for a moment and then threw it open. My flaming dove took one last lap around the dining room, dropping ash and cinders the entire time, and driving Virtus absolutely mad, and then it flew through the window and dove straight into the Lethe. I gathered my hair to one side, pulled it over and across my left shoulder, covering my mark, and turned to face my small audience. Rafe was at the drink cart, pouring himself a brandy, and Fara's attention was focused solely on Virtus.

Behind me the river hissed and steamed.

I thought Delgato would be angry that I'd defied his wishes, but he just laughed and clapped slowly.

"Well done, Nouiomo Onyx," he said. "I have a feeling we'll work well together."

Chapter 12

ꝛ

After dinner, dessert, and my flaming dove trick, I changed into soft linen pants and a high-necked shirt, bandaged my still-bleeding thumb, and fled to the upper sundeck, which, at that time of night, was awash in moonlight and blissfully deserted. Low benches covered in cushions and square pillows outlined the boat's inner railing. I picked a spot as far from the stairs as possible and sat down, hiding myself behind one of the cannons. I tucked my legs up under my chin and stared out at the silver-tinged river and the black hills of the countryside at night.

I was wondering what new perils tomorrow might bring when I heard footsteps on the deck. I wrapped my arms around my legs and buried my face in my knees, groaning. The footsteps grew louder until Ari was standing right in front of me.

"I'm like some abominable jar of pickled hearts," I mumbled, not looking up, thinking of the indelicate spectacle we'd made before my fiery dove thankfully stole the show. "Like the ones behind the curtain at Hyrke street fairs that people pay a quarter to see."

"Maybe, but if that kiss was any indication, you must taste awfully good."

I raised my head, frowning. It was Rafe, not Ari. Suddenly, oddly, unbelievably, I felt like laughing. "Did you just cast a spell over me?"

Rafe feigned innocence. "I told you, I wouldn't dream of casting a spell over you." He sat down on one of the nearby cushions and his expression became serious. "But, actually, I would. That's what I came up here for—to cast a healing spell over you." He motioned to my bandaged thumb.

"So you really can cast useful spells. And the veiling and unveiling of Delgato. Those spells were for real, Rafe. You've been hiding some serious skills. What were you doing with your hands? I've never heard of an Angel that can cast without speaking before."

He shrugged, like it was no big deal.

"Does anyone at the Joshua School know you can do that?" They couldn't possibly. He'd never have been ranked dead last if they knew he could cast silent spells. "You should tell them."

"Why would I want to do that?"

"Don't you want to advance your career?" *What Angel wasn't ambitious?* Well, okay, from what I'd seen of him (or not seen of him, although his blank CV spoke volumes), Raphael Sinclair was the least ambitious Angel I'd ever met. And, sure enough, the next words out of his mouth were:

"I could care less about advancing my career. And besides, the Joshua School kicked me out."

"What—?"

Again, the shrug. Like it was no big deal. And then something occurred to me.

"The letter of introduction. Your name was never on it. You cast a spell over it—a silent one!"

He didn't deny it. I didn't know Rafe well enough to know what he was thinking. And he wasn't a waning magic user with a signature so I couldn't even sense his feelings. He seemed calm, unperturbed. I figured that was just the face he showed everyone. The slacker face. The face that said he didn't give a damn about anything. Or anyone.

"You got kicked out because of me," I said slowly. "Or because of the statue. Justica."

"I guess they didn't like my interpretation of her." He guffawed and it didn't even sound forced. He seemed genuinely amused by the Joshua School's reaction, which was almost unimaginable because now Rafe was completely unemployable, at least as a Guardian. *Wait a minute . . .*

"Did you snake charm your way into being my Guardian just so you could prove to the Joshua School what a mistake they'd made?" If he could prove he'd successfully protected me during this assignment, he would be able to make a fair argument that he should be let back in.

"Come on, firestarter. If I cared about what the Joshua School thought, would I have done what I did in the first place?"

"Why did you come, then?"

He sighed. "It seemed like the thing to do at the time."

I raised my eyebrows. How had he gotten even as far as he had with that sort of attitude? *It seemed like the thing to do at the time . . . Who makes choices that way?*

"You didn't have a Guardian and I didn't have a ward. You clearly need one. Oh, please, you can't possibly be upset by that statement. So I came. Besides, I find you interesting. You're a novelty. You said it yourself. You really *are* like a jar of pickled hearts."

I openly gawked at him. I could *not* tell if he was kidding.

"So . . . are you gonna let me heal you or what?" He motioned to my hand. I looked down at it. I'd actually forgotten about it. Although now that he'd called my attention to it, it throbbed. There was no denying that a healing spell would help me sleep, something that would do me a world of good. And, even though Rafe's methods were unconventional and his attitude was horrible, there was no danger of an Angel with his abilities botching a simple healing spell. So I nodded and started unwrapping the bandage.

"Hold on, I'll do it," Rafe said, getting up. He walked over to one of the railings and pulled down an unlit lantern. He grabbed a small wooden table and walked back toward me carrying both. He sat the table down right next to me, put the lantern on top, and then took a seat so close to me, our hips almost touched. He reached for my hand and I hesitated.

Rafe exhaled, clearly exasperated. "I can heal you without touching you, but it's a lot easier if I can see the cut first. So, do you mind?" He pointed from me to the dark lantern.

Successfully shaping my magic into a flaming dove earlier had given me a confidence boost. The feat, for me, had been quite extraordinary. But then again, my magic had always been capricious. Strong, yes. Predictable, no. So Rafe's small request set my heart beating just a little bit faster. Didn't he realize I could just as easily set his hair on fire as that candlewick? He must, after having seen what I did to Justica! And he had to know the dove was born from provocation as much as peaceful thoughts. Yet there he sat, not an inch from me, calm and unperturbed as ever.

It's not like he hasn't been warned, I thought.

I directed a small, precise blast of magic toward the lantern, focusing on the wick. Just before it caught, however, I twitched, causing a sudden stab of pain in my thumb. I inhaled sharply, not knowing if my small bobble would cause my magic to veer wildly off course, and that's when Rafe gently laid his hand on mine and murmured the words to a spell.

Once, when I was nine, I'd gone swimming in an old abandoned quarry on our estate. It was forbidden, but I went anyway. There were so many things that were forbidden to me as a child, I figured what could be the harm in swimming? And I'd been right. The harm hadn't come from swimming. Nor had it come from demons. It had come from the sun—that bright, yellow, cheery thing that was usually such a good companion to me. I'd fallen asleep under its warm, rosy glow, only to awaken hours later, burned and blistered. Until that moment, I'd never understood the expression *too much of a good thing*. I'd walked home, wincing the whole way, fearful of what further discomforts my mother might have in store for me. But instead of scolding me, she'd soothed my skin with the extract of a plant she'd called Dragon's Tongue.

Rafe's touch was like that: cool, soothing, and soft.

The candlewick burst into life and my magic retracted, for once, as easily as a yo-yo snapping back into my palm. *Huh.*

I looked over at Rafe and he shrugged. "I told you I knew Flame Resistant Blanket." *Well, double huh.* I didn't want him to know how good his stupidly titled spell felt so I took a page from his book. I kept my face perfectly bland as I gave him my hand.

Rafe untied the bloody wrap and placed it on the table next to us. My cut looked nasty, a deeper wound than I'd first thought with ragged edges and oozing puss. My guess was that Delgato's claws were covered in some sort of irritant. Not poison, but something that would likely infect and fester. Rafe held my hand gently in both of his as he murmured a healing spell. After a few moments, the throbbing diminished and then stopped altogether. He let go. I looked down at my hand and flexed.

Amazing! My right hand felt just as strong as my left. And there was only the tiniest scar. I doubted a Mederi could have done better.

I shrugged. Two could play the game of acting like his spells were no big deal.

"I guess you can stay," I said, trying to hide my smile. After all, a little healing couldn't erase the fact that he'd tricked his way on board, was likely still hiding things about himself, and—worst of all—had agreed that I was like a jar of pickled hearts. I mumbled thanks and good night and rushed down the stairs, suddenly eager to get away.

A few minutes later, I found Ari in his cabin. He'd changed as well and was now wearing clothes that looked as comfortable as mine felt. In his hands was a leather-bound book that he closed gently and set aside when I came in. His gaze took in my recently healed hand and my high-necked shirt. He gave me a regretful look.

"I would have come looking for you eventually. I know the kiss made you feel uncomfortable."

"No it didn't," I said too quickly. Ari raised his brows at me.

"Well, maybe just a little," I said, exhaling and laughing quietly. Outside of Ari's small cabin window, I could hear the lap of waves as *Cnawlece* made its way east through the waters of the Lethe. Up top, we heard the soft scuffling of feet on the deck and through the thin wall behind Ari's headboard, we could hear Fara trying to coax Virtus out from under her bed frame. The sounds made us acutely aware that, though no one could see us, everyone could probably hear us.

I walked over to where Ari was sitting on the edge of the bed and straddled him, climbing onto his lap and hooking my legs behind him. I put my arms around him and rested my cheek against his heart.

"There will be paybacks," I said.

"Promise?" Ari's voice was low and throaty, more a purr than a growl.

I smiled and reached for the book he'd been reading before I came in. It was a collection of sonnets first published over two centuries ago by Naberious, a demon poet. Since poetry was usually the province of the Angels, Naberius' work was regarded by some with suspicion. In fact, most Host believed that Naberious had really been a Hyrke who'd invented a pseudonymous identity to increase sales. Either way, fans of Naberious' work were hopeless romantics. It was my turn to raise my brows at Ari. But instead of looking sheepish, he told me in a low voice:

"Your fiery dove was magnificent."

I made some noncommital sound as I pulled off his shirt and pushed him down on the bed. I sat with my hips resting on his, my left hand pressed against his right shoulder and my other hand poised above his demon mark.

"Think you can shape your magic into a symbol of peace?" I said, grinning, my voice more of a growl than a purr.

"I doubt it," Ari said, laughing. "What you did was actually quite remarkable."

I frowned in disappointment as Ari studied my face.

"Nouiomo," he said, suddenly serious, "you're the only one who could ever make me want to try." And then he placed my hand over his heart.

The next night, as promised, Delgato took us up to the sundeck after dinner for our first Manipulation lesson in the field. He had the Angels come too. As he'd said, what was the point of having Guardians if we didn't learn to work with them? The area within which we'd be practicing our fiery craft was as far from the Manipulation dungeon as I could possibly have imagined. Instead of the usual cold, creepy underground dungeon full of torches and Apocalypse-era weapons, we were on top of a dahabiya in hot, sticky summer air, surrounded by lanterns, Angels, claws, and fangs. Luckily, the claws and fangs belonged to Delgato and Virtus.

"Before we start practicing," Delgato said, "we should discuss the demons you're likely to encounter during this field assignment. First off, *rogares*. Do any of you know the type of *rogare* demon that's most prevalent in the areas we'll be passing through?"

"Water wraiths," I said.

"Right," Delgato said, nodding. "And what's the best weapon against them?"

If we were back in Rochester's class, Brunus would surely have shouted out, "Fire!" but thank Luck we weren't. Ari answered instead.

"Salt."

"Exactly. Hopefully, we won't be attacked by a pack of wraiths, but should that occur I want you all to know what to do. Load up the cannons with shot and salt and—"

Delgato clapped his hands together and a huge fire-ball boomed out from one of the cannons on deck. It lobbed over the Lethe and was on its way into the field when it suddenly burst into a shower of harmless ash and dust. It hadn't been a real cannonball; it had been waning magic. But had it landed in the field, it would have burned it all the same.

"If we get attacked by wraiths," Delgato continued, "a possibility about as likely as not, then throw everything at them. Not just shot and salt, but waning magic and"—he turned to the Angels—"every spell you've got."

Everyone nodded. No one was going to make the mistake of holding something back during a wraith attack.

"Okay, so what other demons might we encounter during our trip?"

"Manticores," I said, arching a brow at Delgato. He grinned widely, his sharp canines gleaming white in the moonlight. I didn't trust him (what sane person would trust the Patron Demon of Shadows, Stealth, and Hiding?) but I also didn't think he meant us harm. His signature was still mildly abrasive, but now that I was used to it, it felt a little like Virtus' tongue—spiky and slightly gross, but also full of rough affection.

"You already know everything about me I'm willing to reveal," he said. "Manticores are nocturnal, we love fish, and we're good fighters. What else?"

"A hellcnight," Ari said quietly.

"A hellcnight? I hope not!" Delgato said. "Why do you think we'd encounter one of them? Rochester said the accused was a vodanoy—a water demon."

"He is," I said. "But Vodnik blames Grimasca for his followers' disappearances. Isn't Grimasca a hellcnight?"

Delgato snorted. "Grimasca! He'd sooner be responsible for a crime today than Luck himself. Grimasca's story is even older than Luck's. He's one of the only demons that predates the Apocalypse. No one knows if he was *ever* real. Or if he's just something mothers made up to scare their babes so they wouldn't wander off. Fitting, though, that Grimasca's legend should linger on in a place like the Shallows. The swamps there are full of things that will kill you."

"Maybe it's not Grimasca who's preying on Vodnik's followers," I said. "Maybe it's just a regular ole hellcnight."

"No such thing," Delgato snapped. "Hellcnights are as *rogare* as a demon can get. And they can impersonate anyone, which makes them much more dangerous than the average Haljan demon."

"So any one of us could be a hellcnight right now and we wouldn't even know it?" Rafe said, turning to Fara. "Maybe Virtus is really a hellcnight stowaway."

Fara looked momentarily horrified. Probably because she was worried one of us might actually believe Rafe's casually uttered indictment. We all turned toward Virtus, who was lying on one of the cushions licking his fur clean. When he noticed our sudden interest in him, he stopped, back leg raised, tongue sticking out, and looked at us. He looked preposterously adorable and incapable of harming anything.

"Can a hellcnight really mask its own signature so well that they could pass for a Hyrke around other waning magic users?" *That* was even more impossible to believe than Virtus being a demon imposter, but Delgato nodded.

"And they can manipulate *other* waning magic users' signatures. They use their magic to tap into their victims' memories. If you're sensitive enough to pick up on it, that may be the only warning you have. The first time you encounter a hellcnight, there's a waning magic 'blur' that occurs while the hellcnight is adjusting to its targets' signatures."

"And then what happens?" Fara asked, her voice screechier than usual.

Delgato gave us one of his grinning grimaces as he ticked off the possibilities on his clawed paws. "You'll either be dead, in a deep sleep, or dragged off to be eaten later."

"What happens if the hellcnight comes back?" I asked.

Delgato laughed. "Then there will be no warning, not even a magic blur. If you're very, very lucky, you might be able to fight one off. Which brings us to what we're going to discuss next: using waning magic as a weapon.

"Rochester told me that you have trouble shaping your magic, Nouiomo. But yesterday you shaped it into a flying dove. Not only was the dove a recognizable, fairly complicated shape, but it was an animated one. Your magic is powerful, but you need to learn control and consistency. Could you repeat last night's magic trick?"

"I'm not sure," I said. It wasn't a lie.

Delgato nodded. "Angels only have to worry about one thing when they cast their magic, *potentia*, or how much focus they have left to cast another successful spell." Delgato looked to the Angels for confirmation. Fara nodded and screeched, "'*Potentia* becomes *exponentia* when combined with discipline, study, and practice.' The Book of Joshua, nine, thirteen." Rafe murmured his assent and then yawned. Delgato continued.

"Waning magic users, on the other hand, have myriad aspects of their magic to worry about: speed, strength, accuracy, range, as well as their ability to sustain it and manipulate it. Some aspects can be improved through the use of booster spells and some can only be improved by practicing.

"So let's practice."

Practicing by moonlight on the sundeck of the dahabiya was every bit as miserable as practicing in the Manipulation dungeon back in New Babylon had been. Sparring with

Delgato was just as bad as sparring with Brunus or Sasha would have been. And, to top it off, apparently Rafe knew only two useful spells, the healing spell and the ridiculously titled Flame Resistant Blanket, neither of which was helpful when I was *trying* to throw waning magic. When Delgato finally called an end to the night's practice, I was sweaty, sooty, and so agitated I probably would have set off all of the cannons had they been loaded.

During that first week, we fell into a routine. That is, if anything that felt so tense could be called "routine." The wildflower fields, forests, and rolling hills of the New Babylon countryside gave way to the flat, sprawling rush lands of Halja's river delta. I'd never seen anything so expansive. In the wind, the undulating green rushes ran to the edge of the world, only stopping when the bright blue expanse of heaven rolled down to meet them from above. Looking out from *Cnawlece*'s sundeck, I could almost imagine the curvature of our world. Halja's big sky was like the tinted top of a snow globe, but instead of a sky that rained white sparkles, our earth spawned dark demons. Luckily, our sky stayed cloudless and the demons stayed hidden.

For all its open beauty, though, our world began to feel closed in, in a way it never had back in New Babylon. The snow globe's edge wasn't the limit of what I could see, but the edge of *Cnawlece*'s decks. As inviting as the passing world seemed to be, I couldn't touch it, move in it, explore it, or experience it. In order to survive, we needed to simply pass through it.

And, besides, nighttime disabused us of any notion that the surrounding lands were either empty or bucolic.

Each night, as the sun went down, the dark stole across the land, bathing everything in black. The new moon we experienced on our seventh night out was especially bad. As soon as darkness fell, the sounds and signatures rose, creeping along the edges of our magic and our minds.

Demons make horrible sounds: clicking, clacking, chirping; grunting, braying, snuffling; crying, whistling, rattling. I had no idea, since I couldn't see them, whether my enemies were more or less terrible than I imagined. Over and over again, when I was on night watch, I had to convince myself not to scream out or redline my magic so I wouldn't bring on an attack or burn us all to bits.

Though Delgato and his crew had sailed the eastern Lethe alone before, Delgato told us it would be safer (or less dangerous) if one of us was always on watch. The *rogares* would be able to sense us, he said, just as we would them. Three waning magic users sailing down the Lethe would attract notice. Some demons would be merely curious. Some wouldn't be strong enough to consider an attack. But other demons naturally hunted together and some were quite formidable all on their own. So we divided the day into four shifts of six hours each, the first shift beginning at ten each night.

We trained and practiced during the evening shift. Under Delgato's careful tutelage, my magic control increased at a faster rate than it ever had back in New Babylon. Maybe it was that Delgato wasn't as afraid as Rochester was to mix emotion and magic. Delgato warned Ari against it. Said it was too late for him; he should stick to what he knew. But for me, he agreed it might be the answer. As he put it, "Cheating was the only way to make up twenty-one years of missed practice." After statements like that, I no longer wondered why Delgato wasn't a member of the St. Luck's faculty. Yet, despite my advancements, true magical finesse eluded me. It felt like I was still holding back.

We got used to the boat's motion under our feet. It no longer felt like we were moving, even in rougher waters. Meals were taken in the dining room, although whoever was on watch was always missing.

We ate fish. *Lots* of fish. I got used to filleting. And then I became very skilled at filleting. Every night, as I chopped off a head, ripped out bones, and sliced off skin, I practiced channeling the emotion I would later put to even better use on the moonlit sundeck during our evening training sessions: peace. After all, *si vis pacem, para bellum*, right? *If you want peace, prepare for war.* The fact that we weren't actually headed to war made me feel incrementally better about where we were headed: an investigation that might lead to an execution.

Virtus put on a good ten pounds and thankfully stopped hissing at Rafe every time Rafe tried to pet him, which was annoyingly often. I was still getting to know Mr. TBD but his relationship with Virtus seemed a microcosm of how he related to the world at large. He never cared what others' reactions were to him. He did whatever he wanted. Eventually, things seemed to go his way. If he hadn't ended up knowing some decent spells (albeit with ridiculous names), I might have thrown him overboard.

Fara, on the other hand, grew less confident with each passing mile. Her quoting seemed obsessively focused on fear. We heard "Fear is only as deep as the mind allows" and "The fearful are caught as often as the bold" so many times, I lost count. When she was on watch, she would murmur them, or something similar, under her breath, over and over and *over* again. And she clung to Joshua's book as if it were a baby's binky. If I didn't know her any better (and I really didn't), I'd have thought she was scared.

I was too.

But still, during that first week and a half, it seemed as if Fara's father's wish—*venti secundi, daemones pauca*; fair winds, few demons—was coming true.

All of that changed twelve days into our trip.

Chapter 13

ॐ

The suggested route of passage for the Shallows is fairly straightforward. Or as straightforward as any trip on the eastern Lethe might be. Though the number of streams, tributaries, and rivulets only increases the farther out from New Babylon one gets, our suggested route required only one turn. That turn would occur at First Branch, where the Lethe divided into four nearly equal parts. Each part had its own name: the Concelare, the Blandjan, the Naefre, and the Finthanan. We were supposed to take Blandjan at First Branch. Then, and this was critical, we had to *stay* on Blandjan past Second and Third Branch. The sticky wicket—the place we needed to avoid at all costs—was a place called Ebony's Elbow.

Legend says Ebony was a water demon who gave her memory of hearth and home to her wandering lover so that he could find his way back to her. But losing this memory doomed Ebony to wander the Lethe for centuries until she found a final resting place in the dark waters of the bend in the Lethe that's now named after her. They say the elbow is full of rushing white water that runs black as a blank mind, rocks as sharp as a spinning propeller, and dozens of derelict ships . . . but no one really knows. Anyone who's ever gotten close enough to see it, hasn't survived it.

Oh, there were some tall tales and fish stories in the *Field Guide* I'd brought (stories of how one lone anchor saved an entire ship, pulling it straight out of the treacherously spinning abyss as if it were some ancient Archimedes' claw) and there was some improbable, counterintuitive advice ("in order to pass unharmed, one had to use their anchor"), but generally, reports, route notes, and the map's depiction of the place led to a conclusion as inescapable as the place itself: Ebony's Elbow, a.k.a. Ebony's End, was a graveyard for river vessels and passengers alike. It was like one of those ancient tar pits or the black void of space. It was an area, up or down, where one was sure to encounter the life-sucking sound of death.

To aid travelers, and help them avoid areas like Ebony's Elbow, each Branch was marked with a bonfire frame. Ari, who'd been talking with Delgato, told me all about them on our eleventh night out when he slipped into my cabin a few hours before midnight.

"Who's on watch?" I asked.

"Rafe," Ari said, quietly latching the door behind him. He stood for a moment, leaning against the door, watching me. I was dressed for bed in black lace bloomers and a blush-colored camisole. The alembic rested lightly against my chest. I wasn't sure I believed in its ability to determine guilt or innocence, but I wasn't quite ready to "accidentally" lose it either. With any luck, Vodnik wouldn't have any knowledge of his barbaric, antediluvian right.

"Is Delgato out there with him? He can't sense the demons like we can."

Ari gave a snort that clearly said, *He can't do much of anything.*

"He cast a spell he calls Demon Net," Ari said, rolling his eyes.

Despite the fact that Rafe had proven he could cast some

useful spells, his constant insouciance and lack of serious-
ness bothered Ari tremendously. And I had to admit, if only
to myself, that although I still thought Fara was a fake who
hid behind her glamour and the Book, Rafe was even
worse. His flippancy, his absurdly titled spells, his whole
que sera blah blah blah thing . . . Well, the more it continued, the more I thought it might be a carefully calculated
veneer to hide his true feelings for us: disdain.

I stayed on the other side of the bed, wondering what
Ari had come to talk to me about. Or if he had come to talk
at all. I swallowed and gave him a lopsided smile. Regardless of our romantic history (we'd actually come close to
doing many of the things that were shown in Delgato's dining room pictures), there were still times when I felt nervous
around him. It was crazy. But my reluctance, as Ari sometimes called it, was because no one, *no one*, in my whole
life, had ever made me feel as at risk as Ari did.

When Ari was around, I had to concentrate extra hard
on controlling my magic. It was like I was teetering on the
brink with him. Like I was sitting on a powder keg with a
lit match. And I thought he secretly enjoyed watching me
struggle. How else to explain his casual grazes and meaningful gazes? As much as Ari was always lecturing me
about how I needed to learn control, I thought he loved to
watch me squirm. And what he really loved was to watch
me drop that match every once in a while. And know he
caused the resulting explosion.

Which made me the slightest bit resentful. Oh, sure, I
loved Ari. But falling in love happens to you. You don't
happen to it. So there was a part of me still—that part of
me that wanted to survive—that warned me not to give
myself too completely to him. But was it possible to hold
any part of myself back? I didn't know.

But I kept trying.

"Where's Fara?" I said, ignoring the catch in my throat.

But Ari heard it. He pushed off the back of the door,
grinning. He walked over to me (a very short distance, con-

sidering the size of the room), waving his hand to show how inconsequential everything outside was.

"She's on deck with Rafe, trying to see if she can turn Demon Net into some sort of fishing spell so she can catch more food for Virtus. I guess Burr was complaining about how much he was eating this morning."

"Oh . . ." I said, unable to break eye contact with Ari. I knew the minute I looked away, my cheeks would blush furiously. That would be the sign. The signal Ari would seize upon. Why were flags of surrender white? They really should be red . . .

Ari's signature now felt like a net around me. Without his even touching me, I felt him, all hot and tingly, like a bath full of ice and hot coals. I shivered, but never broke eye contact. It was like one of those staring contests that kids play. Except that I blinked first. And Ari kissed me then, just when my eyes closed.

He wasted no time, taking full advantage of that brief defenseless moment. His mouth captured mine and his tongue swept across my lips. It tickled, on my lips and in my belly. Almost involuntarily, I opened my mouth to him. He pressed me back against the wall of my cabin, eagerly devouring what I offered to him. I knew where this was headed. After that first night, when we'd made the offering to Estes, he'd kept his distance from me, in bed anyway. And then there was the fact that, usually, someone else was sleeping mere feet from where we stood now. Though the thin wall behind me would shield us from sight, it wasn't soundproof. Perhaps even Ari realized that asking me to control more than just my magic during our rowdy exertions was asking one thing too many.

So, with everyone safely on deck, Ari almost feverishly tasted what he'd been denied for the last eleven days. One of his favorite spots to linger over was the back of my neck, just behind my ear. Because his touch there gave me goose bumps, *everywhere*. He brought his hand up to my breast and cupped it firmly, wanting to feel his effect on me.

When he felt it, he made a sound in his throat. It was a sound of pleasure and I let it and Ari's mounting signature pour over and into me. Ari dropped down and, still cupping my breast with his hand, brought his mouth to my nipple and gently bit it through the soft cotton of my camisole top.

I mewled a protest and grabbed Ari's head with both hands, clenching my fists in his hair. But instead of pushing him away, I pressed him closer. He pushed my cami up under my arms. My breasts and demon mark were now bare. He paused and met my gaze, holding it. I leaned back against the wall, breathing heavily. I kept waiting for him to bring his hand up to touch what he'd wanted with no barriers in between us. But he didn't. He just kept staring at me, his signature expanding. Mine too.

And that's when I felt it.

"What's that?"

"An old bonfire frame," Ari said. "Long ago, the routes were lined with bonfires. What you're feeling is the remnants of waning magic fire."

I nodded, not really caring what it was that I felt, now that I knew it wasn't a threat.

"We're going to light it," he said. "Together. Like we did last semester."

"Who keeps it stocked with fresh wood?" I said, my confusion pulling me out of the moment. I reached up to pull my shirt down, but Ari caught my hand.

"The Boatmen," he answered quietly, pushing my hand back down. He returned to the spot behind my ear.

"Won't it be dangerous? It will tell the *rogares* exactly where we are."

Ari laughed, a deep, rumbling, warning sound. "They already know."

He lowered his hands to my hips and pressed his thumbs lightly into my stomach. "And, besides," he said, pulling me tight against him with one hard yank, "aren't the fearful caught as often as the brave?"

"The bold," I corrected breathlessly.

"And which are you, Nouiomo?" Ari whispered, lowering his mouth until it was almost touching mine. "Are you brave or are you bold?"

Neither, I wanted to say, but Ari's mouth on mine prevented it. When he finally released me, I felt boneless and my knees were buckling. *Just once,* I thought, *I'd like to make him feel this way because of something I do.* He laughed and I knew a whiff of what I'd been thinking had reached him through our magic.

"Did you forget?" he said, leading me over to a corner of my room where there was a ladder-back chair. "Half of what you feel is *your* effect on *me.*"

He made me sit down. I was relieved at first, and glad I no longer had to worry about keeping upright while Ari kissed me. But then I realized this positioning might be far, far worse.

Slowly, Ari raised my arms and placed my hands on the top posts of the chair.

"Don't let go." He grinned playfully. "No matter what I do to you."

I was so torn. And Ari knew it. Part of me wanted to stand up, pull my shirt down, and race to the bathroom for a cold shower. We couldn't do this here, now, *like this.* A ladder-back chair? Luck, this was gonna be uncomfortable. But the other part of me (I'm ashamed to say, the greater part) was mesmerized. I gripped the back of the chair and my hands suddenly felt glued in place. I looked away.

"Want to close your eyes?" Ari teased.

"No," I whispered, shaking my head.

He arched a brow, clearly disbelieving, but kept quiet.

He grabbed my hips and pulled them forward so that I was on the edge of my seat, literally. Then he started at the top and worked his way down, taking his time, as if he was going to take an hour for every day that he'd lost. His kisses didn't *quite* feel like when he kissed my mark, but they came so damn close, I knew he'd laced his breath with fire.

He breathed a fiery line down my throat . . . across my

collarbone . . . between my breasts . . . By the time he trailed smoke and fire across my abdomen, I was white-knuckled and glistening with sweat. Ari tucked his finger-tips into the waistline of my bloomers. He winked at me and tugged. When they were fully off, he knelt before me and squeezed my thighs with his hands.

I couldn't move. Couldn't breathe. I knew where his mouth was going next. Just so there was no misunderstand-ing, Ari blew a smoke ring into the air.

"Sure you want to watch?"

I couldn't answer, couldn't even shut my eyes.

"Brave *and* bold. That's what I love about you, Noon." Then I did shut my eyes—squeezed them shut, hard.

"And still a little reluctant."

I braced myself for Ari's kiss, but instead he stood up.

"You can let go," he said softly in my ear.

A second later, he scooped me up and tossed me onto the bed. In the time it took me to shriek my surprise, he'd shucked his clothing and was on top of me, grinning wolf-ishly, his teeth all sparkling and white. There was no trace of fire or smoke. The only evidence of my insane flirtation with the deadly stuff was my racing heartbeat.

Ari nudged my legs apart with his knee. Just before I *really* let go, he whispered, "The Boatmen's bonfire."

We lit it together. And it was magical.

The next day, our twelfth day out, I took a break from studying in the lounge and went up to the sundeck. Rafe was up there, blowing smoke rings. On the table in front of him was a plate of pickles and artichoke hearts.

I kid you not.

I stared at them, and him. He was lounging on the rail bench with one leg bent at the knee, his foot and one dirty shoe placed comfortably on the seat cushion. When I saw him (and what he was doing and eating), I stopped abruptly. *How could he have known? His blowing smoke rings had to be a coincidence. But the pickles and artichokes . . . He*

*had to have requested them because they were the closest
thing the galley had to pickled hearts.*

Suddenly, I was furious.

*What a jerk! He'd tricked his way onto the boat, after
having being thrown out of his own school, and now he
had the gall to make fun of me—the person he was supposed to be working for!*

I walked over to the lunch tray and hurled the food into
the river. Then I smacked his foot off the bench.

"Where did you even get that stuff?" I yelled. "And what
are you doing up here? You should be down in the lounge
studying or in your room practicing spells." Angels had to
constantly study and practice to keep their spellcasting
skills up. The fact that he was doing neither meant he was
risking a botched spell—with me as its target.

But instead of yelling back, or getting angry at my accusation, he laughed. "Such a temper. See? I knew you'd be
interesting." And then he sat up and gave me his full attention, which was more disconcerting than I thought it would
be. In the daylight, his taupe-colored eyes looked almost
yellow, giving them a preternatural look. He puffed on his
cigarette, shaped his mouth into an O, and exhaled. A
plume of smoke slowly billowed out. It grew into an enormous ball until Rafe made a series of small hand gestures
toward it. It grew in size and morphed into a massively
horned, thickly tailed and scaled greenish black demon—
*Jezebeth, the drakon I'd refused to execute at the beginning
of the semester.* Rafe's smoke simulacrum rushed at me,
and even though I knew it wasn't real, my signature pulsed
as the thing passed through me.

Rafe stubbed his cigarette out. He took another one out
of his pocket and tapped it on his sleeve. He held his hand
out so that the tip of it was pointed toward me and flicked
the filter with his thumb. When I stared blankly back at
him, he said, "I'm out of fire. Do you mind?"

"I *hate* those things," I snapped.

"*You* hate fire?"

"No . . . yes . . ." I pursed my lips. I just knew Rafe was

going to be trouble. I tried to remember why I had let him on the boat in the first place. I think I'd felt sorry for him. Unbelievable! "Never mind," I said, turning to go.

"Wait," he said, sighing. Like he'd given in. Like I was the difficult one. "Light this and it will be the last one I smoke."

"Ever?"

"Ever."

I narrowed my eyes at him. "Is this a trick?"

"I want to see if you can light this, *and only this*," he said, giving me a pointed stare. "I've been watching you, Onyx. And I think lighting the tip of one tiny cigarette will actually be harder for you than lighting a big bonfire."

Of course he'd seen the bonfire. Everyone on board had. As well as any *rogares* within ten miles. But that didn't mean they knew what Ari and I were doing when we lit it. (And besides, even if they did, it was no one's business but our own, right?)

"You already know I can do it. I lit a candlewick for you, right here, the first night we were on board." The night he'd agreed I was like a jar of pickled hearts.

"But you would have burned a lot more than just the wick if I hadn't cast Flame Resistant Blanket over you."

I swear, I don't know how he could keep a serious look on his face while he said the name of that spell.

"If you can prove you can control your own fire, that'll give me the freedom to cast other, more useful spells."

"More useful?" I said incredulously. "Rafe, I'm betting you know very few useful spells!"

For a moment, I worried I might have gone too far. His gaze grew sharp and his jaw hardened. But then his face relaxed and, once again, he flicked his filter and waggled the cigarette in my direction. He crossed his legs at the knee, the very picture of patience, the very antithesis of threatening. Fleetingly, I wondered just how powerful a spellcaster Raphael Sinclair really was. Everything about him, even his air of nonchalance, seemed almost overly calculated.

I stood absolutely still and stared at the cigarette. If I let Rafe intimidate me, nothing good would come of this. I'd never thrown magic so precisely before (except for that frighteningly sharp blast that had killed Serafina, the small demon familiar my father had sent me last semester to practice with). I'd lit several bonfires with Ari and I'd inadvertently burned dozens, perhaps hundreds, of things, and I'd lit that candlewick with Rafe's help, but I'd never actually managed to light something as small as a cigarette on my own without burning what was next to it.

Could I do it? Strangely, the first conversation I'd ever had with Rafe came back to me. The one where he asked me if I could, or would, kill Jezebeth in cold blood.

That's what you're telling him, right? That he ought to put his magic where his mouth is. So, what about you? Would you? Could you?

Obviously, lighting a cigarette wasn't proof you could kill something, at least not immediately. But I realized just then that maybe I'd never wanted to perfect my control because it would make me more deadly. It had never occurred to me until then that I might be intentionally sabotaging myself. That I might be subconsciously encouraging my own lack of control.

"It's not easy to kill something, is it, Noon?" Rafe said softly. My head snapped up and I met his gaze, instantly suspicious. How had he known what I was thinking?

"Who said anything about killing?" I said too quickly. "You asked me to light your cigarette."

Rafe tucked the cigarette behind his ear and motioned me over to him. When I was standing in front of him, he turned around, kneeled on the bench, and looked out across the river and rush lands. He patted the rail next to him. Reluctantly, I climbed up next to him. The day was warm and bright and the sun on the water was blindingly beautiful.

"You do realize you threw an entire tray of sandwiches into the Lethe, right?"

I said nothing for the span of about two heartbeats. Then I couldn't help myself, "Sandwiches? But I thought . . ."

"You thought it was a jar of pickled hearts, right?"

"No, not exactly."

Rafe looked surprised. "What did you think it was?"

"I thought it was a tray of . . ." *Oh, Luck, was I really going to admit this?* ". . . artichoke hearts and . . . baby gherkins."

Suddenly, we were both laughing. Hard. Tears welled and rolled down my cheeks. I knew it was a stress release for me. For Rafe, who knew? Maybe he just thought it was "the thing to do at the time." I wiped my face with the sleeve of my shirt.

Rafe murmured under his breath, "Damn," and then a little louder, "Well, that's what I get for trying something new. Fara would have nailed it."

He turned toward me and got serious again. "I'm going to cast Demon Net," he said. "And then I'm going to cast Lure and Aggression."

"What're those?" I said. All traces of former mirth completely disappeared.

"Demon Net tells me where the *rogares* are, Lure brings 'em in, and Aggression riles them up. As they come in," he said, dropping his voice, "you're going to kill them, one by one." He bumped elbows with me. "Think you can do that?"

I turned toward him. Gold and bronze flecks glinted in his yellow irises. Just now, he looked utterly harmless. Long, gray eyelashes framed his eyes and one of them had fallen onto his cheek.

"Why are you always asking me that?" I said softly.

"Why do you never answer?"

We didn't say anything for a while. I fully admitted to myself that I could not figure Rafe out. Finally, I said:

"Why would I want to kill *rogares* that aren't threatening us?"

"That's why I offered to cast Aggression. Once that's cast, your killing them will be in self-defense."

"Is that your idea of Clean Conscience?"

"Maybe it's my idea of practicing."

But there was something in the way he looked at me. Something I was missing that I couldn't quite put my finger on. *Was Rafe really as cold-blooded as his question implied?*

"Well, it's not mine."

He nodded, like he wasn't surprised by my response. He pulled the cigarette down from where he'd tucked it behind his ear and pointed it at me. "That's why you should just light my cigarette."

I blinked. "Are you threatening me?"

"Yes," he said without hesitation. "I have to work with you. Smoke some demons or light this. Your choice."

"You chose to work with me! And besides, I already have one person who pushes me. I don't need another."

"Ari."

I nodded.

"Your 'field partner.'" He smirked when he said it.

"He's more than just my field partner."

"I gathered," Rafe said dryly, and then he obnoxiously pointed from the cigarette to the rush lands.

Would Rafe really bring the demons down on us? Over a cigarette?

"Fine."

I tuned everything out: Rafe, the eyelash that was still on his cheek, the sunlit water, the wooden railing, my fear of failing . . . my fear of succeeding . . . I knew this was it. Prior to now, my magic training had advanced in "two steps forward, one step back" fashion. It may have worked for New Babylon but it wasn't going to work out here. It wasn't that I wanted to be more deadly. It was that I no longer wanted to go backward. This wasn't about surrender. It was about commitment.

I directed a thin, steely flame right to the cigarette's tip and, suddenly, it was lit. Rafe took a big puff and then offered it to me.

"You'd share your last cigarette with me?"

He shrugged. "'Ever' is only as long as I'm working

with you," he said, and then he flicked the unfinished cigarette out into the river. He exhaled, away from me this time,
and when he turned back to me I could resist no longer.

I reached up and plucked the eyelash from his cheek.

"Make a wish," I said. This time, I surprised him. I
could tell. Just as he was about to respond (likely with some
smarty-pants comment like *I wish Estes would regift my
smokes three thousand times over*), we heard a voice from
the top of the stairs.

"You shouldn't play with fire, you know."

It was Fara. As dead serious as I'd ever seen her. I
glanced at Rafe. He actually looked guilty. And then Fara
left as quickly as she'd come.

When I looked down again, the eyelash was gone.

Chapter 14

ਠ

"But I don't understand how drakons can exist in the first place," I said. "Aren't demons spawned from the ground? I mean, Luck creates them . . . because demons can't create anything."

We were sitting in *Cnawlece*'s library with the late afternoon sun shining through stained glass windows depicting some of the most iconic moments in Haljan history: the demon legion and the angel horde's Armageddon battle, Lucifer attempting to rally Mephistopheles' cohort for a final but unsuccessful attempt to pierce the horde's front line with fire, the moment that Lucifer was struck with the lance that killed him, and Lilith's too-late rush to reach him.

We'd been studying *malum in se* versus *malum prohibitum* (and the fact that, in Halja, there really was no difference) and somehow the conversation had segued into drakons. I was glad, because I wanted to know more about them—and because I needed a break. Unfortunately the fact that we were on a boat in the middle of nowhere, possibly heading to our own deaths, didn't mean we could neglect our studies. Dorio, Telford, Copeland, and Meginnis expected Ari and me to be just as knowledgeable about procedures and principles as the rest of the Hyrkes when we got back. It was brutally unfair. *Optimus obligatus*, our Host obligations, really sucked sometimes.

And Ari wasn't even here to study with. He was on watch. Which was why I was studying with Fara. She sat opposite me at the room's two-sided desk in an outfit that was ridiculously ill suited for studying: skintight white cropped pants, black-ribboned platform shoes, and a leopard-print bustier.

A few days into our trip it had become clear, because of the way we'd worked out the watches, that Ari and I couldn't study together all the time. At first, I'd tried to simply fill my solo study time with reading. But the concepts we were supposed to be learning were much better learned through discussion. So, after a few fits and starts, some minor bristling, pouting, stomping out, and slamming of doors, Fara and I had declared a truce and she helped me when Ari was on watch.

I wouldn't go so far as to say Fara and I were friends but, grudgingly, I had to admit that Fara was a decent study partner. She was a natural sponge and, mentally, she was as agile as a gymnast. Rafe, on the other hand, was a terrible study partner. His infrequent time in the library was usually spent loafing on the couch with Virtus.

Fara sat across from me now with one hand resting lightly on the Book of Joshua and the other waggling a pencil. Remembering what she'd done to Sasha, Tosca, and Brunus with her dowsing rod at the beginning of the semester, I eyed the pencil warily.

No one knew better than I how having demon blood prevented one from creating things. Because I'd had the "luck" to inherit a drop of demon blood, I'd inherited the power to light fires, destroy things, and (in theory) control demons. But I'd never be able to grow a garden, heal someone, or have a child. Because demons, and those with demon blood, cause the end of life, not its beginning.

So, if a *drop* of demon blood prevented having a child, how could a creature that was *full* of demon blood have one?

"That's the thing," Fara said, "Luck creates them. As you said. Demons are spawned by Luck—anywhere he likes. So who's to say he can't spawn one in a woman's womb? And when he does, they're born as drakons."

I shuddered. I'd always wanted a child, but I knew beyond the shadow of a demon that I didn't want one in *that way*.

"But there are hundreds of thousands of women in New Babylon," I said. "If drakons are demon children who are born to human mothers, how come I never saw one until three weeks ago?"

"No surprise there. 'Ignorance is bliss until Judas' kiss.' Joshua, fourteen, five. For years you ignored who you were, attended Hyrke schools, and shunned any education that would teach you about the demons you have the power to control."

"This from the woman who is constantly masked," I said dryly.

Fara stared back at me with zero expression. I wondered what emotion her glamour was hiding, if any. For a moment, I worried that she might pick up her Book and leave, as she had during the first few study sessions we'd spent together. But instead, she pointed her pencil at me. I narrowed my eyes at her. But my signature never heated up. She wouldn't dare try to cast a spell over me. Would she?

"How do you know so much about drakons anyway?" I said.

Fara snorted. "A Joshua School education is nothing if not thorough. Drakons were a subunit of the chapter on Estes' cultural impact in my post-Apocalyptic history class."

"Estes? What does Estes have to do with drakons?"

"Most of them are his by-blow. Estes is rather virulent, you know. Delgato's dining room pictures don't lie. Sometimes his affections are returned, sometimes not. But when he lies with a woman, often Luck will gift his lovers with a child."

"Gift?" I said dubiously. "A drakon growing in your belly?"

Fara nodded. "Whether they want one or not. The horrible thing is, it's nearly a death sentence for Hyrkes. A powerful Angel or a Mederi would likely survive such a birth; but then, can you imagine an Angel or a Mederi wanting to raise a drakon?" She laughed, as if what she spoke of were purely academic or theoretical. That we weren't discussing real people, who had lived—and died—as a result of the subject of this subunit in her cultural history class.

"Is it always Estes?"

"No. But it's mostly Luck's greater demons. The ones who rarely take physical form. Or, rather, the ones who rarely take physical form except to ravish some young woman." Her tone was contemptuous.

"You sound like these women deserve what they get."

Fara shrugged. "'If you play in the devil's garden, don't be surprised when a serpent appears . . .'" Her voice trailed off when she saw my expression and where my gaze was directed. At her Book of Joshua.

Had it just occurred to her that I could turn her precious book to ashes in just half a second? That I might even do so by accident?

She looked like she wanted to tuck the Book away in a pocket, but in those pants she didn't even have room for a folded piece of paper. So instead she drummed her fingers on the cover, waiting for me to respond. I had to give it to her. She might be scared of the demons *out there*, but she wasn't easily intimidated by what was in here, on board *Cnawlece*.

"So, except for how they're born, drakons are just like any other demon?"

"That's what I was told. Their magical abilities vary but, like all other demons, they have the power to shift and, as they age, they spend more and more time in their true form."

Remembering Jezebeth's true form, I shuddered.

Had Ynocencia known what she was really getting into when she fell in love with Jezebeth?

But Fara continued, unaware of the splintered direction of my thoughts.

"Just look at Delgato. He'll look like Virtus before long."

"Delgato?" I echoed, not really following her. Our drakon discussion had naturally flowed from our earlier discussion on things that were *malum in se*. But her next words took us completely off the map.

"Do you ever wonder if Delgato is Cattus?"

"Cattus?" I repeatedly blankly. I was beginning to sound like a parrot. "You mean Cattus, as in Curiositas and Cattus?" I said, my tone incredulous. "How could Delgato be Cattus? Curiositas killed Cattus."

"Do you really believe that?"

Well, no. I didn't. I actually thought it was the other way around.

"But Cattus was a demoness," I said.

"Maybe she came back to life as a he. Didn't Cattus have nine lives?"

"Fara, you're not making any sense," I said, exasperated. Now I knew how Ivy felt when she and I discussed that story. "No one comes back to life in Halja."

She shrugged. "Maybe. But with your *Hyrke* upbringing," she said snidely, "you probably remember this one."

She murmured a few words beneath her breath—a spell—and then with a grand flourishing motion reminiscent of a circus ringmaster, she directed my attention to a spot near the center of the room.

Recalling some of Fara's earlier spells, I tensed, but a moment later the most innocuous thing happened. A ghostly girl appeared, maybe age seven or eight, with bangs, pigtails, and a jump rope. Beneath one of the stained glass windows, under the fading brilliance of Lucifer's multi-hued transformation into the Morning Star, the girl started jumping rope. And then she started chanting a rhyme I had long since forgotten:

Curiosity
Killed the cat.

It was knowledge
Brought him back.

Now he seeks
Just one thing:

A trip into
Oblivion.

Fara let the girl chant the rhyme twice before she let the image fade along with the light from the window. Outside, it was dark. Inside, it was quiet.

"Everyone knows Estes is Patron Demon of the Lethe," Fara said softly. "But do you know what the Lethe itself is known for? Do you know what Estes' first followers really wanted?"

I shook my head, completely lost.

"To forget. They sought oblivion. They didn't want to know."

I stared at her, not knowing what to say. Above us, I heard hurried footsteps and Delgato shouting incomprehensible instructions to Russ.

Fara grabbed her Book and stood up, snapping to Virtus, who had been sleeping on the couch. Just before she turned away, I said:

"Fara, I don't understand. What's your point?"

She laughed then and said somewhat spitefully, "If you were *my* ward, I'd tell you straight out. But since you're not, I'll let you figure it out for yourself. Or not . . ." And then she turned and left, taking her own cat with her, leaving me alone in the library.

There's another demon on board," Rafe said, shaking me awake not ten minutes later. I must have fallen asleep in the darkening library after Fara had left.

Correctly guessing my next two immediate moves, Rafe placed a hand on my shoulder to keep me from jumping up out of my chair and said quietly, but firmly, "*Control* your signature."

I swallowed and nodded. He lifted his hand and I stood up, careful not to let my chair squeak on the wooden floor.

"How do you know?" I whispered back.

"A few minutes ago I cast Demon Net. There were three on board . . . and now there are four."

"Three, now four? I don't feel *any*."

Despite the circumstances, he must have found my comment funny because I saw a flash of white teeth as he grinned. "You, Ari, and Delgato were the three. Demon Net tracks *all* waning magic users. Now that you're not going to panic, open up your signature. You'll feel it."

I did. And that's when I felt the fourth. I gasped.

"I can't tell the signatures apart! Or sense where anyone is." It was as if our signatures had been stacked and then mixed, mine included, and now they were just one big blur of waning magic. Although fearful of it, I'd been prepared for a water wraith attack. This was much worse.

"It's a hellcnight," I hissed.

"How do you know?"

I told Rafe about the waning magic blur. "That's why I can't tell anyone apart. Or where anyone is."

"One's on the sundeck, two are on the lower front deck, and one," he said, looking right at me, "is in the library."

"So if you can tell who's who, which one's the hellcnight?"

"I can only tell *where* you are, not *who* you are. You all feel the same to me."

I couldn't resist. "How do we feel?"

Another flash of teeth. "Dangerous." His hand found mine in the dark and he opened the door and prepared to step out, thinking to drag me with him, I guess. But I had other ideas.

I tried to shake his hand loose. "I'll head for the front. You go up top."

But Rafe held tight. He turned toward me. "I may be many things, Onyx. But an oath breaker is not one of them.

'An Angel does whatever is necessary to preserve and protect the life of his ward.' Joshua—"

"Twelve, seven, I know. You sound like Fara."

His only answer was pulling me out into the hallway. I'd be lying if I said I wasn't scared. But I also wanted to find the demon that'd climbed on board before it did something to the boat, the food we had stored on board, or the crew. I felt a brief pang of sympathy for Fara, who was likely to find out soon that one of the demons *out there* was now *in here*. I refused to even think about something happening to Ari, but with his past experience, I thought he'd probably be okay. And, speak of the devil, there he was . . .

Just as Rafe and I neared the end of the hall, Ari came down the stairs. He placed his finger on his mouth, a signal to us that he too was aware of the hellcnight. His gaze traveled the length of me, coming to rest on Rafe's hand, which was still holding on to my arm. I shrugged Rafe off and ran over to Ari.

When I reached him, he said quietly, "There's a hellcnight on board. Do you feel it?"

"I feel the waning magic blur Delgato told us about."

Ari frowned. "We should split up and search the boat."

"Agreed," I said, grabbing Ari's hand. My signature felt odd, like it was thick and full of holes. "Check out the sundeck," I called back to Rafe. "We'll search the front."

I didn't even give Rafe a chance to respond; I just grabbed Ari's hand and headed up the half flight of stairs to the lower front deck. At the top, I stopped. I couldn't see anyone—or anything—here. But this was where we'd loaded most of the crates of food so there was no way to tell if the deck was truly empty without searching it.

"You take the left side," I said to Ari, "I'll take the right."

"Not a chance," he said, following closely at my heels. We started searching the lower front deck hand in hand. Ari's hand in mine grew forged-in-the-fire hot. I recognized the sign. He was preparing for an attack. Did mine feel as hot to him?

We crept around the larger chests and crates, quietly lifting tarp corners, canvas covers, and anything else a demon might hide behind. Nothing. As we neared the front of the boat, I thought I saw a shadow move.

"Come on!" I yelled, dragging Ari forward with me. Fear had suddenly been replaced with anger. *How* dare *this demon come on* my *boat?!*

But when we reached the area where I thought I'd seen the shadow, it turned out to be no more than a piece of untucked cover, flapping in the wind. I bent down and re-fastened it. When I stood up, Ari stood in front of me with a peculiar expression on his face. Disappointment? Maybe, but oddly, it looked more like anticipation.

"It's not here," I said. We'd searched the whole lower deck.

I stood in the last little corner we'd checked. To my left was *Cnawlece*'s front rail and behind and beside me were more crates. The deck was empty, except for us. I started to move forward, thinking to navigate back through the crates in order to get to the stairs to continue the search . . . and that's when it dawned on me.

It might not be Ari standing in front of me. It might be the hellcnight.

"Let's search the rest of the boat," I said, regretting the slight wobble in my voice. But Ari just shook his head and reached for me. The look on his face cinched it. Ari Carmine would never have looked at me that way. As if I were living meat.

Instantly, I tried to bolt, but the creature was faster. It grabbed my hand and yanked me back with a jerk that nearly tore my arm off. Fear and panic made my mind muddled and I could barely think of what weapon I should be shaping my magic into. The hellcnight, on the other hand, suffered no such performance anxiety. Immediately it shaped its magic into a fiery battle flail, which it held threateningly in its right hand as it advanced on me, pushing me back into the corner between rail and crates.

I tried to duck under its arm, but it seized me by the face

and threw me back. My head smashed into the side of a crate. I looked up into its face—Ari's face—slightly dazed. I shook my head, momentarily amazed that my jaw was still attached, and managed to shape my magic into the first weapon that came to mind: a fireball. I threw it toward the hellcnight, but fear gave my magic an erratic elliptical spin. The fireball clipped the side of the demon's ear and blasted a nearby crate. I heard pounding footsteps on the sundeck just as the hellcnight started shifting. It was surreal because the face staring back at me was Ari's. But the expression was one I'd never seen on his face before. *Pure hatred.*

The footsteps got louder and I heard shouting.

"I'm over he—" I tried to shout, but the hellcnight stepped forward and pressed his hand against my mouth. As the demon shifted, its hand grew rougher. Coarse hairs pierced the soft skin of my cheeks. Soon, the hellcnight's hand grew so large it covered my mouth and nose. I couldn't breathe. I threw another fireball at it, but the creature easily deflected it. Another crate of food and a huge war chest went up in flames. Before my eyes, Ari's face—the face of the man I'd given my body to countless times and my heart to once and forever—morphed into a gruesomely pale, blue-veined demon's face with bloodred eyes and a protruding, slavering jaw full of diseased-looking gums and huge, pointy teeth the size of garden stakes.

The hellcnight lowered his mouth to my neck to take a deep bite, but before he could do more than graze my skin with one of his teeth, I heard something that sounded like a lion's roar and then a huge four-legged beast crashed into the hellcnight, knocking him off of me. It was Delgato, who had shifted into his manticore form.

Hellcnight and manticore fell to the deck with a heavy thud. The flames from the chest and crates filled the air with crackling smoke. I gathered my fear and my anger around me like a fiery blanket and then melded them into the same razor-sharp, diamond-strength type of magic that had killed Serafina. My magic always seemed to be strongest when I was defending someone. I had only the briefest second to hope that would be the case now. I thrust my fiery spear right at the hellcnight's heart. It would have worked. I could feel how well shaped it was and how accurately I'd thrown it. Problem was, my target moved. Instead of the hellcnight's heart, it hit Delgato's. He writhed in agony on top of the hellcnight, his scorpion tail twitching, his lion's mane fluttering like the red flames surrounding us, his massively muscled body convulsing.

Burr yelled something to Russ and I felt *Cnawlece* slowing in the water.

I stared as the hellcnight thrust Delgato's limp body off of him. It stood up, glared evilly at me, and then jumped over the railing just as Ari—the real Ari—Rafe, and Fara ran over. A moment later, I heard a splash. Ari took one look at my neck and stepped forward. But even love couldn't prevent my involuntary retreat. The image of Ari's face morphing into the hideously fanged hellcnight was still too fresh in my mind. I held up my hand to stop him.

"Go check on Russ and Burr," I said, waving at him and Fara. Ari looked like he wanted to argue, but one look at my face convinced him otherwise.

"Heal her," he barked to Rafe and then turned on his heel and left. I shuddered. I couldn't help it. Now that the hellcnight had gone, our signatures were released from his hold. One by one they became distinct again. Ari's was chaotic, angry, even murderous—the effect of which was to further terrify me, since it echoed what I'd seen in the hellcnight's face just before it had shifted from "Ari" into the horrifying creature that had attacked me. I didn't want anyone (most of all Ari) to know that the sight of his face scared me, though, so I focused on the third signature—the weakest one—Delgato's.

Rafe stepped over to me with an expression on his face I'd never seen before: concern. *Well, he could take his concern and shove it,* I thought viciously. I think anger and unbelievable regret was making me bitchy. I couldn't bear the thought that instead of saving Delgato, I'd killed him, especially since *he* had been trying to rescue *me*. It wasn't fair to inflict my misery on Rafe, but I could barely stand myself just then, so I couldn't stand the thought of anyone—even Rafe—showing concern for me.

Rafe tilted my head up so he could see my neck and get a better look at the wound he was going to heal. I shoved his hand away.

"Not me," I snarled. "Delgato. That's who you need to heal."

Rafe said nothing, only raised his eyebrows. But he walked over to the manticore and knelt beside him.

"I can't bring people back from the dead, Noon," he said quietly.

"He's not dead. I can still feel his signature."

Rafe looked doubtful and then sighed. "I'm an Angel, not a Mederi."

"You're an oath breaker, that's what." I practically spit the words out. Rafe stared down at the manticore. I couldn't tell if my words had any effect on him. I knew I didn't mean them; I was just being mean. I didn't feel well. My neck hurt where the hellcnight's tooth had nicked me. The cut stung and I felt even angrier than I had before. It felt like my brain was one big buzzing hornets' nest. I reached up to touch my neck. It throbbed. My fingertips brushed the cool silver of the alembic's chain. I would gladly have traded it for what we'd just lost: two crates of food, a war chest full of weapons, and our captain. I slumped to the floor with my back against one of the crates. My last vision was of Rafe trying to heal Delgato.

Chapter 15

ॐ

I woke up three days later. *Cnawlece* was still slowly making her way to the Shallows. We were still on Blandjan. And I was still as impatient as ever to reach our destination. I couldn't help wondering if the fact that we'd been attacked by a hellcnight made Zella Rust's accusation against Grimasca more likely. Hellcnights weren't uncommon (not like drakons were) but they weren't commonplace the way familiars or water wraiths were. What if Grimasca really was preying on fishermen in the Shallows? What if he'd found out that we were on our way to investigate? What if the hellcnight who had attacked us three nights ago was one of Grimasca's minions?

I would have loved to have discussed these questions with Ari or Delgato, but neither was available. Delgato had survived, but barely. He was now sleeping in a comatose state in his cabin. Rafe had healed him enough to save his life, but couldn't wake him from the hellcnight bite–induced sleep. (I'd been incredibly lucky to have just been nicked by the hellcnight's tooth. Three days was better than three months, three years . . . or forever.) Delgato had reverted back to his human form and, oddly, no trace of his former manticore state remained. His pointed ears, sharp teeth, and long claws were all gone. I couldn't even feel his signature. No one knew what it meant, not even Rafe, who'd worked the spells that had saved him (if you could call lying in bed in a coma being saved). One theory was that Delgato's demon attributes were slumbering along with the rest of him. That they'd resurface when he did. Another theory, advanced by Fara, of course, was that he'd used up his nine demonic "cat" lives and there were no more. He was a magic-less human Hyrke now. His next death would be his last.

Who knew? Not us, that's for sure.

Ari was barely speaking with me. It wasn't that he was angry with me. Far from it. It was that he seemed to blame himself for everything that had happened the day of the attack . . . and after. Apparently (I have no memory of it; the Angels and crew told me), Ari came to my room the night of the attack. I went berserk, tried to light him and everything else in my room on fire. Rafe doused it all down with his *stupid* spell Flame Resistant Blanket, but the real damage had been done. Ari was now on watch twenty-four/ seven (to use a favorite Hyrke expression). He refused to switch with anyone. He even slept and took his meals up on the sundeck. To be honest, he was barely speaking to *anyone*.

We were also down two huge crates of food and a chest full of weapons. In hindsight, storing it all together had been a mistake. But these were the sorts of amateur decisions that got first-year MITs like me killed all too often.

The night before we were supposed to reach Second Branch, I couldn't sleep. I kept seeing the hellcnight's grotesque transformation from Ari's beloved features into that gruesome mask of decaying flesh, bulging red eyes, and snapping jaw intent on eating me. Before, Ari was the first person I would have sought comfort from. But now . . . ? Despite being on a boat with a fully functional rudder, I felt adrift. Anchorless.

Sometime around two in the morning, I drifted into the library. Stained glass pictures of a dying deity may not have been the best salve for my mood, but there was nowhere else for me to go. Ari prowled around the sundeck. (I could only feel wispy traces of his signature. After I had attacked him, he'd shut his signature down to practically nothing. I guessed so I wouldn't feel it. It was both sad and terrifying, all the more so because it was also the least bit comforting.) I wanted nothing more to do with the lower front deck. The engine room was off-limits to a waning magic user, so my choices were the galley, dining room, or library. The kitchen didn't have a couch and these darkened stained glass windows were infinitely preferable to the dining room's pictures. *Especially* after the hellcnight's attack.

I lit some candles—with a match; despite my earlier self-admonishment to stop advancing in "two steps forward, one step back" fashion, it just seemed easier and safer considering the recent story about me going berserk—and took out my case file. *If I couldn't sleep, I might as well study,* I thought. In a nutshell, my assignment, and the meager evidence I'd been given so far, amounted to this:

Vodnik, Patron Demon of the Shallows, appeared to have kept his followers safe for over four hundred years. Sure, it's true that things could have happened in those four hundred years that did not reach the Council's ears, but it wasn't likely. As far away as the Shallows was, there was regular, if infrequent, contact between the outpost and New Babylon. And four hundred years was longer than many of the other outposts had lasted. If there'd been trouble before, someone would have eventually heard about it.

So, after *thirteen* generations of harmonious patronage between lord and followers, the first complaint was filed against Vodnik *by an eight-year-old*, Athalie Rust, who accused Vodnik of murder, but she hadn't actually seen it happen (which, considering she was only eight, could only be for the best). She'd accused Vodnik of murdering fifteen of his own fishermen followers, but there was no direct evidence to support her allegation in the file.

The girl's credibility was also an issue. She was a child. And while I didn't necessarily think she was lying, she was probably still learning that, in Halja, bad things happened to good people all the time. Sometimes, there was very little fairness in our world. Eight was still young enough to think that every tragedy needed a villain. And while there was no denying that villains in our world were more numerous than most, just because someone disappeared, didn't necessarily mean that a demon killed them. Even in Halja.

But thinking that the fishermen's disappearances might simply be an accident seemed naive in light of the second complaint, the one written by Zella. The one that said that Athalie took a walk with Vodnik two days after filing her complaint and never came back.

Just then there was a small thud on the outside of one of the stained glass windows. My heart raced and I nearly set the case file on fire. But then I realized Ari was fishing from up top and it was likely a leech or a crawfish or something that had just hit the window on its way down. I briefly wrestled with the idea of going up top, but I couldn't be sure I wouldn't inadvertently do something drastic upon seeing Ari's face in the dark again, so I stayed put and tried to concentrate on the case.

Both Athalie and Zella said in their complaints that Vodnik blamed Grimasca for the fishermen's disappearances. Athalie hadn't believed him. In fact, she'd called Vodnik a liar because "Grimasca wasn't real." Zella, on the other hand, hadn't known what to think. Her best guess was that a demon made Athalie disappear. She just didn't know which one.

I dug out the books I'd collected at Corpus Justica the day before we'd left. Unfortunately, one of the most useful ones, Furious Cinnabar's *Rogare Demons: Survival Strategies* had gone into the water that day in the rain when we were loading. Now that Delgato was in a coma, I felt its loss even more fiercely, but I wasn't going to turn back for a book. Even if Athalie turned out to be the one who was the liar, she was still an eight-year-old girl who was missing in a swamp. If her people hadn't found her by the time we got there . . . Well, let's just say that searching for her, and the fishermen, was just as important to me as figuring out why they'd gone missing in the first place. (Although I had to acknowledge, much as I didn't want to, that they might never be found. When people disappeared in Halja, they usually weren't.)

I found the old beat-up copy of *Oude Rode Ogen, Bicho Papao, and Grimasca: Folktales for Children* that I'd found earlier in the library, oddly tucked into a section full of first-century court decisions and antiquated city surveys. Like Delgato, Grimasca wasn't in the Demon Register. But Delgato was real. Maybe Grimasca was too. I flipped through the tiny book's table of contents and found what I was looking for:

THE GRIM MASK OF GRIMASCA

Once, long ago, there was a war. A terrible war.
The fields around a once great city died.
People grew hungry.
But Grimasca grew fat.

Inside the crumbling walls of the city was a family.
A father and seven children. All boys.
The father couldn't feed them.
So he decided to let Grimasca have them.

One day the father packed a picnic.
He packed all of the food they had left.
Paulus, the oldest son, questioned his father:
"Why are you bringing all the food we have left?"

The father replied: "I am giving away all that I have."
Paulus didn't think this was a good idea.
So he took a loaf of bread from the basket
and hid it in his pocket for the family to have later.

The family spent a nice day on the water.
Paulus' father rowed the boys far away.
They knew not where they were.
Or how to get back.

Paulus' father found a beautiful meadow
between two streams with a large waertree.
He spread a warm blanket on the ground
and took all the food out of the basket.

Eat, drink, and be merry, he said.
Let this always be a pleasant memory.
And they ate, and they drank, and they were merry.
Their bellies were full and they grew tired.

"Lie down and rest," said Paulus' father.
"I will watch over you."
And he did. For as long as he could.
But he knew Grimasca was coming.

When the boys awoke, their father was gone.
They knew not where they were.
They knew not how to get back.
And they were hungry again.

Grimasca came and Paulus offered him the bread.
"I'm a butcher, not a baker," Grimasca said.
"What would I do with bread?"
So the boys ate the bread.

Paulus led his brothers deep into the woods.
Soon they came to a house full of giants.

A whole family of them.
A mother and seven children. All girls.

Paulus explained their predicament.
Was the mother willing to let them spend the night?
The mother was reluctant.
"Grimasca comes here too, you know.

So many children means
Grimasca will come.
But you can stay one night . . .
Upstairs and to the right."

The giantess mother liked to drink.
More than she liked to eat.
That night she got drunk.
Paulus was worried she'd change her mind.

He crept to the left
and dressed all the giantess' daughters
in his brothers' clothing.
Sure enough, the giantess mother changed her mind.

In a drunken stupor,
thinking they were Paulus and his brothers,
she locked her own daughters out in the cold
and waited for Grimasca to come get them.

It took three days and three nights.
The giantess mother never stopped drinking.
When she heard beating on the door, she drank.
When she heard crying on the stoop, she drank.

Finally, the cries stopped.
The giantess mother stopped drinking.
She blinked. And saw Paulus and his brothers.
And she knew what she had done.

She nearly killed herself that night.
But Paulus stopped her.
"Give me all your gold," he said,
"and I'll bring one of them back."

The giantess mother didn't believe him.
But she had no choice.
She gave Paulus all her gold.
And Paulus left with his brothers.

The giantess mother was as lonely as ever.
In the city, Paulus' father was as lonely as ever.
Paulus climbed a tall tree
And saw the crumbling walls.

He led his brothers home
And gave his father the gold.
His father rejoiced.
His brothers rejoiced.

And Paulus rejoiced.
But the next day he left.
He'd made a promise.
To return to the giantess mother.

Before Paulus left the crumbling walls,
he had one more thing to do.
Down the street was another family.
Grimasca was coming for them too.

This family had a mother, a father,
And a daughter, Paulina.
Paulus took Paulina.
And led her to the giantess mother.

And the giantess mother rejoiced.
The next spring, many new babies were born.

Paulina's parents rejoiced.
And Paulus and Paulina rejoiced.

And Grimasca rejoiced.
Because he was coming for . . .
EVERYONE!

Once, long ago, there was a war. A terrible war.
The fields around a once great city died.
People grew hungry. Babies were born.
And Grimasca got fat.

Well, as Haljan bedtime stories went, this one was pretty typical, designed to ensure a plethora of nightmares. It was easy to imagine a mother reading her children this, and then, just at the line "EVERYONE!" scaring them half to death with a mock attack. I'd never heard it, but that didn't mean anything. Our culture was rich in myths. There were likely a hundred different versions of this story and just as many names for Grimasca. The real question was whether Grimasca was real. Was he still living? And, if so, where?

The folktale itself seemed allegorical, rather than literal. The whole point of the story seemed to be that postwar famine killed indiscriminately. Paulus' father deciding to let Grimasca have his boys was probably that character's way of acknowledging he could no longer feed his sons. And the part of the story where Paulus' father took the boys to the meadow definitely seemed to be a wish fulfillment fantasy. No poor New Babylonian family in the immediate post-Apocalyptic era would have been able to row a boat down the Lethe and go for a picnic. (No one did that now!) The "resting" the boys did after their day of merriment was likely a gentle euphemism for death.

Unlike Grimasca, however, I knew giants were real. They were small in number now and weren't very social. There'd never been much written about them—no accounts of heroism during the Apocalypse or anything that you might expect from huge, immensely strong beings. But then again, giants didn't have magic and they generally shunned humans. They lived in the forests and swamps and weren't usually prone to violence. They weren't usually prone to intelligence either, as this story suggested. It was, unfortunately, all too easy to imagine a drunken giantess mother locking her own children out of the house while a monster ate them.

That said, the giant part of the story was probably just a continuation of the allegorical tale about hunger. With fourteen children instead of seven, that would mean that Grimasca (or starvation) would be more likely to come. A story about a giantess mother putting half her kids out to starve (or to be eaten by the Demon of Hunger) made about as much sense as any other Haljan folktale did.

My guess was the author tried for a celebratory tone at the end, what with all the rejoicing over new births, etcetera, but by then they'd been too traumatized by the war and its aftereffects for their efforts to be successful. The author clearly felt that hunger (demon or not) would always be out there waiting and that Hunger, or the Grim Mask of Death, would be the only one really rejoicing after a war.

So did this story prove that Grimasca was real? Hell if I knew.

What I did know was that sleeping after a story like this would be impossible so I packed up my books and shuffled quietly down to the kitchen. Sooner or later, I'd have to make amends with Ari. This distance between us couldn't continue. But, for now, I set my sights on a lesser task: getting through this night.

I pushed open the galley door and froze.

Rafe stood with his back to me, staring at something on the tiny stove in the corner. He turned around when I came in.

"See?" he said, pointing to a small, steaming pot on the stove. "A watched pot *does* boil. But then, you probably already knew that."

My first instinct was to retreat and go back to my room. But I couldn't decide which would be worse: sleeplessness or sleep . . . and the dreams that came with it. I'd come in here thinking to make some tea with the herbs my mother had given me. There was bound to be something in there that would send the drinker into a dreamless sleep. So I stepped into the room and retrieved a box from the shelf. In it were tins and paper envelopes full of the various herbs Aurelia had prepared for us.

Rafe set the pot of boiling water on an unlit burner and walked over to the table where I was sorting through the tea offerings. He leaned down next to me, propping his elbows on the table right next to mine. Silently, we sifted through the box. Rafe pulled one of the envelopes out and turned toward me. Naturally, I too turned, and realized how close we were. Physically anyway. I scooted back.

"Damiana?" Rafe's mouth quirked. Damiana was widely known as an aphrodisiac. "Your mother gave you this?"

I shrugged, fighting to keep my face neutral. Like it was any of his business!

"Obviously, your mother's not a Mederi," I said. If there were two things Mederies weren't shy about, even with their own offspring, it was plants and sex.

"No," Rafe said, laughing, turning back to the box. "I've no Host blood. My mother is an Angel." But something about the way he said it made me think she was anything but.

I glanced over at Rafe, hoping to catch him in an unguarded moment. But no such luck. He appeared as carefully carefree as ever, perusing a box of herbs, hoping to find a soothing combination for tea. Despite the fact that we were on a boat sailing through Wild Territory that was full of *rogare* demons on our way to an outpost known for starvation where sixteen people were missing, the scene before me was undeniably domestic. I let out a sigh—a deep breath I hadn't known I'd been holding. Rafe pulled three envelopes out of the box and shut it. He waved them in the air at me, his silver bracelet glinting in the light of the galley kitchen's lone oil lamp.

"Spearmint, lemongrass, and blackberry leaves."

He poured some of the leaves into an empty teapot, added the water, and then pulled down cups and a strainer. I walked over to him and together we waited for the tea to steep.

"I shouldn't have called you an oath breaker," I said. I braced for the shrug of nonchalance, the sign that he didn't care, but instead he nodded solemnly and said:

"And I should have cast Gold Gorget over you before you went up the stairs with that hellcnight."

I couldn't tell if he was serious. That was the problem with Rafe. I never knew when he was serious. And most of the time, he wasn't. I said nothing else, nor did he. The silence was companionable, though, not tense. Just before the tea was ready, I touched his silver bracelet. It was a small plain cuff, less than an inch wide.

Was it enchanted?

Maybe there was a protective spell written on the inside. I twisted it a bit, trying to see if there were letters engraved on the back. Rafe didn't complain, even when my efforts caused the bracelet to slip off his wrist. I stared at the markings on the inside.

Bhereg 9-2-92

"It's the day my brother died," Rafe said, reaching for the bracelet. He slipped it back on and then poured our tea, taking care with the strainer.

"I'm sorry," I whispered, never meaning anything more.

He handed me a cup and I inhaled, smelling mint and the faintest hint of lemongrass. Tentatively, I took a sip. It made me feel warm and drowsy. Rafe stared at me over the edge of his cup.

"Let me guess," I said. "You ensorcelled this with 'Now I Lay Me Down To Sleep.'"

I thought he'd laugh, but he just shook his head and continued blowing on his tea. After a few moments he said, "I don't know any sleeping spells. But I can sing you a lullaby if you'd like."

Was he serious? He seemed so. I nodded, expecting a song that was as silly as his spells. But his voice was slow and deeply plaintive.

> *Dormi, mi infans . . .*
> *Dormi, certe.*
> *Grimasca venit . . .*
> *Et te vorabit.*

I blinked when he finished. My drowsiness had fled.

"What does it mean?"

He sang it again softly, like a mother might before she kissed her children good night.

"Sleep, my baby . . . sleep, baby do. Grimasca's coming . . . and he will eat you."

I swallowed. "Did your mother used to sing that to you?"

He walked over to the sink and set his cup down. Resting his hands on the edge of the sink, he stared out of the galley's small window. There was nothing to see but darkness.

"Many, many times."

"Who did your mother think Grimasca was?" I said, my throat burning. Rafe walked over to the oil lamp. I set my empty cup down just as Rafe lowered the wick.

"The one demon you never want to meet. Grimasca is whatever you're deeply afraid of." The wick sputtered and went out, plunging us into darkness. Rafe's hand found mine and he led me toward the door.

"Think you'll be able to sleep now?" His quiet laughter echoed in the dark.

Chapter 16

❧

The rain pounding on *Cnawlece*'s now inaptly named sundeck sounded like a thousand *rogares* banging on the back side of Burr's metal pots. It made hearing anything else exceedingly difficult. Earlier this morning, I'd tried to study with Fara, but the rain's incessant beating drowned out the sound of our voices. Discussion had been impossible. Reading, or focusing on anything, had been impossible. The rain rattled everything, and everyone. Even Virtus, who, after a particularly loud thunder crack, had flung himself beneath the dining room table.

In his haste to escape the perceived threat from around and above, he'd crashed into a few chairs on his way under. One of them had fallen into an easel, which had then knocked over a painting of Estes, midshift and (ahem) midthrust, taking the maiden Kora. Since I'd always hated the expression on Kora's face, I was secretly overjoyed when I realized the crash had irreparably damaged the painting. Delgato wasn't conscious to complain so I'd removed the painting's frame, rolled up the ripped canvas, and stuffed the whole thing into a sideboard drawer.

Good riddance, I'd thought, clapping the dust from my hands.

I'd left the dining room with renewed purpose, the drumming rain sparking my determination to put an end to this maddening silence between Ari and me. But when I put my foot on the bottom stair and prepared to ascend the last half flight to the upper deck, I'd started shaking uncontrollably. I'd crept into Delgato's room, the first door I encountered, and here I sat contemplating what seemed to be my endless faults: I'd nearly killed our captain; I'd set our boat on fire, not once, not twice, but three times; I was too yellow-bellied to face my loving boyfriend, whose only fault was looking like the demon who'd attacked me; and I absolutely was not assured, in any way, that I could help anyone in the Shallows, let alone the sixteen people, including one eight-year-old little girl, who were missing or possibly dead.

I gave a sigh of utter abdication and slumped onto the foot of Delgato's bed. No doubt, were the manticore conscious, my prostrate form would have pleased him greatly. But that thought plunged me into an even fouler mood, and so it was that Burr found me about an hour or so later when he came in to check on Delgato.

He gave a shriek and promptly dropped the tray he'd been holding. *Ugh. Great. Yet another calamity I was responsible for.* But then I realized that my self-pity was dangerously close to melodrama so I got down on my hands and knees and helped poor Burr mop up the spilled soup. When we were finished, he promised to return with more, and after an awkward moment when Burr wasn't sure whether to stay or go (there was only one chair in the tiny room), I convinced him to stay by giving him my seat. I stood by the door, holding my soup. I wasn't hungry, but I didn't want to waste it. The soup somehow seemed like an unofficial offering from Burr to me. Hyrkes didn't usually go around making offerings to members of the Host, but ordinary Haljans gave gifts to one another all the time. It showed they cared. I took a sip and Burr smiled. What was that old saying? That the way to someone's heart was through their stomach? I smiled back. The rain had lessened a little so I could finally speak without shouting.

"How long have you been Delgato's cook?"

Burr frowned, concentrating. He was short, but big around the middle. He dwarfed the desk chair he was sitting in and he never would have been able to fit his legs under Delgato's small corner writing desk.

"Maybe six years, give or take. Who knows? Who can remember anything out here? The only way we even know time's passing is because the seasons change. Or because Estes' mood changes. And the Lethe changes with them. But Delgato, he never changed. He was always the same. Until now."

I winced, but Burr continued eating his soup, oblivious to my guilt.

"Have you always been a cook?"

Burr nodded. "I learned to cook from my mam. She cooked mostly over a fire, but she knew how to use a box oven, and she had an iron kettle and some pie irons. She could make a meal out of almost anything. Fish broth, cornmeal, beans. We almost never could afford fish, but she made sure we didn't starve. I had a bunch of brothers and sisters. There were nine of us! My mam cooked for us all, and anyone else who brought her food to cook if they paid her or if they let her keep some.

"When I was thirteen, I realized how hard it was for my mam to feed nine kids. So I told her good-bye. She cried, but she was glad to see me go. She wanted me to see more of Halja than just the street I was born on. So I found work on a dahabiya not unlike *Cnawlece*. My first captain wasn't a bad man, just fairly gruff, as they all are. That captain got killed, when I was sixteen, I think. And so it went. I've worked for more captains than I can remember now. But none so long as *him*."

Burr gestured toward Delgato. It was hard to believe he was the same captain who'd terrified me my first night on board. He looked like a shrunken old man now. There was absolutely nothing sharp left in him.

"Were all your captains killed?" I asked, appalled.

"No, some were maimed. Some just disappeared in the night. I guess they got killed, but I never saw it. Not sure what's worse. Seeing it for yourself or wondering what happened to 'em. Some *rogares* like to toy with their prey. They're like spiders or snakes. Those demons"—Burr shivered—"they eat you *alive*."

"Why do you keep coming back?"

"What else is there? Starving by the docks? Having no purpose? At least out here, I'm my own man. I take orders from the captain, sure. Or I did. But captains never care what food you make as long as it gets to the table on time. It's what I got. It's who I am. You know, I've seen more of Halja than most New Babylonians.

"Demons'll get me one day. When that happens, the only thing I hope is that my mam never finds out. I want her to be thinking I'm always out here. On the river. *Forever*. Always watching over it. And it, and Estes, always watching over me."

I bowed my head. His hope was as close to praying as any Hyrke in Halja would ever get.

Estes wouldn't listen, of course. Because he was a demon. And demons only listen to pleas that are accompanied by sacrifices. But I wasn't going to ruin the moment by reminding Burr of that.

I walked over to Burr and placed my hand on his shoulder. He looked up at me, clearly startled that I'd touched him. But he wasn't fearful of me. He seemed surprised that I'd paid him this much attention.

"Did I tell you how much I love your cooking, Burr? There's only one other person who makes charred red snapper as good as you."

"Who's that?"

I laughed. "Well, maybe not *quite* as well as you. Do you

know Alba? She owns a little café on the corner of River Road and Widow's Walk. It's also known as—"

"The Black Onion. Sure I know Alba. She's my sister! My mam was Alba the Second."

Well, I'll be . . . *Huh*. Go figure. Burr really *did* know Alba the Third. I shook my head in disbelief. What were the odds?

I told Burr to take care and get some rest before dinner. Then I was just about to walk out when I thought of something else.

"Did your mam ever sing to you about Grimasca?"

"Oh, sure. Lots of times."

"What did she say about Grimasca?"

"She said he had three white scars on his cheek that he got from a water wraith and that his lover was the biggest, blackest, most beautiful river serpent anyone had ever seen." Burr sounded grudgingly admiring. But then his voice got lower. "She said they liked to hunt together. That they liked to eat their victims alive. But then one day, Grimasca accidentally bit her and she fell asleep and drowned."

"What do you think?"

"I think he ate her."

P eople always talk about how, when someone is scared, their legs shake, and their heart beats too fast, and their teeth chatter. But, because people *always* talk about those sorts of reactions, it diminishes them. It makes it seem like they're as common as sneezing or coughing or yawning. The truth is, it takes an almost overwhelming sense of *fear* to produce those reactions in a person, even if every bit of it is irrational.

I placed my foot on the last step of the flight of stairs leading to *Cnawlece*'s sundeck. I saw and felt Ari at the same time. He stood at the far, front end of the deck, overlooking the water with his back to me. His signature was hot, but tightly controlled, as if it were the steam stream from a whistling teapot. He had to know I was there. I gripped the stair's rail and stepped forward.

"Ari—"

He turned from *Cnawlece*'s railing and the expression of pain on his face nearly undid me. I rushed to him and he enveloped me in a huge embrace. Suddenly, I was crying and he held me tighter and the teapot just exploded. There was a magical burst and then I felt drenched with magic-laced emotion. The intensity and range of them took my breath away. It was like being bathed in white light, but I was the prism so I felt each and every separate emotion all at once: fear, loneliness, desire, joy, relief . . .

I looked up at Ari's face, half-afraid he might start shifting, but the moment I looked at him, my fear faded. It wasn't just that *this* was truly Ari and not a hellcnight; it was that, in that moment, I finally understood what had disturbed me so deeply about Jezebeth's execution. Yes, the execution itself was horrible. But what made it so personal and unsettling for me was that (and this scared the hell out of me) I identified with *Jezebeth*, not Ynocencia. As my behavior from just three nights ago proved, I too was capable of going berserk. And if going berserk was like a bomb exploding, then love was the match that lit the fuse.

Were any of our actions ever rational when it came to love?

I swiped at my cheeks and glanced up at Ari. I don't know if he'd done it on purpose or not, but he looked completely different. His eyes were sunken from lack of sleep and he had the beginnings of a beard now. I reached up and cupped his cheek with my hand. His whiskers were soft and bristly.

"I'm happy to see you," I said, smiling through my tears.

Ari and I spent the afternoon on the sundeck together. The rain returned and we curled up under the canopy beside one of the cannons. Though we were content just to be in each other's presence, the cannons on deck were an unhappy reminder of what lay beyond the immediate circle of *us*.

"Ari," I said cautiously, eager to apologize but still traumatized enough by the incident not to want to speak of it, "I'm sorry I attacked you the night the hellcnight came on board." My statement was woefully inadequate. *Attack* didn't even come close to describing the magical meltdown I'd had. And saying the hellcnight *came on board* made it sound as if it had stopped by for a drink instead of climbing on board to try and kill me. But Ari seemed to understand that it would take a while for me to fully come to terms with what had happened.

"I'm sorry I stayed away from you for so long after too," I continued. "It's just that . . . well"—I forced myself to hold Ari's gaze and not look away—"when I saw you, or what I thought was you, start to shift . . ." My throat was dry and my voice caught. Ari struggled with his emotions. He likely knew I was still skittish about seeing anger or anything even remotely close to battle rage on his face so he looked away. After a long moment he turned back to me and all I saw in his face was determination.

"And I'm sorry I didn't flay that hellcnight alive and eviscerate it before you ever had a chance to see it," he said resolutely. I had a feeling Ari was successfully hiding even deeper, darker emotions over the whole event.

"Me too," I said automatically.

Ari stilled. "You are?"

I paused and thought about Delgato lying in his bed downstairs. And how much Burr cared for him and how he might never wake again.

"No," I said, sighing. Ari nodded, seemingly content that all was as it had been before, and pulled me to him.

"I wish *I'd* killed the hellcnight," I said. Ari stared intently at me, as if seeing me for the first time. In a way, he was. Then he crushed me to him. And so it was that we were a tangle of arms, legs, and lips when I felt *Cnawlece* slowing in the water some unknown amount of time later. Since *Cnawlece* had slowed only once before (during the hellcnight attack), the slowing of our boat produced immediate dread. I climbed off of Ari's lap and looked out over the rails. Immediately, I knew why we'd stopped.

We were lost.

Everyone came up. To a person, including Virtus, although he was a tiger, we all looked east, over *Cnawlece*'s front rail, to where Second Branch should be. Everyone spoke at once.

"Where are—?"

"What is—?"

"Is that Second—?"

"Luck, which o' them is Blandjan?"

"Are we even *at* Second Branch?"

Russ and I each ran downstairs to get our maps and route notes. In less than two minutes we were back on the sundeck, more winded and worried than before. Quickly, we spread the maps out on a group of small tables that Ari, Rafe, and Russ pushed together into the center of the deck.

Though Delgato's map and mine were slightly different, each highlighted the suggested route of passage for the Shallows. At First Branch (where we'd seen the first bonfire frame), there'd been four choices: the Concelare, the Blandjan, the Naefre, and the Finthanan. We were supposed to take Blandjan, the Lethe's second branch from the left at First Branch. We had. And for days we'd sailed Blandjan, following the map.

At Second Branch, we were supposed to stay on Blandjan. The map showed only two choices: a small rivulet called the Secernere and a wider continuation of Blandjan. It was imperative that we stay on Blandjan because the Secernere led to Ebony's Elbow. (Ebony's Elbow was one of those areas that had a curling whirlpool at its bend; it looked like it led straight into Halja's underground.) But when we looked at Second Branch on the map, it didn't match what we saw on the river. As we stared out across

Cnawlece's bow, there weren't two choices with one clear answer, but three with none.

Had Lucifer not been a lord but a farmer, folks might associate him with a pitchfork instead of a lance. And, had that been the case (although it was not), then surely what we looked at might have been called Lucifer's Pitchfork.

All around us, Halja's vast, expansive rush lands spread out like a bosky blanket. But in front of us, the blanket was shorn, as if a mighty giant had thrown down a massive iron pitchfork with such violence it had burrowed straight into the ground like a meteor. I could almost imagine the crushing impact . . . the shuddering of the rush lands . . . and the sinking of that imaginary hell-forged weapon . . . so that all that remained was a bubbling, oozy stew.

It hadn't really happened like that, but the waters of the pitchfork-shaped branch in front of us still boiled and steamed as if it had. Directly above us, the skies were neither clear, nor raining. The sun was setting, but the sphere was hidden behind haze. Instead of a steady circular glow, the brightest light came from flickering, irregular strikes of lightning. The area seemed caught in some evermore out of time, a place where forward motion, the weather, choices, and maybe even destiny itself were eclipsed, buried beneath the ground, covered with swirling mist and churning waters that streamed in one too many directions.

"Is this really Second Branch?" Fara said, repeating her earlier question. Everyone split from the tables and fanned out around the sundeck's railings. Except for Ari and me.

"Yes," we called together.

It was wispy, and nearly gone, kind of like the smell of smoke from a day's old fire. But we could still feel it. The magical remnants of an old bonfire frame. This one had not been recently stocked with fresh wood (which made me wonder if something had happened to the Boatmen who had stocked the bonfire at First Branch). But waning magic users don't need wood to start fires. And I didn't want anyone wasting even one second on whether we were actually at Second Branch. So, almost as cavalierly as I might wave a fly out of my face, I lit the bonfire and turned back to the table. Without the wood, it wouldn't burn long after I left, but for now it served its purpose. Russ and Burr gasped in surprise and everyone refocused their attention on the fork.

"We all know the Lethe reforges itself from time to time," I said, addressing the group. "Who knows when Second Branch became a three-pronged branch instead of a two-pronged branch. It could have been weeks or months ago, or it could have just happened today, as a result of all this rain. What matters is that we now have a choice to make."

The exact location of the bonfire frame wasn't marked on the map. But the bonfires had been markers at one time. So it seemed to me, the only real question was: did we take the path that was marked with fire . . . or not?

While everyone else bickered and dithered, I remembered what Ari had said to me the first time we'd lit a bonfire together: *Lucem in tenebras ferimus*. Into the darkness, we bring light.

He'd likely not meant the words to have any meaning beyond us and that single dark Beltane eve that had occurred last semester. But in the time since, I'd often thought of his words as a Maegester's rallying cry.

Because wasn't that our purpose? And wasn't that what we were trying to do just now? Bring the light of justice into the darkness of Halja's hinterlands?

For me, there was only one clear choice.

We chose the path marked with light.

Chapter 17

The mood that evening was restless. It was the first time we'd ever not been sure of our path. Sure, everyone agreed with my suggestion that we take the marked route, but no one really knew if it was the right one.

Since Ari and I had made up, and everyone was just the least bit on edge about where we were going, Burr suggested a casual dinner up top on the sundeck. The dining room had long ago lost its appeal (if it had ever had any to begin with) and, this way, no one would need to stand watch alone. So it was, on a late-summer evening sometime around twilight, that I found myself dining alfresco on the deck of a dahabiya halfway between New Babylon and the sea.

The demons' nighttime noises were quieter here (a fact I did not dwell overly on—if the *rogare* demons avoided this branch, what did that mean for us?) and, sometime after eight, a slight northeasterly breeze started blowing. Russ raised the sails and Burr set up a folding table, draping it with colorful batik tablecloths and mismatched sets of chunky kitchen china in azure, indigo, and chartreuse. I found it touching that Burr didn't want to risk Delgato's fragile matched dining room set for our impromptu picnic and hoped Delgato appreciated Burr half as much as I was starting to.

Despite our circumstances, the scene Burr set for us was undeniably beautiful. Below us, the last of the sun's rays sparked across the Lethe like a million muted firecrackers while, on deck, nearly a hundred lanterns, votives, and tea lights twinkled and winked at us, a warmer, closer version of the soon-to-be starlit sky. I smiled at the menu (Burr had to have made it for me): charred red snapper, new potatoes with rosemary, and a few bottles of Mumblehead Perry. That Burr was a sly one—by serving pear wine, he neatly sidestepped the question of grapes versus apples for the exactly half Host, half Angel dinner party.

No one had formally dressed for dinner since that first night so Fara and Rafe appeared exactly as they had earlier in the day with Fara wearing black snakeskin pants, high leather boots, and a silver chain-mail jacket, and Rafe wearing a red flannel outer shirt, a faded gray undershirt, and mustard-colored pants splotched with engine oil. With her white gold locks and silver jacket, Fara almost looked like the moon personified, while Rafe . . . looked like he'd just climbed out of a Haljan oil well.

"Are we having engine trouble?" I asked.

"Nothing for you two to worry about," Rafe said, giving Ari and me a peremptory wave.

Ari said nothing. I was absolutely certain that he wasn't insulted. Unlike me, Ari was completely comfortable with what he could and couldn't do as a waning magic user. As he'd told me more than once, it was his younger Hyrke brother who was the mechanic in the family. Machines had never even held a passing interest for Ari. But I was also absolutely certain that Ari barely tolerated Rafe. I knew the only reason he hadn't started pressing me to replace him was because, out here, there were no other options.

I waited for everyone to be seated, fiddling with my filleting knife, meeting the dead fish's gaze straight on. (This time I wasn't worried about getting fish goo on me. I was wearing canvas pants and an old shirt I'd bought at a secondhand store with Ivy. It was white with a huge bouquet of black lilies on the front. When I'd seen it, I'd just had to have it, although the image provoked conflicting emotions in me. Ari had loved it, of course.)

Ari reached under the table and squeezed my hand, his signature flowing into mine like honey, sweet and slow. He looked almost as scrumptious as the meal. His dark looks and partial beard, combined with his rugged fishermen's sweater and his not insignificant size, made him a strong, solid, and utterly attractive presence by my side. I squeezed back.

"How about a toast?" he said.

I looked expectantly at our Angel friends. Those sorts of things were very much their bailiwick. Fara nodded and cleared her throat, which did nothing to ameliorate the hoarseness of her voice. I sighed inwardly when she picked up her Book of Joshua and flipped it open. "A battlefield blessing," she croaked.

> Sitting, clutching, aching,
> My death is in the making.
> Drumming heart, stop your riot!
> I want my end quick and quiet.
>
> Cold, gray sky, hear my cries.
> No time for why or further lies.
> With the dead and dying all around,
> It's to the bleeding, I am honor bound.
>
> Only one thing left to do,
> Tell my friends—that's you!
> All you meant and more.
> In needing, we were rich; in wanting, we were poor.

During Fara's toast, my mild annoyance had turned to grudging respect for a well-chosen toast I'd never heard before to a feeling of surprise and then suspicion. Had she really meant the sentiment of the blessing? Or had the toast simply been a rote recitation of someone else's words and feelings?

I hardly had time to ponder. Not to be outdone, Rafe also raised his glass, although his toast turned out to be one I'd heard:

> Here's to a long life and a merry one;
>> A quick death and an easy one;
>> A pretty girl and an honest one;
>> A cold drink—and another one!

Rafe winked at both Fara and I during his toast, but he'd gotten us confused, winking first to me and then to her. And, typical of Rafe, he changed the last line to make it even more irreverent. It was supposed to be *a purpose and a happy one*.

No matter, we all raised our glasses and drank. I began deboning my fish. There was much less spattering and splattering this time. The beginning of the dinner passed peacefully enough. Angels were good conversationalists and Ari, at least ever since I'd known him, had always been charming and gracious, even in mixed company. If I was the quietest member of our little group, no one remarked on it. Our dinner continued amid the softened tones of low conversation, the tinkling of silverware, the flapping of the sails, and, always, the lapping sound of the Lethe's murky waters . . . somehow hypnotic and soothing and forlorn and lonely all at the same time.

Around midmeal, we started to sense that something was wrong. We couldn't see them yet, but all around us, we could feel them gathering. Always, at nightfall, the demons' sounds were worse, but before, those sounds had been scattered around Halja's countryside, like the low buzz of bees fertilizing a field. Now the low buzz was more like an angry hiss. It was as if, by choosing this route, we had inadvertently poked a hive. And now an aggressive, lethal swarm was on its ways to attack us.

"Do you feel that?" I asked.

Ari nodded, looking straight at me.

"Nine of them so far," Rafe said, gazing out into the still-empty, nearly dark rush lands.

Fara narrowed her eyes. "Best to cast up," she said, glancing at Ari. "I can cast at least three good shielding or cloaking spells and still have enough *potentia* for offensive casting."

If she'd lose the glamour, she'd have even more, I thought. But I didn't say it. I had the feeling if things got dire enough we'd see the real Fara soon enough. We all scraped our chairs back at the same time and stood up. It was hard to know what to do first: rush to the remaining weapons chest, warn Burr and Russ, lower the sails, close and lock the shutters, arm the cannons with salt and shot . . . Before I could decide, however, I heard a new sound. And this one didn't come from a demon, though it was infinitely more scary. Because that sound told me, even in the dark, exactly where we were going and how much danger we were in. It was the sound of rushing, gushing water—the kind that spins in a great big sloshing circle before gurgling out of sight into a deep, dark, watery maw.

My signature zinged and I viciously clamped down on it. No way was I going to panic and go berserk like I had after the hellnight attack. That would only make this worse. Hearing the sound of that churning, spine-twisting, lung-crushing water grow closer made me realize we'd never be able to pass through this river bend unharmed. I didn't give a grand flapping sail what one addled *Field Guide* contributor's fallacious advice was. No anchor would save us. There was only one way out. We had to reverse course—*now*!

It would take the Angels a few minutes to "cast up," as Fara had said. Most spells took time to cast and I didn't want to waste it standing around having Rafe cast something stupid like Someone To Watch Over Me while we drifted closer to the heart of oblivion.

"I chose the wrong branch," I said in a rush. "This must be the Secernere. *That*," I said, pointing out into the dark toward the front of the boat and the increasingly loud sound of rushing water, "must be Ebony's Elbow. That's why the *rogares* are coming. It's a trap."

To their credit, no one else panicked either. Not that I expected them to. Fara's glamour prevented us from seeing her unwanted expressions. While Ari must have felt as I did: that we still stood a chance of reversing *Cnawlece*'s direction and escaping. And Rafe, well, he just looked as carefully carefree as always, damn the man. *Did nothing faze him?*

I grabbed Rafe's arm.

"Come on! You need to get to the engine room and slow us down. I'm going to tell Russ what's going on so he can try to turn us. Ari, you should load the cannons and have Fara cast some defensive spells over you, Burr, and Russ."

"What about you?" Ari said. "Fara can cast Ascendancy and Impenetrable over you before you go."

Fara bristled and I winced.

An Angel's first duty is to their ward. That's who they take the oath to protect. So it's unfair to ask them to deplete their *potentia* on someone they're not assigned to protect. On the other hand, it happens all the time. There's no rule saying Angels can't cast spells over someone who isn't their ward (so long as that person agrees). But, since Angel's recoup their *potentia* with time and rest, it doesn't usually happen when you're facing twenty-nine demons and a watery grave. Plus Ari's statement was as good as saying Rafe's spellcasting was useless.

The problem was, I wasn't sure I disagreed. Compared to battle spells, Rafe's silent hand gestures were mere parlor tricks, and while there was no denying he could smother a fire and heal someone, those weren't the sort of spells you wanted your Guardian casting when you were facing a demon horde or death by drowning.

I looked up at Rafe. For once, he didn't look carefree. He looked angry.

"Load the cannons," he said to Ari. "I'm going to see if I can reverse our course."

And then he was off without even a glance in my direction. *Some Guardian he was.*

I dashed after him, biting the inside of my cheek, hoping I'd live to see the day when Ari chewed me out for not letting Fara cast some useful spells over me before I took off to warn Burr and Russ of the danger we were in.

A few minutes later *Cnawlece* had full knowledge of her predicament. Russ informed me that turning in these waters would be impossible. *Cnawlece* was too big, the current was too strong, and the water too littered with unseen rocks. If he tried to turn us now, the boat would get snagged, list, fill with water, and sink. The best we could hope for was to reverse the engine. As if on cue, I heard a tremendous rumble and the deck shuddered beneath my feet. A moment later, we hit our first rock. The bump tossed me against the wall.

I regained my footing and ran upstairs, shouting for Fara. She met me at the top, looking finally, just the least little bit, in dishabille. Her chain-mail jacket was gone and her long, blond hair was now caught up in a ponytail. Salt dusted her face, arms, and shirt.

"Can you cast Impenetrable over *Cnawlece*?" I asked Fara breathlessly.

"The whole boat?" she said incredulously, looking around its upper deck and then down the stairs. She paled as she considered, wrestling with some internal decision. What could possibly be worse than a pack of *rogares* and a giant whirlpool?

"Yes, the whole boat!" I said. "It will prevent the hull from being ripped to pieces by the rocks and the decks from being overrun with demons."

She shook her head. "Even if I could cast it over the whole of *Cnawlece*, it wouldn't keep an army of *rogares* off for more than a few minutes. Maybe with Rafe's help—"

I rolled my eyes. But Fara shook my shoulder. "He knows more spells than you think. Ask him!" She glanced back over her shoulder toward Ari and the cannons. He was loading one with shot and salt. I felt another bump as a watery mist hit my face. At first I thought it had started raining again, but then—with my heart lurching up to my throat and my stomach falling to my knees—I realized we must be close enough for me to feel the gurgle and spit of the Secernere in the watery mouth of the bend.

Along the banks, I felt the *rogares* numbers swell. *Water wraiths,* I thought. *There had to be at least fifty of them out there by now.* Their shrieking cries pierced my ears just as their collective signatures started to smother mine. Instinctively, I pressed back but it was like being the shortest person in a packed bar—one that was going to catch fire soon. Panicking a little, I pulsed my signature. That's when the shrieking turned to hoarse braying and roaring.

"Stop!" Ari yelled from across the deck. "Don't engage them yet." The back of his shirt was wet with sweat and he barely had time to give me a glance as he finished loading the last of the cannons. Fara stood in the center of the deck mouthing the words to Impenetrable. I hoped the spell wasn't a long one . . . How much of the boat could she cover on her own?

A hideous yowl rose up to my left. *They're on board!* I thought, nearly sending a blast of fire to the source of the sound. But then I saw it was Virtus, finally living up to his name. He stood on *Cnawlece*'s bow like a living figurehead, scowling and snarling at the advancing army of wraiths, who were now wading into the water toward us.

As the water wraiths got closer, I got my first glimpse of them. Cold dread raced through my limbs like water sluicing off a melting icicle. If I hadn't grabbed the railing, my knees would have buckled. Their fire was the first thing I focused on. It wasn't warm and golden like the waning magic fire I was used to. Instead, it looked sickly and malignant in shades of glowing green and sulfurous yellow. Each wraith carried a fiery war club or a blazing spiked flail. Their skin was little more than an ash-tinted membrane stretched taut over a skeleton of sharp bones and grisly innards. And the size of them. Each one of them was easily twice Ari's size. Their webbed, clawed feet sank in the mud under their weight, but that didn't slow them. More of them appeared on the horizon. I'd never seen this many demons before. Knowing Halja was full of demons and seeing them were two totally different things.

Had this *been what Armageddon had been like?* I thought crazily, momentarily giddy with my own battle response. *How amazing would it be to control something like this?* The Angels had never stood a chance. But, as the wraith horde drew closer, I realized how foolish my thoughts were. I couldn't control this. No one could *ever* control this. Staring out at the sea of evil and anger, at creatures with claws the size of grappling hooks and horns as wide and sharp as two-bladed plows, I realized the Host's immense mistake. The Apocalypse was *Cnawlece* sailing the Secernere. It was me pressing back against the wraiths' smothering signatures. It was Virtus standing at the bow, snarling. It was us, the Host, poking a hive—a hive full of demons that was still buzzing two thousand years later.

I raced downstairs to look for Rafe. By this time, *Cnawlece* was shaking so severely that I nearly fell down the stairs. I gripped the rail, climbed down into the hallway, and put my hands up to steady myself. Below deck, *Cnawlece*'s hallways were empty. Burr was likely still lowering the sails and Russ was probably in the engine room with Rafe. I didn't want to go in there, for fear my waning magic might make whatever engine problems we were having worse, but I had to get close enough to yell to Rafe so that I could get him back up top. If he didn't help Fara with Impenetrable soon, it wouldn't matter whether we could reverse course or not.

I stumbled down the hall and opened the small door at the end. Behind it was a circular stair leading down into darkness. *Did I dare try to light a small fireball to see?* Yes. For once, fire was not my top concern. Five steps from the bottom, *Cnawlece* hit another rock. I slipped and fell. My fireball went out and I landed in an inch of water, my head banging against the metal steps behind me. I pulled myself up, rubbed my head, feeling the sticky squish of blood, and relit my fireball. Shaking now (and not just from *Cnawlece*'s shuddering), I sloshed my way to the engine room door and pounded on it.

"Rafe!" I called, my hand stinging from the force of my pounding. The roar of the engine down here was much louder. *Could he even hear me?* Now the water was up to my ankles.

"Rafe!" I shouted again, pounding louder. I had my hand on the knob to open the door when it suddenly opened. Rafe stood there, covered in engine oil.

"What are you doing down here?" he yelled. "Get away from the door. You'll just make things worse."

Could things be any worse?

I grabbed Rafe before he could disappear back inside. "You have to come upstairs. Russ will have to figure out the engine problems by himself. You have to help Fara cast Impenetrable over *Cnawlece*."

"Over the whole ship?"

I nodded.

"You don't do things by halves, Onyx." But there was a look on his face that hadn't been there before. A spark of humor. He grabbed my arm and led me away from the engine room. "We can't reverse," he yelled to me as we walked. "*Cnawlece*'s engines weren't designed to fight a current like this. The best we can do is try to hold our position while we figure out another plan."

"Can't you cast a spell? Something like Reverse or Backward or something?"

Rafe's spark of humor turned into a full-fledged laugh. *Only Rafe could laugh at a time like this.*

He didn't bother answering. It had been a stupid, desperate question anyway. If Rafe knew any spells that would help, he would have cast them. Besides, casting spells in an engine room was only slightly less risky than using waning magic would have been. Damn machines. Problem was, they'd been designed by man, not Luck or the Savior.

"So what spells can you cast?" I asked Rafe once we'd climbed up out of the circular stairwell into the middle hallway.

"Offensive or defensive?"

"There's an army of wraith *rogares* out there," I yelled, equal parts exasperated, incredulous, and scared. "*Offensive*, Rafe."

"Nouiomo Onyx," he said, almost to himself, "is asking me for offensive spells. Hmm . . . well, you didn't seem too impressed by them during *Voir Dire* but I can offer you Painfall, Damage Cascade, and Hemorrhage—"

"Those are Holden Pierce's spells," I said, cutting him off. "Rafe, can't you be serious for once?"

"I am," he said quietly, and despite all the noise, I finally heard him. "Pierce doesn't own those spells. He just listed them on his CV. I know all the spells on Lambert Jeffries' and Melyn Danika's too, if you're interested."

It was a moment of time we didn't have. But I couldn't help it. I stared at Rafe, realization dawning. Raphael Sinclair should have been ranked first out of eleven.

"Why didn't you—"

"Why didn't I say something? Why should I have? The last thing I ever wanted was a ward. It wasn't until—"

BOOM! The firing of the first cannon nearly deafened me, knocking me right off my feet. I fell against Rafe and he caught me under my arms. He quickly righted me and pushed me to my feet. I heard Ari yelling to Fara and footsteps heading in this direction. No doubt Ari was frantic to find me by now.

I ran up the stairs to the sundeck, pulling Rafe with me, worried that we'd already wasted too much time below.

Emerging onto *Cnawlece*'s upper deck was like coming up out of a cave into the middle of an active battlefield. Although Russ and Burr's efforts had managed to slow *Cnawlece*, we were now close enough to see the gaping hole of water we were headed for. The spray was relentless. Standing on deck was almost like standing under a waterfall. Fara was manning the cannons and Ari was throwing fireballs. In the time it took me to reach him, he threw three separate blasts, which killed two wraiths and mortally wounded another. Still, they kept coming. I saw immediately that our priority was keeping them off the boat. If anyone had ever questioned whether feeding Virtus all those pounds of fish had been worth it, they now had their answer. He paced the edges of the deck, snarling and spitting at any wraith that got too close. This was how Ari knew who to fire at next.

I turned to Rafe.

"Fine," I said, more to myself than him. *Make me more deadly.* "I want you to cast them all over me: Painfall, Damage Cascade, and Hemorrhage. Then you and Fara work on trying to cast Impenetrable over as much of *Cnawlece* as you can." Maybe if we held out until dawn, we'd make it. I tried not to think about the fact that dawn was seven hours away.

If Rafe had any reaction to my request, he kept it to himself. He locked his hands together and then beneath his breath, he calmly murmured a series of words. One by one, I felt the spells settle into place. My signature suddenly felt longer, stronger, and slicker, like I was wielding a flaming scorpion tail whip. The next time Virtus snarled at one of the wraiths, I ran over to him.

There it was. In the water, not three yards from us.

I shaped my magic into a fiery sling and then used it to whip a fireball directly into the wraith's chest. I didn't know how Rafe's spells would work and I didn't want to take any chances so I'd thrown my magic hard and fast. The effect was more than enough. More than I wanted to witness. The wraith burst into flames, shrieking, and then collapsed into a liquefied puddle of demon stew. On deck, Fara shuddered and reached for her Book. She knelt down with Rafe and together they tried to cast Impenetrable over all of *Cnawlece*.

It didn't work. The wraiths started throwing fireballs that looked like radioactive will-o'-the-wisp. Some of them reached the deck. Fara screamed and I turned from my disgusting wraith blasting to put the fires out. After the smoke cleared, I saw Fara lying on the ground next to Rafe. He had her head in his lap and was stroking her hair, murmuring something to her. I ran over to them.

Fara was horribly burned. Over much of her body. In fact, it was hard to imagine she'd gotten this injured from the hot, but brief, fires I'd just put out. And that's when I realized it wasn't recent burns I was looking at. As I'd predicted earlier, things had finally become so dire that Fara had been forced to drop her glamour. *This* was the real Fara. At some point in the past, Fara Vanderlin had been consumed by fire and then had been unable to heal herself or reach a Mederi.

I'd utterly and thoroughly misjudged her. My guess was Fara's glamour kept more than emotional scars at bay. Looking at her writhing in pain now, I could only imagine that her daily glamour also helped her deal with some lingering physical pain as well.

I looked at Rafe, grievously ashamed of all the times I'd accused Fara of being fake.

"She'll be okay," he said. "Her *potentia*'s gone, but Impenetrable is up, at least for now." He pointed toward the sky. Two iridescent green glowballs exploded in midair. The sparks rained down over our heads but then fell to *Cnawlece*'s side, like they'd hit a great big clear umbrella. I seized the moment, clutching at this tiny sliver of hope, only to have it shatter in the next second.

Cnawlece lurched forward from the position we'd been holding and started drifting toward the bend again.

"The engine just failed," Rafe said. But he didn't move. Just sat there, still cradling Fara's head in his lap. "You should find Ari." His tone was entirely too fatalistic for me. I remembered Fara's battlefield blessing from dinner. How fitting it had turned out to be.

Only one thing left to do, tell my friends—that's you! All you meant and more . . .

Well, I wasn't ready to say good-bye just yet.

"Lower the anchor!" I yelled, jumping up. *What had the*

Field Guide *said? Something about an anchor being the only way to escape Ebony's End?*

I ran to Ari, who was covered in salt. He looked miserable. His eyes were more sunken than before and his skin was greasy and pale. He shook and was so out of breath, he could barely speak. I should have been doing more to help him.

"The engine just slipped and we're drifting toward the hole again," I told him. "I'm going to drop the anchor."

He nodded and followed me over to it. After a moment or two of struggling, we finally unhooked it. It fell into the water with a great big splash and I heard the gratifying sound of the chain clanking as the anchor dropped lower and lower into the water. A moment later, the clanking stopped. There was no more chain. The anchor had been lowered, but we were still drifting . . .

The *Field Guide* had been wrong.

Luck must want us to die, I thought. There could be no other explanation. The water here was too deep to anchor in and now, suddenly, after hitting rock after rock, we seemed to have passed all the snags.

"Time to abandon ship," I said to Ari. "At least in the dinghy we can row."

It was madness. Pure folly. Abandoning *Cnawlece* meant a slow death instead of a fast one. If we didn't die at the hands of the wraiths tonight, we would die at the hands of other *rogares* later. It had taken us nearly three weeks to get to this point by boat. I didn't even want to contemplate how long walking back would take. And, honestly, how would we even get there? We had no land maps; we were abandoning most of the food (even the food we'd brought for the Shallows settlers, which made my heart break). We had to leave the weapons chest. There was no room in the dinghy for that. All our books, our clothes . . . Everything, left behind. That's what *abandoning ship* means.

In the end, each of us grabbed what we could. I told Burr to get some food. I managed to pocket Alba's black onion. After a quick trip back to his cabin to retrieve Luck knew

what, Rafe carried Fara off the ship. She brought her Book
and Virtus. Russ busted open the weapons chest and pulled
out five daggers and a sword. The alembic full of waerwater
was still fastened around my neck. I guess Ari had been
right; it was the safest place for it.

Ari and I went below to retrieve Delgato. While we were
down there, I told Ari to grab whatever else he thought
he needed. He looked at me long and hard and I knew what
he was thinking. *I* was the only thing he needed. Despite
everything, I smiled at him. I wasn't ready to say good-bye.
Didn't want to say good-bye. But I did want him to know I
felt the same way he did.

We carried Delgato upstairs together and lowered him
into the dinghy. The wraiths had spotted us getting into
the dinghy but seemed to be waiting to attack until we
pushed off.

"Will you be able to cast Impenetrable over the dinghy
once we're clear of *Cnawlece*?" I asked Rafe. He gave a
curt nod, his face tight. I had to hand it to him. Tense as he
was, his *potentia* seemed limitless.

Russ was just about to shove off when I noticed Burr
was missing.

"Wait!" I cried. "Where's Burr?" I wished I'd never
asked him to go back for food. It wasn't as if we could take
enough anyway. Sooner or later, if we lived (which was
starting to look doubtful anyway) we'd have to learn to live
off the rush lands if we were going to make it back home.
But then, thankfully, Burr appeared a second later, holding
several sacks and packages. He threw the larger ones directly into the dinghy and then he tossed a small tin into my
lap. My mother's dried herbs. The ones we used to make tea.

That Burr had risked his life to retrieve something so
small, something so insignificant . . . was both touching
and confusing to me. But I supposed, to Burr, the herbs
weren't insignificant.

It's what I got. It's who I am.

Burr had gone back inside for what was important to

him and he'd gathered the things that brought other people comfort.

I made room for him in the dinghy, nervously eyeing the wraiths in the water, but they didn't move any closer. In fact, they seemed to move farther away. I don't know if they were afraid of getting caught in the current or something else, but they actually seemed to retreat as Burr made his way down the ladder toward the waiting dinghy. I gripped the handle of my paddle, ready to row with every ounce of willpower I had left.

But then something happened that stripped it all away.

The bow of *Cnawlece* hit the edge of the whirlpool, causing the boat to turn suddenly away from us. At the same time, Russ started to push us clear. Even so, Burr would have had enough time. But just as he was stepping from the ladder to the dinghy, a massive black river serpent rose up out of the water and grabbed Burr by the leg. He screamed—a horrible, heart-piercing shriek—and managed to cling to the ladder for a split second before being pulled down into the water. A second later I felt a waning magic blur and then something heavy dropped in my lap. I picked it up, stupefied with shock. It was Burr's filleting knife. The only thing that was left of him.

I will never forget that moment. Not because I killed something. But because I didn't.

Burr popped up out of the water twenty yards from us, and then thirty, and then sixty. Each time his screams grew quieter as he lost more breath, but somehow I knew the black river serpent (which had to be another hellcnight impersonating the long-dead Ebony) wasn't going to kill him. Not just yet. It would eat him alive. But instead of killing Burr to prevent that, I wept. I didn't want to roast Burr into oblivion like I'd roasted the wraiths. I was sick enough over them. But then Ari put an end to Burr's suffering. The next time he resurfaced, Ari threw a fiery arrow straight through Burr's heart. Instead of feeling relief, I retched over the side of the dinghy into the water.

Aut amat aut odit mulier. A woman either loves or hates. That's what Sarah Meginnis, our Evil Deeds professor, was always telling us about domestic clients. Well, in that moment I hated *everything*. In my all-consuming rage I did something I'd never done before. I blasted the rush lands and all of the wraiths within it with fury, fire, and *darkness*. I poured all of my hatred into that blast. I thought I'd likely never be able to look at my own reflection again. The blackening of my soul (if I had one) was surely nothing compared to the fiery blackening I rained down over our enemies.

But I needn't have worried. Not only had my mirror gone down with our ship, the wraiths had left as well. We sat, silhouetted against a wall of flaming rush land, stunned and unmoving in our tiny rowboat—the only life left on the Secernere.

Despite the insanity of it, we started rowing toward the fire. Not that any of us were capable of rational thought, but I guess we thought our chances were better against the flames and the demons we knew than a watery death and the demons we didn't. But it didn't matter. Nothing did. After all our struggles, spells, defensive maneuvers, attempted rescues, and other efforts, we were all going to die anyway. Because we couldn't row against this current. Further strength and endurance spells failed. Our oars broke. Ari and Rafe finally collapsed, sweating and shaking. We reached the event horizon for Ebony's End.

We were going in. We were going under.

We were going to drown.

II

Neither should a ship rely on one small anchor,
nor should life rest on a single hope.

—EPICTETUS

Chapter 18

I felt heavy, and very small. The whooshing sound in my ears made it seem like the Archangel was giving the eulogy underwater, but I knew it was just the wind. It wasn't stuffiness. I hadn't cried. I never cried. Only babies cried.

I looked out across the wide, gray river toward the big city.

Someday, I thought, I'm gonna leave here and go there and never look back. And I won't care . . . ever again!

"Raphael," my mother said, her voice barely above a whisper, but somehow louder than the wind. The Archangel paused, waiting for my attention. My mother pointed to the ground beside her. I moved closer and the Archangel continued.

> Then thou the mother of so sweet a child,
>   her false imagined loss cease to lament,
>   and wisely learn to curb they sorrows wild.
>   Think what a present thou to Him has sent.

The Archangel looked straight at me, but everyone else looked toward the river. How could they not? That was where I'd sent him, just like the Archangel had just said. Above us, the trees swayed with the wind, dropping their leaves. But leaves didn't sink.

I watched one fall through the air as the Archangel spoke his hushed words. It swirled and curled, twisting and spinning. Even though it fell, it floated. It didn't sink like a rock, straight to the bottom.

I watched another. This one from the very tip of a black branch that had no other leaves. The wind plucked at this last leaf and, with one flick of its pointy end, the branch let go. The leaf was pushed out onto the wind. It whirled and swished. A flight I couldn't take.

The Archangel finished just as the wind blew one of the leaves into my cheek. It pressed against my skin, cold and wet. I peeled it off.

If it wasn't dead yet, it would be soon.

Everyone started walking back to the house. It would take a while. The cemetery was down by the river and the house was high up on the hill. As they passed us, I could hear them.

". . . accident . . ."

". . . he tripped . . ."

". . . baby fell . . . drowned . . ."

I ignored them and kept walking. At the top of the hill, I looked back. The long wooden pier jutted out into the Lethe, its weathered boards as warped and twisted as the claws of a crow. I stumbled in the grass, remembering . . .

Right when I'd felt the boat dropping away from beneath me, I'd felt a rip in the fabric of my mind, like someone plucking hair from my scalp—but from inside my head, not on top of it. I experienced the most profound sense that something had been taken from me, something substantial and weighty, something meaningful and defining. And that's when the memory of Rafe's brother's funeral had come to me, slipping into the place that had been previously occupied by the now-unremembered memory.

When my true sight returned, we were still spinning in the dinghy, caught in Ebony's whirlpool. But now I knew: these were the last moments of my life. I don't know why I'd suddenly seen Rafe's memory of his brother's funeral, but nothing seemed more fitting. It seemed natural that my last thoughts would be of a funeral, even if it was someone else's.

But Fara must have seen a different memory. Because instead of quiet acceptance, whatever she'd seen galvanized her. Her *potentia* was restored; her glamour was back. She looked at me, grinning.

"Noon, I know what will save us!" she cried. "*You* showed me." And then with what appeared to be almost superhuman strength she reached into her jacket pocket and withdrew her Book. She flung it into the water, shouting:

Nil desperandum; crede Joshua!

If I had to write an ending for Fara, it would have been exactly that one. Her shouting: "Don't despair; trust in Joshua!" Except she didn't die. None of us did. We passed through unharmed, except for those sore spots in our memory—the gaps that now held the stolen moments from someone else's memory.

When we finally arrived on the other side it was morning. The reedy rush lands on either side of the water were bathed in the pink glow of sunrise. Our clothes and hair were sopping wet and there was standing water in the bottom of the dinghy, but we were on the surface of the river, not beneath it. Behind us, the river gurgled contentedly, satisfied that it had delivered us—from what fate or for what future, we didn't know. These were the sorts of experiences that, while uncommon, were not completely unheard of in Halja. Haljan magic resided mostly in people, but every now and then we'd discover magic in a place or thing: the Angels' ensorcelled apple wines, Alba's black onions, Lucifer's Tomb . . . and now Ebony's Elbow.

What exactly had just happened to us? Had Fara's Book really saved us? And, most importantly . . .

Where in Halja were we now?

I surveyed our dinghy and its occupants. Delgato's still form was sprawled in the muck on the bottom of the dinghy. Ari's gaze swept briefly over me before he turned toward the surrounding countryside. Fara kept a tight hold on Virtus, who looked absolutely miserable. I remembered how much cats hated the water. Virtus' ears were back and he looked about half his usual size. His fur clung wetly to him as a low growl burbled up from his throat, an odd accompaniment to the river's gurgling behind us.

I glanced back at the bubbling spot. I guess that's where we'd come from. It seemed impossible to believe. But before I could ask Fara what she'd meant when she'd shouted that *I'd* showed her how to save us, Rafe leapt out of the dinghy and into the water. Virtus' low growling and the river's quiet gurgling were momentarily eclipsed by the sound of splashing. A moment later, Russ joined him.

"Where are you two going?" I cried. My gut instinct was that everyone should just sit tight. But then I laughed at myself. Sit tight for what? For someone to come along and rescue us? I snorted at my own stupidity.

"We need to drain the water in the bottom of the boat," Rafe said, "make repairs, and build some new oars."

I nodded. I hadn't realized it, until just then, but passing through the Elbow had somehow made my magic feel expanded, frozen, and constricted all at the same time. Like I was an ice cube with a piece of string wrapped around it . . . and inside of it. I forced myself to relax. My signature thawed just as Rafe and Russ beached the dinghy on the river's edge.

Russ was holding up remarkably well for a young man with no magic who'd been nearly drowned and then mysteriously transported to an unfamiliar place. But then again, he was the one with all the river experience. Maybe something similar had happened to him before.

I let my signature melt into the surrounding land so I could feel, magically, what might be in store for us, but thankfully, there were no demons here. The only signature I sensed was Ari's. I still couldn't feel Delgato's, although he was still alive at least.

Ari jumped out of the boat and offered me a hand. I eyed the tall grasses warily. Just because there were no demons here didn't mean there weren't other things that might still kill us. The rush lands were full of crocodiles (the *rogares'* main food source), venomous snakes, and poisonous frogs, just to name a few of the dangerous, unseen things creeping around out there. But I'd been the one who'd been pushing everyone to take every possible survival option prior to entering the Elbow, so I could hardly give up now that we'd actually made it through.

I accepted Ari's hand and hopped out of the boat. Rafe and Russ had already disappeared into the rush lands, presumably to find materials for new oars.

"What about Delgato?" I asked.

"He'll be safest in the boat until we find somewhere to camp for the night," Ari said. "Fara, you and Virtus can stay with Delgato." She nodded. She either didn't care that she'd be left alone, or she thought a comatose ex-captain and waterlogged tiger were company enough. That's when I noticed what else was missing from the boat—the food and weapons. I nearly cried out in frustration. What else could we possibly lose? First our clothes, books, maps, case file, and letters of introduction, then *Cnawlece*, which had been both shelter and transportation, the food we'd brought for the people of the Shallows, then Burr, the most selfless member of the crew. As if that weren't enough, it seemed that Luck wanted to strip us of everything. Fara'd given her Book of Joshua, and now the last of our food and weapons were gone. I raised my hand to my chest to feel for the alembic. It was still hanging on its chain, but the catch had come undone. It was empty. The waerwater was gone.

I yanked hard on the alembic's chain, pulling it free. I held it up to show Ari. He just shook his head.

Was *everything* gone?

Of course not. We still had our lives and our magic. I patted my jacket pocket, feeling a tiny bulge and two larger, sharper-shaped ones. The tin full of tea herbs Burr had risked his life going back for had made it, as had his fillet-ing knife and Alba's black onion. I was consumed with a nearly overpowering urge to ask it, "How will we get back home?" but I figured the onion wasn't big enough to hold the answer. I sighed.

Aut viam inveniam aut faciam. I would either find a way or I would make one.

By late afternoon, much had been accomplished. We'd cleared a small camp area near the river's sandy edge; we'd moved Delgato out of the dinghy, bailed out the water and patched its holes; we'd made new oars out of wood and reeds, collected firewood, and, with Virtus' help, managed to capture a few nonpoisonous marsh creatures, among them a half dozen geese and two swans. Our hair and clothes were now dry (it was the end of Ghrun; the day's heat, for once, had been welcome) and whatever storm had blown through last night was entirely gone. Even the de-mons were keeping their distance. I hadn't felt a single un-familiar signature since we'd passed through Ebony's Elbow. Still, the last thing I felt was safe or comfortable. Especially since there was not just one, but *two* hellcnights who had now "adjusted" to my signature. I didn't think, based on what Delgato had told us during our first training session with him, that I'd be able to sense either one of them if they decided to attack us again.

The five of us (six, if you counted Virtus) huddled around the small fire Ari and I had made, while Delgato continued his odd slumber off to one side. The geese and swans were roasting on spits and the sun was just be-ginning its descent. I'd started to nervously eye the grass again, half expecting to see a crocodile or snake head emerge. The cynical, fatalistic part of me had to admit it would be pretty funny if, after all I'd been through, I died from an attack by something as mundane as a nonmagical swamp beast. But then I thought of Athalie, the girl from the Shallows whose demon complaint had started this whole journey.

No, there was nothing funny at all about being lost in the swamp for her, I thought, glancing around at my surroundings. If the girl was still alive, I was going to find her.

"I still want to try and find the Shallows," I blurted out.

Five sets of eyes turned toward me. I was happy to see that no one looked angry about the suggestion, even Russ, although Virtus just looked hungry. He quickly shifted his gaze from me to the swans.

"You know we have no map, right?" Ari said, pointing out the obvious. I nodded and he continued. "And you know there's no way of knowing where we are, except that we're probably, hopefully, still somewhere in the Lethe's river delta." I nodded again. (If we weren't still in the delta, we weren't in Halja anymore, and I don't think any of us wanted to consider that possibility.)

"And you know the delta's over a hundred miles wide?"

This time I took more time to nod. I knew what Ari was saying. It could take the rest of our lives, or at least the better part of our youth, to find the Shallows. But I couldn't give up. If there was even the smallest chance we could still reach the Shallows and find Athalie, or prevent further disappearances, then I was determined to try.

I was also beginning to think that not only might Grimasca be real, but he was probably the demon who was behind both the hellcnight attacks on us and the disappearances in the Shallows. The fact that both demon complaints named him as a suspect combined with the fact that we'd been attacked twice by hellcnights on the way to investigate those complaints was too much of a coincidence to ignore. I shared my thoughts with the group. No one argued, but no one looked particularly convinced either.

"I felt the waning magic blur too," Ari said. "Just before Burr was attacked."

"That's the other thing," I said, pausing because I was much less sure of my analysis with respect to this part of my hypothesis. "I was talking to Burr yesterday about Grimasca." I dug in the sand with a stick, hardly believing I'd sat in Delgato's room with Burr only yesterday. "Burr said his mother told him Grimasca's mate had been a big, black river serpent. Sound familiar? Burr believed Grimasca killed his mate. Well, I think Grimasca's mate may have been Ebony and *that's* why Grimasca's hellcnights can impersonate her at the Elbow."

This last theory of mine was met with varying degrees of skepticism. Russ had never even heard of Grimasca (I guess his mother, like Aurelia Onyx and Joy Carmine, had not felt it necessary to terrify young Russ with the stories of Luck's hungry, serpent-loving, spy assassin in order to make him go to bed).

"Why does it matter what Burr's mother thought?" asked Ari. "Why are her thoughts so much more important than Tosca's mother's or Mercator's or Sasha's?"

I told them Burr's mother had been Alba the Second. "The Albas and their onions go way back. If an Alba is saying something is true, I'm at least going to seriously consider it."

No one spoke as they digested this new information. Rafe, for once, seemed to be paying attention to the discussion, even if he wasn't actively participating.

Ari frowned. "Weren't you the one who said you wouldn't execute a demon based on the words revealed to you by 'one tiny vegetable'?"

"I still wouldn't. But that doesn't mean I wouldn't *ever* use a black onion either. In fact"—I slipped my hand into my pocket and pulled out the onion—"we can use *this* to find the Shallows." I held it up so that everyone could see it. Then I neatly tossed it in the air and caught it again. I was just about to peel it when Russ stopped me.

"Save it," he said. "Once night falls, I think I can figure

out where we are." He pulled two small instruments and a tiny leather-bound notebook out of his pocket.

"What are those?" I asked. "Navigational tools?"

Russ nodded. "Sextant, chronometer, almanac," he said, pointing to each in turn.

I grinned at him, ready to cling to any good news, even if it was news that we now had the tools to tell us we were a hundred miles off course.

Later that night, after the geese and swans had been eaten and the fire banked, Russ announced that, with all the tall grass surrounding us on land, the best place for him to see the horizon would be from the middle of the river. Ari volunteered to go with him, both as oarsman to keep the boat still while Russ made his calculations, and as protection should something nasty pop up out of the water. Of course, this possibility prompted Fara to declare that she too was going, which naturally meant that either Virtus would go or that he'd wait for her return caterwauling at the water's edge. Neither of those options suited, so after a brief verbal scuffle, it was decided that, oath or no, Fara and Virtus would stay behind.

Fara and I stood on the shallow, sandy beach of the river's edge, watching Ari row Russ out. As soon as they'd left, Rafe had flopped down on the ground in between Virtus and Delgato. The three of them were now sprawled behind us in various states of consciousness.

Whichever tributary this was, it was about a mile or so wide here. Luckily, it was a clear night. Similar to last night, when we'd dined alfresco on the deck of the dahabiya, I was once again struck by how beauty could find one at the oddest moments. The black silhouette of two young muscled men rowing a dinghy amongst the soft silvery moonlit waves was . . . well, a magical sight. But then the image of Ebony's posthumous, gaping black and red maw rising out of the water just before the hellcnight who'd been impersonating her clamped down on Burr's leg and dragged him under ruined my peaceful reverie. I reached into my pocket and withdrew Burr's filleting knife. I was just about to make a shallow cut on my palm as an offering to Estes for Ari and Russ' safety when Fara placed her hand over mine.

"They'll be fine," she said with quiet conviction.

I paused and looked up at her. I realized she hadn't quoted the Book *once* since we'd passed through the Elbow.

"What happened back there?" I said, pointing behind me, toward the still-bubbling spot in the river. "Why did you throw your Book of Joshua into the water?"

What I really wanted to ask was whether that book had saved us. But I wasn't sure I was ready to hear the answer.

"Noon, did anything unusual happen to you when you passed through Ebony's Elbow?"

Besides surviving? I thought, but didn't say. I knew what she meant. The memory grafts. Or rather, the memory lifts and grafts. Because, even though the soreness was going away, it still felt like a part of my memory was missing. That there was something I should be able to remember but couldn't, because it was gone. And when I tried to remember it, all I could remember was Rafe's brother's funeral, which was sad and weird and disturbing. I shouldn't be able to remember that.

What had Alba said to me in her café the day of Jezebeth's execution? That Hyrkes liked to have a little fun with magic too. *Really? Did they have any idea how warped and twisted magic could actually be?* I shook my head.

"Yeah," I confided to Fara. "I now remember something I shouldn't."

But, surprisingly, she smiled at me. "Exactly. Me too." She looked at me expectantly, but there was no way I was going to share Rafe's memory with her. Just the fact that I possessed it made me feel like I'd somehow betrayed the fragile trust that had started to develop between Rafe and me.

"After finals last semester," Fara said, "you and Ari

hiked out to Lucifer's Tomb. You remember finding Lucifer's Tomb, right?"

I nodded emphatically, remembering the stormy night Peter Aster and I had discovered Lucifer's Tomb. Locating it had been a momentous occasion with professional and personal repercussions for both Peter and me. I couldn't imagine a trip down a watery rabbit hole would erase *that* memory. But did that mean the memory that *had* been erased was even more meaningful? I scrambled to remember a late-semester hike out to the tomb with Ari and couldn't.

"I don't remember it," I croaked, worried. What had happened then? And what did it have to do with Fara tossing her Book in the river? But Fara looked anything but worried. She looked . . . invigorated.

"When you and Ari hiked out to the tomb, you went with a purpose: to bring life back to the land around it. You went to try to remove the blight from Armageddon's battlefield."

I looked at her blankly. "I did? And did I?"

Fara laughed, somewhat giddily, remembering *my* memory. "Yes! *Lucem in tenebras ferimus*, Noon. Or rather, *lucem in tenebras tulisti*."

"Into the darkness, we bring light?" It was what Ari had said to me the first time we'd lit a bonfire together with our magic. "*I* brought light?"

She nodded excitedly. "Right! Well, you brought fire."

"I used waning magic to bring something back to life?" The tone of my voice conveyed just how preposterous I found the whole idea.

"No, of course not!" Fara laughed so hard that Rafe looked over. He removed his arm from where he'd flung it across his eyes and peeked over at us. Sufficiently reassured that we weren't being attacked by demons or monstrous reptilian swamp creatures, he turned the other way. But by now I was well and truly vexed with Fara.

"Just tell me what happened," I said.

"You lit a bonfire, Noon."

"So what?"

"On ground that hadn't seen fire for two millennia, since Armageddon! But you know what's even more remarkable?"

I just stared at her, desperately wishing she didn't have an Angel's love for All Things Dramatic.

"You didn't use magic. You used faith! Well, faith and a match." She cleared her throat. "But *that's* how I knew. How to save us from Ebony and the Elbow. I used faith and a book. *The* Book."

It was then that I realized Fara was waiting for me to remember. She thought that by telling me about the experience, it would somehow trigger its return. But the memory was gone. It was like it had never happened. And now whatever I'd learned from it resided in someone else's memory. Fara's. Where she'd used it to save our lives.

If indeed that's what had happened. I had my doubts. Apparently, Fara now had my faith. Well, she could keep it.

I patted her shoulder. "Thanks for telling me," I said. "And for saving us."

She gave me a wicked smile and then snickered. "The bonfire wasn't exactly the hottest part of the memory."

Virtus saved me from responding. He walked over and sat down next to Fara, rubbing his head against her leg for a pat. Fara gave Virtus what he wanted, sighing contentedly and gazing out across the river toward the silhouetted skiff. Ari and Russ were still at it. I glanced back at Rafe, who still had his arm draped across his eyes.

How much of our discussion had he heard?

I pressed my lips together. Time to give him back his memory.

Chapter 19

ॐ

I took a seat next to Rafe's sprawled form. Now was as good a time as any. I didn't know when we'd have a chance to be alone again. I sensed instinctively from the mood of the memory that it wasn't something he'd ever shared with anyone. Tentatively, I reached out to touch Rafe's silver bracelet. The moment my hand made contact, he started. Sometimes I forgot he couldn't sense me the way Ari could. He couldn't have been sleeping, right? He sat up and crossed his legs together, facing me on the ground. I looked at Delgato's sleeping form and then Fara's back over at the water's edge and then into Rafe's eyes.

Maybe he didn't want the memory back. It wasn't as if it was a happy one. Why had Fara been given a memory that galvanized her, invigorated her, made her laugh? Whereas I'd been given one that was infinitely sad and heartbreaking? Each of the moments seemed significant, defining even. But why had the magic of Ebony's Elbow worked the way it had? Legend said that Ebony gave her memory of how to get home to her wandering lover so that he could find his way back to her. It was a romantically fictitious tale for a creature that'd been horridly real. And yet . . . was the tale that hard to believe? What if Ebony's lover *had* been Grimasca? Maybe Alba the Second's story was true. Maybe Grimasca accidentally bit Ebony and she drowned in the Elbow. It didn't excuse Grimasca from any sins he'd committed, but it did cause me to feel just the slightest pang of sympathy for the two doomed lovers. If Ari's destiny was to wander Halja's hinterlands, wouldn't I give him anything, even my most cherished memory, in the hope that he might somehow use it to find his way back to me?

I thought about the *Field Guide*'s advice for passing through Ebony's Elbow unharmed. What if the contributor who'd written about using an anchor to save himself hadn't been writing about ship anchors? What if he'd been writing about memories? The types of memories that define us, anchor us, and make us who we are. Apparently the rushing white water in the bend of Ebony's Elbow took our "anchor memories" away and gave them to someone else.

Why? Who knew?

I only knew I had to try to give Rafe's anchor memory back, even if it was one he might be better off without.

In the bluish black of night, Rafe's taupe eyes appeared darker than usual, almost iron gray. He was still wearing his oil-splotched, mustard-colored pants, although now they were even filthier. Sometime during last night's fight for survival he'd lost his flannel outer shirt. Now all he had on was a thin, sleeveless undershirt. Somehow it didn't surprise me, but being dunked and nearly drowned hadn't wrecked Raphael Sinclair's carefully carefree countenance. His sandy blond hair fell in riotous uncombed waves to his bare, and—I couldn't help noticing—well-sculpted shoulders.

"You know we never finished our conversation in the hallway," he said.

"What conversation?"

"The one where I was telling you the last thing I ever wanted was a ward."

"Oh," I said, frowning and leaning back. Maybe now wasn't such a good time after all.

But he smiled at me, his white teeth gleaming in the moonlight. "Just before Ari and Fara started firing the cannons, I was telling you that it wasn't until I met you that I was even remotely interested in having a ward."

I blinked. He hadn't said that. I narrowed my eyes. "I know, I know," I said, waving a hand in the air. "I'm like a jar of pickled hearts."

"Something like that," Rafe murmured, his gaze never leaving mine. Something occurred to me.

"Rafe, do you remember something now that you shouldn't?"

His smile was so *knowing* that a slow blush started creeping up my cheeks.

"What did you see?"

"You, Noon. I saw you."

We stared at each other for a few moments. Oh, Luck. Had Rafe been given a memory like the one Fara had been given?

The bonfire wasn't exactly the hottest part of the memory . . .

Had Rafe been given one of Ari's memories? Of me? I squirmed and broke eye contact. But the tall reedy wall surrounding us offered no inspiration on how to extricate myself from this perilously awkward social situation so I turned back to Rafe. He was still looking at me, but his carefully carefree look was gone. I didn't know what this new expression meant. I'd never seen it on Rafe's face before. I glanced out at the river. Ari was rowing the boat back toward the shore.

"I think I figured it out," I said quickly. Rafe raised his eyebrows. His lips curved in the slightest hint of a smile.

"The whirlpool at Ebony's End mashed up our memories," I continued. "It took one from each of us and gave it to someone else."

Rafe's smile fell. The carefully carefree look was back.

"I got yours," I said.

"Oh?" His tone was flat.

I wasn't sure how to begin. I glanced at his silver bracelet again. The one with the word "Bhereg" etched on it and the date his brother died.

Rafe's gaze followed mine. "Which memory was it, Noon?" His voice was harsher. "You know, I have so many *happy* ones."

I winced. "It was your brother's funeral." When he didn't say anything, I said, "I know what happened, Rafe."

He looked at me disbelievingly. Ari dragged the skiff onto the beach.

"You couldn't possibly. Or you wouldn't still be sitting here." I couldn't sense Rafe's mood or feelings the way I could with Ari, but it was pretty clear he was in pain. I pointed to the bracelet. The fact that Rafe wore it told me I was doing the right thing. Even though the memory was painful, he *wanted* to remember.

"Does Bhereg mean 'brother' or was that his name?"

Rafe clenched his fist and stood up, glancing over at Ari and Russ. He looked back down at me, his expression contemplative. After a few moments, he offered his hands to help me up. I slipped my hands into his. They were rough and strong and smooth and gentle all at the same time.

"It means 'white' or 'bright,'" he said, pulling me to my feet. "I named him."

We stood for a minute, hand in hand, staring at each other. Somehow, I felt guilty that I couldn't feel his pain. But then again, that wasn't really true. Because I could. Through his own memory.

"It was an accident," I whispered, lightly squeezing his hands. Although it wasn't part of the memory, I imagined six-year-old Rafe holding his infant brother, trying to soothe the crying child so his mother could rest, walking down the uneven boards of his family's weathered pier . . . tripping . . . falling . . . and Bhereg . . . tumbling from Rafe's arms into the Lethe. Had Rafe dived in after him?

"Can you even swim?" I blurted out. Rafe squeezed my

hands then, but way too hard. I flinched, instinctively yanking them back.

"I can now." He laughed viciously and stuffed his hands in his back pockets. "What was the funeral like?"

"Sad."

Rafe nodded. His expression edged back into nonchalance. But I knew now that his outward attitude of uncaring was as much a mask of his true self as the glamour Fara wore.

He turned to go.

"Wait!" I said, grabbing his arm. He looked down at my hand and then back at me. "Rafe . . ."

I didn't know what I wanted to say to him. That I was sorry? Of course I was. But I'd already said that to him once already and now it didn't seem nearly enough. That he shouldn't feel guilty? Who wouldn't? That I wished the accident hadn't happened? But it had and nothing I said would change that.

"I wish I'd been given your memory of the accident and not just the funeral," I finally said. "I wish . . . I wish I could take away your pain, Rafe. There are some things we're better off not remembering."

Oddly, impossibly, he laughed. "So now *you* want to cast Clean Conscience over *me*? There's a reason I never learned that spell, Noon. There are some things even an Angel can't believe in."

"Don't say that."

"I guess what Peter Aster said about you is true."

I stiffened. "What's that?"

"That you've got a healer's heart."

It was impossible to tell if it was a compliment or a criticism. We stood, staring at each other in the dark, nearly squaring off. About what, I couldn't have said. Something had changed between us. Finally I said:

"Are you going to give Ari back his memory?"

"The one of you?" Rafe said softly.

Before I could answer, Ari walked over to us.

Rafe winked at me. "Not a chance," he murmured and slipped off in the direction of Russ and Fara.

Ari gave me a puzzled look. His signature felt fizzy, like sparkling wine. The kind that went to your head, made you giddy and do questionable things. He smiled and reached for me.

"You'll never guess where we are."

"The deepest part of the Secernere."

Ari raised his eyebrows in surprise. "How'd you know?"

Turned out the deepest part of the Secernere was only a very long day's row from the Shallows. Between Russ' calculations and the rudimentary map on the cover page of his almanac, Russ was able to direct us to our original destination by late afternoon the next day. Throughout that day, as we rowed farther and farther east, the land around us got greener and greener. It was a color I wasn't used to seeing in such abundance. Last semester, it might have enchanted me, but now it just felt . . . wrong. Off. Which was silly because these eastern hinterlands looked exactly as they should: swampy, heavy, wet, and dripping in myriad shades of olive-tinged sepia, sage, ash, and iron.

Cypress and tupelo gum trees crowded the swamp. They stood tall and straight, flanking one another, nearly as numerous, and as forbidding looking, as the demons must have looked in Luck's lost Host army. The trees thickened the farther we went into the swamp so that it appeared almost as if they were advancing on us, pressing in on us, more than the demons of the rush lands ever had. The trees grew right up to the edge of the Secernere. Some even dipped so low over the water's edge, we had to duck under them to pass.

Moss hung from the trees like greenish gray hair or the frayed and faded cloaks of folks caught and hung here. It was very disconcerting. No fewer than six times an hour I swore I saw someone moving toward us, on the ground or in the trees, but when I turned to gaze at them directly, I saw only moss . . . hanging, swaying, swinging, though there was no wind that I could feel. It became exhausting. My heart would seize, my hands would clench, my signature would redline . . . and then, when the movement turned out to be imagined, I had to force myself to relax. Slow my breathing, unclench my fists, and expand my signature from the tight little ready-to-explode ball it had wrapped itself into.

My muscles became cramped. With six people in the boat, plus Virtus, there was no room to move around. Standing up was out of the question. Luck forbid an ill-chosen step dumped everyone into the water. I peered over the edge of the boat for the nth time that day, half-fearful of and half-wanting to lower my hand into the water and kill all the green duckweed coating the surface of the river. Rowing down this section of the Secernere was like rowing down the back of a thick green snake. Each piece of duckweed was as shiny and shimmery as a scale. For one wild moment, I imagined the whole river might be one giant slithering water demon. But then I blinked and the illusion vanished. But not the tension.

After going through Ebony's Elbow, I'd said I wanted to push on to the Shallows because, if there was any chance of still finding Athalie, or preventing further disappearances out here in the swamp, I wanted to do that. But as we got closer and closer to the Shallows, I became less and less sure of my plan. I'd started to think Grimasca might be behind the attacks on us and the disappearances in the Shallows. But I'd based that theory on nothing more than coincidence and hearsay. I needed to begin my investigation with Vodnik, the accused.

What exactly was I going to say to him when we arrived?

Prior to the catastrophic losses from two nights ago, we'd at least have shown up on equal footing with the outpost lord. Arriving in the Shallows on the luxuriously appointed dahabiya *Cnawlece* would have made a statement about who we were, what we represented, and the power and authority behind our visit. Forget about the lost letter of introduction. My inability to fulfill that social and legal formality was laughable compared to the other grave breaches of protocol I'd be making when I showed up in a twelve-foot wooden dinghy with no food or clothing, seeking shelter for my investigative team, a former *Cnawlece* crew member, and care for its unnaturally unconscious demon captain.

Oh, and by the way, Lord Vodnik, I'm also here to determine if you killed your own followers and, if so, to execute you for it.

Yeah, right. The new introduction I imagined for tonight's landing in the Shallows was bound to be even worse than the one I'd imagined at the start of our trip. Luckily, I didn't have to wait long for it to occur.

Sometime around late afternoon, I noticed a thinning in the vegetation off to the right side of the Secernere. Ten minutes, two twists of the river, and at least a hundred more oar strokes and an unmistakable clearing appeared. The swampy land from here until the next turn in the river was brown, instead of green. Instead of trees, there were small wooden huts on raised platforms with roofs made from thatched grass or jagged pieces of rusty tin. I wondered idly if Rafe knew the spell Unlockjaw.

As our tiny boat made its way east past the settlement, the only sound I could hear was the sound of our dripping oars as Ari slowly rowed us closer to the shore. The slowing splashes broke my traveling trance as much as the transition from green to brown had.

We were here.

It was a mark of our exhaustion (or a visceral reaction to our visibly depressing destination) that there was no show of excitement. Everyone stayed quiet and still. The whole trip had been that way, what with the cramped conditions of the boat, taking turns at the oars, having slept on the ground out in the open last night, not to mention the still-recent shock of having lost nearly everything but our lives.

The thing was, though, it was quiet and still in the settlement next to us. There wasn't a sound coming from those huts or the cleared area beyond them. It made the hair stand up on my arms. Just before the Secernere made a sharp turn to the right, a small, rickety-looking wooden pier jutted out into the river. When I saw it, my first irrational thought was that maybe it was best that we hadn't arrived on *Cnawlece* because if *Cnawlece* had tried to dock there it would have ripped it clean out of its moorings. The dock itself was only the tiniest bit bigger than the boat we were in.

At the end of the short dock was a wooden shack. This one had a tin roof, although it looked slightly less rusty than the others we'd seen while rowing, and the building itself was bigger. But not by much. Ari maneuvered the dinghy right up to the side of the pier. Rafe stepped out of the boat and held it next to the dock. There were no ropes, either on the dock or in the boat. Virtus leapt out immediately. The fact that Virtus wasn't hissing, spitting, or growling meant there was likely no immediate danger. But that still left all the hours until nightfall and every single one of them after that to worry about.

"Do you feel any demons?" I asked Rafe. I'd poked fun of Rafe and his silly spell titles, but the fact was, Demon Net might be the only thing that would alert us to the presence of either of the two hellcnights that had already attacked us. If the hellcnight who'd climbed on board *Cnawlece* or the one that had impersonated Ebony and killed Burr had used those encounters to adjust to Ari's and my signatures, then they could now mask themselves around us and we wouldn't be able to sense them the next time we encountered them.

Rafe nodded. "There's a demon on the other side of that shack, some distance away, but coming toward us." I felt it too. I tensed and swallowed. I didn't feel any waning magic blur, which meant the demon coming toward us had to be either Vodnik or one of the hellcnights who'd already attacked us. Or possibly Grimasca himself, if he was powerful enough to mask himself during a first encounter with no telltale hellcnight blur.

Fara cast a simple levitation spell to lift Delgato out of

the boat and then she and Rafe cast Impenetrable over everyone, even Virtus, just as a precaution. Ari dragged the dinghy over to the shallow muddy edge of the river next to the pier and pulled it up on the bank. Together we walked over to the shack's small, wooden door.

Should we knock?

Some outposts had guardhouses, but this ramshackle building hardly looked up to that task. I thought it much more likely that, due to the unusual nature of the route we'd taken to get here, we'd inadvertently arrived at the Shallows' back door. My guess was that this rickety hut was a storage area for fishing supplies, crab pots, and the like. I reached out to clasp the latch and paused.

What if the door was enchanted?

Before I could touch it, Rafe reached for it.

"Heraldry is an Angel's job. Allow me"—and he brushed my hand aside and stepped in front of me.

Chapter 20

ಶ

The door was locked, which gave Rafe pause for only a moment before he murmured a spell and the latch popped like the buckle on a too-tight pair of pants. Tentatively, he pressed the door open and peered inside. All I could see through the door was blackness. The little shed had no windows.

Rafe pushed his way in and then motioned for us to follow. Once we were inside and my eyes adjusted to the darkness, I could see the contents of the shed were exactly as I'd suspected, which eased my fears not at all. I couldn't imagine the rest of this visit would go as predictably, or that our findings would be as innocuous as a few fishing poles, a tackle box, ten crab pots, and two birdcages.

Slowly, our group made our way through the tiny shed to the door on the other side. That one wasn't locked. The five of us, plus Virtus and Delgato's uncannily levitating form, exited the shed into what lay beyond, which was, for a moment, the reverse of what we'd experienced entering the shed. We stood clustered together, blinded by bright sunlight. For one brief second, I was paralyzed by fear.

Nearly every demon I'd ever met had been horrible. Serafina had been small, but had burned Ivy and almost killed her. I shuddered recalling Nergal, my client from last semester. Lamia, his wife, had been even worse. Jezebeth may have been loved by Ynocencia but he'd killed multiple people, and his horns, claws, and jaws had inspired a healthy dose of fear in me. Delgato had been the only decent demon I'd ever met and even he had induced mild heart palpitations the first time we'd met. So, needless to say, I was braced for someone awful.

The demon that stood before me was awful, but not as bad as I'd braced for. He was large and imposing, with well-muscled arms and a strong face. His hair and beard flowed nearly to the ground, looking creepily like the moss that had hung from the trees we'd just rowed through. His skin had a slick sheen to it that reminded me of the Secernere's duckweed, but its color was darker, duller. He wore a dark brown, leather-belted tunic with a small, short, rust-colored cloak. The cloak was fastened with an elaborate iron pin. His eyes were greenish gold with thin black slits for pupils. We blinked at each other and instinctively I stepped back. The demon's signature felt sluggish, but there was definitely *something* about him that warned he could strike at any moment.

Surrounding the demon, in a great big hovering flock, was a gaggle of children. They appeared to range in age from two to twelve and were covered in mud. It was on their clothes, their skin, even in their hair. But they looked happy enough and, I was surprised and pleased to see, they didn't look nearly as thin as I'd thought the children of the Shallows might be. They hopped up and down, chirping and chattering excitedly, and pointing at us with crooked fingers and flailing arms.

The demon opened his mouth and uttered a greeting—in a language I'd never heard before. I have no idea what he said, but the children rushed to us then, laughing, and those who could get near enough to do so, embraced us. I nearly fell over from the force of their exuberance. Ari's signature was steady and alert. I sensed from him that he was slightly bemused by this welcome but still wary. I doubted Ari ever let down his guard for long, and certainly not while meeting outpost lords accused of murdering their own people.

At first, the children kept a respectful distance from Virtus. I imagined none of them had ever seen a tiger before. Natural beasts were much more common in Warja than in Halja. But it was clear they had the same fascination with Virtus that Russ had had when he'd first laid eyes on him when we were loading up in New Babylon almost six weeks ago. In the time since, Virtus had grown bigger. His coat was sleeker and his frame leaner. Fara motioned to the children who were closest to Virtus, encouraging them to approach him and give him a pat. For his part, Virtus looked positively smitten with all the attention. I swore I could almost hear the rumble of his throaty purr over the incomprehensible high-pitched chirps and squeals of the children. I glanced at Rafe and Fara.

What language was spoken here in the Shallows?

The demon complaints had both been written in the Haljan common tongue. So some of these children must know it. Though I realized, while listening to all the squawking and screeching, that it probably wasn't their first language. Rafe was leaning over toward a group of children, conversing fluently, apparently telling them something amazing because their eyes grew as wide as the whirlpool we'd passed through to get here. After answering a few more questions in this strange-sounding language of theirs, Rafe ruffled the top of one of the boys' heads, a wistful expression on his face, and stood up, looking toward me.

"Avian," he said, answering my unspoken but assumed question.

Interesting, I thought. *Who would have guessed?* Even if Lambert Jeffries had agreed to work with me, his Aquaian would have been useless here. Somehow it didn't surprise me that Rafe knew Avian. I was betting he knew lots of demon languages that he hadn't yet told me about.

Rafe grinned at me and then turned to address Vodnik formally. Since Rafe was my Guardian and I was the lead investigator, it fell to him. He raised his hands above his head, palms down, and immediately the children grew quiet. Vodnik eyed Rafe with rapt attention. In a strong, clear voice Rafe uttered a series of guttural whorls and warbles, interspersed with a few tweets and chirps. Knowing the Angels' penchant for theatrics in general and Rafe's preference for silliness in particular (regardless of the number of life-threatening situations we'd faced together, or the somberness of some of his own memories, I could never forget that this was the man who'd said he knew the spells Pat on the Back, Ladies Man, and Wet 'n Wild), Rafe could have made a mockery of the introduction. But instead he appeared to infuse his unnatural speech patterns with all of the gravitas appropriate for the situation.

As he had when making our introduction to Delgato, he made a few sounds, likely noises describing our names, places of origin, and family connections, and then gestured to each of us so that we could acknowledge Vodnik and his crowd of tiny followers. As each of us nodded or bowed, Rafe chirped a few extra words. In response, the children's faces reflected varying levels of amusement, awe, horror, or fascination. I got the impression Rafe was telling them the story of how we'd arrived there, as well as each of our parts in the story (no doubt with a healthy amount of exaltation and glorification). When it was my turn, I nodded to Vodnik, and Rafe added whatever chirpy codicil he'd come up with for me. It was longer than the others and throughout there were audible cries of alarm and then, finally, sighs of delight. At the end, Rafe clasped his hands to his heart in an intentionally exaggerated romantic gesture reminiscent of a swooning lover as he once again gestured toward me. The children laughed and I felt the barest uptick in Ari's signature. He narrowed his eyes at Rafe. Like me, I'm sure he wondered what was being said about us, but since the audience for Rafe's show was mostly children, I couldn't imagine it was anything too untoward.

Throughout all of it, Vodnik appeared expressionless and patient. I could not have said what he thought about either Rafe's introduction or our presence in his outpost. But then he made his position clear.

"Welcome, friends," Vodnik said haltingly in words I recognized. "We have been waiting for you. I know Zella wrote to the Council for help. The Demon of Hunger has found his way to the Shallows and has taken many."

I worked hard to keep my expression neutral and my signature steady. Vodnik didn't realize we were here to investigate *him*. That Zella's complaint named him as a possible suspect. Or that Athalie's complaint named him as the accused. Of course, it was equally possible that Vodnik knew those things and he was just a good liar.

"Ask Lord Vodnik who he believes the Demon of Hunger is," I instructed Rafe. Even before Rafe finished interpreting Vodnik's response, though, I had a partial answer. The look on the children's faces when Vodnik uttered the sounds that must have meant "Grimasca" was a mirroring of the demon's other moniker, "The Grim Mask of Death."

Ari asked, "Why does Lord Vodnik think it was Grimasca, a legendary and mythical figure who is so old no one is even certain he's real, and not another hellcnight or some other *rogare* demon, that caused the disappearance of his followers?"

Rafe interpreted Ari's question. I was beginning to worry we might stand here all night, swapping chirpy questions with a demon who was under heavy suspicion, and get nowhere with the investigation, an eventuality I could barely bear to contemplate after all we'd been through. But instead, in response to Ari's question, Vodnik pulled two items out of the pocket of his brown tunic and showed them to us. One was a butcher's knife. The other was a small silver spice box with the words "For Ebony" engraved on it. I stared at them, not understanding.

Vodnik and Rafe thereafter engaged in a lengthy Avian

discussion. After a few moments, Rafe turned to the rest of us and explained. Apparently Vodnik's lawman Stillwater had found these items out in the Meadow where the men had been fishing. Everyone knew Grimasca's favorite alias was a butcher, although not as many knew Ebony had been his lover. Regardless, the two items were Grimasca's and finding them at the scene of the sin the day after it happened was evidence enough for Vodnik of Grimasca's guilt.

Well, huh. After that tortured analysis, interpretation, and explanation, I was half-inclined to dig Alba's black onion out of my pocket and ask it what *it* thought. I would have loved to have gotten a better view of both the butcher knife and the silver spice box but Vodnik had already re-pocketed them. Vodnik observed me keenly. I wondered if his next question would be about the fact that I was a woman with waning magic. But the outpost lord surprised me. He chirped a few notes to Rafe, who then said to me:

"He wants to know what saved us in the Elbow. What saved us from drowning?"

I looked over at Fara. She'd changed her glamour when we'd arrived. She was now dressed in white pants and a mottled brown and white feather vest. Her hair was slicked back and her eyes were ringed with great big black kohl circles. She looked wise and owl-like. I smiled at her and winked.

"Faith and an anchor," I said.

Vodnik scowled. "They say Ebony was Grimasca's anchor," he croaked in the common tongue. I stared at him.

"How do you know so much about Ebony and Grimasca?" I said, suddenly suspicious. Vodnik screeched a curt answer to Rafe.

"He said the Shallows are less than a day's row from the Elbow. Do we think we're the first people to have passed through it on the way here?"

There was another exchange between Vodnik and Rafe and Rafe continued.

"We can stay the night. Tomorrow, Stillwater, the outpost gerefa, will take us out to the Meadow where the fishermen disappeared. We can start our hunt there."

As bucolic as "the Meadow" sounded, I couldn't help wondering if we would end up disappearing there too . . .

The Shallows was a large triangular piece of land bordered by the Secernere, the Blandjan, and a low stone wall that ran for approximately half a mile between them. We'd come into the settlement from its back door on the Secernere. I gathered the fact that we'd arrived via Ebony's Elbow gave us just as much, if not more, notoriety than the fact that we'd been sent by the Council "to help."

On the Blandjan side of the Shallows, there was a much larger pier, one that, while nothing like its counterparts in New Babylon, would have been sufficient for docking *Cnawlece* alongside. As I'd suspected, since Vodnik made his home here and his own waning magic would have killed off any vegetation long ago, the interior of the Shallows was completely devoid of the trees, moss, weeds, and reeds we'd seen so much of on the way here. Instead, the ground was either mud, standing water, dried wood chips, or some combination of all three. The settlers' homes were small wooden huts that stood elevated on six-foot-high pilings. Front "doors" were made of cloth in various shades of mud-splattered olive, lichen, rust, and root. Often, laundry lines were hung across the fronts of the huts, and clothes (looking like they'd been sewn from the same cloth as the door curtains) hung on the lines to dry. It was going to take a while. Because the humidity here was even worse than it had been on the river.

At least on the river, there'd been occasional breezes. Here, the air was still. The numerous puddles of standing water throughout the settlement acted like giant mirrors, reflecting the grim, dull, gray existence that I imagined was the settlers' lives.

No one else greeted us, which seemed strange, so I asked Rafe to ask one of the children where their parents were. I didn't know whether to be relieved or worried when I found out most of the men were on the river fishing and most of the women were in the swamp tending gardens or gathering food. The rest were at Stone Pointe, an old giants' house that had been built at the tip of the Shallows' triangle.

Stone Pointe was now Vodnik's keep. It wasn't quite a castle (the home I'd grown up in looked more like a true castle than this structure), but it looked like it had wanted to be one, like it might have been one, had it been allowed to grow old somewhere else. But instead it had grown old here, on soft muddy ground, in an area where most buildings' life spans were half a man's, if that.

Stone Pointe was surrounded by a moat, but as I looked more closely, I thought it hadn't been an intentional one. The keep was made of stone. Here and there I could see half-submerged window frames—open holes in the foundation that allowed a watery sludge to flow in and out, under, and all around the slowly sinking building. My guess was that the weight of the walls had caused them to sink into the mud. And, over time, with repeated flooding, what once may have been high ground became low ground. I imagined, after the first few floods, the early settlers might have even tried to dig this keep back out of the muck, an unfortunate practice that likely contributed to the building's odd moat and all but guaranteed further flooding of the lower floors.

The moat had two arms, both of which stretched to the Blandjan, but in opposite directions, one east, one west, nearly paralleling the course of the river a few acres away. Here, on the eastern Lethe, the thick, stagnant muck of the moat was just one hard rain away from being rushing white water. Someday, if the Lethe chose to spawn a new tributary for itself as it had at Second Branch, then the Shallows would likely be cut in half or completely submerged, the foundation of this old stone keep, and maybe even its people, lost forever.

Mercator had told us earlier this semester that Vodnik had established the Shallows in 1593, over four centuries ago. But this keep looked even older than that. I tipped my

head back to gaze at the crumbling stone leviathan that
must have been the settlers' first home.

*How many floors of this keep had sunk by 1593? How
many times had it flooded since? How many times had it
been rebuilt? How many men had it taken? Had anyone died doing it? Who had drowned here? Been born
here? Married here? Loved . . . lost . . . cried . . . plotted
revenge . . . granted forgiveness?*

I stared at it, thinking that this hulking, half-whole, inanimate chimera was the unbeating heart of the Shallows—
and probably the key to understanding its people. They'd
built their settlement in the shadow of a giant's house. My
guess was the Hyrkes of the Shallows would stay until
Stone Pointe washed away.

We walked across the small wooden bridge (it was
really little more than a few dozen boards held together
with dried vines) that had been constructed over the moat.
While crossing, I peered at the bubbly sludge on either side.
Could things live in there? If so, it must be like swimming
in quicksand. Stone Pointe grew bigger. I heard the clomping of footsteps, duller sounding than they'd been on the
pier, as Fara, Virtus, and Russ crossed behind me. Rafe and
Ari were in front, following Vodnik. The children waited
until we were across and then they scampered over in twos
and threes, scattering around us as we clustered in a group
in front of the keep's entrance.

Vodnik sent one of the children into the keep. A few
moments later a young woman emerged. She was much
cleaner than the mud-caked child who'd gone to fetch her.
In fact, she looked bleached, almost anemic. Despite that,
and the lean circumstances of the settlement she lived in,
she looked well fed and had a fragile beauty that seemed at
home here in the swamps. She reminded me of pearlescent
featherfoil, the floating river plant with translucent stems
and small white flowers that we'd seen so much of on our
way here. The woman wore a shapeless dress and her thin,
chamomile-colored hair was held back by a plain leather
tie. She smiled at us, but it was strained and uneasy. She

had no signature, but even I could sense something wasn't quite right. She stood away and apart from us, and from Vodnik.

And that's when I realized she was pregnant. *That's* why she wasn't coming any closer.

I forced myself to relax. Obviously, she knew to stay back. The people of the Shallows wouldn't have survived this long if they didn't know to keep their breeding females away from waning magic users. Vodnik and Rafe exchanged a few words in Avian. Rafe nodded in understanding and approached the young woman, uttering a series of squawks. Despite the language barrier, even I could understand Rafe's message: *Beware!* The woman, looked at Ari and then at me, her face a mixture of morbid curiosity and trepidation. Ari glanced over at me, concerned, I supposed, about how I was taking this less than warm welcome. He needn't have worried. It was a reaction I now expected in one out of every three introductions. Further and more importantly, Vodnik's next words, a stuttering introduction of the girl in our language, had my mind skipping ahead like a gramophone needle over an analog disc record.

"This is my inamorata, Zella," Vodnik said, motioning to the fair-haired, pregnant woman.

Huh, I thought, *now that's information that wasn't in the case file.*

Zella Rust, the woman who'd written the second demon complaint—the one that had stopped a mere hairsbreadth away from accusing Vodnik outright of murdering her eight-year-old sister—was Vodnik's lover. I stared at her bulging belly in horror wondering if the child had a Hyrke father . . . or if Luck had "gifted" her with a drakon child for lying with Vodnik. Hadn't Fara said it was usually only the inamoratas of greater demons that were "favored" that way? I hoped so! And I imagined Zella did too since there were no Mederies within a few thousand miles of this place . . .

Chapter 21

ཚ

We were given huts to sleep in. I gathered that, due to the unfortunate disappearance of the fishermen earlier in the spring, there were more than enough. They were as sparse on the inside as they looked from the outside, but at least their thatched roofs would keep the rain off at night. Delgato was given into the care of Meghan Brun, the outpost cearian or nurse. Meghan looked slightly older and less wary of us than Vodnik's other followers had. I'd thought that a good thing since she was on my list of people to speak with. (Both her and Thomas Stillwater, the outpost gerefa, or lawman, had been listed as possible witnesses in my now-lost case file.) On the whole, I thought our introduction and immersion into this strange place had gone well. It was a feeling I tried to ignore. Past experience made me realize that acknowledging good fortune in the midst of an assignment usually resulted in reversing it.

We were invited to dine at Stone Pointe. Meghan gave us all clean clothes and let us wash up in the med shack. The water in the wooden tub was cold, but the soap was more than welcome and I sat there shivering and scrubbing, just grateful to finally be getting the smell of the river off my skin and out of my hair. Getting it out of my nose and memory would take at least as long as it took to get back to New Babylon, perhaps a lifetime.

I toweled off and put on the loose linen pants and long-sleeved tunic that Meghan had left, glancing at Delgato out of the corner of my eye. He was sleeping peacefully on the cot farthest from the door. I tied a thin leather cord around my tunic as a belt, tied my hair back with another, and walked over to him. I leaned down and put my hand on his chest. *Nothing.* I couldn't even feel a whiff of his signature. *When would he wake up?* I'd only slept for three days. But then again, the hellcnight had only nicked my neck, whereas it had severely bitten Delgato.

When I emerged from the med shack, Ari was waiting for me. He'd cleaned up as well and now wore the same earthly colored pants and tunic that I did. His tunic wasn't belted, though, and his shoulder-length chestnut-colored hair was unbound. After the hellcnight's attack, he'd let his beard grow out. His chin and cheeks were now completely obscured by a full, black beard.

His signature softened when he saw me and he offered me an elbow. Together, we walked from the med shack to an area near the center of the Shallows, a large cleared patch of ground where a campfire had been lit in the shadow of the stone keep. I'd been told that this was where Vodnik and his followers ate every night, so long as the weather didn't drive everyone inside. It certainly wouldn't tonight, although there were hints that another storm like the one we'd seen only two nights ago might be on its way.

To the west, the inky silhouettes of the shaggy swamp trees swayed against the iridescent amethyst hue of early nightfall. To the north, black human shapes gathered around the crisp, crackling orange red light of the fire. Specks of black, gray, and silver ash floated in lazy circles amidst a swirling haze of smoke. I couldn't help thinking that I was looking at a scene that had repeated itself for over four hundred years. Surely, if Vodnik was capable of killing his own people, scenes of simple communal domestic tranquility such as the one I was watching would be impossible. Right?

"Noon," Ari said, stopping me before we reached the campfire, or the area within which anyone might overhear us. "If it comes to it, I can execute Vodnik for you."

He might just as well have splashed freezing cold water in my face.

I sputtered. "We don't even know that Vodnik's guilty."

Ari gave me a tight smile. His signature receded. I recognized the signs. He was going to say something I wouldn't like.

"How likely is it that *Grimasca* killed those fishermen and that girl?"

I frowned. It was impossible to miss the sarcasm in Ari's voice. "What about the fact that we were attacked—twice—on the way here by hellcnights? Don't you think that's a little too coincidental?"

"Hellcnights exist. I'm not saying *they* don't. I'm just saying I don't think their legendary leader exists. Or ever did. I think Grimasca is a bedtime story mothers made up," he said.

"Rafe said Grimasca was the one demon you never wanted to meet, the one demon you'd be deeply afraid of."

Ari's patient, slightly patronizing expression transformed into one of slight disbelief and mild humor, with just the slightest hint of jealousy. "You'd take Raphael Sinclair's advice about a demon over mine?"

"Maybe they drowned or got lost," I said. I didn't really believe it, but I felt we had to consider every possibility.

Ari raised his brows. "How likely is it that a group of fifteen men, born and raised here in the swamps, all drowned or got lost?"

"Very," I argued. "What if they stumbled into quicksand or stepped into a newly formed tributary that was covered with weeds and reeds?"

"Then how do you explain the butcher knife and the silver spice box that was found where the fishermen disappeared?"

I frowned in confusion. "If you think those items are vital clues, why do you think Vodnik is the demon who's responsible for the disappearances?"

Ari exhaled and looked away. I could tell from his stance and signature that he wasn't any more certain of his theory than I'd been of mine. Which was to say, we'd each formed a gut opinion about which demon was responsible based on the evidence so far. It just happened to be that we each thought a different demon did it.

Finally, Ari sighed and met my gaze. "I think Vodnik found the butcher knife and the spice box near the Elbow and planted them in the Meadow for Stillwater to find. I think he's lying. I think he knows that Zella suspects him and he's desperate to pin the blame on another demon."

"Vodnik has been the outpost lord here for four hundred years, Ari. That's over thirteen generations of harmonious living thrown away because . . . why? What's his motive? Why kill those fishermen? And why an eight-year-old girl? It doesn't make sense."

Ari paused, considering my words. Then he shrugged. "Maybe he just needed fewer mouths to feed. You know what they say about lying? 'The best lies are the truth in disguise.' Vodnik said, 'The Demon of Hunger found his way to the Shallows and took many.' Maybe he wasn't lying when he said that. But, if so, he meant the *mythical* Grimasca, not the real one."

It was my turn to pause and consider. Ari's arguments were as convincing as mine. I realized the worst thing that could happen in this investigation would be to speak to everyone, investigate the Meadow, turn out every shack in the Shallows, and the Stone Pointe keep, and find *nothing*. Nothing else to go on but the evidence we currently had. My choice would then be to execute a potentially innocent outpost lord or leave these people with their possibly murderous patron.

I made a sound of disgust, knowing we wouldn't solve anything tonight. But there was one more thing I had to say.

"Ari . . ." I said slowly, "I couldn't be more grateful for your presence here. But I'm *Primoris* and I'm going to make the final decision. And . . ." I looked over at the purple sky, wondering why it had to look so pretty when we were talking about something so ugly. I looked back at Ari and stared him straight in the eyes. "I don't want you covering for me the way you did with Jezebeth's execution. Whatever needs to be done . . . *I'll* do it."

We stared at each other for a few minutes. Then he nodded and kissed my forehead.

"Know what they're roasting for dinner tonight?"

I shook my head.

"River slugs." And then he laughed and pulled me in the direction of Vodnik, his followers, and the fire.

Thankfully, even in the Shallows where food was extraordinarily scarce, there was more on the menu than just river slugs. There was also bloodfish, bonemeal grits, and stewed swamp greens. I don't know what Burr or Alba would have made of it all. It was hard to complain when these people so willingly shared their food with us.

The campfire was lined with huge logs that had been pulled from the swamp so long ago the bark had been worn down to a shiny smooth surface. I estimated that there were a little over a hundred and fifty people gathered around the site. A core group of about twenty congregated around the fire and the rest ate on logs, blankets, or just while standing, in groups of threes and fours all around the edges. It looked like the outer groups were families, catching up with one another after being apart for the day.

Their cooing, warbling, whistling, and trilling were infinitely preferable to the dry clacking and wet snuffling sounds the *rogare* demons made at night, but I did wonder what they were all talking about. It wasn't like they were complaining about the Lethe commuter ferries or the amount of work that was still waiting for them back at the office. But then again, none of them had that frazzled, harried, one-beat-short-of-a-heart-attack look that most New Babylonians had either. Maybe we were all on our way to an early grave and it was just a matter of how we wanted to accomplish it.

After choking down a bowl of swamp greens and a few bites of bloodfish, I suggested that Ari keep Vodnik occupied so that I could speak with some of his followers. He agreed and I walked over to where Rafe stood to enlist his help. Even if some of these people spoke the common tongue, it was clear that Avian was their preferred language.

"What are they all saying?" I said without preamble when I reached Rafe. "You never translate anything they say *verbatim*. I want to know what they're talking about."

Rafe looked at me quizzically. He always seemed to be evaluating me. *Shouldn't it be the other way around?*

"Do you think it would help your investigation?"

"Maybe," I said, turning toward the settlers.

Rafe gave me a funny little smile. "*Verbatim*'s not a word in their vocabulary."

"Well, what is?"

He looked around, assessing candidates, and finally zeroed in on a young couple standing at the edge of the group. They were facing each other, speaking Avian in low chirps and long sonorous notes. Rafe listened intently to them for a few minutes and then turned to me.

He gently took my hand in his and placed it on his chest, as the young man had just done to the woman. The fire reflected back in Rafe's bronze-flecked, fawn-colored eyes, making them look like shimmering bits of gold.

"Shelter with me tonight," he said. I blinked, forgetting for a moment that he was repeating what the man had said to the woman.

When I didn't react, Rafe leaned toward me until he was close enough for his breath to tickle my face. Then he winked and whispered, "She said, 'Kiss me and convince me.'" He looked expectantly at me, like I might actually repeat his words and play the part.

I yanked my hand free. "You're a terrible Angel, Raphael Sinclair. All I asked was for you to translate what some of these people were saying. And you can't even do that without turning it into a joke!"

He grinned at me. "Who says I was joking? I was just doing my job. Translating, like you asked me to." He motioned back to the couple, who were now kissing passionately, ardently.

I rolled my eyes. "Rafe, get serious. It's time to work. I want to interview Zella Rust. Tonight. And Meghan Brun too if we can."

He nodded and appeared to get serious (with Rafe you could never tell) and looked around the campfire area. We spotted the women at the same time. Conveniently, they were sitting together on a ratty-looking blanket near the edge of the clearing.

"Come on, then," Rafe said, motioning me toward them. We walked over to where the two women sat eating their dinner (I saw that Zella had chosen the same meal I had, whereas Meghan had gone for the roasted slugs). Not wanting to get too close to Zella, I sat down on an empty log that was a few feet away from where they were sitting. They'd stopped talking when they saw us approach and now eyed us cautiously. I couldn't blame Zella, but it was interesting that Rafe got the same look. Their body language was very unwelcoming. Zella gave Vodnik a nervous glance.

Uh-oh. Was she afraid to speak with us? If so, that was definitely another mark against Vodnik.

As we'd agreed, Ari was occupying Vodnik's attention so he hadn't yet glanced our way, but I had a feeling he knew I was over here. Vodnik could feel my signature same as I could his.

"Ms. Rust, I'd like to talk to you about why we're here. Would you rather we speak alone?" I knew Zella spoke the common tongue. She'd written her demon complaint in it.

Meghan, I wasn't sure about. Our brief interactions earlier had been accomplished with few words, and those we had exchanged had been translated by Rafe.

"I didn't think you'd come," Zella said. Her voice was so soft I had to strain to hear it. Scooting closer was out of the question, though. I glanced at Meghan. If Zella didn't want to talk in front of her, she would have said so by now.

"You filed a demon complaint with the Council. Why didn't you think someone would come?"

Zella took a while to answer. Finally she said, "We've never met anyone in Halja outside of the Shallows. Even our Boatman was raised here. He told me the Council existed and that there really were more people in New Babylon, but I wasn't sure I believed him—until I saw you."

I tried—and likely failed—to keep the surprised look off my face. To Zella, Maegesters were as legendary as Grimasca. I gave her what I hoped was a reassuring smile.

"We exist. And we're here to help. You said your sister was missing. I assume she's still missing?"

Zella nodded, her eyes tearing slightly. I bit my lip and tried to think of the questions I wanted to ask. Seeing Zella's face and imagining the eight-year-old Athalie either dead or out in the dark swamps alone made concentrating that much harder. But I was supposed to be the "legendary" Council Maegester, right?

"Zella, do *you* believe in Grimasca?"

Zella turned to Meghan and the two exchanged a look. Meghan grunted. She'd recognized the name "Grimasca" at least, or maybe she'd understood everything so far.

"I didn't. I don't know . . . Maybe I still don't." Zella sighed. "My father and husband were among the fishermen that disappeared that day," she said. "I'll never forget the sight of Vodnik and Stillwater returning home from the Meadow alone. I just knew something horrible had happened. And all Vodnik would say about it was 'Grimasca got them.' Lots of us were . . ." She struggled to find the right word.

"Skeptical?" I said. Zella frowned. Maybe she didn't know what that word meant. "Doubting?" I prompted.

"Yes," she said gratefully, but then grew immediately somber again. "Until the next day when Stillwater returned from the Meadow with Grimasca's butcher knife and spice box."

I cleared my throat. I found it ironic that I was about to make Ari's argument. "Do you think Vodnik might have found those items somewhere else and then planted them there for Stillwater to find, so that he could blame another demon for the fishermen's disappearances?"

Zella appeared to give this suggestion serious consideration. "I don't know. Maybe." She shifted on the ground, clearly uncomfortable.

"When is your baby due?"

"Any day now." But she looked fearful instead of excited. I knew that childbirth could be risky, but there seemed more to it than that.

"Vodnik called you his inamorata. When did that relationship start? After your husband disappeared? In your condition, you can't possibly have consummated the relationship. Is he just hopeful for a future with you?"

Zella laughed harshly and looked away. Meghan squeezed her shoulder and spoke for the first time. Her voice wasn't quite as raspy as Fara's, but it was close.

"The disappearances weren't your fault," Meghan said, lightly shaking Zella as if to convince her. Zella blew out her breath and clenched the hem of her tunic in her fist. She struggled not to cry. I hated to press her, but she was the one who'd written for help. If she didn't tell me what she knew, it would be that much more difficult for me to figure out what had happened here.

"Yes, Vodnik's hopeful for a future with me," she said. "But it's not one I want." Again, she glanced nervously at Vodnik, who was still sitting with Ari. Fara had joined them. Angels were natural bards and the practice of singing for one's supper was practically pre-Apocalyptic it was so old. No one in the Shallows had ever even seen an Angel perform so, needless to say, Fara was in her element. Her crowd of twenty may as well have been twenty thousand for all the gusto, flair, and glamour she appeared to be putting into her story. No one would be looking over here anytime soon.

"Last fall we were celebrating the First Day of Darkening," Zella continued. "I had too much bog water. Antony and I had a fight and he left the fire. Vodnik asked me to come back to Stone Pointe with him." She looked up at me to gauge my reaction. I kept my face neutral. I thought I knew where the story was going, and I couldn't say I would have encouraged her, but nor was I here to pass judgment on *her* sins. Besides, no one knew more than me how easily small slipups could become monstrous mistakes.

"So you slept with Vodnik," I said softly. "And now that Antony's gone, he wants you back. For good."

Zella nodded. Meghan looked upset with me and fiercely protective of Zella. Somehow I just knew if she'd been born with waxing magic, Meghan would have been a Mederi to reckon with. But I had to ask my next question.

"Do you think Vodnik killed Antony out of jealousy?"

"No!" Meghan said. "Even if Vodnik was capable of that—and I'm not saying he is—he wouldn't kill fourteen other men and her sister to cover it up!"

I looked up at Rafe, curious to see how he was taking all this. He shrugged. At first I thought that would be his only contribution, but then he said:

"Why did Athalie go with Vodnik to check the traps the morning she disappeared? If she suspected Vodnik of killing her father, uncle, and a dozen or so other men, why did she walk into the swamps alone with him?"

"I don't know," Zella said finally. "I was on the Blandjan dock checking lines when they left."

"So she could have been forced to go?" I asked.

The two women looked at each other, considering. Then Meghan said, "I don't think so. Not without someone noticing. But there's something else you should know. I don't know if it's related or not. About a month before the fisher-men disappeared, another group of men, a smaller group, was down in the Meadow fishing by the waertree—"

"There's a waertree in the Meadow?" I said, surprised. Although I don't know why. They had to grow somewhere.

"Yes," Meghan said, waving her hand to indicate the waertree had nothing to do with what she was about to tell me. "Something bit one of the fishermen while they were fishing there. No one saw what it was, but the bite was big and nasty looking. They carried the man home. Cephas was his name. By the time they got him back here, he was al-ready passed out from the pain. I cleaned out the wound and sewed him up, but he never woke up again. Just like your captain . . . What bit him? Do you know?"

My stomach suddenly felt like it was full of ice water and someone had stuck a pin in it. The cold leaked out from my middle and into my arms and legs.

"A hellcnight," I croaked. "Where's Cephas now?"

"After three months, his family gave him to Estes," Meghan said.

I frowned. "What do you mean?"

"They put his body on a raft and floated him out into the Lethe."

"But—" *Oh, Luck. He probably drowned, then.* But thinking such thoughts was akin to blasphemy. I was a member of the Host. If anyone should believe in the exis-tence of the greater demons, it was me, right? I realized then, though, just how small my sacrifices to Estes had al-ways been. Drops of blood, small trinkets, tokens really, more representations of sacrifice than anything real. I couldn't help wondering, though . . .

If it was my last resort, would I be able to float a sleep-ing, helpless person out into the Lethe in the hope that Estes might save them?

Probably not.

"People are saying we should do the same thing for Del-gato," Meghan said.

I was just about to demur, to say something tolerant and

respectful while politely refusing, when Rafe beat me to it. But his response was seething with quiet fury.

"The Patron Demon of the Lethe will not save the Patron Demon of Shadows. If anyone here tries to float Delgato out into the river, I will turn them into a frog. And then I will step on them. Do either of you have anything else to add that may be helpful to Ms. Onyx?"

Rafe had clearly made an enemy of Meghan, but he didn't seem to care. She looked insulted and upset. Zella just looked worried.

"Grimasca was a hellcnight, right?" Zella said, close to tears again. "If Cephas was bitten by Grimasca, then it's possible that Athalie and Antony and my father and everyone else were too, and if so, they might still be out there, bitten and sleeping, instead of dead. I think"—Zella's voice got even softer—"if it were me, I'd rather be dead."

Chapter 22

ও

The snap of a twig in the dead of night sounds as loud as the mast of a tall ship breaking at the base. A thousand times that night I awoke, covered in sweat, a shiver of fear racing down my spine, whorling around my waist and into my belly, and then bursting near my navel. A thousand times, I clenched my fist and pressed it into my thigh, willing my signature not to go supernova. Sleeping in the Shallows, for me, was near impossible.

We'd regrouped after the interview with Zella Rust and Meghan Brun and swapped information. Though unsurprising, Ari and Fara confirmed my guess that they'd learned nothing while distracting Vodnik. Rafe and I shared what we'd been told, including the fact that a former follower had likely been bit by a hellcnight the month before the fishermen disappeared. In light of this unsettling revelation and our continuing mistrust of Vodnik, we'd decided, cramped though it would be, to bunk together in a hut. Between the unfamiliar outside sounds, the noise of three snoring people (Russ had elected to stay in the med

shack with Delgato) and a tiger inside, plus a running list of
questions in my head that was as long as my leg, sleep
eluded me. I pulled out Alba's black onion and stared at it.
What should I ask it? I could answer at least one of my
questions right now. But which one?

*What happened to the fifteen fishermen and Athalie?
Did they drown or get lost?* (That would be a waste of the
black onion. There was no way I was going to ask it that.)
*Did Vodnik kill them? Did Grimasca? Did another hellc-
night? Were they bitten? Were they still alive somewhere?
If so, where?* And then, once the questions started, I
couldn't stop them. They poured into my head like the river
water had poured into the boat the night *Cnawlece* went
down.

*Did Curiositas really kill Cattus? Was Delgato Cattus?
Was Grimasca real? Had he lived? If so, when? If he lived,
was he now dead? Or was he just a bedtime story mothers
told their children to make them listen?*

*Had Ebony been Grimasca's lover? Had he killed her?
If so, why? Why did Fara never quote the Book anymore? Would Rafe ever forgive himself for his brother's
death? Had Ynocencia really not known that Jezebeth
was a drakon? Did waerwater really work? Could a demon
survive a trial by waerwater and, if so, did that really
mean that he was innocent?*

*Would this black onion tell me something that would
actually help me? Or would it give me a vague nonanswer
like Fortuna's wisdom from the beginning of the semester?*
"When traveling into the unknown, sometimes the biggest
danger is the one you bring with you . . ." *What did that
even mean anyway? Had* we *brought the hellcnight to the
Shallows?*

*Would I ever remember the memory I lost when we
passed through the Elbow? What memory had Rafe been
given of me? Would Delgato ever wake up? Would we ever
make it back to New Babylon? Alive?*

I put the black onion back in my pocket. Questions were

worse than a hydra's head. If you answered one, a dozen more just sprang up in its place. Needless to say, I hardly slept that night. When we woke the next morning, low thunder was already sounding. But it seemed far off and no one (least of all me) wanted to put off the walk to the Meadow. After a quick breakfast of fried pieces of small insects and other critters I was glad not to have seen whole, we waited at Stone Pointe to meet Vodnik and his gerefa, Thomas Stillwater, who would be escorting us out to the Meadow.

We spotted Russ with Meghan. She'd apparently taken him under her wing and was now showing him how to draw water from one of the rainwater cisterns. Zella made a brief breakfast appearance and somehow managed to scarf down an entire plate of fried . . . spider legs? Lizard tails?

"I thought pregnancy made women nauseated," I said to Fara, who was standing next to me. Among the drab brown and gray of our surroundings, Fara stood out like a bright bromeliad. Her glamour this morning was peacock-patterned pants paired with a short silk cranberry red blouse and matching lip gloss. Her dowsing stick was back too.

Fara deepened her frown while watching Zella and was on the verge of responding when Vodnik approached with a man I hadn't yet met. The man was stocky and strong looking with close-cropped salt-and-pepper hair. He wore a leather cuirass, the only one I'd seen in all of the Shallows. It immediately proclaimed him as a man of stature.

"This is Thomas Stillwater, our gerefa," Vodnik said.

We introduced ourselves (I thought it would be far less time-consuming than having Rafe do it). Stillwater gave me a look that ran head to toe. "Were you really born with waning magic?" he asked in a clipped, chirpy voice.

I answered his question with a curt nod. Stillwater shook his head in disbelief, but then said, "Well, come on, then. There's a storm coming and we'd all best be back before it starts." He marched off then, glancing back only once, at

Virtus. I couldn't tell if he was wary of him or if he thought Virtus might make a good meal. I followed Stillwater, catching up to him quickly.

"How far is it to the Meadow?" But Stillwater didn't answer. He just kept on walking.

We walked from Stone Pointe, across the moat, and through the Shallows toward the stone boundary wall that separated the Shallows from the Dark Waters beyond. Except for Stillwater and me, and Fara and Virtus, our hunting party formed a straight line marching through the camp. The people of the Shallows turned out to watch us go. The children scampered up ahead of us as their parents watched from the side. Some looked up from where they were repairing tools or clothes, while others peeked out from behind their door curtains. Their faces were grim and it wasn't just the dirt. They looked like they were watching us being led to the gallows.

I think it was that, and my annoyance over Stillwater's ignoring me, that made me do it.

I lit a small fireball in my hand and held it, as if it were a toy ball I were going to throw to a dog, and then I tossed it up in the air and caught it again. I rolled the ball to the tips of my fingers, balancing it there for a moment, and then flipped my hand over and rocked the ball back and forth on the back of my hand. I gave the ball one final toss in the air. This next trick was the toughest for me—retracting my magic without a fireworks show.

I didn't even bother. I let the ball burst into a hundred small colorful sparks in the air, each one sounding louder than the last in the quiet of the morning. The children came running over to me, grinning, tweeting, and chirping. Their pleasure over my magic "trick" was heartwarming, but I hadn't performed for them. I turned to see Stillwater's reaction. Indeed, he was reassessing me with a look similar to the one he'd given Virtus earlier. I cocked an eyebrow at him.

"A morning's walk," he said. I nodded and we tromped through the wide opening in the wall. The children stayed behind.

No attempt had been made to erect a gate. We slipped through the wall without even thinking. But as we moved into the other side, a prickly feeling of apprehension came over me. It felt very much like the pre-hum of an electric storm and, indeed, as if on cue, another low rumble of thunder sounded. Beyond the wall were the gardens and gathering areas for the Shallows. I was relieved to see that a wide dirt path had already been carved out of the shallow lands we passed through. Farther off, to our left and right, I could see neat rows of unfamiliar vegetables. I couldn't be sure, but some looked blighted. Yet another reminder that hunger was as much an enemy of these people as the *rogares* and crocodiles were. We passed spindly orchards full of trees strung with cobweb-like moss and low-hanging black fruit. Whatever the fruit was, it stunk, and I actually pinched my nose shut while we passed to avoid the smell of stinging pepper laced with mold.

The dirt path turned into a rickety, sometimes rotted, boardwalk that wound and twisted through the swamp with myriad shallow sets of stairs and numerous two-, three-, even four-way forks. I tried to keep track of our route but it became increasingly difficult the deeper we went into the Dark Waters. I was tempted to ask Rafe if he knew the spell Breadcrumbs, but I knew of something better. Just as a precaution, I touched a leaf at every fork, turning it into a black marker. Should something happen to Stillwater, I wanted to make sure we could find our way back.

Beneath and beside us the swamp bubbled up in various shades of ochre, puce, and rust. It reminded me of the "water" in the moat around Stone Pointe. *Was the entire peninsula sinking?* In a hundred years (or next week) the Secernere and the Blandjan might end up merging much farther west and this whole area would then be underwater.

"Did you see Grimasca when he attacked the fishermen?" I asked Stillwater.

He grinned. His teeth were remarkably white and straight for a man who'd grown up in an area that was known for its dietary shortages.

"Course not. Wouldn't be here if I had. The bastard threw me against a tree. Knocked me out cold." Stillwater pulled a knife out of his pocket. A large one. Metal weapons weren't exactly my specialty but I thought it might have been a falchion, one of those old, single-sided short swords.

"Don't you think it's odd that you're the only one to have survived?"

Stillwater narrowed his eyes at me. We both knew what I was really saying. His survival made him a suspect as well.

"Vodnik survived. Luck must have saved us for a reason."

I grunted. It wouldn't do to question Luck's judgment and yet . . . well . . . Stillwater's survival smelled fishy to me.

The boardwalk narrowed and walking side by side became impossible. Stillwater dropped behind me. I was thankful that he couldn't sense my signature because he made me nervous creeping along behind me like that, with his unsheathed knife and his hulking, slightly unfriendly presence eyeing my rear. My magic was exponentially more powerful than him or his sword, but one sharp blow to my head would render me unconscious and unable to use it. I suddenly wished I'd taken the rear so I could stare at *his* butt, preferably with a threatening fireball in my hand.

Of course, I had no reason to believe that Stillwater intended us harm. As far as I knew, he still believed we were here solely to help him and Vodnik hunt down Grimasca. To my knowledge, neither he nor his outpost lord knew that the Rust sisters had filed demon complaints alleging that Vodnik might be murdering his own people. But it was equally possible they did and were leading us out here to be ambushed.

As we walked, that prickly feeling I'd felt along the back of my neck as we'd left the Shallows intensified. I couldn't say exactly what the impetus was, whether it was the silent Stillwater at my back, the rumbling storm threat from above, or the oozing stew of the Dark Waters all around me. But Ari must have sensed the growing tension in my signature. He called out from the front: "Angels, cast up."

* * *

It's possible that "the Meadow" was older than even Lucifer's Tomb, the archeological site that Peter and I had found last semester. If Haljan legend is to be believed, Babylonians sailed the Lethe long before Armageddon. The route to the sea was long, even then, and there were many stops. Legend says one of them was a beautiful meadow, about halfway between Babylon and the sea. The area was immense, naturally flat and cleared of all trees save one, a large tree that grew right up through its middle. It was said that the meadow's tree was awe-inspiring, nearly fifty feet around and towering hundreds of feet into the air.

It was almost impossible to believe that anything could grow beneath such massive shade, and yet, legends say that grass and flowers grew in the meadow abundantly. In late summer especially, white asphodels dotted the verdant green ground, marking it as a calm, cool place of respite for weary sailors. They say that Asphodel Meadow was a mirror image of heaven. That children played there, picnicking among the flowers, sleeping beneath the tree. But over time, the meadow grew swampy. People stopped coming, except for the Boatmen, who later used it as a different kind of resting place—one for the plague and famine victims who died following the war.

Legend says the dead loved Asphodel Meadow a hundred times more than the living ever had. For years the Boatmen's boats came bearing visitors who would never leave. Hundreds of corpses, thousands, maybe even hundreds of thousands, the sheer number of them being so vast that the ground sank beneath their weight. It was said, when Asphodel Meadow was full and could accept no more, it flooded, not with water, but with tar.

I clomped along the boardwalk that twisted through the Dark Waters in my leather boots and borrowed linen clothes, damp from perspiration and humidity, heavy in body and mind, mulishly dredging up every shred of memory I'd ever had on the legendary Asphodel Meadow or any other meadow between New Babylon and the sea.

Hadn't that tale about Grimasca from *Oude Rode Ogen, Bicho Papao, and Grimasca: Folktales for Children* had a verse in it about a meadow? One with a waertree and two streams? Maybe the two streams were the Secernere and the Blandjan. Maybe the waertree was the towering tree that had grown up in Asphodel Meadow. Maybe the meadow from "The Grim Mask of Grimasca" was Asphodel Meadow and that's where we were headed now.

"Meghan Brun told me that one of the young men from the Shallows, Cephas, was bitten by something at the Meadow. Possibly a hellcnight. Why did the fishermen come to the Meadow to fish after that?" I asked Stillwater. "Even if Vodnik came to protect them, there must have been other fishing areas. Safer ones."

"Because *Acipenser Paulus* lives in the shallow waters around the Meadow."

"Acipenser Paulus?" Not *another* demon, surely?

"A species of small swamp sturgeon. 'Small' being a relative term. They can grow to be twelve hundred pounds or more. One *Acipenser Paulus* will feed the people of the Shallows for nearly a week."

"What about Athalie?" I said. "Why did she go to the Meadow? Seems like a dangerous place to bring an eight-year-old for a walk."

"She wanted to see the place where her father died."

"You mean 'disappeared.'"

Stillwater shrugged. It was clear he thought there was no difference.

"What was Antony Rust, Zella's husband, like? Did he and Vodnik get along?"

Stillwater snorted. "Everyone in the Shallows gets along with Vodnik. He's our patron. Without him, we'd be dead. The Shallows wouldn't even exist."

But surely, even relations between a demon and his follower could become strained, especially if said demon slept with said follower's wife.

I cleared my throat, warning Stillwater that I thought his answers were evasive at best, but he didn't elaborate or provide any other information. I decided to treat him as a hostile witness.

"My Guardian knows the spell Veracity," I lied. "I can ask him to cast it over you, but there can be unintended consequences."

Stillwater stopped walking and we squared off. Everyone else stopped too. I don't know how much of our discussion they'd heard with all the thunder and our clomping on the boards and the fact that we'd been traveling in a line, but they could tell from my stance, and Ari could tell from my signature, that Stillwater wasn't being cooperative.

"Such as?" Stillwater said, calling my bluff. I glanced at Rafe, suddenly inspired by his threat from last night.

"It's been known to turn some Hyrkes into frogs." I shrugged. "But he knows Amphibian too so I'm sure we'd still be able to understand your answers. I'm sure they'd be fascinating, *and forthcoming*, with a boot pressed to your head."

Rafe flexed his hand, which made me wonder if he really did know a spell that could turn someone into a frog. Only Rafe Sinclair would learn a spell like that.

"I know why you're here," Stillwater said. "You think Vodnik killed those men. And that girl. But it's not true." I sensed a change in Stillwater then. Resignation? Cooperation? His earlier belligerence seemed to deflate before my eyes.

"What do you want to know?" he asked. "That Antony was Vodnik's most outspoken critic? Well, it's true, but it doesn't mean Vodnik killed him or his friends."

"Then tell us what happened," I said, motioning for everyone to continue walking. I wanted to reach the Meadow before the storm broke.

"When the old gerefa died last year, Antony and I both put ourselves up for the position. When Vodnik chose me over him, Antony started making trouble."

"What kind of trouble?"

"He started spreading rumors about Vodnik. That Vodnik was getting too old to rule the Shallows."

I inhaled sharply. Those were serious accusations by a follower.

"Antony said we needed to find another demon patron to watch over us—because if Vodnik died before we found one, the *rogares* would get us."

Unfortunately, it was true. That would be the fate of these people if their patron demon died before they found another.

"Antony's suggestion made him unpopular," Stillwater continued. "Vodnik's been Patron Demon of the Shallows for over four hundred years. He's raised us, watched over us, been our protector for so long no one can remember or imagine life without him. Even so, some believed as Antony did. A handful of men said they'd already seen signs that Vodnik was approaching his end."

"What signs?"

Stillwater scoffed. "How should I know? I wasn't one of them. They just complained. Said Vodnik couldn't provide for his people anymore. That he'd lost his ability to lead the fishermen to the fish."

We reached another fork in the boardwalk. Stillwater led us to the right and I casually grazed a leaf, turning it black. A year ago it would have been unthinkable that I'd be out in Halja's hinterlands on my way to a legendary meadow tracking a mythological monster—and casually killing greenery as I went. But the fact was, these trees would survive. One leaf wasn't going to make a difference to anyone but us.

"The truth is"—Stillwater paused, as if making a decision about how much he was going to reveal—"Vodnik *is* dying. About three months ago, Vodnik gathered up the men who'd been the most vocal about his age and diminishing abilities. He told them he didn't want to frighten everyone else, but it was true—what they were saying.

"He said he knew a demon that could help. Someone who'd been hiding for centuries. A demon that was lonely and needed followers to look after. He asked them if they would be willing to help Vodnik find the demon and speak with him, to see if he'd be willing to become their new patron when Vodnik was no longer able. The group was full of malcontents. All the young men who loved to complain. About being hungry, about having to walk too far into the Dark Waters to find fish, about the frequent floods."

Stillwater snorted disgustedly. "They didn't deserve to be called fishermen. They were born *in* the Shallows, but they weren't born *of* the Shallows, you know?"

I paused, but then nodded. I knew what he meant. It was the same way with waning magic. It wasn't a happy kind of magic, but it made me who I was. It defined me. Without it, I would be someone else. Regardless of which outpost my history lessons had focused on, I'd always understood why settlers *left* New Babylon. Who didn't dream of something better? Those who actually sought it were to be admired. But what I'd always had trouble understanding—until now—was why they stayed away. Why they didn't come back once they found out there was nothing better in the outposts. But Stillwater made me realize that settlers stay for the same reason I continued to train as a Maegester. It was the same reason Burr had continued sailing on the Lethe. It was what we had. It was who we were.

"We set off that morning," Stillwater said, "to find him, the demon that might agree to be our new patron when the time came."

"Who was it?"

"Grimasca. Vodnik said he'd changed. That he wasn't the monster everyone said he was. But Vodnik was wrong. And he lost sixteen of his followers because of it."

Was Stillwater lying to me? Had Vodnik lied to Stillwater? Or was Stillwater's story the truth? I couldn't help thinking of what Ari had said earlier. *The best lies are the truth in disguise.*

Chapter 23

❧

Around midday we came to the Meadow. The entrance wasn't marked, but it was unmistakable. After a wobbly walk across a portion of boardwalk suspended with ropes over a particularly watery section, we descended a set of six steps, the longest yet. At the bottom, the boardwalk split in two opposite directions, each curving around into the green swampy brush. The boardwalk here had railings and, if I had to guess, had been built to encircle the area in its middle, which was the blackest, ugliest lake I'd ever seen. Of course, it was no lake. It was a tar pit.

Slowly, almost reluctantly, I walked over to the edge of the rail and gazed out across the great expanse of bubbling blackness. The light here was different. It was greener, blacker. I looked up, knowing why before I even saw it. Still, it was a thing to behold. I'd never seen a waertree. They were few in number and waning magic users weren't in the habit of taking nature walks. It was humbling to stare at something that was both so ancient and so strong. I'd probably have to stand at its base, touching it for at least a month before it would show any sign of weakening.

I craned my neck, shielding my eyes from the weird light, and squinted at the tree's canopy. From my vantage point, it appeared to cover the sky. It didn't, of course. Not even close. But it did cover the entire enclosed tar pit. Shafts of yellow sunlight pierced through small holes, making it look like a giant was up there, shining a flashlight through a huge spinach-colored colander. The tar looked like kale or collard greens that had been left in the icebox too long. It was a liquefied greenish black stew, full of bits and pieces of vine, twigs, and other long, thin things that looked disquietingly like human humerus, radius, fibula, and tibia bones.

I shuddered. If there'd once been flowers here, they were long gone.

The canopy's leaves rustled and swayed with the wind, sounding as loud as a small waterfall. A thunderous crack told me the storm was getting closer. Recalling the many low-lying areas we'd just walked through to get here, I vowed to search this area quickly. The storm that had sunk *Cnawlece* three nights ago had started with similar rumbling, crackling thunder.

"We should hurry," I said. No one argued. Stillwater glanced nervously at the sky. He seemed to be as afraid of the storm as any demon that might still be lurking in the Meadow, which gave me a new appreciation for the storm's ability to possibly flood this area. "Can you show me where you were attacked?" I asked him. "And where you later found the butcher knife and spice box?" He nodded and motioned for us to follow him to the right. I started to follow but Ari stopped me.

"I don't feel any demons here, do you?"

I'd been keeping my signature as wide as I dared and hadn't felt anything except Ari the whole way here.

"No. How about you?" I said, turning to Rafe. "Do you sense any waning magic users with Demon Net?" Ironically, his spell would be the best chance we'd have to sense a hellcnight before it attacked us. I had to hand it to him. He'd known some useful spells after all.

"Just you and Ari."

So that meant there weren't any demons here. At least not now.

"Let's split up, then," Ari suggested. "We'll cover more ground that way. Fara, Virtus, and I will head this way"—he pointed to the left—"and you three head to the right. We'll refill the alembic and you can search the area where the attack occurred."

"Okay," I said. Ordinarily I would have been reluctant about splitting up, but it made sense with the storm coming.

Ari, Fara, and Virtus walked off in the other direction and Rafe, Stillwater, and I were left to circumnavigate this black cesspit of death as a threesome. I squared my shoulders and glanced at Rafe. He flicked his fingers toward me and I felt another spell slipping into place.

"You might ask first," I grumbled. Protection spells were one thing, but I'd really like to know if Rafe had just cast Hemorrhage or Painfall over me.

Nearly an hour later we were exhausted and soaked. It was a feeling I was starting to associate with *bad things*, which didn't help my mood. My hair and clothes were plastered to my skull and body. We'd found nothing. The landscape around us never changed. Nor did the boardwalk. It was equally rotted around what seemed like an endless perimeter. There were no footprints in the mud, no bloodstains on the deck, no pieces of torn fabric hanging from a branch, no dropped fishing rod, tackle box, bait, hook, or lines. There weren't even any broken branches anywhere. There was absolutely nothing to suggest that any struggle had occurred at any point along this path. Of course, it had been months since the attack occurred, so I don't know what I'd been expecting to find. I only know that I'd hoped to find *something*. And that's when I saw her. Up ahead, crouched on the boardwalk, was a small mud-caked girl with tangled hair and a wild look in her eyes.

Athalie. It had to be her.

The girl took one look at us and started running. In the other direction.

"Wait!" I cried. Without thinking, I took off after her, ignoring Rafe's shouted warnings behind me. *She's what I came to find,* I thought, madly dashing after her. I wasn't leaving without her.

I tore down the rotted boardwalk, the urgency of my chase giving the edges of my magic a dangerous orange glow. Small flames briefly flared to life on leaves in front of me. Running past, I quickly smothered them. Up ahead, I caught glimpses only of her, flashes of her wheat-colored hair, flashes of her sun-bronzed skin. Behind me, I heard a brief scuffle and then a huge thump. I kept running. I *had* to catch her.

It was just me and the girl. Running. Endlessly running. Around the endless perimeter of the pit full of things I didn't want to think about. The pit full of people I'd never met and possibly the one demon I never wanted to. And then it was just me and the girl again. Both of us scared and running. Her likely scared because she'd been alone out here in the swamp for three months and me scared because I was afraid I wouldn't catch her.

"Athalie!" I called. "I'm here to—"

My boot hit a warped board and I tripped. Forward momentum sent the rest of my body pitching forward and I crashed through the rail, somersaulted in the air, and landed feet first in the thick, oozing tar. Too late I realized what I'd done. I glanced back up at the boardwalk. The girl was gone.

Around me, there was only an endless expanse of black, gooey muck covered with a thin film of leaves, twigs, and sticks. I was trapped. And the more I struggled, the faster I sank. There was nothing substantial to grab onto and the boardwalk was just out of reach. The tar was like quicksand.

I willed myself to be still. A few minutes later and a few inches deeper into the muck, I realized how stupid I'd been.

I desperately hoped Rafe wasn't lying in a pool of blood up there on the boardwalk just out of sight, dying from a gash wound caused by Stillwater's falchion.

Had Stillwater clomped Rafe over the head? Is that what I'd heard? Is that why he wasn't coming? Had we been lured out here to be dealt with in the same way that the young group of malcontents had been? Or had they both been attacked by a hellcnight? Or worse—Grimasca himself?

I called out, hoping someone might hear me. After a few more moments of silence and sinking, I finally heard light footsteps up on the boardwalk, accompanied by a strange dragging sound. The girl came back. At first, she did nothing to help me. Just stood there watching. But then she leaned down toward me. Suddenly, I wasn't sure I wanted her near me.

What if this girl was a hellcnight? What was that old saying? Fool me once, shame on you. Fool me twice, shame on me. Was dying too great a price to pay for being foolish? Apparently, Luck didn't think so.

I thrashed in the muck trying to free myself but only managed to sink farther. My head, neck, and left arm were now the only parts of me that were above the surface.

The girl pulled a long tree branch from behind her back where she must have been dragging it and managed to maneuver it down into the pit toward me. I grabbed it (instinct telling me to run from the girl, logic telling me she was my only hope). The girl tugged and tugged, pulling me toward her and the edge of the tar pit. It was slow going, but after a few minutes of further struggling, I was close enough for her to reach out to me with her hand. But she didn't. Instead, she leaned toward me and opened her mouth. Her jaws grew big and wide, expanding before my eyes. She started shifting and suddenly I wondered if I was looking at Grimasca himself.

Rafe had said Grimasca was "the one demon you never wanted to meet, the one demon you'd be deeply afraid of." So the fact that she first appeared to me looking like the child I'd been too late to save made a sort of macabre, mad sense. But what she morphed into next was even worse. It was a hideous hellcnight chimera of nearly every demon I'd encountered on this trip: it had Ebony's black twisting tail, Vodnik's greenish gold snake eyes, and Ari's face, which was heartbreaking and horrifying all at once. *Why hadn't I lost that horrible memory of the hellcnight attacking me when we'd come through the Elbow?* If I lived beyond the next three seconds I'd have nightmares again for weeks. Months. Possibly forever.

The thing grinned and snapped its head back, preparing to strike. I fired a blast of magic right at its head but it swerved serpent-like and the blast exploded into the brush, instantly igniting it. I flailed in the muck and lost my hold on the branch. The demon's long, sharp claws grasped the branch and swung it toward my head. Struggling to remember Rochester and Delgato's lessons, I tried to shape my magic like the falchion Stillwater carried and thrust the force of it toward the branch, deflecting the blow. My magic exploded into angry bits of orange red sparks. They fell into the tar pit and soon the entire surface of dried leaves, twigs, and brush was alight. The flames from my own magic wouldn't burn me so long as I kept my wits about me, but I'd soon suffocate one way or another. Ironic, in a way. If it wasn't the tar, it'd be the smoke that killed me. I spent my remaining energy on trying to smother the flames with my magic.

The demon stood at the edge of the pit, eyeing me hungrily, like a great western *ursus* eyeing a fluke trapped in a deep stream it couldn't reach. It definitely either wanted to eat me—or it wanted to save me for later. I shivered and sank farther. My nose finally went under. The last thing I saw before sinking completely was the hellcnight pacing the edge, watching me. I was only conscious for a minute or so after that. They say the last minute of your life lasts the longest. Well, it isn't true. It's over in an instant. No time for regrets because fear is the only thing your mind makes room for. When you're breathing in something that's as thick as porridge, *that's* the only thing you're thinking of.

I came to sometime later, lying on the boardwalk with Rafe draped over my front, his lips pressed against mine, trying to resuscitate me. When I started gagging he moved off quickly and held me as I wretched the mud stew from my lungs.

"How long was I under?"

"Only a minute or two." Another bout of nausea overtook me and I leaned over the boardwalk and wretched up more tar porridge. When I finished, I sat up. Rafe stretched his hand out and wiped off my cheek. It was gross but sweet. He held my cheek cupped in his hand for a second longer than he had to and I remembered that, before I'd woken up and gotten sick, his lips had been on mine. It was weird to think of it.

"Where's the hellcnight?"

"Gone."

"Where's Stillwater?"

He rolled his eyes. "Lying unconscious on the boardwalk. How did you end up in the tar pit?"

"I tripped."

We stared at each other for a few moments. Rafe's taupe-eyed, lion-like stare became serious and then he said, "You should be more careful."

It was my turn to roll my eyes. "You think?" I struggled to stand up, Rafe helped me, and a few moments later we found Stillwater's unconscious form lying on the boardwalk.

"What happened to him?"

"I hit him over the head with his falchion."

I looked up at him, surprised. "Why?"

"He tried to stop me from running after you," Rafe said, shaking his head. I'd seen that look on his face before. It was the look he gave to people who acted ridiculous, preposterous, more outlandish than he ever could hope to be. "Said there was no reason for us both to die. As if the threat of death would stop me. Does he not *understand* an Angel's oath?" Rafe's words were grumpily muttered, like someone complaining that his bootlaces kept coming untied. But they had a profound effect on me. Until now, I hadn't been sure *Rafe* had understood an Angel's oath. Clearly, I continued to underestimate him at every opportunity.

"We'll have to bring him back with us," I said. Rafe sighed, but then nodded.

"Can you heal him enough so that he can walk back?"

"Maybe." He looked at me uncomfortably for a moment and then made a shooing motion with his hand. "Do you mind?"

Oh. Right. Even a Mederi would have a harder time healing with a Maegester lurking by her patient's side. I stepped away.

"But stay where I can see you," he said, quirking a smile, and then he got to work. Stillwater came to a few minutes later, rubbing his head and moaning. When he seemed coherent enough to understand where he was, he squinted up at me with a look of shock.

"You survived," he croaked. "How?"

"My Guardian Angel," I said. I fully intended to glare at Stillwater then, to show him how mad I was that he'd tried to stop Rafe from helping me, but I surprised myself by smiling at Rafe instead. I supposed Rafe would do something egregiously irritating tomorrow but, for now, I couldn't deny that I felt all warm and fuzzy toward him. He'd saved my life after all. A girl was allowed to feel grateful.

Chapter 24

❧

An hour or so later the place where we'd left Ari, Fara, and Virtus was in sight. The storm had picked up, as I'd known it would. Overhead the leaves, moss, vines, and branches fought one another in the wind. The whooshing sounds of the trees' leafy rattling competed with the creaking sounds of their swaying trunks. The rain fell in swift, straight shafts that felt strong enough to nearly pierce our skulls. I longed desperately for a hooded cloak or a hat. No such luck, though, so I kept spitting rainwater out of my mouth. I kept my head down and tromped to the foot of the shallow set of stairs we'd descended when we'd first arrived at the Meadow.

I peered into the mist and saw three figures approaching from the other end of the boardwalk perimeter. In seconds, Ari, Fara, and Virtus joined us. Virtus looked miserable, as he always did in the rain. Fara, on the other hand, looked perfect, as she always did, under almost any circumstance. Ari just looked grim and determined. He held the alembic out to me. I noticed the catch was fastened, but the alembic itself was crushed and twisted.

"Were you able to refill it?"

Ari barked out a laugh. "Yeah, but what a job. I had to use the alembic itself as a spile." He shook his head and I knew he was regretting the fact that he never carried iron weapons.

"What happened to you?" he said, eyeing all the mud and tar on my clothes and in my hair. I felt his signature start to zing in alarm.

"I'm fine," I reassured him. And then I brought him up to speed, filling him in on all of the details of the hellcnight attack, except the part about Stillwater trying to stop Rafe and Rafe clomping Stillwater over the head with his own falchion. We needed to get back to the Shallows. I couldn't be sure, but I thought the water level around the boardwalk where we were standing had already risen. I took the lead on the way back, following the black leaf marks I'd left for us. If Stillwater was impressed by my ability to find my way out of the swampy labyrinth he'd led us into, he didn't say. But then again, he was likely still dazed from being hit on the head. Or maybe he was just grateful to have some-one else in charge for a change.

It began to feel like the night *Cnawlece* had gone down. The only difference was that the boardwalk—for now—felt steady beneath our feet instead of shifting. But lots of low-lying parts were flooded by the time we reached them. Whole sections of the walkway were underwater. I found myself sloshing through brown swamp water that came up to my ankles. My boots became heavier; the bottoms of my pant legs became soaked, as did the rest of me. Torrential rain poured down from above, splattering my head and hair, rolling underneath my shirt collar and down my back. For over an hour we retraced our footsteps back through the swamp.

Along the way I thought about the clues we'd gathered so far and what it all meant. Mentally, I tallied them up, as

I would have for class with Telford or Copeland. The six clues that summed up the entire investigation for me were: (1) Cephas, a young man from the Shallows, had been bitten by a hellcnight out in the Meadow approximately four months ago; (2) a group of fifteen fishermen and one girl from the Shallows disappeared from the Meadow approximately three months ago; (3) the fishermen had supposedly been on their way to meet Grimasca, a notorious, albeit possibly mythological, hellcnight; (4) two hellcnights had attacked us on the way to the Shallows; (5) I'd been attacked by a hellcnight out in the Meadow while investigating the aforementioned disappearances; and (6) Vodnik was in possession of two artifacts, a butcher knife and a spice box labeled "For Ebony" that he claimed were Grimasca's.

At this point in the investigation it was clear that hellcnights were involved. To argue otherwise would be, as Darius Dorio would say, *tauri merdam*. So my remaining questions were (amazing what a raging storm and one demon attack will do to whittle your list of questions down; last night I'd had over thirty, now I had just three):

#1—Where were the hellcnights hiding?
#2—Was one of them Grimasca?
#3—If so, was *Vodnik* Grimasca?

I realized contemplating question number three was long overdue. The various settler stories I'd unearthed about First Day of Darkness transgressions and grumpy groups of young men were just red herrings. The hellcnight's attack on me earlier today proved that. Vodnik *alone* couldn't be the demon responsible for everything that had happened because he was a water demon, not a hellcnight. And it was highly unlikely that Vodnik was working with another hellcnight to attack his own followers. Demons were dangerous, but patrons who'd successfully managed their flock for four hundred years usually didn't start suddenly preying on their own people. So that meant Vodnik was a possible victim, not suspect. I'd asked Stillwater earlier today whether he thought it odd that he was the only one to have survived Grimasca's attack on the fishermen. He'd corrected me and said he wasn't—that Vodnik had survived too. But maybe Vodnik hadn't.

Fact was, it was entirely possible that Grimasca killed Vodnik three months ago along with the fishermen. Stillwater could be the lone survivor of that ill-fated outing. And if Grimasca masquerading as Vodnik found out about Athalie's demon complaint, well, it didn't take much of a mental leap to deduce that he'd have wanted to silence her.

The way back to the Shallows took forever, and yet it happened in a millisecond. The rain, trees, wind, and water drowned out all further thoughts except where our next footstep would fall. I kept my signature open so that I could sense if there were any *rogares* lurking just out of sight, but the only signature I could feel was Ari's behind me. His signature floated around the edges of mine, soft, thick, and meandering, like weft yarn in a weaving. But I could sense the warp underneath, the threads of his magic that were stretched thin, too tight and nearly breaking.

When we returned to the Shallows, Stillwater left us, which was a relief. I didn't think *he* was a hellcnight in disguise, but I didn't trust him. Based on our earlier discussion, he was obviously very loyal to Vodnik and I had no idea how he would take my new theory that Vodnik might actually have been killed by Grimasca and that Grimasca might be masquerading as Vodnik now. Further, I didn't want a lawman on my team who tried to stop Guardian Angels from helping their wards when there was trouble. Stillwater may not have had much practice at tracking down villains, but neither had I. I didn't need sheriffs like him riding at my side.

"We need to find Vodnik," I said to our group. "Obviously, there's a hellcnight, possibly two, preying on the people of the Shallows." I explained my newest theory— that Grimasca was real, that he might be the demon responsible for all of the attacks so far, and that he could be masquerading as Vodnik.

As before when we'd discussed this case, reactions to my theory were mixed. Everyone agreed that my logic was sound, but my evidence was thin. What we'd discovered so far wasn't enough to pass judgment on "Vodnik," let alone execute him. Even Ari (who'd executed an untold number of demons before enrolling at St. Luck's) agreed. I looked at Fara.

"You're the gap filler and glamour expert. Know any spells that will strip a glamour? Or that will reveal a demon's true face? If we could cast something like that over Vodnik it would at least tell us whether he's really who he says he is."

Ari's signature zinged painfully and he gave Fara a piercing look. "Do you? I thought only Archangels knew revelation spells."

"That's right," Fara confirmed.

"I know Revelare Lucere," Rafe said quietly.

"Really?" Fara looked impressed. Ari's signature flared. But then again, Ari had made his position on unauthorized spellcasting clear last semester. He didn't approve of it. Thought it was wildly dangerous. Thought it could result in all kinds of unintended consequences.

"A botched spell is no joke," he said to Rafe. "Just ask Fara." I inhaled sharply. *Is that what happened to Fara? A botched spell?*

"I don't have to cast it," Rafe said. "I'm just telling Noon I know it."

"And you can cast it without botching it?" Ari said dubiously.

Rafe shrugged. And *that*, I thought, was the difference between Peter Aster and Raphael Sinclair. Peter would have bristled and been insulted, tried to convince whoever was calling his competence into question that they were ignorant and incorrect. Rafe, on the other hand, didn't care what anyone else thought about his spellcasting abilities. Which (combined with what he'd shown he could do so far) had me trusting him that much more.

"What's Revelare Lucere?" I asked. "What does it do?"

"It's a revelation spell," Rafe said. "Its name means 'to reveal a shining brightness.' The brightness being a reference to Lucifer's Morning Star. It's one of the oldest spells there is. Some Angels think it's the spell Joshua was referring to in Joshua, one, twenty—" Rafe looked pointedly at Fara.

"'We must look demons in the face,'" she said. It was the first time she'd quoted the Book since the Elbow. But, though her voice had the same scratchy tone it always did, it sounded far less preachy now and much more self-assured.

"It's good to see you quoting again, Fara," I said.

"I never stopped believing, Noon," she said huffily. "I just realized that it's the truth behind the words that matter more than the words themselves."

Personally, I'd never been able to decide if Joshua 1:20 was my favorite or least favorite Joshua quote. But that was probably because, as Fara had just suggested, it was the one I felt was the most truthful. And therefore the most frightening.

"How is it that you know an Archangel spell, Rafe?" I asked. It wasn't that I didn't believe he could cast it, but I did want to know how he'd learned it.

He cleared his throat and gave me a self-deprecating smile. "Right after I was kicked out of the Joshua School, I stole Friedrich Vanderlin's spell book." Everyone looked shocked. Rafe had to be the boldest—or the stupidest—Angel I had ever known. "Anyway," he continued, like he was telling the story of how he'd elected to take an extra sugar cube for his coffee instead of the story of how he'd pilfered an Archangel's most prized possession, "after you were attacked by the hellcnight," he said to me, "I spent some time in *Cnawlece*'s library, studying, because you always said I never did. I learned some new spells. Revelare Lucere was one of them."

Well, huh.

"In any case," Rafe continued, ignoring our stunned expressions, "if it's cast over a demon, it will force them to reveal their true form. Revelare Lucere is the spell Karanos Onyx ordered the Angels to use to unveil Jezebeth before he was executed. So . . . what's our plan, then? Find Vodnik, cast Revelare Lucere over him, and if he shifts into Grimasca, kill him?"

He looked straight at me when he asked it. In an instant, we were back to the first day of the semester. The first day I'd met him.

I take it you'd rather get this over with . . . Do it right. Put the guy out of his misery without all this pomp and . . . circumvention . . . That's what you're telling him, right? So, what about you? Would you do it? Could you do it?

"Yes," I said, meeting Rafe's taupe-eyed gaze. "That's the plan." Rafe held my gaze for a moment and then shrugged.

"Okay, then. Let's do it."

Ari's signature was chaotic. I was sure it was in part because we were possibly headed into a lethal demon fight, but also because big, ancient spells had always bothered him.

When we reached Stone Pointe, the dirt courtyard inside the moat was deserted. Considering the weather, I imagined everyone was deep within their own small shelters, hiding behind their door curtain and hoping their thatched roof didn't leak. We crossed the wooden bridge over the moat and walked up to the keep's large front door.

This time I didn't wait for Rafe to open it for me. I grabbed the iron ring and pulled.

Vodnik and Zella were waiting for us inside.

Vodnik sat on a huge bone throne. There was no other way to describe it. The massive skeleton of some immense sea creature had been used to construct the one and only oversized chair in the room. The dead fish's macabrely twisted spine formed the back of the throne while its empty rib bones formed impressive wings at its side. At the top, nearly three stories above our heads, the leviathan head of this great sea monster towered above the throne and appeared poised to devour every occupant in the room. Its jaws were unhinged and its multiple rows of teeth were still intact. Clearly, the throne had been built to intimidate any-one and everyone standing before it.

I imagined this was the throne of the giant king who had once ruled here. Because the throne dwarfed Vodnik, its effect might have been diminished but for Vodnik's signa-ture. It was furnace hot, which made it feel like—to Ari and me anyway—the belly-of-the-beast throne where Vodnik sat was a kiln of white-hot waning magic. I willed myself not to raise my hand up to shield my face. It wouldn't do any good and would only call attention to the fact that Vod-nik's signature felt blazingly hot to me. Zella sat off to one side, on some stone debris that had fallen from the keep sometime in the distant past.

Stone Pointe was even more dilapidated than I'd previ-ously thought. Part of the roof was missing, as well as half of one of the back walls. As I'd guessed from looking at the outside, the keep had once been many stories tall. But in present times, much of it had sunk in the muck. Glancing around this crumbling, makeshift throne room, I realized the rest of the keep had long since fallen apart. The floor I stood on, which looked like it may have been reinforced with stone blocks and some sort of lime mortar, was littered with fallen beams, dirt, and dead leaves. Above us, nestled into walls that no longer enclosed rooms, were remnants of the keep's formerly grand features. Large ornate fireplaces, gaping window holes, iron hooks that might have once held enormous tapestries, deep decorative niches, massive stone carvings . . . There were at least three oversized stories of these crumbling architectural details.

How fine this keep must have once been!

This keep must be as old as the Meadow. In fact, Stone Pointe had likely been whole and glorious when aspho-del flowers had still bloomed in the Meadow. Hadn't that boy Paulus from the children's tale "The Grim Mask of Grimasca" stayed in a giantess' house? Maybe the giantess' house had been one of the homes surrounding this keep's castle. If "Vodnik" was Grimasca, it seemed only too fitting that a demon who was rumored to be older than the Apocalypse would try to take over an ancient pre-Apocalyptic keep.

"What do you think?" Vodnik said, gesturing to his huge bone throne. "I dug it out of the bottom of the keep last month."

I kept my face neutral. What did he expect me to say? Words like *intimidating* and *impressively disgusting* sprang to mind along with *over-the-top* and *can't possibly be real*.

Thankfully, though, Vodnik didn't seem overly interested in my reaction to his keep's decor. "We're waiting to hear what you found at the Meadow," he said, eyeing the four of us and Virtus. Zella sat facing Vodnik and looking miserably uncomfortable. I was sure the last place she wanted to be was in a room with three waning magic users. She wouldn't have been able to feel the waning magic radiating off of Vodnik, but her gut instincts to avoid it were spot-on.

"Ms. Rust can hear what we have to say later," I said as casually as I could. I wanted Zella, a defenseless pregnant Hyrke, as far away as possible from the likely line of waning magic fire that would soon erupt. But Vodnik waved off my concerns for his inamorata.

"What did you find?" he asked impatiently.

"Nothing," I said. "But we *were* attacked by a hellcnight."

Vodnik's eyes narrowed and his signature pulsed. "*You're* alive so I gather *it* isn't." Vodnik still had a heavy Avian accent, but he didn't seem to stumble over his words as much as he had last night.

I shook my head. "The demon lives," I said. Vodnik's eyebrows rose in disbelief. Virtus growled.

"Two Maegesters, two Angels, *and a tiger* couldn't kill one hellcnight?" He tsked mockingly and rose from his throne. Rain poured in through the collapsed parts of the ceiling. *Now probably wouldn't be a good time to tell him that we weren't in fact Maegesters but rather Maegesters-in-Training.*

Vodnik ratcheted up his signature and I realized "white-hot" had merely been "pre-heat" for him. Ari's signature fired in response, gaining heat at an alarming rate. Suddenly, it was crackling and blisteringly hot. I felt the spell Impenetrable slip over me just as I was shaping a waning magic shield. But Vodnik didn't walk toward me. He walked toward Zella, who jumped up from her seat and started backing away.

Vodnik grinned maliciously. "I know what you said in your complaint," he said to her, almost near enough to touch her. "*And* I know what your sister said in hers." Vodnik grabbed the hem of Zella's dress. She stifled a shriek. "I know," he said, pulling her slowly toward him, "because the Boatman told me."

"Now," I murmured to Rafe, giving him the sign to cast Revelare Lucere. I was a second away from blasting Vodnik anyway. It was clear that the demon in front of us was no kind and benevolent patron and I wanted to know which demon we were dealing with.

I screamed at Zella to "Run!" She looked terrified, but managed to extricate her dress from Vodnik's grasp before he actually touched her. She scrambled toward the heavy oak doors we'd just come through, but in her haste to get away she stumbled headlong onto the ground. Virtus paced and growled and Zella started shrieking. Rafe began to cast Revelare Lucere. It wasn't a spell he could cast with the flick of his wrist so while he was muttering what seemed like an endless string of ancient words and phrases, Vodnik had a chance to shape his magic into a great big flaming spear. He threw it straight toward me.

Zella got up from the floor and mercifully made it to the door. She struggled to push it open. Her legs were cut and bleeding and she clutched at her middle, grimacing in pain. Vodnik's spear soared toward me, its shaft fiery and *dark*. I remembered how effective some of my darker magic blasts had been. Fear laced through my veins the way frost forms on a windowpane. Fara cast something over Ari.

Vodnik's fiery spear glanced off my waning magic shield with such force, my teeth knocked together. The reverberation of magical spear against shield doubled my

vision for a moment. Thank Luck I'd avoided a direct hit.
But I underestimated the demon in front of me. Most demons who throw magic (versus shaping it for hand-to-hand
combat) need time to "reload." Most waning magic users
weren't powerful enough to throw two near-simultaneous
blasts. Unfortunately, Vodnik (or Grimasca) was atypical.
He threw a second, darker fiery spear almost immediately
after the first. The second one hit me.

Right in my thigh, which exploded in pain. I howled and
fell to the floor. My face bounced off the corner of a rock,
slashing the skin on my cheek. Three inches higher and it
would have hit my temple and been the end of me. I looked
up and shook my head to clear it. Blood dripped down my
cheek, jaw, and neck. Zella finally escaped from the room.
Vodnik took a flying leap toward me. He snarled fero-
ciously, wielding a flaming sword that was aimed right at
my neck. Ari gave me a look so fleeting and so full of regret
that I later thought I might have imagined it. And then he
leapt up to meet Vodnik wielding a flaming sword of his
own. Rafe finished casting Revelare Lucere over Vodnik
just as he and Ari's swords clashed. There was a snapping,
crackling sound and then a burst of fuchsia, gold, and aqua-
marine sparks filled the air. Vodnik and Ari fell to the
ground together and started shifting.

Both of them.

I stared in horror as Vodnik's slick, dark green skin
turned translucent and his snake eyes changed from gold to
red. His mossy beard disappeared as he grew what looked
like an infinite number of jagged teeth in an oversized jaw.
But Ari's transformation was even more shocking. He
morphed into a demon that looked like Jezebeth had, with
greenish black scales, a long, thick tail, and those half
dozen long, ridged, lance-like spirals. And *wings.* Ari had
wings. He'd shifted into a drakon.

"You botched the spell!" I shouted to Rafe, who looked
as stupefied as the rest of us.

Ari tipped his beast head back, opened his now massively large jaw, and brayed. The sound of it reverberated off of the stone walls and escaped out into the darkening evening. If the people of the Shallows weren't hiding in their huts before, they would be now. Ari unfurled his wings, almost as if he were stretching them or testing them for the first time. Then he curled them back in and lowered his head toward the hellcnight in front of him. The lance-like spirals were now aimed toward the hellcnight like scythes on reaping day. The hellcnight, whose form had remained humanoid, still held his fiery sword as it advanced on Ari's drakon form.

"Exsignare!"—*Extinguish his signature*—I called to our group, firing up my own fiery weapon, a flaming falchion like the one I'd shaped in the Meadow earlier today. I'd deal with Ari the drakon and Rafe's botched spell after we killed the hellcnight.

As a group we converged on the hellcnight. It was over in seconds. The hellcnight rushed Ari. Ari didn't even spare us a glance. He ran the hellcnight threw on one of his lance-like bone spirals and reared. Gravity impaled the hellcnight further. Ari brought his forelegs to the ground with a thunderous rumble and shook the hellcnight off. The hellcnight's lifeless body landed a few feet from where Ari stood. I thought he would leave off then but either battle rage or confusion over the botched spell got the better of him and he stomped on the hellcnight once more and then—and this was the part I could never forget—Ari bit the hellcnight's head off. Some measure of humanity must have reasserted itself then because he did nothing else. He opened his mouth and dropped the head. It rolled to a stop a foot or so from where I lay, panting in shock, the pain in my thigh nearly undoing me. Ari stared at the hellcnight's head and then at me.

Ari wouldn't attack me, *would he?*

But then he gave a raucous cry and was gone. He unfurled his wings and flew off. I was left staring at the place where Ari had once stood, completely and utterly dumbfounded. And then the full impact of what had just happened started to sink in. If Rafe had botched the spell, Ari might never be human again.

I rounded on Rafe, who also still looked fairly stupefied by it all. Suddenly, I didn't care that Rafe was a powerful spellcaster who had taken an oath to serve as my Guardian. I didn't care that we'd fought *rogare* demons and nearly drowned together. I didn't care that I'd been given the memory of his dead brother's funeral. Or that he'd been nice to me on occasion, like the night he'd made tea for me when I couldn't sleep or the day we laughed over me throwing that sandwich tray into the Lethe. I didn't care that he'd tried to help me learn to control my fire, or that he knew a stupidly titled spell that could safely douse me when I couldn't. I didn't care that his touch had healed me. Or that he'd saved Delgato's life or that he still tried to make friends with Virtus no matter how many times Virtus hissed and spit at him. I didn't care that if I cut ties with him he'd never be paired with another ward. That he'd never be accepted back into the Joshua School, never accompany another Maegester into the field again. I didn't care that he'd spend the rest of his life researching dull, theoretical academic questions in some dusty archive library or that his only company would be an endless stack of books. Because that's all he was fit for. That was as it should be.

"You botched the spell, Rafe," I said, barely repressing my magic.

"I didn't," he said in a hollow voice. And then he swallowed and looked away. "Ari *shifted*. The spell worked. It just revealed two demons instead of one."

I don't know what I'd expected him to say. Well, that's not exactly true. I had expected some sort of apology or maybe a vague denial, but not this.

"Members of the Host don't shift."

"Demons do."

"Ari's not a demon! I know he's not. Why would he hide something like that?" I said, getting more hysterical by the moment. "What would he *possibly* have to gain?" I shouted, my voice hoarse with emotion. "We live in a world where demons are *worshipped*, Rafe. If Ari were a demon, why wouldn't he want to be adored?"

Fara placed her hand gently on my arm. "You need to be healed and then we can talk about this."

Her calmness frightened me. The fact that she wasn't aghast at what Rafe had done. *Was this just the Angels closing ranks?* The cold spot in the pit of my stomach told me otherwise.

"Fara," I said, my voice scared. "You know what a botched spell looks like." I could barely ask my next question. But I *had* to know.

"Did Rafe botch Revelare Lucere just now?" I whispered.

Slowly, she shook her head. Tears formed in the corners of her eyes. But they weren't real. *None* of this was, right? A high-pitched, strangled keening sound came out of my mouth and I collapsed to my knees. But I didn't want to burn the keep, or Luck forbid the settlers' huts outside, so I focused all of my waning magic into a fiery ball of *rage* and *regret* and *sadness* and even *hate*, and I blasted that damned bone throne all to hell. Rain poured from the open parts of the ceiling and bone dust poured down from the rest. In a matter of seconds the entire thing was reduced to ashes.

"Do *not* remake it," I hissed to Rafe.

"Wouldn't dream of it," he murmured.

Virtus came over to me then and butted his head against my leg, purring loudly. Somewhat surreally, I remembered that cats purr when they are in distress. Virtus was still a cub. Maybe he was even more traumatized by what had happened here than I was.

I gave him a reassuring pat on the head and then held my hand out to Fara, who helped me up.

"You can heal me," I said, hobbling toward the door, motioning to the Angels, "but let's do it outside."

Even the bubbling ooze of the moat would be preferable to *this* place.

Chapter 25

ॷ

S ome lesser demons aren't adored. They live in anonymity. Maybe that's why he wanted to be a Maegester."

A few hours later, the rain had stopped and we were sitting in the dirt courtyard inside the Stone Pointe moat. I'd sent Fara to check on Zella. I was worried she might already be in labor. Fara wasn't a Mederi, but she knew some spells that might provide relief and comfort at least. Rafe had partially healed the wound in my thigh. Since it had been made with waning magic, I'd need a Mederi to finish the job, but at least I was now well enough to walk. In the time it had taken Rafe to cast the healing spell, the night had darkened. With the darkness, the questions had returned and we were now discussing, in various states of antagonism, Ari's shocking betrayal. I'd nearly set fire to the moat a half dozen times (and Rafe had stopped me the same number of times with Flame Resistant Blanket) so, with my permission, Rafe had finally cast his most ridiculously titled spell to date—Chillax. He said he'd originally designed it to chill drinks but had inadvertently discovered a hidden benefit. Apparently, it also acted as a muscle and mood relaxant. Because I recalled only too vividly how I'd burned acres of rush lands the night Burr had died, I finally agreed to let him cast it over me. Just this once.

"Rafe," I said incredulously, "do you hear yourself?!" Chillax took the edge off so I didn't burn down the Shallows, but it hadn't left me completely emotionless either.

"Demons may be worshipped in Halja, Noon, but who do you think really runs this country? The greater demons may not even exist. Have *you* ever seen them?"

I was speechless with disbelief. Disbelief at both what he was saying and the audacity it must have taken to say it in the first place. But Rafe persisted.

"*Your father* runs Halja. The executive to the Demon Council—*a Maegester*—rules this country, supposedly as the administrative head of a council of demons no one has ever actually seen, who themselves are regents for an absent demon king. Ari's positioned himself well, attaching himself to you—Karanos' only daughter. In fact, I'd argue that since Karanos has dozens of demon executioners, but only one daughter, Ari's in an even better position this year than he was last year."

Rafe suddenly seemed to realize that he'd gone too far. That he'd said too much. I sat on the ground with my arms clutched around my bent knees and my face buried in them. I didn't believe what Rafe had just said. It was outrageous, just like Rafe. But, unfortunately, there was also no way to refute it, and it highlighted all of the insecurities I'd thought I'd long since banished. *Was Ari only interested in me because I was Karanos Onyx's daughter?*

"Do you think Jezebeth told Ynocencia the truth at first?" Rafe asked softly.

"Jezebeth . . . ?" I said, shaking my head, confused.

"The drakon your father had executed in Timothy's Square at the beginning of the semester."

"I know who Jezebeth was," I snapped.

"You asked why Ari would hide, what would he have to gain. Why did Jezebeth pretend to be Ynocencia's husband?

Did you really think he was trying to steal her farm? Isn't it much more likely that he simply wanted a life that he hadn't been born to? Not unlike you, Nouiomo. Until recently."

"Don't call me that."

"Look," Rafe said, sighing, "I think we both know I've got no love for the Joshua School or the Divinity. And, as an Angel, I don't feel particularly beholden to the Council either, except that as a resident of Halja, I generally follow the rules. But you tell me. You're the future Maegester. Is Ari breaking any rules by not telling anyone?"

I didn't answer. Jezebeth hadn't been executed for his duplicity. He'd been executed because he was a murderer. But then, Jezebeth had only pretended to be a Hyrke. He hadn't put his name on the List and tried to train as a Maegester.

Rafe shrugged, interpreting my silence as "no."

"So keep his secret. I don't care. I'll keep it too."

"Do you think he'll come back?"

"Revelare Lucere will wear off eventually, just like any other well-cast spell, if that's what you mean." It wasn't, but Rafe couldn't answer my question anyway.

"When?"

"When will it wear off?"

I nodded.

"I don't know. A day maybe. At the most."

Would Ari come back then?

Did I want him to?

L ater that night, Fara met up with us. She'd checked in on Zella. As I'd suspected, the woman was in labor, but wanted no part of Fara or her spells. Considering the fact that Zella likely associated Fara with what had happened in the keep, I didn't blame her. In any case, Meghan was with Zella and had assured Fara that the mother-to-be was in no real danger.

Fara declared her oath to Ari broken. Angels were under

no obligation to guard demons. The post-Apocalyptic treaty terms were clear. Angels were only required to serve Host warlords and their descendants. Not "the demon horde rabble," as Fara had put it. She'd clapped her hands together too, as she'd said it, as if *just like that* she could wipe Ari out of existence—swish him away in the wind, brush him off her hands, and be done with him. *I should be so lucky*, I thought, fighting back tears and hating myself for it.

Personally, now that the effects of Rafe's calming spell had worn off, I wasn't doing too well. The revelation that Ari had really been a demon, that he'd had a lot more than just the "drop of demon blood" most future Maegesters have, that he'd been fooling me, as Jezebeth had fooled Ynocencia, messed with my mind. It wasn't, necessarily, the fact that he had shifted into a horrifying-looking beast (although I'd never forget the image of him biting the hellc-night's head off). And it wasn't, necessarily, the fact that he hadn't told me (although that was huge). It was the fact that I should have known. Looking back there were myriad clues, and I'd willingly ignored each and every one of them. Oh, sure, I could blame my own ignorance. Any knowledge of magic gleaned in childhood was used for the sole pur-pose of avoiding detection, not ferreting out other waning magic users who might be hiding secrets of their own. No, it was my *willful* ignorance I blamed.

When I'd first arrived at St. Luck's, Ari had been the one who'd been ranked *Primoris*. Why? Because his magic was so much stronger than everyone else's. And what had Ari done before enrolling at St. Luck's? He'd been a demon executioner. Apparently, one of my father's favorites. And yet he'd never once requested the services of a Guardian Angel. Why? Because he didn't really need one. He'd told me himself, he'd chosen Fara as his Guardian *for me*.

"So what's our plan now?" Fara asked. "Just wait for the Boatman and catch a ride back to New Babylon?" She looked unhappy. I couldn't tell if she were reflecting on recent events or future ones. A trip back to New Babylon with the Boatman would take far longer than the trip out here, be much less comfortable, and just as dangerous.

"We can't leave," I said quietly.

Rafe and Fara spoke at the same time.

"Wha—?"

"You're not suggesting that we stay here . . . indefinitely, are you?"

"No," I said. "But there are two reasons we can't leave with the next Boatman—or I can't." I swept my arm in a wide gesture encompassing all of the Shallows. "What do you think would happen to these people if we left them here, without an outpost lord?"

Comprehension dawned for the Angels. It might not happen right away, but eventually a *rogare* would figure out that there was no patron demon protecting the Hyrkes here. It would be a slaughter, and there was no way I was leaving the settlers here to face that alone.

"So you—a first-year MIT who's spent most of her life sequestered in the tiny village of Etincelle—are going to be the new defender of these people?" Rafe said. Again, that appraising look. Like he was seeing me for the first time or just wondering what I was really made of.

"Not forever," I said hastily. "Just until the Council can send someone else out, or figure out a way to relocate everyone here."

"They'll probably refuse," Fara said.

I sighed. "First things first. The other reason we can't leave is that I think there's a second hellcnight hiding here."

"Really?" Fara asked, her eyes wide. "Do you feel another demon?"

"No, but we were attacked by two hellcnights on the way here. And the hellcnight that Ari killed earlier wasn't Grimasca. Grimasca has three parallel scars slashed across his face." I told them what Sasha had said during class in the beginning of the semester and what Burr had told me the day before he died. They'd each had conflicting stories about how the scars had gotten there, but each agreed that

Grimasca's cheek was marked. "And that hellcnight's cheek wasn't," I said, pointing toward the keep.

"That means he wasn't Grimasca, just an ordinary garden-variety hellcnight." *As if there were such a thing.*

"So you still think Grimasca is behind all this?" Rafe asked.

I shrugged. "I don't know. I only know that, one, Vodnik is dead. He was killed by the hellcnight in there, or the hellcnight's partner, at some point in the past—most likely out in the Meadow the day the fishermen disappeared. And, two, I know that one hellcnight is dead. The one in there. And, three, I know there *may* be another one hiding here who may or may not be Grimasca."

The Angels sat silently, contemplating the fact that our demon fights for this assignment might not be over.

"How long has it been since you cast Demon Net?" I asked Rafe.

"Not since the Meadow earlier today."

"You should cast it again. I won't be able to feel another hellcnight hiding here if it's one of the ones that attacked us from before."

He did as I asked. Thankfully, Demon Net didn't take as long to cast as Revelare Lucere had.

His gaze met mine. He looked grim and somber. I couldn't help remembering the lines from the song he'd sung to me the night we'd made tea together on *Cnawlece. Sleep, my baby . . . sleep, baby do. Grimasca's coming . . . and he will eat you.*

"There's a demon hiding under the keep," he said. "But it might be Ari."

I'd almost forgotten that Rafe could only sense a waning magic user's presence with Demon Net, not their identity.

"No, I would feel Ari's signature if he were anywhere near, but I don't. The fact that I can't feel *this* demon means it's one of the hellcnights that attacked us on the way here. So . . ." I said, blowing my breath out and clapping my hands together. I could hardly believe I was thinking about doing what I was just about to do. I eyed the dark, half-sunk, water-filled, lower windows of the keep and finally said, "Who's willing to crawl in there with me?"

Rafe scoffed. "You have to ask? I gave you an oath. Of course I'm in."

I turned to Fara. She leaned down and whispered something to Virtus. She scratched him behind the ear and pretended to listen to something he said. I tried not to roll my eyes. Over the course of this trip I'd grown to genuinely like Fara, but she could be . . . well . . . different. But then, who of us wasn't? She looked up at me.

"I'm in, but Virtus is going to wait with Russ. If anything happens to us, he knows Russ will take good care of him."

Right. Well, I put the odds of our surviving at fifty-fifty. And, since cats didn't like water anyway, Fara's plan was actually more thought out than mine.

So that was that. We were going in.

Chapter 26

◌

The three of us stood in front of the keep deciding which opening we were going to wade into. The sun had set long ago and the Shallows were completely dark. A slight, damp breeze stirred the far-off trees and my hair. I licked my lips and clutched Burr's knife, wondering crazily if I should give the Angels some sort of "eve of battle" speech. I still wore the clothes Meghan had generously given me when we first arrived in the Shallows: loose linen pants and a slim-fitting tunic with a low-slung belt. I'd managed to keep the boots I'd been wearing when *Cnawlece* sank. I debated unlacing them and taking them off—they would make swimming more difficult—but I couldn't be sure we'd be swimming instead of wading so I left them on. I took the belt off, though. No need for that extra weight. And I tore the long bell sleeves off of my shirt. They'd only get wet and get in my way. I didn't necessarily need my hands to throw magic, but having my hands free would help me to focus.

Rafe immediately followed my lead and shed his belt. Fara shed her glamour, which weighed nothing but the *potentia* she might need for other spells. She stood before us clothed in simple canvas pants and a nondescript shirt, not unlike the clothes we had on. She still had her scars but they looked less shocking now. Maybe it was because our circumstances weren't quite as drastic as they'd been before, or maybe it was because I'd seen them already.

Rafe cast the spells I'd come to think of as the "Pierce Triumvirate" (Painfall, Damage Cascade, and Hemorrhage) over me. He then cast Impenetrable and a cloaking spell before I stopped him and told him to shield himself and then preserve his *potentia*.

I turned to Fara, motioning. "Come on, then. Don't be shy. I hear you've got some spells I might be interested in too."

She looked confused. "Clean Conscience?"

"No," I said quickly, barking out a laugh. "Not that one. I meant Ascendancy. And I know you also have an AIR Boost. If I remember correctly, you learned them for me, so let's see how they work, shall we?"

She grinned and cast me up. Her spells felt different from Rafe's. They seemed to have an expansive feel rather than a focused feel. I didn't know whether the different feelings were because they were different spells or different casters. *How had my life come to this?*

For most of my life I'd wanted to be a Mederi, to have waxing magic. I'd given up that dream last semester. For the most part, willingly. (Oh sure, there were some days when I still wanted a garden, but I'd genuinely tried to make my peace with the magic Luck had given me.) So it was fairly shocking to realize that my life had come to the point where I also willingly let two Angels cast me up with the most deadly spells imaginable while I shaped my own death magic into a fiery filleting knife so that we could crawl into a dark, watery hole in order to drag a demon out of it—or possibly kill it. I mean I'm the type of girl who obsesses over writing assignments, class attendance, and due dates for library books. I don't think of myself as a monster fighter, defender of justice, or people savior.

But then, life and Luck are funny partners. I guess they give you the life they think you can handle, not the one you necessarily wanted. Deep down, I knew I was doing the right thing (there was no way I was going to allow a demon to continue preying on these people if I could prevent it) but that didn't make what I was doing any less frightening.

We elected to enter the lower level through one of its largest openings. If the Angels were thinking along the same lines as me, it was because we all wanted our escape hatch to be as big as possible. Despite the fact that it was midsummer, the water in the moat was cold. As soon as I stepped into it, it rose to midcalf, completely covering my already soaked boots. As careful as we were, a certain amount of splashing was unavoidable. The opaque water made me uneasy. It was impossible to see what was in it. The changing patterns looked like a giant thumbprint, a whorl of swirling browns, coated with a shiny, reflective egg wash. Every foot or so, I stumbled over a fallen stone from the crumbling keep or a large river rock that the Blandjan's current had probably washed into the moat during a flood. I sheathed Burr's knife and ducked under the crumbling stone archway of the opening, gritting my teeth against the cold as the water level rose to my waist. Inside, the floor kept sloping downward. We were going to have to swim.

Once in, we all lit lights. After a deep focusing breath, I lit a fireball and was momentarily happy to see a well-controlled, flickering yellow fireball light in my hand. Rafe and Fara cast Angel light, which was more silver and steady than my flame. We used the light to take our first peek at the watery bowels of the Stone Pointe keep.

I wished I hadn't had to look.

The walls were plastered, top to bottom, with huge skulls. Not human skulls—they were far too large for that. And yet, they had human features, not demon ones. *Giants*, I thought, pushing out into the water as I reached the end of the area within which I could stand. *They were giant skulls*. I kicked in the water with my boots, careful to keep my right hand, the one that held the fireball, above the surface. I gazed at the skulls—there were hundreds of them—with a sense of macabre wonder. And then it occurred to me that these walls weren't the walls of subterranean catacombs, but rather were the walls of floors of the house that were once aboveground. *Huh.* Well, magic or no, I guess those ancient giants knew a thing or two about intimidation. *Nothing like receiving visitors in rooms decorated with the skulls of your conquered. Or the skulls of your loved ones. Either way* . . . I shuddered and my hand dipped beneath the surface of the water, extinguishing my light.

"Noon?" Rafe called. He was only a few feet behind me. I could see the angles in his face, all oddly lit by his silvery light.

"I'm all right," I said, relighting the fireball. Every now and then (although it was odd when it happened), I found my fire comforting. *This* was one of those times.

The next three hundred seconds felt like three hundred years. Rafe, Fara, and I explored the flooded keep bottom, searching for any sign of the demon presence Rafe had sensed with his magic. His sense of it grew stronger the farther in we got, which made continuing that much harder. I knew this was supposed to be my job (tracking down errant demons, even if it meant crawling into their hidey-holes) but that didn't make it any easier. Every instinct told me to turn around and start swimming *out* before it was too late.

Navigating the area was like navigating a labyrinth. There were just as many turns to recall as there had been when we'd been out in the swamp navigating the board-walks, but unlike the swamp, this semi-subterranean space felt quite claustrophobic. Instead of a sky above us, there was a huge stone keep, and in some of the areas we had to half crawl, half swim through, the stone ceiling was only inches above our heads. And the twists and turns were infinitely closer together. We'd no sooner make a turn from one narrow twisty passage, than we'd find ourselves facing another. As we'd continued in, I realized that not all of the walls had been plastered with skulls. It seemed that, over the years, additional walls had been added. Whether to serve as support for the collapsing keep above or to confuse anyone seeking to find what was hidden here, I had no idea.

Though the place was dark and watery—nearly the opposite of a sunlit garden in every possible way—I couldn't help feeling like we were climbing through a giant spiderweb. These narrow passageways were the webbing and we were slowly making our way to the center. The murkiness of the water, which in some places reached my chin, continued to unnerve me. I hadn't felt the signature of the hellcnight who'd masqueraded as Ebony until he'd been right under us. Until seconds before he'd snatched Burr right off of *Cnawlece*'s ladder and into the water. What if we were attacked again in the same way?

Finally, we reached a turn that took us into a room, not just another passage. The walls here were also lined with skulls—and something else I'd never expected to find.

Bodies.

But they didn't look dead. They looked like they were sleeping. I took a chance and increased the glow of my fire. In its flickering light, we counted twelve of them. One of them was a young girl. *Athalie*. It had to be her.

I splashed over to the body that was closest to me, oblivious to the noise. It was a man, probably around thirty years of age, although it was hard to tell in this light. He, and the others, were resting on narrow shelves that had been cut out around the room. Had this place once been used for burial? Maybe by Vodnik and his early settlers? But these people hadn't been buried. Or rather, they hadn't been buried in any traditional way.

They'd been entombed down here—alive.

I felt for a pulse at the man's neck but couldn't feel anything. Still, he wasn't stiff and the room didn't stink of death. Instead it just smelled dank, almost like dirt, which was weird since the whole room was full of water. *Ugh*. I wondered when I was going to get the assignment that didn't involve a deep, dark hole in the ground that some demon had dragged people into. I peeled back the man's shirt so I could see more of his upper torso. Sure enough, there was a hellcnight bite just beneath his left collarbone.

"He's been bitten by a hellcnight," I said. No need to speak loudly in here. Every sound echoed.

Fara and Rafe, who'd moved away to check other bodies, confirmed bite marks on three others. My guess was they'd all been bitten somewhere. While the Angels continued examining bodies, I surveyed the room. The splashing from our movement and the drips from the walls and ceiling barely drowned out the sound of my breathing. I was scared.

"It's in here," Rafe murmured.

I fought the urge to shout or to spin around shining the light every which way. Panicking now would only get everyone killed. Slowly, I turned around, shining the light of my fireball into the dark areas of the room. At the same time, I opened up my signature as wide as I possibly could. My body shook, as did my magic. The fireball sputtered and my signature wavered.

Just before my fireball went out, I saw it.

It wasn't underneath us, in the water; it was on top of us, on the ceiling.

It was the most hideously frightening thing I'd ever seen. The hellcnight had Ebony's shape, but the black serpent body now had hundreds of tiny claws that anchored its massive weight into the stone ceiling above us. Its eyes were as big as my fireball had been and suddenly just as glowing. The sight of it flushed my magic like water spilling from a slashed water pouch. It didn't matter that Rafe and Fara had cast me up with no fewer than seven spells between them; I couldn't move. Couldn't speak.

Couldn't see.

My light had gone out.

"Raf—!" I managed to squawk before the thing jumped at me.

The water and the weight of the thing crashed down on

me. Claws pierced my arms and legs. Water covered my head, pouring into my ears and mouth as I was pressed beneath the water. In the second it took me to react, I finished calling Rafe's name. But it came out as a string of shouted bubbles. I thrashed and twisted in the water, trying to break free. My arms and legs felt like someone had driven nails into them. Every attempt to wrench myself out of the thing's clutches just drove the nails deeper into my flesh. My eyes watered, but little difference it made.

Finally, just as my head slammed into a stone, I threw a blast of magic at the beast. It shrieked, the high burble of it sounding positively unholy in the water, and squeezed me tighter.

Where were Rafe and Fara? Could they not hear all my splashing and thrashing?!

I felt woozy and slightly numb, surely the effects of hitting my head. I had an unfortunate history of blacking out at inopportune moments such as these. This time, I *refused* to succumb.

Even though I was still underwater and likely bleeding from a hundred tiny holes by now, I willed myself to be calm. I stilled . . . and concentrated. I shaped my magic like Burr's filleting knife and plunged it into the beast's belly. Instantly the claws withdrew and the weight that had been pressing me into the water lifted.

I rose up out of the water gasping. Above the water, all was a cacophony of sound. I realized only a few seconds had passed. Rafe and Fara hadn't been ignoring me; they'd been casting spells at the demon. I hadn't worked with either of them long enough to recognize what they were throwing, but it was impressive. The Angel army at Armageddon must have been formidable. The air was alight with sparks of magic, spitting bursts of fiery electric blasts, frantic splashing, and incomprehensible shouting. I rubbed my head where I'd hit it on the rock and looked around to see where the demon had gone.

It had disappeared.

"Noon, are you all right?" Rafe asked, rushing over to me. He motioned to Fara to follow. She did, but kept a wary eye out for another attack.

"Did you see where it went?" I asked.

"No," Rafe murmured, distracted. He was looking at my injuries. He put his hand behind my head, cradling it. At once I felt stronger, less light-headed. He'd cast a healing spell. My arms and legs still throbbed and I felt the trickle of blood oozing out of too many cuts to count. But I pushed Rafe's hand away and started walking toward the center of the room. There would be plenty of time for healing later.

Again, I lit a fireball, but this time I let it grow as large as the giant skulls we'd passed on the way in here. The room was now nearly as light as the Angel restaurant Empyr with its thousands and thousands of candles. I looked around the room, taking care to inspect the ceiling carefully. Behind me, Rafe and Fara were still. Looking. Listening.

Nothing.

I swallowed.

It was still here. I felt it still, hiding, lurking, waiting.

I glanced around at the bodies again. Wait—!

There were thirteen of them now. Hadn't there been twelve before?

But which one was the hellcnight?

The hellcnight was doing what hellcnights did best, masking its signature. Demon Net must have only told Rafe that it was in this room because he was still searching the ceiling.

I caught Rafe's eye and pointed toward the bodies. I held up one finger, then three, then put my finger on my mouth and started walking toward one of them. The flaming knife I'd shaped with my magic was still holding strong so I felt only slightly unhinged at the thought of examining these bodies yet again, knowing this time one of them didn't belong and it was really a demon that wanted to kill me . . . Or bite me and feed off of my sleeping form later.

As it was, it didn't take long to focus in on the demon we

were looking for. As soon as I approached the young man in the corner farthest from where we came in, it sat up.

It was Ari.

I switched my flaming knife from hand to hand, suddenly nervous in a whole different way than I had been before.

"It's not him," Fara hissed. "It's the hellcnight." She readied a sparking, electric bolt of blue and held it in her hand, looking at me, waiting for my okay. Rafe did the same.

There I was, flanked by two Angels, their blue Angel light contrasting sharply with the orange red glow of my fire, facing a demon that had to be put down . . . and I wavered. My fire flickered.

"You don't really want to kill me, do you?" Ari said.

I gritted my teeth. How could the voice be the same too?

"Let's go outside," I said. "We can talk up there."

"Noon . . ." Rafe growled, his voice a low warning. "You *know* that's not Ari."

"Who are you?" I said to the demon. "Who are you really? Are you Grimasca?"

"Grimasca!" The thing shifted again and stood before us as the other hellcnight had, a pale, blue-veined, sharp-toothed demon with glowing red eyes. But now it had a scorpion-like tail that whipped around behind it like a snake. "Grimasca is just a name for all hellcnights, like the Legion is the name for all demons. Grimasca is a romantic legend for those of us who like *dark* tales." The hellcnight took a step toward me. "Where is my partner, the hellcnight who was impersonating Vodnik?"

"Dead," I said. The hellcnight looked angry, but also frustrated and possibly the least little bit scared. It had to be a trick. Everything about hellcnights was a trick. I glanced at the end of the hellcnight's tail and raised my flaming knife. *Best to go for the end of the tail first and then its belly,* I thought, marveling at my own thoughts.

I heard splashing as the Angels shifted in the water. But instead of attacking, the hellcnight pointed to my alembic.

"Is that full of waerwater?"

I raised my left hand to the partially crushed alembic.
The catch was still in place. I had a sudden urge to rip it
from my neck and blast it with fire. *Was the hellcnight's
question a trick?*

And then the hellcnight shifted again. Into a man. An
ordinary man. No one I had ever seen before. But someone
I could have seen a thousand times before. The man standing in front of me could have been any man in the Shallows
or any man in all of Halja. The hellcnight had intentionally
chosen a less threatening form. But it was a calculated act
of nonaggression.

"I want to confess," the man said. I glanced at Rafe, who
gave me a guarded look in return. Fara's gaze was locked
on the hellcnight. I had a feeling she was still feeling pretty
angry about Ari's betrayal and refused to be fooled again.
She didn't trust the hellcnight, even in its innocuous and
nonthreatening form. I didn't blame her one bit.

"Confess to what?" I said warily.

The hellcnight smiled. "I want to make a formal confession," it said. "I will tell you my name. My real name. And
your Angels will act as witnesses. I will confess to my sins
here in the Shallows and then you will try me—with waerwater."

I tried not to look surprised. I doubt I was successful.
This definitely had to be a trick. Ari had said he'd seen
"more than a few" demons die from drinking waerwater
and none who had lived. Ari's credibility might be somewhat shot now, but I doubted he'd have lied about that.
Did this hellcnight just want a chance to die "honorably"?
I didn't think hellcnights were honorable. Maegesters were
supposed to be the honorable ones. We were the ones
descended from Luck's right hand. Hellcnights were the
demons that carried out the dirty work of Luck's left.

I had two choices. I could either kill this thing now or I
could allow it to confess and be tried with waerwater. Since
I wasn't too keen on killing in the first place, the second
option seemed like the way to go. Sure, I'd likely have to
hear all kinds of gruesome details (or possibly heartfelt ex-

cuses) about what had gone down out in the Meadow three months ago, but I'd have all my answers, the case could be closed, and the waerwater would nicely take care of the demon so I wouldn't have to.

With a cautious glance at the Angels to make sure they were ready to move if necessary, I doused my flaming knife. It retracted with just the slightest bit of smoke. I reached up and unfastened the necklace's catch. I held up the alembic, which swung suspended in the air by the silver chain. But I didn't offer it to the hellcnight. Not yet.

"Let's hear it," I said.

"I am Beetiennik, Patron Demon of Springtails, Mayflies, and Water Beetles. The hellcnight who I hunt with—who you say is now dead—was Biviennik, the Patron Demon of Shipworms, Squids, and Slugs."

Before Rafe could jump in, I made my own introduction, "And I am Nouiomo Onyx, future Maegester for the Demon Council."

Beetiennik raised an eyebrow, no doubt at the "future" part of my introduction, but he continued with his confession.

"Three months ago, Vodnik and a group of his followers called upon Grimasca, the Grim Mask of Death, out in the Meadow near here. You can be the judge of whether the demon they called really came or not. After all, it all depends on who, or what, you believe 'Grimasca' to be. If you believe Grimasca to be death itself, then he came." Beetiennik sneered evilly.

"Biviennik and I attacked Vodnik and his fishermen out in the Meadow that day. Why? Because we were hungry. Because we were tired of eating bugs and slugs. Vodnik and one of his followers were killed in the attack."

"What about Stillwater, Vodnik's gerefa? Why did you leave him there?"

Beetiennik barked out a laugh. "He was a surprise. We thought we got everyone. And then he comes out of the swamps two hours later, ranting about how *Grimasca* had gotten everyone."

So Stillwater had been telling the truth. Luck really *had* saved him that day.

"What about Cephas? The fisherman who was bitten in the Meadow the month before you attacked Vodnik and his group?"

"That was Biviennik. Being too hungry to wait for the right time." I narrowed my eyes. Beetiennik ignored me.

"We moved our catch down here," he continued, "to keep it cold, and then Biviennik took over for Vodnik 'upstairs.' We didn't want to spook our new school of fish with any big changes to their environment." I was beginning to think waerwater would be too merciful for this demon. "And then we found out the girl had sent word to the Council—to you." Beetiennik shook his head disappointedly. "So Biviennik took her out to the Meadow and I bit her there and dragged her back here." He looked expectantly at me. I said nothing. "We knew you, or someone like you, would be heading out to the Shallows, so Biviennik kept watch for you while I stayed back here pretending to be Vodnik. Biviennik was the hellcnight that attacked you on your boat."

"But you were the one who pretended to be Ebony that night at the Elbow," I said.

"That's right," Beetiennik said.

"You were the demon that killed Burr."

"Who?" Beetiennik looked confused. He also looked mildly aggravated with my continued questions. Like he couldn't believe I would care about the identities of his Hyrke victims. His lack of compassion galled me. It angered me. It *enraged* me. That Beetiennik could end a life without even knowing the sort of person they were, good or bad, was incomprehensible to me.

"Beetiennik, Patron Demon of Springtails, Mayflies, and Water Beetles, I have heard your confession and find you guilty of murdering five human Hyrkes and an outpost demon lord."

"And I appreciate your judgment, Nouiomo Onyx, *future* Maegester for the Demon Council, but yours is not the judgment I'm looking for. Lucifer's judgment is what I seek. I demand to be tried by the absent king himself. I demand my right to a trial by waerwater."

Part of me felt like a coward, handing over the waerwater. I'd told myself before Jezebeth's execution that I hadn't wanted Ari to throw my stones for me. Well, giving Beetiennik waerwater to drink was letting Luck throw my stones for me. Still, the only alternative was to become a lawbreaker myself. Definitely not something I wanted to do. I wasn't entirely sure I believed in the divining power of waerwater—wasn't sure that I believed it really was Luck passing judgment on the accused—but since the outcome would be just, I wasn't going to quibble with the method.

Not trusting the hellcnight enough to get close to it, I tossed the alembic to it. Beetiennik caught it and wasted no time. He unfastened the catch and, after only the briefest hesitation, tipped back his head and poured the contents of the alembic down his throat.

The effects were as awful as I'd been led to believe they would be. Beetiennik immediately shifted back into his true hellcnight form—a horridly pale demon with bloodred eyes and an oversized jaw—and collapsed into the water shaking. I resisted my first instinct, which was to help him. He'd asked for this "trial." He thrashed in the water, making horrific squealing noises, clutching at his throat and bashing his head and limbs every which way on the rocks and debris. Before our eyes, he seemed to shrink like a plum left in the sun. His claws grasped at the air and he struggled for breath. The water around him bloomed like a crimson rose. We could see the stain of the demon's blood in the water even in the half-dark room. Eventually, Beetiennik's squealing ended. But then the truly horrific thing happened. I thought he would stop thrashing and lie there, dead in the water. But instead, he got up. He wasn't laughing. Instead he was panting and wheezing, but he was alive.

Beetiennik was alive.

What did it mean? That he was innocent? I didn't believe that and wouldn't no matter how many divination tools told me otherwise. Did the fact that Beetiennik lived really mean that Luck had saved him? Or that Luck was still testing me?

When Beetiennik's wheezing subsided and he could finally speak again he said, "You are free to go now, Ms. Onyx. You've come to the Shallows and completed your assignment. You can go back to New Babylon now. The Boatman should be here in a week or two. Your Angels can bear witness to both my testimony and trial. There are no further crimes that need to be tried here."

Was he mad? Of course he was mad.

I couldn't leave him here! And wouldn't. I didn't care that Luck may have deemed him innocent. I realized then that even if Beetiennik promised to go somewhere very far away, I wouldn't let him do it. It was blasphemous to put my judgment before Luck's, but I was too afraid Beetiennik would do it again. To another Hyrke—or even another demon—somewhere else. And what would that make me? As guilty of that future murder as Beetiennik would be.

I took a deep breath, because what I was contemplating was so very grave. I wanted to make sure I could live with my decision. If I executed Beetiennik now, *I* would be the one committing a sin, arguably against Luck himself.

"You're free to go," I said to the Angels. I didn't want them to be witnesses to anything they didn't want to be a part of. To anything that could get them into serious trouble later, should the truth come out. But they didn't move. Instead they readied two blue bolts of Angel light.

For this execution, however, I was going to strike first. Because if anyone was going to take the blame for casting the first stone against an "innocent," it was going to be me.

I reshaped my magic from a filleting knife into a huge amorphous blast—exactly the kind of blast both Rochester and Delgato had warned me never to throw. Because, though they are hot and blinding, they are almost never deadly. Beetiennik laughed, an odd warbling gurgle that sounded like a bubble being dislodged from his throat. He thought I'd made a mistake. But I hadn't. I knew, without the element of surprise, my magic wouldn't kill this demon. It was far too powerful. So while the demon laughed over my apparent magical miscalculation, I unsheathed Burr's knife and stepped close. Just as its laughter was fading, I plunged Burr's knife, his real one, deep into the demon's heart.

Beetiennik had been prepared for magic, but steel worked just as well.

"*Now*, you can blast it with Angel light," I said, stepping back. I didn't want a slow death. It wasn't torture I was after. And, truth be known, it wasn't justice either. I wanted an end.

Beetiennik shifted several times before he died, convulsing in ghastly paroxysms from the black, slithering water serpent Ebony to the moss-bearded Vodnik to Ari and then Athalie, as I'd first seen her in the Meadow. Only it hadn't been her. It had been Beetiennik. Or Biviennik. It had been them all along.

When the creature finally died, I found myself staring at myself. The hellcnight's last transformation was into Noon Onyx.

Rafe's mother had said Grimasca was the one demon you never wanted to meet. The one demon you were deeply afraid of. Well, Grimasca wasn't real. But hellcnights were. So how fitting was it that this hellcnight had died looking like me, the one "demon" I'd never wanted to meet? Again, the first conversation I'd ever had with Rafe came back to me. The one we'd had at the *Carne Vale* when I'd taunted Sasha for hiding behind its "pomp and circumvention." Rafe had asked me if I ever would, or could, kill an accused in cold blood.

That's what you're telling him, right? That he ought to put his magic where his mouth is? So, what about you? Would you do it? Could you do it?

I hadn't wanted to know the answer then, but I knew now.

Luck, how I wished I didn't.

Chapter 27

ॐ

It took us until morning to move all of the victims out of the bottom of the keep. There were twelve in all, including Athalie and Antony Rust. The Shallows settlers soon discovered what had happened. Everyone was in a state of shock. Many were overjoyed that loved ones had been found alive, but that joy was tempered by the knowledge that their loved ones had been bitten by hellcnights and now were in a deep state of sleep. Everyone knew about Delgato, who was still resting in the med shack, and no one had forgotten poor Cephas. And the relatives of those whose bodies were not recovered were, understandably, near inconsolable. Zella and Athalie's father had not been one of the twelve. Honestly, if I'd not had the recovery effort to focus on, I might have succumbed to hysteria or grief-induced apathy myself. To say the situation at the Shallows was depressing was as much of an understatement as saying Armageddon had been a small skirmish.

Sometime after we'd removed the ninth body, the rain had started again. This time, it seemed like Halja's heavens were serious. Yesterday's downpour had been a mere throat clearing. In a matter of minutes, the sky opened as if Ebony's Elbow were above us in the clouds, swirling, twisting, turning, and spitting out water and spray at a relentless, waterfall rate. The moat started rising. Those victims who had been pulled out already were moved into the med shack or relatives' huts. Over the sound of the storm, I yelled for volunteers. We had one more chance to pull the last three people out before the water level rose too high to crawl back in there.

Stillwater and Russ volunteered to go in with us for the last rescue effort. Swimming back into the demons' watery hidey-hole for one last go-round was both more and less harrowing than before. This time, there was no threat of attack, but the water was so high in some of the passages, we had to tip our heads back to breathe in the few inches of air that was left between water and ceiling. I gained a new appreciation for the Angels' efforts. Oath or no, they were risking their lives to pull people out that may never wake again. And Stillwater and Russ! Stillwater proved over and over again, as he kept his cool in the dark, narrow, skull-lined, quickly-filling-with-water passages, that he'd been the right choice for outpost gerefa. I honestly don't know where Russ got his steely grit from. I knew Hyrkes could be tenacious, but I was starting to realize that Hyrke sailors were in a courage class all their own.

When we reached the central interior room, Rafe took one body, Stillwater and Russ another, while Fara and I walked over to the third and last victim. This victim had been placed farthest from the door and closest to where the hellcnight had fallen. I couldn't help taking one last glance. The hellcnight had, thankfully, reverted to its true demon form. It was ghastly to look at, but not quite as awful as seeing my own dead face stare back at me. Its hand clutched the handle of a butcher knife. I hadn't noticed before, but apparently its dying plan had been to fight steel with steel. The demon must have been in the process of withdrawing the knife when it had been blasted by Angel light.

I don't know why I did it. I suppose if it had been Beetiennik's knife I would have left it. But I remembered
Beetiennik (or maybe it had been Biviennik) showing it
to us when we'd first been introduced to him as "Vodnik."
I didn't know who the knife really belonged to, but I
knew it wasn't this demon's. And then—just as I heard a
sharp cracking sound, followed immediately by a deep
rumbling—I remembered the silver spice box. The floor
shook and the water in the room sloshed. This time, though,
it wasn't because there were feet splashing around in it. It
was because the Stone Pointe keep was falling. After millennia, it was finally giving in to the combined effects of
time, rain, and, more recently, magic blasts. With frantic
fingers, I searched the hellcnight's dead body.

"Noon!" Fara shouted. "Impenetrable won't save us if
the whole keep falls. We have to get out *now*."

My fingers closed around the silver spice box and I
snatched it out of the dead demon's pocket. Rescuing that
box made about as much sense as rescuing the victims who
would never wake. Maybe I was becoming as romantic as
the Hyrkes. But that box had belonged to someone else, and
my guess was that someone had been Ebony's lover. If not
Grimasca, then another demon who'd likely been wronged
by Beetiennik. It seemed wrong to leave the spoils of Beetiennik's sins with him when he died. Beetiennik deserved
nothing but the death he'd gotten.

On the way back out I had many instances to regret my
romanticism. On multiple occasions, I figured Fara and I
(and the poor sleeping person we carried between us) would
die because of my stupidity. I didn't regret it on my behalf.
But I did regret getting Fara into this. At one particularly
tricky spot, when I truly thought we'd drown, I told Fara
how wrong I'd been, how sorry I was, and what an extraordinary Angel she'd turned out to be.

She'd smiled sweetly and then said through gritted teeth,
"Noon, I *swear* if you take any more time out for self-
recrimination or *anything* else, I will blast you with Angel
light. If Luck, or the Savior, had wanted to drown us, we

would have died at the Elbow. Now take a deep breath and *swim!*"

Right. I took a deep breath and ducked under the water, pulling on the arm of the settler we were rescuing and dragging him with me. I kicked as hard as I could, with one hand stretched in front of me, hoping we wouldn't crash into an unseen wall.

We emerged from the moat a minute or so later, panting and gasping for breath. Strong arms pulled us out of the water. I raised myself up on my elbows just in time to see the keep fall. It reminded me of Beetiennik just after he'd drank the waerwater. The keep just seemed to shrivel up on itself, collapsing from the inside, then imploding, and sinking into the moat. The ground shook as if it were an earthquake. I looked around at the settlers' expressions. Their faces were full of terror-filled wonder and frightened awe.

After confirming that everyone else was out and accounted for, I dragged myself into an empty hut and fell asleep. I did *not* pass out. But, after the day's events—finding out my boyfriend was really a winged demon in disguise, confronting two murderers, executing one of them, coordinating the rescue efforts for a dozen Hyrkes, and witnessing the fall of a structure that was old enough to have once housed *giants*—I was allowed to be tired.

I woke up next to a fanged, clawed, and tailed hairy beast. Luckily his purr told me right away who it was so I didn't singe Virtus into ashes. He wasn't the only one who had crawled into the hut and gone to sleep. I looked around the room and saw that the Angels had also managed to find room in here. It was cramped, and I was more than sore, but we were alive and, under the circumstances, that was no small miracle. I took out the silver spice box I'd risked our lives over at the end. *Had it been worth it?* Certainly not, but curiosity compelled me to examine it. Etched on its front were the words:

For Ebony

But much more interesting were the words that were etched on the back, the ones I hadn't been able to see the first time I'd seen this box:

"Better late than never" is a lie.

What did that mean? I was just about to open the box, when Rafe's voice interrupted my thoughts, startling me enough so that I almost dropped it. I glared at him. He grinned.

"You know what they say, right?"

"What?"

"Curiosity killed the cat."

"It's 'Curiositas killed Cattus,'" I said.

"But it's a parable. About the dangers of opening small boxes."

"No, that's another one," I said. I thought about what Fara had said when I'd told her what a great Angel she was, that neither Luck nor the Savior wanted us dead or we would have died at the Elbow, and decided to open the box. After all, hadn't faith saved us at the Elbow?

"Noon . . ." Rafe warned. I pressed the catch and the box sprang open.

Inside was a chalky white powder. *Huh.* My first guess was ashes, but the substance was too white. It was a spice box, so maybe salt? Or sugar? I licked my finger and dipped it into the powder—

Rafe hissed my name again and Virtus growled. Fara woke up groggy, rubbing her eyes, and stretching. Her glamour was back, but it was slightly more subdued than usual. When she saw what I was about to do, she frowned.

"What are you doing?"

"Testing a theory."

"What theory is that?"

"That this isn't salt or sugar."

Then they both started protesting at the same time, but by then it was too late. I'd already tasted it.

Well, it wasn't salt. And it wasn't sugar. Whatever it was, it was bitter as hell. But that's all I could definitively say about it. I clicked the box shut again and put it back in my pocket.

By evening, we felt rested enough to make our way around the camp and see how others were faring. Meghan, Stillwater, and Russ had segued into the leadership vacuum. If they realized the danger they were in now with no outpost lord (and not even a keep to hide in), they gave no sign of it. I saw anew how these people had survived for four hundred years in the swamps. New Babylonians could learn a thing or two from them. Frustration over a missed *hourly* ferry, impatience over a "long" cabriolet ride from one side of town to the other, or irritation over burned bread at the Black Onion, all seemed ludicrous and laughable out here.

We stopped by Zella's hut to see how she was doing. I was worried she might not want to see us, but her response was by far the warmest. It had to have been the fact that we'd found Athalie and Antony, combined with the fact that her labor was now over and her baby had been delivered safely.

"What's her name?" I asked, happy that I could now approach both mother and child without fear of endangering them. Zella had paused and then smiled shyly at me.

"Nona," she said.

I swear, I almost started crying. "Nona" was another nickname for Nouiomo. Once the tears had formed, betraying my emotions for all the world—or at least Fara, Rafe, Zella, and Meghan—to see, I was half-afraid that Zella would say something like, "We named her after her birth time," but then, just so there was no misunderstanding,

Zella asked *if I wanted to hold her* because, after all, *she'd been named after me.*

I accepted with tears fully rolling down my cheeks. It was embarrassing, but something I was also willing to endure. Because I'd never held a baby before. And it sure beat most of the rest of the experiences this trip had given me.

On the way out, I spotted the baby's reed basket. I stopped so suddenly upon seeing it that Rafe bumped into me from behind.

"Are you okay, Noon?"

I nodded, but my thoughts had scattered to earlier discussions about mothers, baskets, babies, and floating things—and people—back to Estes on the Lethe. Rather abruptly, several memories came back to me at once.

The memory of an idyllic, sunny afternoon with Ari last semester in Bradbury:

"What's with the basket?"

"Joy found me at the riverfront one morning, floating around in that basket. If she hadn't come along, I would have drowned . . . At first, my parents thought it was someone from Bradbury who couldn't afford a child . . . But then, when it became clear I was no ordinary Hyrke child, they looked to Etincelle. There are a few Host families in New Babylon, but not many, and the current flows in the opposite direction. It was pretty clear that basket had come from your side of the river."

"Then who are your real parents?"

"Steve and Joy Carmine."

"But . . . don't you want to know?"

"No. As far as I'm concerned, I was born in that basket."

And a discussion I'd had with Fara in *Cnawlece*'s library just last week:

"But I don't understand how drakons can exist in the first place. Aren't demons spawned from the ground? I mean, Luck creates them . . . because demons can't create anything."

"Demons are spawned by Luck, anywhere he likes. So

who's to say he can't spawn one in a woman's womb? And when he does, they're born as drakons . . . Estes is rather virulent, you know. Delgato's dining room pictures don't lie. Sometimes his affections are returned, sometimes not. But when he lies with a woman, often Luck will gift his lovers with a child."

"Gift? A drakon growing in your belly?"

"Whether they want one or not. The horrible thing is, it's nearly a death sentence for Hyrkes. A powerful Angel or a Mederi would likely survive such a birth, but then, can you imagine an Angel or a Mederi wanting to raise a drakon?"

And then finally, my discussion with Meghan about Cephas night before last:

"Where's Cephas now?"

"His family gave him to Estes."

"What do you mean?"

"They put his body on a raft and floated him out into the Lethe."

Had Ari's birth mother tried to do the same with him? Had she tried to give him back to the demon that was responsible for his spawning? I shuddered. I wasn't sure I was prepared to think of Ari again *in any light*—infant or adult—for a long, long time.

But Luck has a habit of ignoring my wishes. When I ducked my head out from behind Zella's door hut curtain, I felt him.

Ari was here again. In the Shallows.

Chapter 28

ॐ

H e's back," I said.

"Who?" Fara asked.

"Ari," Rafe said. He'd known who I'd meant. Maybe both of us had been more aware of the time than we'd wanted to admit. We'd probably both been waiting to see what would happen when Revelare Lucere wore off.

If Rafe was nervous about Ari being angry with him for uncovering his secret, he showed no sign of it.

"Oh," said Fara. And then *she* looked angry. I realized then what a mess the whole thing could become if I sought out Ari flanked by the Angels we'd brought. He and I needed to sort out our differences on our own. But the Angels refused to leave my side. Rafe blathered on about his oath and Fara harped about what a huge bone she had to pick with Ari—*huge, bigger than the bones from the keep!*—and I realized she'd been wronged by him as well. Not nearly as much as me, obviously, but enough, I suppose, to justify accompanying me to meet him. And, truth be told, my knees were starting to shake just a little. Having some support if things went awry might not be a bad idea.

We found Ari in the dirt courtyard of the collapsed keep at Stone Pointe. He was (not that I'd expected anything but) in human form. I guess he'd found clothes from some unsuspecting and generous Shallows settler. Now that we'd found him, he'd turned his signature down to the lowest hum. I could barely feel it. I guessed he was being courteous. He had to know how volatile my emotions were right now. He must have correctly guessed that had I felt even the slightest uptick in his signature, anything might have been possible, from a full-scale Stone-Pointe-keep type of collapse to an all-out conflagration, Ebony's Elbow–style.

I kept my gaze averted from his, as well as my signature. I didn't trust myself to look at him yet. I didn't want to see *anything* in his face. No hurt or pain or loss or regret . . . because the next thing I'd wonder was if those emotions were real.

The Angels and I stood on one side of the planked bridge and Ari on the other. It would have been fairly melodramatic had the moat bridge been constructed anywhere but the Shallows. But it was hard to have a big dramatic showdown across the three or four boards we'd been walking over for the past two days, which were tied together with only a few pieces of vine. I wondered if someone would be able to tie me together like that . . . Maybe Rafe knew a spell called Vine or Tie or Bridge or . . .

"Noon." Ari's voice jerked me out of my reverie. My gaze locked with his. In the light of the sinking sun, his eyes looked almost mulberry. I wanted to blast him with waning magic. I wanted to more than I'd ever wanted to blast anything in my entire life. I wanted to sob uncontrollably and I wanted to yell until I was hoarser than Fara. But none of that would make yesterday go away. I was stuck with that memory, forever. Oh, I'm sure an Angel could find a spell to take it from me. But if I wanted to live a real life—and I did—then I couldn't use magic to intentionally erase things. So I decided *I* would dismantle my relationship with Ari, and in an organized way. I didn't want a collapse or an implosion or any kind of sinking into the muck. I swallowed.

"You need to apologize to Fara," I said.

"To Fara?"

"Yes."

After a brief pause, Ari cleared his throat. And then he said, "I'm sorry, Fara."

I don't know what I expected. Maybe for Fara to say *for what?* just to get the ball rolling for me. Or maybe for her to start badgering Ari on my behalf. But she must have seen through my stall tactic—breaking up with Ari was *hard*—and decided to leave us to it.

"Come on," she said to Rafe. "Let's stand somewhere where we can't hear them." And then they walked off. So they didn't (quite) leave me alone with him.

When they left, Ari's signature cracked the least little bit. It was like putting my cheek next to a crack in a kiln. Instinctively, I threw up a shield, but my emotions quickly turned it into an aggressive thrust. Ari redirected it harmlessly into the pile of ruins behind him. I ratcheted down my output. The last thing I wanted was to turn this into a magic fight. We'd both lose that, in more ways than one.

"Did you know what you were before Rafe cast Revelare Lucere?"

He could have lied. He could have said no, that this whole thing had been as surprising and shocking and horrifying to him as it had been to me. But he didn't hesitate.

"Yes, I knew. I've always known."

"Why didn't you tell me?"

"What would you have said? You're still dealing with the fact that I executed demons for your father *before* enrolling at St. Luck's."

"You never would tell me how many. Would you have told me about this?"

"About the fact that I'm a drakon? Go on, Noon, you can say it."

We glared at each other. *What right did he have to be angry?*

"Yes, I would have told you about it. I wanted to tell you about it. I was just waiting for the right time. And, no, I'll never tell you how many demons I killed before St. Luck's because I don't know. A lot, Noon. A Hundred. *Hundreds.* But they all deserved to die. Just like Jezebeth and just like this one." He pointed with his thumb behind his back toward the rubble. "What happened here? After I . . . left?"

"Shifted, you mean," I sneered. "Go ahead, Ari, you can say it." Luck, I couldn't believe I was stooping to this level with him. "His name was Biviennik, by the way."

"Who?" And then I lost it for a moment, because Ari's question reminded me of Beetiennik's when he'd asked who Burr was. And then I thought, what's the difference, really, between any of us? How many years would it take before *I* couldn't remember the names of those I'd killed?

"The demon you killed!" I shrieked. But no magic was thrown. I wiped a stray tear away from the corner of my eye and made sure I looked away until they were dry. I turned back toward him with my hands clenched. Ari's face was painful to look at. It was hard to believe he was faking the emotion I saw on his face. It was too raw. He took a step toward me, but something he must have seen in my face made him step back again. He must have known if he tried to come near me, this conversation was over.

"I killed the other one," I finally said, once I had my voice and my emotions under control again. "Beetiennik."

"You executed a demon?"

"Yes, Ari. Me. With Rafe and Fara's help."

He continued to look surprised for a moment and then he shook his head.

"I'm sorry I wasn't there to help."

I laughed, a sort of herniated hiccup. Of all the things I was mad at him about, that one hadn't occurred to me.

"You know, you didn't tell me what you were either when we first met," Ari said. "You pretended to be a Hyrke."

My mouth opened to respond, but no words came out.

"You didn't declare your magic until the threat of death forced you to," he said. "How is that different than my true form being revealed by Revelare Lucere?"

I blinked. *How was this about me?*

"What if we'd met a year ago, Noon? A year before you were *forced* to declare your magic? Would you have told me about it?"

"I declared," I hissed. "It may not have been what I wanted at the time, but no one had to cast a spell over me to reveal what I was. I finally decided I was sick of being a coward and I plucked up the courage and declared my magic to the world."

Ari grimaced.

"Besides," I pressed, "we hadn't even *kissed* before you knew what I was. In fact, you claimed to know from the very first moment you met me. Well, I *didn't* know *about you*!" I was yelling again.

But, instead of looking guilty or backing down, Ari went right for my emotional jugular.

"So maybe you're better than I am," he said. "Or maybe you're just less afraid of losing me than I am you."

He tried to take another step toward me. This time, I held my hand out. "Ari, please. Stop. I don't know how I feel about you anymore. I don't know if anything about you is real or what things about you to trust. And what you did to that hellcnight . . . Well, it's a lot to take in."

Ari looked away for one moment. Clearly there was some small part of him that regretted that he'd bitten Biviennik's head off while in drakon form. But my guess is he was only sorry I'd seen it, not that he'd done it. Sure enough, a second later he turned back to me and all traces of guilt or embarrassment or repentance were wiped clean.

"I guess you would have rather I teased him or toyed with him, or bit him and dragged him off to be eaten later, or done at least *one* of the atrocious and horrific things that *demons* do to their victims. Right?"

I fumed. The killing had been brutal. But it hadn't been cruel. It had been quick. Was his kill more gruesome because he'd done it with drakon teeth and jaws whereas I'd performed mine with magic and steel? I elected to forgo arguing with Ari over Biviennik.

Because I wasn't breaking up with Ari over Biviennik. I was breaking up with him because I couldn't trust him.

"Ari, you said you felt my magic the moment we met, that 'I could never hide from you, any more than you could ever hide from me' because 'that's just the way our magic works.' But that's not the way it works. I *never* knew about you, Ari. I never had even the slightest suspicion that you were a drakon. I should have. But *should have* just makes me wrong."

Ari's eyes glistened, but I was sure it was a trick of the light. I had never, ever seen him shed a single tear.

After some time had passed, during which neither of us said anything, Ari finally asked, "So where do we go from here?"

"Where do we . . ." I echoed crazily. "We don't." I put my hands on my hips. "What was *your* plan? Go back to St. Luck's and just pretend this never happened? Are you really going to continue training as a Maegester after this? You're a drakon!"

"And you're a woman." Ari looked me square in the face. I sputtered.

Another moment passed. It would be midnight before anything was settled between us.

"Why do you want to train as a Maegester anyway?" I asked, remembering Rafe's theory about Ari somehow using me and St. Luck's as a path to rule the world. It had seemed pretty far-fetched even when I was tanked up on his spell. But I still wanted to hear Ari's answer.

"It was Joy's idea." I nodded. That actually made sense. "And your father's."

I stilled. "Does my father know? About you?"

"I don't know," Ari said slowly.

"Ari," I said, thinking of Rafe's theory again. "Why are you dating me?"

Would he tell me the truth? Would I know if he was?

"Noon," he said carefully. "I'm going to answer your question, but I want you to do one thing for me before I do."

I looked across at the man who'd been my lover, the man I'd loved, and still loved, who was now a stranger, and wondered how many more revelations I could take. *Here* was when he would tell me that, though he'd started dating me to get closer to Karanos, he'd fallen in love with me. And I would have no idea whether to believe him or not.

"What?" I said stonily, bracing myself for the worst.

"Open up your signature. I want you to feel what I'm saying."

"Signatures aren't lie detectors, Ari."

"I'm not talking about lies, or even words, although I'm going to talk. I just want you to feel."

I knew, in the bottom of my heart, that I'd regret it. But I did it. I opened up my signature.

If feeling his signature before had felt like feeling the heat from the crack in a kiln, *this* was stepping into liquid fire. All the emotions that I'd expected to feel when I'd first seen him tonight were there: hurt, pain, loss, and regret. Those emotions swirled around me ready to flay me alive. But at the center of all that fiery darkness was a white-hot core. It was love. I could feel it.

I nearly shut my signature down because I didn't *want* to feel it. But Ari ran across the bridge and grabbed me by the arms.

"I never dated you to get closer to your father, Noon." I stepped back, but Ari stepped with me, keeping hold. Out of the corner of my eye, I saw Rafe and Fara walk toward us.

"I don't love Nouiomo *Onyx*," Ari said, rushing now to get his words out. "I love *Noon*, the woman who hates fire but wields it anyway, the woman who wanted to grow flowers but couldn't, the woman who offers sacrifices to deities she's not sure she believes in, the woman who hates to kill. Or cause pain. The woman who wanted to be a healer, but had the courage to embrace the dark magic she'd been born with."

The Angels arrived.

"I love *you*, Noon," Ari said.

I didn't respond. I couldn't. At least not to that.

"You're wrong about one thing, Ari. I do believe. I just believe in living, breathing people more than I believe in magic. I want to be my own waerwater, my own black onion. I want my head and my heart to determine someone's fate."

"Your heart, huh?" Ari said softly. "Well, you heard what I had to say, and you felt what I feel for you. What does your heart say about me?"

I swallowed. My throat hurt.

"It says it's broken, Ari." I pushed his hands away. "What do you think it says?"

"And what do you say?" Ari's voice was immeasurably quiet, but even the Angels must have heard the unshed emotion in his voice. I knew they were ready to cast.

"I can't be with you anymore. I'm sorry."

Just before he closed up his signature I felt the liquid fire rush into the kiln. I imagined the whole thing was internally combusting right now. But all he said was, "I'm sorry too."

He walked backward across the bridge, never taking his eyes off me. And then he shifted. He suddenly grew five times his human size and crouched before us on four legs instead of two. His dove-colored skin turned greenish black. His tail lengthened, its thick base extending a good twelve feet or so into a narrow, pointed tip. At least there wasn't a scorpion's stinger on its end. I shuddered. Ari reared and then lowered those lance-like spiral ridges at us. The Angels stiffened. I stood my ground.

I'd said I didn't trust him. But I knew he wouldn't hurt us. At least, not with his body or his magic.

"What was that spell you cast over Sasha, Tosca, and Brunus at the beginning of the semester, Fara?" I said, "The one where you turned them all to ghosts and swished them away?"

On the other side of the bridge, Ari snorted fire. It

reminded me of Serafina. But Ari was at least a thousand times bigger than she'd been. If he chose to singe something with fire, the effect would be far greater than a few tiny burn marks created by a sneeze of blown embers. Fara glanced between Ari and me and shook her head. "Let him leave his own way," she said.

Ari's massive wings beat the air, ruffling my hair. I felt a final puff of warm air and a fleeting echo of his white-hot signature core, and he was gone.

We stood for a moment looking at the ruined keep. Finally, I broke down. Fara pulled me into a fierce embrace and, inspired by my spell request, I suppose, quoted the verse from Joshua 5:34: "We are all but pale spirits to be poured over the land until the time shall come to be made whole again."

"You *will* feel whole again someday, Noon," she whispered hoarsely. "I promise."

Chapter 29

❧

Rafe found me the next day in the small tin-roofed storage shed on the Secernere side of the Shallows, the one we'd walked through when we'd first arrived. I was sitting cross-legged on the floor amongst the fishing poles, tackle boxes, crab pots, and birdcages contemplating the silver spice box with the words "For Ebony" on it. I'd been contemplating it, for hours. I'm sure it's because the box conjured up the fatalistic sentiment I'd been feeding myself since Ari had left yesterday. "'Better late than never' is a lie." No kidding. *On time* is definitely best. Like the fact that Ari should have revealed to me *before yesterday* that he was a drakon and not just a human member of the Host like me.

Rafe came in quietly at one point and sat next to me. It reminded me of the time we'd made tea together on board *Cnawlece*. Our silence was companionable, not uncomfortable. After a while he said:

"I really do know the spell Pat on the Back."

Despite everything, I laughed. "Who taught it to you?"

He shrugged. "I learn most of my spells on my own. Or I design them myself. None of the traditional ones ever seem to do what you need them to do."

"Maybe you should have been a gap filler."

"Maybe."

"What *is* your specialty, Rafe?"

He fiddled with one of the birdcage doors, pressing it open, then shut, then open again.

"Looking out for you, Onyx. Luck knows you need it. So how 'bout it?"

"How about what?"

"Pat on the Back," he said, just the tiniest put out that I'd seemed to have forgotten the spell that he'd offered.

I smiled, playing along. "How long does it last?"

Rafe's taupe-eyed gaze met mine. "As long as you want it to."

He left a few moments later. He wasn't insulted when I didn't take him up on his offer. I think he realized I needed exactly what we all suddenly had so much of—time. We had at least a week before the Boatman was due to arrive. So I spent the rest of the afternoon trying to unravel the mystery of the spice box.

What had *"Better late than never" is a lie* meant to the person who'd engraved this box? What had been too late for Ebony? Legend said she was a water demon who gave her memory of home to her wandering lover so he could find his way back to her. But why had her lover been wandering in the first place?

Burr's mother (the near-incontrovertible Alba) had said that Grimasca's lover was a big black river serpent who liked to hunt with him. According to her tale, Grimasca had bitten her and she'd drowned.

I had no hard evidence, but I thought it likely that Grimasca and Ebony had been the two lovers both Alba and the legends spoke of. So if Grimasca bit Ebony and then she drowned, it seemed safe to assume she'd drowned from a hellcnight bite.

Ebony's final resting place had been the Elbow. According to legends, that's just where she succumbed. The legends were always vague about what she'd succumbed to. But couldn't it have been a hellcnight bite? But if so, why hadn't Grimasca been with her? If he'd bitten her, why wouldn't he have been with her at the end?

But then I thought about the wandering part again. The fact that Ebony's lover had been a wanderer. And that she'd given him her memory of home *so that he could find his way back to her.* Well, had he? Had Grimasca found Ebony before she died? Ebony's legends say she died alone.

And then it hit me. What the quote might mean and what the powder might be. An antidote. A cure for Grimasca's bite. Maybe Grimasca had been wandering, looking for a cure, but when he finally found it, he didn't make it back in time to use it. Maybe that's what *"Better late than never" is a lie* meant.

I ran out of the shed, found Rafe and Fara, and told them my theory. They both thought it was at least worth seeing what Meghan, Stillwater, and Russ thought of it. Depending on what their take was, we could decide whether we wanted to try it out on Delgato. It took us the better part of an hour to round them up (scattered as they were in various parts of the camp), but when we were all assembled outside of the med shack, I once again explained my theory. That the white powder was really an antidote to a hellcnight bite. That the silver spice box had been Grimasca's and he'd found the cure for his lover Ebony but he'd been too late to use it.

Frankly, they all thought it was pretty far-fetched. Russ didn't believe in Grimasca at all. But the fact that I'd tested the powder already on myself, and no harm had come to me, impressed Meghan mightily. She asked us if we thought Delgato would rather die sleeping in his cot after Luck knew how many years lying like that, be floated out into the river and given to Estes (Rafe cleared his throat, narrowed his eyes, and shook his head at Meghan over that option, making his position clear), or take a chance on this mysterious powder. To a person, we all agreed that Captain

Delgato would rather take his chances with the powder. We had nothing to lose. If it didn't work, nothing would happen.

Late that night, Meghan mixed a small amount of the powder with warm water and managed to get most of it down Delgato's throat. He was still for so long after, I feared we'd failed, that my theory was bunk, and I was no closer to figuring out the mystery of the powder, the box, or the quote than before. But then he coughed. The first real movement he'd made since the night the hellcnight attacked us on board *Cnawlece*. And I knew I'd been right. And I knew then that we could save everyone, or at least the twelve settlers we'd pulled out of the keep. After that, everything happened fairly quickly. It took half the night and the rest of the powder to wake everyone up, but we did. By the darkest hour in the Shallows, not a single person was sleeping.

A few days later nearly everyone in the Shallows was gathered for breakfast on the Blandjan dock. We'd been gathering here for meals since the keep had fallen. No one in the camp wanted to eat their meals (even if those meals consisted of bloodfish, bonemeal and/or other various and sundry "edible" marshland offerings) while looking at the pile of debris that had almost become a tomb for at least a dozen of them. In the dirt next to the dock were small campfires here and there where settlers were frying or roasting fish. The dock itself was covered with people, kids especially, who sat at its edge, legs dangling over the water, with makeshift poles and lines. Athalie, who'd turned out to be a precocious eight-year-old with wide brown eyes and wild, corkscrew curly hair, sat off to one side on a blanket with Zella, Antony, and her new niece, Nona. Stillwater, Meghan, and Russ were standing at the very end of the dock looking east toward the mouth of the Lethe and the sea. At dinner last night, Antony had casually suggested that the group relocate once a new patron was found. The idea had met with immediate resistance from a few folks, including Stillwater. I smiled to myself. Those two would likely continue their feud long after I was gone, but it didn't involve demons or seem anything more than two men who had differing views on what was best for their community. A healthy sort of problem, in my opinion. And one their new patron could deal with.

The morning was already hot and humid, but without a cloud in the sky. The rising sun on the Blandjan had been blinding, which I thought fitting since Blandjan meant "blind." Rafe had been continually casting Demon Net so we'd know if anything tried to sneak up on us, either on land or from underneath the water. But he'd felt nothing. Nor had I, not even Ari. I had no idea whether I'd see him again in New Babylon when we finally made it back or not, but I was determined not to think of it. Besides, I had enough to keep my body busy and my mind occupied. Like convincing Delgato he should become the new Patron Demon of the Shallows.

Delgato had been told about *Cnawlece*'s sinking and Burr's death. He was more grief stricken over Burr, which I found touching. Apparently, Delgato *had* appreciated Burr as much as I'd started to during our brief voyage. We filled Delgato in on recent events in the Shallows, Beetiennik and Biviennik, the rescue and revival of their victims, and the collapse of the keep. He was told about Ari. Delgato seemed less surprised by that revelation than by the tales of my heroism. I tried not to be insulted about either.

Fara outdid herself on her glamour that morning. I think she knew her time in the Shallows was almost up and so she had a limited number of further opportunities to create lasting dramatic impressions. Inspired by tales of Lethe sirens, she chose to appear in a glimmering sheath of oyster shells. Freshwater pearls adorned her lustrously wavy hair and glitter sparkled on her eyelashes like sunlight sparkling on the surface of the river. She'd even gone so far as to "grow" webbing between her fingers and toes. Soon every young girl at the docks had a fish tail or iridescent scaled skin. The boys then asked to be turned into giant toads, snails, or lizards. Within minutes, Virtus was left alone at the edge of the dock, peering into the sun-flecked water, hungrily eyeing its surface for any evidence of the fish lurking beneath. Sometimes his ears would twitch. Sometimes his tail. Sometimes his eyes would grow big as saucers and his haunches would wriggle in anticipation . . . But he stayed out of the water.

And so it was when I asked Delgato that fateful question one sunny summer morning during Haita, Halja's seventh month (which was named after what it felt like, *hot*) while standing on a wooden dock halfway between New Babylon and the sea.

"So what do you say, *Captain* Delgato? Would you like to be *Lord* Delgato and look after these people?" I asked him.

What demon would say no to that?

But he didn't answer right away. Instead, he looked around and carefully considered each of the settlers, assessing them as he'd once assessed me. He made a sound that was half-grunt, half-growl. Delgato's catlike characteristics (the pointy ears, furry paws, and sharp teeth) had all come back with his consciousness.

"Not sure what the Council would have to say about it," he said.

"The Council's back in New Babylon. You're here; the settlers are here. You've got no boat and they've got no patron. It makes perfect sense so long as everyone's in agreement."

"What do you think their take on it will be?" Delgato asked, making a gesture that included everyone on the docks and in the dirt behind it.

I shrugged. "You'll have to ask them how they would feel about following the Patron Demon of Shadows, Stealth, and Hiding. Course, you could always become the patron of something else," I said, grinning. "Like rainbows, sunshine, and wide-open spaces."

"It wouldn't be the first time, would it?" Rafe said quietly.

Delgato looked at him queerly. "What do you mean?" he growled.

"I mean, it wouldn't be the first time you've reinvented yourself."

The two stared at each other and I realized I'd missed something important. "What are you talking about?" I asked.

"Delgato is Grimasca," Rafe said.

To my shock, Delgato didn't deny it. I turned to him in dismay. "*You're* Grimasca? Grimasca actually exists?"

"No," Delgato said emphatically. "Grimasca does *not* exist. Grimasca died a long time ago. I killed myself—drowned myself in the Elbow—centuries ago."

"That's impossible," I cried. "Nobody comes back to life in Halja."

Again, Delgato shrugged. Clearly, he couldn't care less whether I believed him or not. "I did. Or rather, I came back to life as someone else. After the Elbow spit me back out, I was no longer a hellcnight; I was a manticore. But I still possessed each and every one of my accursed hellc- night memories. How? Why? Beats the hell out of me. Maybe because I drowned alone. Like she did. Or maybe because Luck wants me to suffer."

"How did you know?" I said to Rafe.

"It was just a guess," he said. "Until now."

We all stood looking at one another for a moment. No one said anything. It was weird, though, because even though it was nice and sunny out, I suddenly felt a shadow pass over us. I looked at Delgato, and for a single second I could have sworn his eyes glowed red. I shivered and rubbed my arms.

"Still think I'm the right demon to watch over these people?" Delgato growled, glancing back at the innocent and unknowing settlers.

"That depends," I said slowly, pulling out the butcher knife and the silver spice box. "Are these yours?"

He stared at the knife and the box, transfixed. Finally, he reached for the box, waving off my offer of the knife. "Keep it," he said peremptorily. And then, as if the box were made of the finest, most delicate blown glass, he gingerly examined it. Lovingly, he caressed the words "For Ebony" and then scowled at the quote he'd engraved on the back. *"'Better late than never' is a lie."*

I found his actions telling. He'd rejected his old butcher knife, instead reaching for a momento of lost love.

"When we met, you said you both adored and abhorred secrets. Want to swap answers? I want to know what happened with Ebony. And you want . . . well, an answer limited only by your question, I imagine. I can give you the answer to *any* question about anyone, anyplace, or anything in Halja."

"*Any* question?" he asked. I nodded.

"You've still got it, don't you?" he said. "The black onion."

I smiled and pulled it out of my pocket. "I told you it was yours at the end of this trip."

"You said it was mine if everyone made it back safely. Burr died, and you're still here."

I shrugged. "It's mine to use as I choose."

"Don't *you* want to ask it a question?" he said, eyeing me closely. "You've certainly earned the right. Sounds like you've done far more than just sail the Lethe on this trip."

I thought about what I might ask. *When was the Boatman coming? Would we make it back alive? Where was Ari? Did he still love me? When would I be able to forget him? Who should become the new patron demon of these people? Was Delgato the right choice?*

I realized, though, that some of my questions could be answered with time, not magic, and that others probably shouldn't be asked. I might have welcomed some help with the last two *if* I knew I could trust the black onion to provide helpful information. But, the truth was, I'd never known magic to work straightforwardly or exactly as one wished it to. And hadn't I told Ari just a few nights ago that

I believed in living, breathing people more than magic? That I wanted my own head and heart to determine some-one's fate, not things like waerwater and black onions?

"You can have it," I said, never meaning anything more. But he didn't accept it.

"What do you want to know about Ebony?"

Once again, I thought of all my unanswered questions. Had he really loved her? Had he bitten her? Had it been an accident? How had it happened? I didn't believe for a single second that he'd eaten her, as Burr had believed. That em-bellishment was Grimasca/Delgato's punishment for hav-ing been such a horrible creature to begin with. But he wasn't anymore. I *knew* he wasn't. And really the only rea-son I wanted to know about Ebony was because I wanted to ask him how he did it. How did he keep on living without her? But how would *his* answer help *me*? I had to find my own answer.

"Never mind," I said. I grabbed Delgato's paw and pressed the black onion into it. "Keep your painful memo-ries. I've got my own."

A little over a week later the Boatman came in a small, narrow riverboat. By that time, I was unbelievably sick of bloodfish and bonemeal. But I'd miss everyone in the Shallows. Delgato had agreed to stay on as patron. The people had willingly embraced him. Stillwater and Antony Rust were still at it, with Stillwater advocating that they stay in the Shallows and rebuild the keep and Antony pressing for the sea. Russ chose to stay with Delgato. Our parting gift to the people of the Shallows was the Mederi-blessed pack-age of seeds we'd brought. The night *Cnawlece* had sank, *that* was what Rafe had gone back for. He presented them to Russ to hold as our official farewell gift. I had never meant any sentiment more.

Fare well, I thought so fiercely, it was almost a prayer. As we rounded the bend in the Blandjan that would take us out of sight of the Shallows, I turned to ask Fara if she

remembered any farewell blessings from the Book of
Joshua but her face was buried in Virtus' fur. She was
weeping. I glanced over at Rafe. His carefully carefree look
was back.

It took us two months to get home. By the time I set foot
on campus the weather had completely changed. During
our trip back, Haita had become Draugr, the month of dry-
ness, and then Ciele, the month of frost. The leaves on the
trees changed color. There weren't any trees at St. Luck's,
but here and there, scattered around the city sidewalks in
tree wells, were a few elm, birch, and beech trees. After all
the drab iron, moss, and sage of the swamp and lower
Lethe, their blazing golds and sanguine reds were as bracing as the cool wind that blew us back to the New Babylon
docks.

In time Ciele, the month of frost, turned to Fyr, the
month of fire. The crimson and canary-colored leaves fell
from the trees, the days grew darker, and the nights colder.
Apples were harvested and the smell of bonfires filled the
air. Ari did not return. I gave Rochester a full report on
what happened in the Shallows, but I "modified" the facts
for two of the most significant events. I told Rochester that
Ari had disappeared during the investigation. It was techni-
cally true (I had no idea where he was) but I also knew it
was a lie by omission. I didn't care. While I couldn't forgive
Ari for his deception, I didn't feel it was my place to reveal
his secret. And I told Rochester that my alembic had been
lost the night *Cnawlece* sank. Another lie? Yes, undoubt-
edly. But I'd made my peace with that earlier, after Beetiennik's trial by waerwater when I executed him despite
Luck's pardon. If I was a sinner, so be it. At least I was a
sinner who could look herself in the mirror while brushing
her teeth.

Rafe was admitted back into the Joshua School. Typical
of Rafe, he'd shrugged and said it made no difference to
him where he slept. Freidrich was still deciding whether he
would be allowed to continue training as my Guardian. I'd

heard that relations between Friedrich and my father had become strained. But since Karanos wasn't in the habit of cultivating close relationships, I didn't read into it overmuch. Fara was going to be assigned to someone new. I would miss working with her. Thanks to the time I'd spent with her studying in the library on board *Cnawlece* and the massive cram sessions with Ivy and Fitz upon my return, I passed all of my classes.

Over drinks one night at Marduk's, I introduced Fara and Rafe to Ivy and Fitz. It was awkward at first, only because I had so much shared history among all of them, but not together. But I think they realized how important it was to me to feel like my closest friends got along so they tried extra hard. Before long (and a few boilermakers later) no one was trying anymore. Fitz was egging Fara on to pull off increasingly outrageous illusions, put on ever more outlandish glamours, and asking if he could "borrow" Virtus for some insane future purpose. Ivy offered to redraft Rafe's CV for him. She was intensely curious about all of the spells he'd made up. Since Rafe had proven he could cast the likes of hottie Holden Pierce under the table, Ivy thought Rafe's ridiculously titled spells were *exceptionally charming* and *effortlessly inventive*.

I took a few days off and went back to Etincelle. I visited my mother's black garden. It was a blackened area just outside my bedroom window that my mother had torched with a can of gasoline and a match the day after my brother and I were born. I knew (because my mother had told me of things she'd done in the garden and because in nearly twenty-two years the garden had never grown back) that there was magic in it. But I thought it best not to dwell on what kind. The place didn't feel malignant. It just felt hazy, slow, and muted, like a dream with no color.

I knelt in the ashes and took out Burr's filleting knife and Grimasca's butcher knife. I carved each of their names on the handles and then plunged them deep into the ground, side by side, so they looked like miniature tomb markers.

Among the black ash, cinders, broken glass, shards of splintered wood, and other debris in the garden, the two knives looked right at home. Burr was dead, as was Grimasca. But Delgato lived, the people of the Shallows lived, and *I* lived and would continue living. Every day it got a little easier to breathe.

A few days later, to celebrate the end of the semester, I met Ivy, Fitz, Fara, and Rafe at the Black Onion. I'd been worried I might not feel like eating there anymore, but then I surprised myself by ordering the fish special. (It was charred red snapper. How could I not?) Midway through the meal, I pulled Alba aside and told her about Burr. I expressed my deepest sympathies. She expressed her deepest gratitude. She'd expected nothing less from Nouiomo Onyx than a swift execution of the demon that was responsible. I was just about to give her the three black onions I'd found for her in my mother's garden when Aurelia herself walked in. But infinitely more surprising than seeing *her* was seeing who was with her—my father. They almost never went anywhere together anymore.

As before when Karanos Onyx entered the Black Onion, the din stopped and all eyes turned toward him. But then he cleared his throat and everyone got back to the business of eating and talking. My parents walked over to where Alba and I were standing.

"You've been digging in my garden, Nouiomo," Aurelia said.

Alba narrowed her eyes at me. *Who would want to be caught stealing vegetables from the executive's wife's garden?*

But then my mother said to Alba, "Next time you need something, let me know. I can't promise you anything *fresh*, but black onions shouldn't be a problem. In fact, I think I saw some black garlic and black shallots out there last week . . ." Alba couldn't get my mother into the corner fast enough to discuss the terms of their future partnership. Which left me standing alone for a moment with Karanos, who spared no time, per his usual, on idle chitchat.

"Did Aristos really disappear in the Shallows, Nouiomo?"

I looked into his eerie, unreflective eyes.

Did he know about Ari? If he didn't, did I trust him enough to tell him the truth? How much trouble would Ari be in if the Council found out that he'd been a drakon training to be a Maegester? Karanos was my father and the executive . . . But something made me hesitate (natural caution? misplaced loyalty?) and I merely said, "I haven't seen him since then. What other explanation could there be?"

We stared at each other. "And the alembic?" Karanos asked. "Rochester said you never used the waerwater. That you lost it at the Elbow . . ."

The best lies were the truth in disguise . . .

"That's right," I said, chin up, gaze steady. To my utter shock, Karanos laughed then. It was little more than a cough, really, that happened coincidentally while he was smirking. But that's what it was.

"Well then," he said, nodding, "looks like you're ready for a new assignment."

Afterward, Rafe walked me back to Megiddo. On the way, he sang me the *silliest* song. It was about a cat who was sitting on a roof when he discovers that his true love has been unfaithful to him. In his madness, after having discovered her betrayal, he falls off the roof and breaks his solar plexus—

"What the heck is a solar plexus?"

"The pit of your stomach," Rafe said. "Ever had the wind knocked out of you?"

Many, many times . . . In fact, after this most recent time, I was still trying to catch my breath. Rafe nodded. "Then you've been hit in the solar plexus. Anyway, this cat, he broke his solar plexus and died."

"Died? From getting the wind knocked out of him?"

Rafe shrugged. "Cats," he said, like that explained everything.

"Is that the end of his story?" I asked.

Rafe shook his head. "He came back to life."

"No one comes back to life in Halja, Rafe."

"Some people don't," he said sadly. "But you will, Noon." And then he put his hands in his pockets and started whistling, like he didn't have a care in the world.

I followed his lead. Two could play at that game.